D0961057

Perfume of Paradise

ALSO BY JENNIFER BLAKE

Love's Wild Desire

Tender Betrayal

The Storm and the Splendor

Golden Fancy

Embrace and Conquer

Royal Seduction

Surrender in Moonlight

Midnight Waltz

Fierce Eden

Royal Passion

Prisoner of Desire

Southern Rapture

Louisiana Dawn

Perfume of Paradise

JENNIFER BLAKE

FAWCETT COLUMBINE
New York

A Fawcett Columbine Book
Published by Ballantine Books

Copyright © 1988 by Patricia Maxwell

All rights reserved under International and Pan-American
Copyright Conventions. Published in the United States by
Ballantine Books, a division of Random House, Inc., New
York, and simultaneously in Canada by Random House of
Canada Limited, Toronto.

Cover painting by Jim Griffin
Cover design by James R. Harris

Manufactured in the United States of America

Perfume of Paradise

CHAPTER 1

THE sun had set at last, though beyond the French windows flung open to the evening air the long tropical dusk lingered. It was close and warm in the bedchamber where Elene Marie Larpent was being dressed for her wedding. The candles burning on either side of the dressing table mirror added their heat to that of the waning day and sent thin gray columns of smoke rising toward the lofty ceiling. Elene's face was flushed, and there was dampness darkening the edges of her hair that had the color and fine texture of spun gold. However, the distress that shone in the clear gray of her eyes had nothing to do with the temperature.

"I can't do it, Devota," she cried in tones of soft despair as she met her maid's gaze in the mirror, "I can't."

Devota never faltered in her task of brushing the long, straight curtain of her charge's hair. "Don't upset yourself, *chère*. It will soon be over. It won't be so bad, you'll see."

"I can't think why Papa is so set on it now."

"It was decided long ago."

"So it was, but not by me."

The maid surveyed the pale oval of the younger woman's face with its hectic flush across the high cheekbones, the too firm set of the delicately molded mouth, the pinched look about the straight nose with its slightly retroussé tip. Finally she said, "You aren't afraid, are you, *chère*?"

"Of course I am! To have so large a wedding in times such as these is madness. Why could we not have been married quietly, with just you and Papa and one or two friends for witnesses? There is no need to flaunt our extravagance in the faces of the renegades."

"I think your papa has accepted at last that things are never going to be as they were, and so he means, for one last time, to pretend that they are."

"And Durant supports him in it." The tone in which Elene spoke the name of the man she was to marry held nothing of loving anticipation and little of respect.

"They are two of a kind."

Devota's quiet voice was soothing. The implied criticism of both her master and Elene's groom was not unusual; the mulatto maid was in fact Elene's aunt, a younger half-sister to her dead mother. The relationship was readily acknowledged, and by no means uncommon. A tall woman with skin a soft golden brown, aquiline features, and crisply waving hair tied up in the kerchief of the islands called a tignon, she had cultured speech reflecting the education she had received along with Elene's mother. She had been Elene's constant companion since her birth, when her own mother had died in childbed.

Devota said now, "But I spoke not of fear for the dangers of our situation, but of your groom. You are not ignorant of what will be expected of you on this night, nor can you doubt Durant Gambier's experience. Surely you can't dread what he may do?"

"No, not the thing itself, or at least only a little, but, oh, Devota, what if he isn't—isn't kind?"

"He is a gentleman—"

"That doesn't mean anything!"

"He will honor you as his wife, the mother of the children you will have together."

"Yes, but will he be gentle? Will he care whether he gives me pain or pleasure? Will he be patient, or will he force me to do his bidding?"

"In short, will he use you with love? This is what you want to know?"

"I suppose it is," Elene said, her voice low.

"What if it could be assured beyond doubt? What if Durant could be made so mad with love that he would become a slave to his desire for you only?"

Elene looked up with a wry smile lighting her eyes, bringing out the flecks that swirled like silver dust motes around the pupils. "Somehow it seems unlikely."

"Wait only a small moment." The maid, her lips pressed together in a line of determination, swung around and left the room.

Elene stared after the woman with a puzzled frown. What could Devota mean? With her it was not always possible to guess; she could be strange at times. Certainly it was not like her to be so abrupt or to interrupt so important a toilette. There was little time to waste if the bride was to appear at the appointed moment.

Suddenly restless, Elene got to her feet and moved to the window. The back gallery on which it opened was empty. The evening gathering outside was still, with an oppressive, muffled quiet. The insects and night birds that usually filled the air with their muted din were silent. The only sounds to be heard were caused by humans, the crunch of carriage wheels in the seashells that surfaced the drive of the house and voices raised in greeting as arriving guests were welcomed at the front door. On the terrace beneath the gallery, where the ceremony would be held, the trio of Negro musicians hired for the occasion could be heard tuning their instruments, playing snatches of melody. And far off there could also be caught, like a bass rumble of distant thunder, the beat of drums in the hills. Elene shivered.

From the direction of the kitchen drifted the aroma of roasting meat, mingling with the scent of flowers and fruit and the salt tang of the sea that was always present here on Saint-Domingue. Elene breathed deeply, deliberately, trying to calm herself. These were the smells of her childhood, one of the things about the island she had missed most while in France.

It was while she was away that her father had arranged this marriage. Actually, she thought it had been discussed between the groom's father, M'sieur Gambier, and her own when she was less than a year old and Durant only six. The lands of the two men lay together, and it had seemed a fine thing to join them by the marriage of their offspring. That had been twenty-three years ago. Things had been very different then, before the revolt of the slaves.

Elene had been at boarding school in France when the Negro slaves had risen against their masters on Saint-Domingue. Her father had not been on the island either, but en route to France to take her away from the dangers of the bloody revolution taking place there. It had seemed for a time that everything they had known was being destroyed, that there was no safety anywhere.

Regardless of the numbers of slaves involved in the first rash of attacks on the plantation owners on the island, in spite of the atrocities committed and the tremendous loss of life, no one had expected the slave revolt to last. Elene's father had removed her from the boarding school near Paris and made arrangements for Elene to stay with distant relatives, solid bourgeois merchants at Le Havre who were carefully neutral in the struggle in France. He had then left for New Orleans to join the community of refugees in the city while waiting for the opportunity to return to the island.

Elene had wanted to join her father when at last he had returned home, but matters had remained too unsettled. It was just as well she had not; those had been years of danger, of shifting loyalties and precarious fortune amid near constant fighting.

In the beginning, the Negroes and mulattoes, those of half-white, half-black blood, had joined together against the whites, raping, mutilating, killing, and pillaging. The French government, in the throes of upheaval itself, had been unable to send sufficient troops to put down the uprising, and so it met with a large degree of success. However, the mulattoes despised the Negroes as animals, and the Negroes hated the mulattoes for holding themselves above them, so that any time one of the two groups appeared to be gaining ascendancy the other turned on them. When republican France was finally able to send an army to reestablish its authority, the mulattoes joined with the troops in opposition to the Negroes. The Negroes then, in a bizarre *volte-face*, joined with the royalist French planters, their old masters, against this new threat. Later, as the Spanish and British brought the war in Europe into the Caribbean, the Negroes, under their leaders Toussaint L'Ouverture and Jean Jacques Dessalines, allied themselves with these French foes.

The British were weakened by the disease-ridden climate and overextended supply lines. With more important battles looming in Europe, they had withdrawn at last. Toussaint L'Ouverture, declaring himself governor-general for life, had then turned on his former Spanish allies and driven them from the country. He paid lip service to French sovereignty, but was in effect the supreme ruler of the island.

A period of peace had descended with the elevation of Toussaint. The governor-general had tried to revive the sugar and cotton commerce. Toward that end, he had invited the planters in exile to return and had forced the former slaves back into the fields. For the first time in over ten years, conditions on Saint-Domingue had seemed stable at last.

That had been just over a year and a half before, in 1801. Elene's father had waited a few months, until he felt certain the conflict was over at last, then he had sent for Elene. She had been instructed to bring with her all the frills and furbelows she would need for a wedding.

Elene had complied with her father's order, though it had meant more delay in returning home. When she had finally reached Saint-Domingue, the army of Napoleon under his brother-in-law, General Leclerc, a force 20,000 strong, had been on her heels, also bound for the island. Napoleon, having consolidated his position as consul, had decided France was in need of the rich produce of this island paradise, and would not tolerate Governor-General Toussaint controlling the shipments. The fighting had commenced once more.

After months of fierce conflict, Toussaint had accepted terms of peace, only to be treacherously arrested and sent to France. The renegade Negroes had been forced into the mountains, from which they launched savage and bloody raids against isolated plantation houses. General Leclerc had reestablished the hated slavery that had been abolished under Toussaint, along with many of the restraints upon the mulattoes.

The unrest was palpable, the dull rumble of drums from the renegade bases in the mountains—Voudou drums that carried messages among the scattered bands of the Negro army—was a near constant undertone. It was unsafe to travel at night without an armed escort. The ranks of Napoleon's soldiers, like the British and Spanish before them, were being slowly depleted, not so much by the rebels as by the virulent tropical diseases such as yellow fever and cholera, malaria and typhoid. The latest victim had been General Leclerc himself.

With the perilous conditions on the island, the wedding had been postponed for a time. Both Elene's father and her prospective groom were in the militia and had been involved in numerous skirmishes. The French army, though larger than any force sent against the Negroes so far, was still outnumbered by nearly twenty to one. If the Negroes under their new leader Dessalines could manage to coordinate their forces, or perhaps find a cause to rally around, they might still win the day. The position of the whites would then be dangerous indeed, for Dessalines was known as a brutal and vengeful man, with a virulent hatred for anyone with white skin.

Elene had been glad of the postponement, even if, after all the delays, she could be considered an old maid, past the freshest age for marriage. As much as she wished to please her father, she had been in no hurry to wed. She had wanted time to get to know him again, time to explore the house and lands she had thought gone forever and to adjust to the hazards of living on the island. But most of all, she had needed time to become acquainted with the man she was to marry.

The wait had proved instructive. Her father had changed beyond recognition, becoming bitter and vindictive. So strict was he in his behavior toward his slaves, so fearful of their treachery, that he would not tolerate so much as a straight look from one of them without ordering the whip. Even with Elene, he could not seem to behave as a loving parent; he lashed out immediately with scathing anger if she voiced a difference of opinion or failed to agree at once to his suggestions for household management or her own activities. It was as if he could not accept the slightest encroachment on what he considered his authority.

As for Durant, Elene had to admit he had charm and gallantry, and could be quite likable when he relaxed his guard. Certainly he was handsome enough in a dark and satanic fashion. Regardless, he was tainted by the same need to prove his manhood and his power as her father. He had a habit of telling her when he would come to call, rather than asking when it would be convenient for her to receive him; of instructing her in where she could visit and when she could go on her outings. He stated his preferences that amounted to orders about the style of her gowns and bonnets, how she should wear her hair, and even what music she must play in the evening. He had already decided when they would have children and how many, and had chosen their names. He made it plain that he expected a well-run household and an excellent kitchen, both centered around his own likes and dislikes.

He did not like it when Elene appeared uneasy in his presence. She need not fear that he would mistreat her, he said; he would handle her like the most fragile of ornaments.

Such a promise would have offered more comfort to Elene if Durant had not felt it necessary to make it. He was as much aware as she was, however, that his reputation with his horses and his slaves was not the best; it was even whispered that his mistress Serephine sometimes showed a livid bruise or two.

It had been the arrest of Toussaint and his imprisonment in France that had caused the date for the wedding finally to be set. But it was, Elene thought, the arrogance of her father and her groom that required it to be turned into a lavish entertainment for the countryside. They meant to show the world they did not fear calling attention to themselves, that they scorned to modify their traditional arrangements for mere safety's sake.

Elene, returning to the dressing table, stared at her reflection in the mirror and felt a fleeting scorn for her supine acceptance of the marriage arrangement. There must have been some way she could have made her father understand her reluctance, something she could have done to prevent the plans from going forward. Her cousins in France had scolded her often for her high spirits, her combative energy that caused her to defy curtailment of her movements.

But when she had tried to speak to her father, he had flown into such a rage that she had been afraid he meant to send her to the whipping post like the lowliest of his slaves. She might have run away, certainly, but there were few places to hide on an island, and she had no means, no funds of her own with which to leave it. In any case, for a white woman, or even one of color, to venture out onto the roads alone in these troubled times was like issuing an invitation to grief.

These were not the only reasons, however. The truth was, she wanted to please her father, to bring back the warm and loving man she had known as a girl. She had missed him so dreadfully while in France, had so longed to be with him. Now she could only do as he wished in an effort to gain his love and approval.

Elene's reverie was interrupted as Devota returned, swinging into the room and closing the door carefully behind her. Elene turned. "Where did you go? We must hurry or I'll be late, and you know how Papa is."

"Never mind. This is more important, much more important, *chère*."

"What is it?"

"A secret that will protect you."

The woman reached into her apron pocket and brought out a small, jade-green bottle with a cork stopper. She released the cork with a deft twist, and the fragrance of gardenias and roses, jasmine and frangipani and sandalwood wafted on the still, warm air, along with other subtle scents that defied identification.

"Perfume?" Elene inhaled it with appreciation, but shook her head. "It's lovely, but I doubt Durant will be impressed. I've heard his mistress bathes in scented water every day."

"Not in perfume like this."

"How can you be so sure?"

"There is no other like it."

It really was a delicious fragrance. Alluring in its combination of flower and wood fragrances, it was delicate and yet richly exotic, intense but fresh, while floating above the recognizable essences was a grace note of haunting, ineluctable mystery. It lingered on the air and in the mind with rare persistence, a soft, vibrant presence.

Elene held out her hand. "Using it can do no harm."

"One moment, *chère*. Open your dressing gown, if you please."

"What?"

"This is an oil, a very light one, and should be massaged into your shoulders and arms. It will make your skin supple and like satin to the touch, as well as fragrant."

Devota was only trying to help, Elene knew, with her talk of enslaving Durant and softening her skin. It would be unkind to show open scepticism. Besides, Elene could not deny that she needed any aid she could find to boost her spirits and allow her to walk with confidence to the altar where she and Durant would exchange their vows.

With a faint shrugging motion, Elene slipped her dressing gown from her shoulders, then held out her cupped hand for Devota to pour a small amount of the perfumed oil into it. Following the maid's instructions, she carefully transferred some of the fragrant liquid to her other hand, then smoothed her palms over her shoulders and the hollow of her throat, then down her arms to the bends of wrists and elbows. This application was not enough for Devota. The woman gave her a few drops more, and insisted that Elene spread them over the white globes of her breasts and down the flat plane of her abdomen to the juncture of her thighs.

As Elene massaged it into her skin, Devota began a low, monotone chant not unlike a prayer or a blessing. The sound of it recalled whispers Elene had heard years ago, whispers about Devota being involved with the Voudou cults, the worship of the old gods brought from Africa, whispers that she served sometimes as priestess for the pagan rites. Such priestesses were said to have strange powers, including the ability to cause death with a curse or a doll stuck with pins, to bring the dead to life, to concoct potions to turn love to hate or hate to love. There were many who believed, black and white alike.

Stories, nothing but stories. Devota looked so normal there in the candlelight, with her neatly starched white apron and tignon and her dark brown eyes warm with affection and concern. The whispered tales could not be true. It was the height of folly to think they might be.

The fragrance of the oil enveloped Elene, mounting to her head in near overpowering strength for an instant before it faded to a rich and lovely aura surrounding her.

"Good, good," the maid said softly. "Now when your husband holds you to him in the act of love, he will receive the perfume, increased in power a hundredfold by the added essence of your body, upon his own skin. And when that is done, there will be no escape for him. He will be in thrall to you, and will wish only to please you in all ways. His need for you will be insatiable. No other woman can attract him."

"That's all very well," Elene said with the faintest quiver of humor in her voice, "but what if he takes a bath? Or I do?"

Devota frowned. "You must not take this lightly, *chère*. Of course the perfume will be removed by bathing. You have only to apply it again, and the effect will be the same."

"Suppose I touch some other man. Will he also be enthralled?"

"You must take care that doesn't happen—unless you are sure it's what you want."

The things Devota was saying did not seem real. However, Elene thought, she might as well play the game. She tipped her head. "And what of me? Does it have no affect on me at all?"

"To you it is only a perfume. Yet it is best for a woman who wishes to hold a man not to fall too deeply in love with him."

"That sounds so calculating." A frown creased Elene's brow.

"It is. What I speak of is control, control of your life with your husband, not of perfect happiness. If you must have happiness, then seek love without any aid except a loving heart."

"I'm not certain a loving heart is what Durant wants," Elene said. "More likely, it's a suitable wife and Papa's land."

"Trust me, *chère*. Now we must hurry to dress you, or your papa will be angry."

The fashion in women's dress, as dictated by Paris, was patterned after the simple, draped lines of the clothing of ancient Greece and Rome as it had been for more than a decade. Elene's wedding gown was of the same order, in cream-colored tissue silk with puffed sleeves and a flowing skirt falling from just under the bust, and embroidery in gold thread at the hem and around the deep, square decolletage in a pattern of scrolls and leaves. Her hair was swept up in a shining coronet formed of a single thick braid that had been interwoven with a length of metallic gold ribbon. Her only jewelry was an exquisite cameo necklace that had belonged to her mother and a pair of gold earrings shaped like leaves that, along with a Kashmir shawl and a fan with ivory sticks, had been sent to her in the *corbeille de noce*, the basket of bridal gifts from the groom.

Elene did not, ordinarily, care for face painting, but she looked so pale this evening that she agreed to a little carmine cream on her lips and a brush of red Spanish paper across each cheekbone. Her brows and lashes were naturally dark, in spite of the pale color of her hair, so that they needed no more than a touch of oil to give them a soft sheen.

Devota was lavish with her compliments when at last Elene stood ready. Elene thanked her, but could feel no gratification. It did not matter what anyone thought of her appearance, including Durant. She felt more like a sacrifice than a bride, and all the praise and platitudes that usually surrounded such affairs were not going to change that. If she must go through with this wedding, all she really wanted was for it to be over.

There came a faint tap on the door. "It's time, mam'zelle," the butler called from the other side.

Devota told him they were ready. Suddenly flustered, she looked around for Elene's fan, in case she should be overcome by the heat, and also the nosegay of yellow roses and fern she would carry. Placing these things in Elene's hands, Devota gave her a quick, fierce hug, then moved to open the door.

The music heralding the coming of the bride rose from below, sweeping up the outside stairway and along the gallery to where Elene stood. She took a deep breath, then started forward.

"Remember," Devota said, her voice low, "your man will love you beyond life itself. He cannot help himself."

"Yes," Elene whispered, and stepped through the door and out onto the gallery.

The Larpent house was built of limestone cut and hauled laboriously from the mountains of the island. It had escaped burning in the years when Elene's father was in exile, but had not been free from looting or from damage. Most of the once grand furniture was gone from the rooms, and the gallery floor was scarred by the dragging of heavy objects from the house. The railing of the gallery, carved of the same soft limestone, had been hacked by machete and bayonet, and several of the urn-shaped balusters across its width were missing, doubtless knocked out by carelessness or carried away for some other use. The carved pineapple that had once decorated the newel post of the stone stairs that descended to the terrace was gone. To cover the jagged hole where it had been ripped away was a large porcelain jardiniere filled with cascading pink geraniums. More of the same flowers sat at intervals down the stair steps and were grouped about the bottom newel post.

Elene paused at the head of the stairs. Below her were the wedding guests seated on small gold-painted chairs in a semicircle about the altar. Among them, in the first row, was her father. The altar itself was draped with gold and red and set about with ferns. The priest in his surplice stood ready in front of it, watching, as were they all, for her arrival.

The faint murmur of conversation died away and clothing rustled as those congregated below discovered her presence and turned in their seats. It suddenly came to Elene as she stood there, the focus of attention, that she could no longer hear the beat of the drums in the hills.

The music of the trio of musicians swelled. Below her, the guests rose to their feet in her honor. There was a flicker of movement and Durant stepped from beneath the gallery to the newel post at the foot of the stairs. He stood waiting, a handsome figure in his wedding attire of a gold satin swallow-tailed coat and white knee breeches. On his mouth was a smile of satisfaction.

Elene stared down at him, at his thick brown hair, which he wore rather long, and his deep-set black eyes. His face was square, with a long lower jaw, a Roman nose, and muscular lips. Though of average height, with a stocky build, there was about him an air of supreme self-assurance that intimidated some men and infuriated others. A man of refinement, he was used to the best and would tolerate no less, whether in a glass of wine or a woman. He would not be an easy husband to please, she thought, though he might be one other women would envy.

Durant put his foot on the bottom stair and rested his hand on the stone bannister, ready to reach out to Elene, to lead her to the altar. Elene moved down one step, then another, striving for poise, trying to ignore the stiff reluctance in her muscles that threatened to trip her.

It was then a woman screamed.

The cry, shivering with a knife-edge of horror and hysteria, rang out from the back row of guests. Immediately it was echoed by savage yells and undulating war cries of a kind that lived in nightmare-haunted dreams. It was an attack of the Negro renegades.

The guests leaped up and stared around them, shouting, uttering exclamations of terrified disbelief. Women began to scream. There came the rasping sounds of men drawing the dress swords that hung at their sides. Others sprinted for pistols and muskets left in the house. Across the lawn the black figures ran, waving their weapons, their teeth bared in ferocious blood lust.

In an instant, the terrace was a mass of struggling, flailing bodies from which rose curses and grunts, desperate cries and the sickening sound of blades slicing flesh to the bone. Bright red droplets of blood splashed on the paving stones.

Elene, standing in stunned disbelief, saw Durant fling away from the stairs to grapple with a wiry Negro in a loincloth. Her groom wrestled the man's machete from a grasp slippery with blood. Hacking, slashing around him, Durant was lost in the melee as Elene swung her gaze toward her father. She was in time to see him struck down, an ax buried in his neck, half severing his head.

She screamed, the sound rising unbidden in her throat in her horror and sick rage. She stumbled downward a step, her gaze on the fallen body of her father. Below her, a pockmarked attacker turned, then started at a lope up the stairs. There was a knife held blade uppermost in his fist and a glaze of murderous fury in his eyes.

Elene hurled her nosegay and fan at him, then spun around, snatching up her skirts as she leaped back up the stairs. She could hear the thud of the man's bare feet on the treads below her. The noise acted like a goad. Nearing the top, she dropped her skirts and reached for the heavy jardiniere of flowers on the newel post. Dragging it from its place, she wrenched around and heaved it down upon her pursuer. It crashed into him in a spill of dirt and geraniums. He howled as he tumbled backward down the stairs amid broken crockery. Elene did not wait to see the damage, but whirled once more.

There was a dark face above her. Her heart gave a painful leap, then recognition came. Devota. The maid grasped her arm, pulling at her.

"This way! Quickly!"

They plunged across the gallery and through the main doors of the house, coming to a skidding halt in the stair hall. Ahead lay the broad width of the grand staircase that led down to the front entrance, while to the right was the dark, twisting well of the servant's stairs. They swung to the right, diving down the narrow steps in a headlong scramble until they reached the bottom.

There was a small door closing off the stairs, one that opened into the butler's pantry that in turn was connected to the formal dining room. Devota turned the knob and eased the door ajar. She looked and listened for an instant, then gave a beckoning nod.

Once more they were running, crossing the pantry and dining room, thrusting through the French windows that opened onto a secluded side garden. They clattered down the steps of the small terrace and, fleeing across a stretch of lawn, threw themselves among the tall hibiscus of the shrubbery border. Using that concealment, they angled away from the house toward the cane fields, scurrying like hunted animals across open spaces, glancing over their shoulders, gasping for breath. Then they were plunging between the first tall stalks of the sugarcane, thrusting into the protection of its great, waving stand.

They could not stop, even then. They pounded down the rows, like long green tunnels with broad, grasslike leaves of cane arching above them. They held up their arms before their faces to protect themselves from the dry and viciously sharp lower blades, ducking under or leaping over the canes that were so thick and heavy with juice that they leaned into the rows. Sometimes they slowed to a walk to catch their breaths, but quickly pushed on again. Behind them, the screams and yells, blasts of gunshots, and tinkling of broken glass receded. It was both a relief and a torment when they could hear the sounds no longer.

The fields seemed to go on forever, mile after endless mile. They crisscrossed one another, running with the lay of the land and of the irrigation ditches. Now and then there was a cane patch gone to seed, choked with weeds and wild coffee bushes and vigorously growing vines, or else a stretch that had not been planted since the first uprising and was already being reclaimed by the forest. These patches grew more and more frequent, turning at last into the forest itself.

The two women moved more slowly after a time, partly from exhaustion, partly from the fear of running into a remnant of the attacking Negroes or else another band altogether. When they were well into trees, they stopped at last. This section of wooded land was no more than a strip of perhaps a mile and a half in width, with the cane fields through which they had come on one side and the main road leading to Port-au-Prince on the other.

They pushed into its depths. When they could go no farther, they staggered underneath a great tree and dropped to the ground. They sat with their backs to the trunk, their heads tilted back and eyes closed as they sought to draw air into their lungs and ease the ache in their heaving sides. It was some moments before they could move or speak.

At last, Elene opened her eyes. The first thing she saw was that somehow, without her noticing, darkness had fallen. The second thing was the flickering red glow in the sky back the way they had come. She tested the warm air and smelled the unmistakable taint of smoke.

"The house, they're burning the house," she said in flat tones.

"Yes," Devota answered without opening her eyes.

"And look over there. Is that—can it be another house on fire?"

Devota peered through the canopy of leaves above them. "Where?"

Elene pointed. "There, you can see the glow reflecting against the clouds."

"It must be an islandwide uprising, then," the maid said. "What can have set it off?"

Elene shook her head, letting her eyelids fall shut again. "Does it matter? The question is: What are we going to do?"

Her father was dead. She had seen him die. She should feel terrible grief, but beyond that first instant of horror, all she could feel was a pervasive numbness. She shuddered from the scenes of carnage as they passed through her mind; still they seemed without reality. In the lethargy that held her, she could not seem to think what would be the best means to reach safety. As far as she could see, there was no such thing.

"It may be we could go to the French soldiers at Port-au-Prince." Devota's tone was tentative.

Elene felt the brief stir of an emotion she had not known since before she had learned she was to be married. It jolted along her veins, then faded, but in that brief moment, she recognized it in something near shock as interest in the future. She said slowly, "Perhaps we could."

"We would have to take care."

"Yes," Elene agreed. "The road will most likely be too dangerous. It would help if we could discover just what is happening."

"I might find out," Devota said.

"What do you mean?"

"If I could come upon some of the slaves from the house, they might be able to tell me what Dessalines is up to, or at least give some idea of why these attacks have been ordered."

"It's too risky," Elene said with decision. She had known the slaves from her home must have taken part in the uprising, the people she had tended with her own hands in their illnesses, the men and women who cleaned and dusted in the house and pruned and raked in the gardens, the hands who sang in the fields. She had known, but had not wanted to face it.

"There's no great risk, not for someone of my color."

It was seldom Elene thought of Devota as being nonwhite, just as she hardly ever thought of her as being related. She was just Devota, always there, ever thoughtful, ever wise. Was it possible the woman might have known what was to happen tonight, could have warned her father and the others? No, it could not be. There were some things that had to be taken on trust.

"Suppose you are recognized as my maid? It might be enough to put you in jeopardy."

"It's a chance I'll have to take. We must know something, and soon.

If this really is a general uprising, we will need a place of hiding, need it desperately, by morning."

Devota pushed to her feet and straightened her apron and tignon. Elene watched her shadowy movements there in the darkness. She could order Devota to stay, as mistress to slave, but that had never been their relationship. In any case, Elene was by no means certain Devota would obey, particularly now, or that she herself would want her to stay for that reason.

"If you must go, I'll come with you, at least part of the way."

"What good will there be in that, *chère*? No, no, it will be easier if you remain here. I won't be long."

"I could keep watch—" Elene began, then stopped abruptly. Where Devota had been standing seconds before there was only darkness. She had disappeared into the night.

The other woman was used to moving about in the dark countryside, Elene told herself. As a follower of the Voudou rites, or perhaps even a leader of them as a priestess, she must have left the house often in the midnight hours to travel to the gatherings in the hills. Devota would be all right.

Time crept past. Elene became aware of soft rustlings around her. It was only the stirring of small night creatures, or perhaps the fall of a dead twig or limb or the drift of a vagrant breeze through the thick tropical foliage. There was nothing to alarm her. Once she caught the sound of voices raised in drunken celebration. It was some distance away, however, perhaps on the main road beyond the wooded strip where she stood. The noise grew no louder. After a time, it faded out of hearing.

The night was without a cloud. Moonglow brightened the horizon beyond the far-stretching cane fields. The moon itself cleared the tree-tops and lifted slowly into the sky to filter its beams through the leaves overhead. It made the shadows under the spreading limbs appear darker, while shafting odd-shaped puddles of silver light poured down onto the forest floor. A spot the size of a man's hand penetrated the branches above where Elene sat. Its brilliant gleam pooled in her lap of cream silk, turning the material of her skirts to shimmering tissue of gold. The radiance, soft as it was, dazzled her eyes.

It might as well be a signal light, directing the renegades to her.

Elene scrambled to her feet and whisked herself into the shadows. Even there, the fabric of her gown seemed like a beacon, and the gold of the chain that held her mother's cameo glinted back and forth along its length with her every breath, her every movement. She removed the cameo and thrust it into her petticoat pocket. She thought of discarding the gown, but her petticoats underneath were hardly less lustrous. She wished she had thought to snatch a cloak, a blanket, anything to hide the pale sheen of what she was wearing.

Perhaps if she smeared her gown with dirt? There would be dampness under the mulch of leaves on the forest floor, but would it be enough? And her skin with its pearl sheen caught the light nearly as well as her clothing. It could use dulling also.

She knelt down, raking at the leaves at her feet, scraping the earth with her cupped hand. The rich, fecund smell of it filled her nostrils while the rustling she was making sounded loud in her ears. She scratched up a handful of the damp dirt and smeared it along one arm. Its moisture acted on the perfumed oil she wore, drawing out its scent so that it mingled with that of the earth. The crumbling black soil fell back to the ground, leaving no more than a smudge. She reached for more.

A short, sharp exclamation brought her head up. Standing not ten yards away was a pair of Negro men, one squat, one tall. They wore only rough breeches, leaving their upper bodies bare. The designs they had painted on their chests and faces in orange and white made them appear cruel and inhuman. One carried a silver pitcher by its handle in his left hand and a machete in his right. The other man had no trophies, but hefted an ax on a short handle.

Elene rose slowly erect and took a step backward. The movement brought her into a direct flood of moonlight. She felt it pour over her, glinting, shimmering on her hair, her skin, her dress. She stood at bay, but held her head high and regal with her determination not to show the terror that coursed along her veins.

The two men drew in their breaths with a rasping noise of amazement, as if they had seen a vision. The one with the silver pitcher muttered what might have been a prayer. The other with the ax flung him a short hard glance. He spat.

"Get her," he said.

CHAPTER 2

ELENE held her ground until they were upon her. The instant they touched her, such fury erupted inside she could not contain herself. She struck out, clawing, kicking, screaming in throat-searing defiance.

It availed her little. After the first instant of surprise, the men were entertained by her ferocity. The one with the machete laughed as he snatched her nails away from his face and twisted her wrist, forcing her to her knees. They called her she-cat and bitch and worse things, and wrapped the pale gold braid of her hair, as it came loose from its pins, around their hands like a rope, hauling her this way and that before they threw her to the ground among the leaves.

Still Elene struggled, writhing and twisting from side to side with her breath coming in harsh gasps against the pain of their hold on her wrists and ankles. In the back of her mind she wondered why they did not strike her with cane knife or ax, why they did not kill her, and knew the reason even as the questions formed. She heard the silk of her gown tear loose at one sleeve, felt the neckline give. There rose in her mind a red haze of distress and disbelief. This could not be happening. It could not.

The man kneeling at her feet stiffened, then gave a strangled cry. Her ankles were released. The one at her head looked up, cursing, then flung her from him so that she rolled in the crackling leaves. She wrenched herself over, pushing to her knees. Before her there was a third man in the moonlit darkness of the small clearing. Tall and wide-shouldered, pale of skin in the dimness and lean of form, he faced the burly Negro

who wielded the cane knife with a flashing sword in his own hand that
he gripped as if he knew how to use it. Not far away, the second Negro
lay sprawled on the ground with his ax beside him. He did not move.

The attacker and the newcomer circled each other, their movements
stiff with caution. The breathing of the big dark-skinned man was rough
in the night stillness, and his feet made a scuffling sound among the
leaves. The other was quiet, watchful, with tense alertness in his movements. The Negro lunged with a slash of the machete that cut through
the air with a vicious, wafting whine. Metal clanged on metal. There
was a flurry of blows and counterblows too swift to follow in the uncertain light. The man with the sword leaned forward in full extension,
then drew back. His sword glistened. The attacker cried out, stumbled.
The cane knife thudded to the ground. The Negro fell on top of it.

At the edge of the small clearing, a shadow moved. Elene swung
toward it in alarm. Devota stepped forward into the moonlight. Touching the man with the sword lightly on his shoulder in approval, ignoring
the bodies of the others, the maid came straight to Elene. She knelt
before her, catching her arms as she exclaimed in concern, "Are you all
right? Speak to me, *chère*, tell me you are unhurt."

"Yes, yes, only let me get up." To regain her feet, it seemed to Elene,
would be to regain her dignity, and perhaps her inviolability.

"Of course, let me help you. What trash you have in your hair, and
there is a sleeve half out of your gown. *Sacré*, but what animals! I can't
bear to think what I would have found if I had returned a moment
later."

"Nor I!" Elene pulled away from her maid as the older woman
brushed at her gown and tried to pick bits of sticks and leaves from her
hair. "Please, Devota. I love you dearly and thank God and all the
saints that you came, but will you have done so that I may speak to this
gentleman?"

Her rescuer had wiped his sword on a handful of leaves and replaced
it in its sheath that hung at his side. He stood waiting with his hand on
the hilt and his legs spread in a stance that indicated no great patience.

"Yes, of course. *Chère*, this is M'sieur Ryan Bayard of New Orleans.
We met most opportunely on the road."

Elene dropped a curtsy as best she could there in the darkness in
answer to the brief bow he sketched in her direction. "You were well
met, M'sieur. I am more grateful than I can express for your—your
intervention just now."

"I am delighted to have been of service," he answered, his voice deep and more than a little brusque. "Now that we have the courtesies out of the way, could we please go? I have no desire to fight all of Dessalines's army single-handedly."

"Forgive me if I delayed you—" Elene began, at a loss.

"It's of no consequence, so long as you do so no longer." He moved toward her and took her arm. "Can you walk?"

"Of course I can walk," she said, attempting to release herself from his strong grasp.

"It would not be surprising if you were a bit shaken. I could carry you, if you like."

"I don't like! Carry me where, M'sieur?"

"Away from here."

"*Chère*," Devota said.

Elene wrenched her arm back, trying to free it, but with little result. "You are a complete stranger to me, and though saving me from . . . from harm may entitle you to an interest in my welfare, it does not give you the right to direct my movements or to manhandle me."

"*Chère*?" The maid's tone was admonitory, though not hopeful.

"Forgive me, Mademoiselle," Ryan Bayard said with terrible politeness as he released his hold. "I was under the impression you wanted to go with me."

"I can't think how you gained such an idea."

"*Chère*, no!" Devota's protest was anxious.

"Nor can I. I will bid you good-night."

Elene drew herself up. "I extend you the same."

"He has a horse and carriage, *Chère*," Devota cried, "and a place to hide us!"

Elene turned to look at the older woman. A place to hide. For an instant, she wanted to deny that she needed such a thing, then the reality of the events of the evening were borne in upon her with sickening force. She did not need to see Devota's face to know that her maid thought they should go with this man, that he was their best hope of safety. It could well be so; it was almost certainly so. She swung back toward her rescuer. He was walking away, a tall, straight shape in the dimness with a broad back tapering to narrow hips, and a free-swinging stride. She had been too hasty. It was not a mistake she made often.

She took a step forward, calling out, "M'sieur!"

He stopped, turned.

"Wait, please, I—" The last word was tight, wobbling, then her throat closed, making it impossible to speak.

He came back a stride, then another, staring at her through the darkness. Ryan Bayard, seeing the gallantry in the straight shoulders of that bright, disheveled figure, hearing the choked appeal in her voice, was suddenly ashamed of his preoccupation with his own concerns.

His voice quiet, he said, "I believe, Mademoiselle, that you are more shaken than you know; this is a night to shake the strongest of us. I tender you my apologies for my conduct, and beg you will believe that I would be honored to be of service to you, if you will permit it."

Elene cleared her throat. "Again."

"Pardon, Mademoiselle?"

"You will be of service again." She indicated briefly the still forms on the ground. "We accept your offer with gratitude, M'sieur, my maid and I. You are—very kind."

Ryan Bayard had been called many things in the past few years, but no one had accused him of being kind. He was not sure he liked it.

"Shall we go then?"

It was not nearly so far through the woods to the main road as Elene had thought. The carriage was hidden at the edge of the shell-covered road, a phaeton pulled by a shining bay. Built for speed, the open vehicle offered little comfort, having only a thinly padded seat designed for the driver and perhaps one slender passenger at most. The three of them only managed to fit on it by Elene sitting in the middle and holding tightly to both Devota and M'sieur Bayard. Even so, each time a wheel dropped into a pothole or they rounded a curve on two wheels, she thought they would all go flying off the seat or over the carriage's kick board in front of them. The only thing that prevented it, she was sure, was the hard arm of the man at her side to which she clung.

It was an odd thing to occur to her, but Elene did not think she had been so close to a man not of her own family in her twenty-three years. Even Durant had been kept at a distance by her father's presence or Devota's chaperonage. The body of the man who had killed for her was taut and hard with corded muscle. There was no hint of an easy or indolent style of living about him; rather, it seemed that he must engage in physical labor. His speech and his manners were those of a gentleman, however, as was his expertise with a sword. He was a puzzle, one that might serve to keep her from dwelling on sights and sounds and deeds she would as soon not bring to mind.

Was Ryan Bayard trustworthy? That was a question indeed. He had stopped his carriage for Devota on a night when people of her color were massacring whites, when he would have had every right to suspect a trap. That indicated either overweening confidence in his own ability to protect himself, or above-average concern for his fellow human beings. He had come to Elene's aid at the risk of his own life, with hardly a moment's hesitation, without knowing who she was, certainly without hope of reward. It was not possible that he could have any base reason for it, nor was there any cause to think he might take advantage of the situation.

Still, there was something about the man that disturbed Elene. She wanted to think she had heard his name before, and not merely in a fable about the ancient family of Bayard renowned in France for their prowess in war. She wished she could see his face, to search for some resemblance to someone she knew perhaps, or else to test his intentions.

The road they traveled remained clear in the bright moonlight. They passed one or two plantation houses with lamplight showing on the galleries, as if the owners were out staring at the red haze of fires and dark clouds of smoke boiling into the night sky. There was no sign of destruction here as yet, however, nor of the army of Dessalines.

"Do we have far to go?" Elene asked.

"Three or four miles. We will be off this main road soon."

His effort toward reassurance was made, she supposed, because he had noticed the way she looked back at the two or three small groups of Negroes they met, groups that faded into the woods as they bowled past. It appeared the uprising was localized for the time being, but those not involved were shifting from place to place in the night in defiance of the restrictions on movement.

"It's so quiet along here. Shouldn't we stop and warn people that there has been an attack?"

"Anybody who can see the fires ought to know."

That was certainly true enough. Those who were still on the island were veterans of such atrocities after ten years of what could only be termed civil war.

"The wedding, that is why they chose us, why were we singled out?"

Ryan lifted a shoulder, his attention on controlling the bay as it shied at the swoop of a bat across the road. "I would say you attracted attention by the wedding, from what your maid tells me. But it was only an excuse for a place to start."

"You mean—"

"It looks as if only a few houses, those three or four closest to yours, have been hit. The road was fairly clear from the house where I was visiting, maybe two miles from where I was stopped for you, and I saw no sign of any large body of men. It's my bet the order for all hands to rise hasn't gone out. That will come in the morning, or maybe tomorrow night."

"Things have been so quiet lately," Elene said, almost to herself. "What has brought all this on?"

Ryan turned his head toward her. "Haven't you heard? News arrived yesterday that Governor-General Toussaint died in prison at Joux."

Toussaint, dead. There had been something paternal and statesmanlike in his rule and, though he had been defeated, in his brief reign he had accomplished much for his people. He had been respected, even loved. With all these things, combined with the trickery that had brought about his arrest, it was not to be wondered at that his death in a French prison should be the tinder that set Saint-Domingue aflame once more.

This conflagration would spread, there could be little doubt of it. What was she to do then? She had no home, no family other than Devota; she did not know if her fiancé was alive. The only valuables she owned were the earrings in her ears and the cameo necklace in her petticoat pocket.

"Where are Leclerc's soldiers?" she asked. "When will they march?"

"The question is, will they march at all?" Ryan said. "Their ranks have been so thinned by dysentery and yellow fever that they'll be lucky to muster a good company of men to put into the field."

"But something must be done to stop Dessalines!" Elene cried.

"Possibly, but not any time soon. The best thing I can see for you or any other whites is to get off the island as quickly as possible."

He could be right. If matters reached the pass they had during the first uprising twelve years before, the only safety would be in leaving until the situation cooled, or until the French army could regain control.

"But how can we? What of our lands, the crops?"

"They aren't much use to you if you're dead," Ryan said simply.

Before Elene could frame an answer, the carriage swung into a drive and bowled up it toward a darkened house. Ryan did not draw the horse up before the front door, but continued on around to the stable area in the back where he sent the bay through the arched opening of a barn before stopping. He unhitched the animal and turned him into a stall, then dragged the phaeton into a corner. Only then did he turn to the two women with him.

Elene, while waiting for Ryan to remember the presence of her maid and herself, had had time to catch her breath and look around her. This house where they had wound up was not only conveniently off the road, but stood on a headland above the sea. She could hear the sound of the waves in the still night, taste the salt in the air. The stables and barns seemed large compared to the size of the house, and in a near corner there was a wagon too massive to be used for anything except freight.

"What are we doing here?" she asked, keeping her voice low as she walked quickly along beside Ryan.

"This place belongs to a business associate. I'm staying with him for a few days."

Elene sent him a swift glance. She had learned enough of the island in the year and a half she had been back to know that the house belonged to a mulatto merchant named Favier. She had never met the man. The mulattoes did not move in the same social circles, if Saint-Domingue could be said to have such a thing as society these days, and in any case, Favier had a reputation for keeping to himself. It was popularly supposed that, in addition to his more legitimate interests, he dealt in smuggled goods.

Something shifted in Elene's mind, and she knew with abrupt clarity where she had heard the name Bayard. There was a privateer of no small notoriety—some even called him a pirate—who went under that cognomen.

The back door of the house swung open before they could reach it. It was no servant who stood in the opening, but the master himself. He carried a candle with a shield affixed. As they neared, he drew them urgently into the house and slammed the door behind them.

They called him a mulatto, but it was likely that Favier had only one-quarter Negro blood in his veins, instead of half, for his skin was the color of old parchment. He was short and stout, bordering on corpulence, and his hair was curled and pomaded with all the care of a dandy. It was also plain that he was badly frightened, for the candle he held shook in his hand and there were beads of sweat on his upper lip.

"Did anyone see you turn in here?" he asked, his liquid brown gaze wide as it fastened on Ryan.

"Not that I know of. I hope you won't mind that I have brought guests back with me, Mademoiselle Larpent and her woman Devota." Ryan turned to Elene. "Mademoiselle, permit me to present to you M'sieur Favier."

"M'sieur," Elene dropped a curtsy.

"Mademoiselle." Favier sketched a clumsy bow, his gaze lingering on the disarray of her gown and hair only an instant. He spoke no words of welcome before he turned back to Ryan. "I expected you hours ago. Where have you been?"

"There was some disturbance along the road. I had to make a slight detour once or twice, and then it was necessary to take up Mademoiselle Larpent."

"Was it indeed? Do you realize the danger you have put me in?"

"You?"

"I have managed to keep out of the fight between white and black and to maintain friendly relations with Dessalines, but if he finds out I'm harboring a white man, not to mention this Larpent woman, he will tear this place apart. And me also."

"Then you will have to make certain Dessalines doesn't find out, won't you?" Ryan said quietly.

Elene watched Ryan Bayard. In the candlelight, she saw that he had hair as dark and polished as walnut and a face burned by the sun to a color at least two shades darker than that of the mulatto. His features were rugged, with a firm, heavily chiseled mouth and a nose that had been broken at some time in the distant past so that it gave him the predatory look of a hawk. His eyes were as blue as the midnight sea, and protected by heavy brows and a screen of thick dark lashes. He could not be called handsome, and yet there was something compelling in the cast of his features that caught and held attention. The force that she had sensed in him was there in his stance as he faced his host. It was not surprising that Favier was nervous, for Bayard did not appear to be an easy man to cross.

The mulatto's terror of Dessalines was greater than his wariness of Ryan, however, for he licked his lips, then burst out, "You can't stay here!"

"Where do you suggest we go?" Ryan's gaze was hard, but his voice carried almost a conversational tone.

"Into town. To the French army."

"And shall I take my business there also?"

Favier moaned, as if the suggestion gave him physical pain. He drew out a handkerchief and mopped his forehead. "You don't understand."

"I think I do. I risk a great deal for you with every voyage, but you decline to return the favor when needed."

"The French soldiers can protect you."

"Possibly, if the lady and I could get there," Ryan said. "But you could hide us. And get word to my ship, so I can be taken off the island.

The French would not be so obliging. For some reason, they don't seem to approve of me."

His ship. Ryan Bayard was indeed the privateer then, and it was apparent that Favier was in league with him, that he received and sold the goods Bayard brought to the island. Elene had heard much of these merchant-adventurers who sailed under letters of marque to plunder the shipping of countries at war with each other then sell it to the highest bidder. Those of French blood, one would think, would molest only British ships, but it was said that Bayard sometimes turned a blind eye to the color of the flag if the prize was a rich one.

She stared at him, at his coat of dark blue cloth and conservative white on white striped waistcoat, his cravat that had been somewhat disarranged by his fight with the Negroes, his closely fitted doeskin breeches and brightly polished boots. Even with the sword at his side, that was somewhat heavier than the dress blades affected by most men, he looked not so much like a corsair, a terror of the seas, as a gentleman planter. Except for the bronze of his skin. No gentleman of her acquaintance would allow his face to be so exposed to the sun, any more than would a lady. Such sun-darkened skin could give rise to rumors of a touch of what was known as *café au lait*, an admixture of African blood. Not that she suspected it of this man. Rather, the bronze of his skin was further proof of his calling.

Ryan, glancing at Elene, saw the censure on her face. The cause was not difficult to find. Annoyance pricked at him. She might have at least given him the benefit of the doubt, considering the trouble he had been put to on her account. She moved a little under his narrow gaze, turning to glance at her maid. A breath of her perfume was wafted toward him. He had noticed it earlier as she sat pressed against him on the seat of the phaeton, a scent like a tropical garden under the moon. It was absurd but he had a strong impulse to step closer to her, the better to inhale it.

The inclination, when the woman so obviously disapproved of him, did nothing to soothe Ryan's temper. He turned on Favier. "Well, what is it to be? Will you whistle your profits down the wind out of fear for your yellow hide or will you act the man? Make up your mind. I know one or two others who might find your receipts worth a risk or two."

A spasm passed over Favier's face, then he threw up his hands. "All right, all right. But I will take no unnecessary chances. If you want to be hidden, that is exactly what you will be. Come this way, quickly, before one of the servants comes snooping, wondering what the noise is about."

The house was not as large as the Larpent house, or as pretentious. It consisted of six rooms, three upstairs and three downstairs, that were surrounded on all four sides by galleries that protected the inside walls from the hot sun or windblown rain while permitting the circulation of air through floor-to-ceiling windows. The interior was furnished with an eye to comfort, and even a touch here and there of luxury. In the dining room where they were led, the room to the right on the bottom floor, there was a Beauvais rug in jewel colors on which was centered a long table and matching chairs of rosewood. On the table itself was a Meissen fruit bowl and a pair of matching candelabra, while ranged upon a sideboard was a collection of silver serving pieces and a set of decanters holding wines and brandies.

Favier set the candlestick he was holding on the tabletop and began drawing the chairs back one by one. Elene looked at Devota, who shrugged her incomprehension.

Ryan was not so reticent. "If you are about to offer us the hospitality of your kitchen, we appreciate it, but I, for one, am not hungry. We require your quietest rooms, a pair of them. Are there no servant's accommodations or attic rooms we could use?"

Favier gave him a belligerent look. "For what you require, the only thing I can offer you is here. Anything else is entirely too exposed. I have an old woman who keeps house for me who snoops into every room, and if told to keep out would only try to see what I am trying to hide."

"So shut her up somewhere for a few days, or send her away."

"I can't," Favier said shortly. "She's my mother."

"In that case, she would hardly betray you."

"You don't know her." Favier gave a pettish shrug as he continued to draw back the chairs.

When they were all out of the way, Favier lifted one end of the table and kicked the rug from under the legs. He then rolled the rug back, revealing a trapdoor.

"I begin to understand," Ryan said.

"I hope you like it," Favier answered, a touch of malice in his voice. Grunting with effort, he lifted the door by an inset ring and laid it back on its hinges.

There was nothing to be seen at first except a dark hole. Then Devota reached for the candle and held it low under the table. The space that was exposed was too small to be called a cellar, too small even to qualify as a room. Hewed out of the limestone on which the house sat, it must have been used to store contraband from time to time, for a faint odor of wine and spices and tea rose from it. However, it looked like nothing so much as a large grave.

Ryan rose from where he had gone down on one knee to look. "There must be some other place."

"Nowhere that you won't be discovered, and, just maybe, reported to Dessalines."

"Don't tell me," Elene said with asperity, "that your mother doesn't know about this?"

"She knows, but it hasn't been used for some time, and she would have no reason to think there was anybody down there now."

"Show us somewhere else." Ryan's voice was hard.

"There is nowhere else, I promise you! It's this or nothing!"

Elene spoke almost to herself. "There is no reason Devota and I should not go to the army at Port-au-Prince."

"Oh, yes," Ryan said as he swung on her, "as you were doing when I came along an hour or two ago."

Elene gave him a cold look, one that had no visible effect there in the candlelit dimness.

Favier glanced from one to the other and wiped sweat from his brow. "Every moment that we stand here arguing is a danger. It will only be for a few days, three, four at most, until I can send word to your ship."

"You don't know for certain that matters are so serious," Elene pointed out. "We are all of us only guessing that Dessalines will order a mass attack. Perhaps we could wait and see what happens."

"Yes, and by that time every slave on the place will know where to look for you, supposing Dessalines wants to hunt down whites. Do you know what he does to white women? Do you?"

Devota set the candle she held down on the table and stepped in front of Elene. "She knows, you fool. Only look at her."

Favier smiled grimly. "She hasn't been tortured, that I can see. Yet."

The older woman turned her back on him, speaking to Elene. "Perhaps it would be bearable for a day or two, *chère*. Then if matters don't turn out as we think, we could go on to Port-au-Prince, you and I."

"And then what?" Ryan said in rasping tones. "The word among the men at sea is that the Treaty of Amiens has failed. War with the British will be declared any day, and I don't doubt they will aid Dessalines against the French this time by blockading the island. That will turn

Saint-Domingue into a charnel house from which there is no escape. Dessalines can raise more than 100,000 men by beating a drum. Of the fine French army of 20,000 sent out by Napoleon, over a quarter are dead of fevers, and another quarter, maybe more, aren't fit to fight. That makes the odds against victory somewhat higher than a hundred to one. What will you do if there is a rout, or a surrender?"

Elene gave him a hard stare. "I don't know, M'sieur, but what choice have I? I have no family, no friends, no money. There is no ship waiting for me!"

"You could come with me."

Ryan had no idea where the suggestion had come from; certainly he had not known he would make it. It had simply presented itself full-blown in his mind, and he had spoken it aloud. He was an idiot. It would cause problems, but he supposed he could attend to them when they arose. For now he waited for his answer.

"Go with you?" Elene's voice was blank.

"To New Orleans."

"But I don't—"

"For the love of God!" Favier cried. "You can discuss where you will go and what you will do afterward for the next three days. Will you conceal yourselves before we are all discovered and dismembered for Dessalines's pleasure?"

Ryan cursed softly, then with abrupt decision, bent his tall form into a crouch and ducked under the table. He sprang down into the gaping hole and turned, waiting to help Elene. She went to her knees, then hesitated, eyeing the way he had been nearly swallowed up in the darkness.

"Go on," Favier moaned in exasperation.

There seemed nothing else to be done, except perhaps to curse as had Ryan Bayard. Pressing her lips tightly together, Elene crawled to the edge of the hole and swung her legs down into it. Ryan reached for her. She put her hands on his shoulders and felt his hard hands close around her waist. She fell against him as she jumped down, the soft curves of her body pressing into his long length, their faces inches apart. Then he set her carefully on her feet, and together they turned toward the light.

Favier, panting in his eagerness and effort, folded himself up under the table and reached for the trapdoor.

"Wait!" Elene called. "Devota, come on."

"You'll be too crowded," Favier protested.

"Yes, but—"

Devota shook her tignon-wrapped head. "Don't worry, *chère*, I'll be all right. To hide like this isn't necessary for one of my color. And I will be able to see to your needs if I am free to move around." This was said with a challenging glance at Favier, as if the maid dared him to try to stop her, or suspected he might allow Ryan and Elene to starve if not watched.

"People will know you are from the Larpent place. They will want to know why you are here," Elene said. She was concerned for Devota's safety, but she also felt as if a vital protection was being stripped from her.

"I'll make up some story, never fear," Devota said calmly.

Favier was closing the door. His voice was false with heartiness as he said, "She'll be fine."

Ryan put up a hand to stop the descending door. "Leave us the candle."

Grumbling, Favier passed it down. "You must only use it for emergencies. There may be cracks in the floor where it will shine through."

"We are not idiots," the privateer answered in hard tones, then had to lower his head quickly as the trapdoor thudded shut.

Outside they heard Devota call out, "I'll bring food and drink and a few things for your comfort in a moment."

There came the sound of Favier telling the maid to be quiet, then there was nothing but silence.

The candle flickered in the gloom. Both Elene and Ryan looked at it, measuring its length. Around them, the walls seemed to close in. Elene, of no more than average height for a woman, could stand upright, though the top of her head brushed the trapdoor. Ryan was forced to stoop with his neck at what looked to be an uncomfortable angle. The space in which they stood was perhaps ten feet long, but no more than four feet wide. The trapdoor was fitted into the wood floor above them, rather than into the stone itself, so there was a narrow space the width of a floor joist that opened out under the house. This space allowed the circulation of air, though it also seemed to encourage spiders, for the wood beams and floorboards above them were festooned with dust-coated webs.

The space was bare except for what appeared to be a small pile of jute bags in one corner. Ryan set the candle he held on the floor and stepped to pick up the bags, shaking them out. There were five or six of them. He spread them out in two neat piles against one wall, then lowered himself to one of the piles.

His tone laced with irony, he said, "Sit down. It appears we may as well make ourselves comfortable."

"So it does." Elene moved with stiff muscles to accept the seat he had made.

She had not realized how exhausted she was until she was off her feet. Her strength seemed to vanish, leaving her drained and with a near uncontrollable tendency to shiver. She leaned her head back against the stone wall and closed her eyes. Instantly, images she would as soon not see began to flood her mind. She opened her eyes quickly. Directly before her was the candle, its rich yellow light a comfort and a worry.

Elene moistened her lips. "Do you think we should put out the light?"

"When your maid returns."

She was aware of a sense of reprieve. Keeping her mind carefully blank, she sat watching the wavering flame, marveling at the colors it contained, blue and orange and yellow, the black of the wick, the cream of the wax, the gray where the smoke left its stain. The shadows cast by the light flickered over the walls, overlapping each other. The rising warmth wafted the spider webs above them with gentle languor.

Ryan glanced at the woman beside him. Something in her stillness disturbed him. He thought of all that had happened to her in the last hours, most of it gathered from what the woman Devota had said in her tumbled plea for his help, and knew an instant of surprise that he did not have an hysterical female on his hands. It would be amazing if she wasn't in some kind of shock. That fool Favier could at least have offered them a drink. He could do with a tot of brandy himself.

"I'm sorry," he said aloud. "This isn't precisely what I had in mind when I offered you shelter here."

Her lips twisted in a wry smile, then were still. "It's a great deal better than the alternative."

"Some people have a fear of close places. If you do, you have only to say so and I'll force that weasel Favier to find us some other place."

It was an instant before she replied. "I can't say I like it, but I think I can bear it. We will find out, won't we."

It was so precisely his own view of the matter that she rose another notch in his estimation. She had courage. He remembered, suddenly, the wild fury with which she had been fighting the Negroes holding her.

"I meant what I said about New Orleans," he went on. "I have friends there who can help you get settled. You will have no trouble making a place for yourself."

Privately he thought there would be a great many of his friends who would like nothing better than taking care of a woman who looked as this one did. She really was beautiful. The wonder was that she had not been married for a half dozen years already, instead of just going to the altar.

Elene made no reply, though she considered what he had said. Her father had lived in New Orleans for a time, as a refugee. He had enjoyed himself there, she thought, when he was not worrying about returning to Saint-Domingue. He should have stayed. If he had, he might still be alive. But he had not, and so—

The trapdoor opened above them. Ryan got to his feet and took the things Devota handed down, an armful of quilted coverlets, a loaf of bread, a roasted chicken and several fried fruit pies wrapped in a napkin, plus bottles of brandy and wine and a jug of water and drinking glasses. When he had passed these things one by one to Elene, the maid gave him the last item of convenience, a porcelain chamber pot with a lid painted with roses.

Devota called softly, "Is there anything else you can think of you need?"

Ryan looked to Elene who shook her head. He relayed the answer.

"Then Favier says I am to tell you to lower your voices. He thinks he can hear you talking."

"We'll do that," Ryan said, his tone grim.

"It may be tomorrow night before I can bring anything else. If it is, don't think I have forgotten you," Devota whispered.

"No, we won't."

"Then sleep well."

Ryan made a sound through his nose that might have been a snort. The trapdoor closed down on them again.

Ryan set the chamber pot in the far corner, then kneeling on the floor, began to arrange the food and drink in the other. "Would you care for something to eat?"

"Thank you, no."

Elene turned her back and began to spread out the quilts over the jute bags. There was simply no room to make more than a single pallet out of them, not if they were both going to be able to lie down. And lie down they must; they could not sit up, sleepless, for three days. She and the privateer would have to stretch out side by side. Together. Down here in this hole. She sat back on her heels, staring at the spread quilts.

Behind her there was the clink of glass on glass, the gurgle of liquid. "Here," Ryan said, his voice rough, "drink this."

She turned to look at him as he knelt so close beside her. She met his dark blue gaze, and saw the flame of the candle glowing there. His presence, the sheer force of him as a man, was suddenly overpowering. She swallowed hard, and reached with fingers that trembled for the glass of brandy he was holding out to her.

Her lips were cold against its rim. The fumes of the liquor rose to catch in the back of her nose. Still, the fire of the brandy spread life-giving warmth in its slide down her throat to her stomach. A shiver of reaction rippled over her. She drank again, cautiously, cradling the glass in both hands.

Ryan gave a faint nod of satisfaction and raised his glass. "To New Orleans."

She had not said she would go. She could not refuse to drink to his home, however. "To New Orleans," she repeated, and sipped once more from her glass.

Ryan shifted his position, easing onto the pallet she had made, though he only sat as before with his back against the stone wall. He swirled the liquor in his glass, his thick lashes shielding his eyes as he stared at it.

Elene looked at him out of the corner of her eye, then looked away again. The situation they were in had every appearance of one that was going to be embarrassing in the extreme. It was not something either of them had caused or that either could do anything about, however. That being so, there was no point in being silly about it. She took a deep breath and let it out, then moved gingerly to settle beside him.

"I expect," Ryan said in neutral tones, "that we had better save our candle. There's nothing to say that Favier will give us another."

"Yes, I suppose so," she answered.

He reached out one long arm and pinched the candle flame with his fingers. Blackness descended.

They were alone in the dark.

CHAPTER 3

THE effects of the brandy seemed stronger without the light. Elene felt a welcome easing in her mind and a warm sense of relaxation in her muscles. She was not inebriated by any means, only aware that she easily could become so.

She did not blame Ryan Bayard for her state. He had given her the brandy, true enough, but he had not forced her to drink it, and she certainly did not suspect him of having any ulterior reason for offering it. She was, in fact, grateful to him for the impulse. He might not be aware of it, but she had been close to the edge of her composure.

Probably, he knew it very well. A man such as he must have had a great deal of experience with women, quite likely women in the grip of emotion. In addition, a privateer must often meet with overwrought people of both sexes, those none too pleased at having their valuables taken from them.

Ryan Bayard's experience with women or anyone else was not, of course, a concern of hers. The three days they must spend together would soon pass. It was unlikely that, once they were over, the two of them would ever meet again.

She did not approve of him. She hoped she had not made that fact too obvious; it would not be very polite to sit in judgment of the man who had saved one's life and honor. Nonetheless, she could not change the way she felt. A man should have some allegiance to his country, some loyalty to the land of his forefathers, if not of his birth. Ryan Bayard was of French blood, or so she assumed from his surname and the fact that he spoke the language as if he had learned it in his cradle. Why would he attack French merchant ships when he should, if anything, have been hounding the enemies of France?

It was difficult to know, of course, which faction of the French government to support these days. Her father had been a staunch royalist who had castigated First Consul Napoleon Bonaparte as a Corsican upstart with pretensions to glory. She herself, after her sojourn in France, had a certain sympathy with the cause of *liberté, egalité, et fraternité*, though the excesses of the revolution had sickened her as surely as those on Saint-Domingue. She could never forget, however, that she was a Frenchwoman. Regardless of who ruled, that would not change.

Beside her, Ryan spoke in quiet tones. "This woman of yours, Devota, can she be trusted?"

"Of course she can!"

"There's no 'of course' about it. Just because you've known her all her life doesn't mean she wouldn't like to see your throat slit."

"If she had wanted that, all she would have had to do is leave me this evening," Elene said, shivering. "I doubt if I could have gotten away from the plantation house in time without her, or out of the woods. Besides, she isn't merely a slave."

"If you mean by the last that she's a blood relative, that's no guarantee of loving kindness. However, I'll take your word that she's as devoted as her name."

"Given our position," Elene said with some tartness, though keeping her voice low, "I hardly think you can do anything else."

"On the contrary. If one is forewarned, there's a great deal that can be done to eliminate a danger."

The dispassionate timbre of his voice was an indication of his intent. She swung her head toward him in the darkness. "How can you think of injuring Devota when she has just brought us food and every available comfort?"

"How many of those who joined in the attack on your home this evening have seen to your comfort in other days?"

She turned away again, staring at nothing. "I . . . I would rather not think of that."

He muttered an imprecation under his breath. "Nor did I intend to remind you."

The scent of her perfume came stealing to Ryan out of the darkness. It mounted to his head along with the fumes of the brandy, curling in his throat and lungs, lingering in his mind. There crept in upon him an insidious image of himself opening the bodice of Elene's torn gown, burying his face in the soft valley between her breasts, and inhaling the tantalizing essence, seeking its source. The impulse was amazing, unlike anything he had ever felt before. It grew in intensity, becoming so overpowering that he was forced to set his glass down and clench his hands into fists to control it.

After a long moment, he let his breath out in silent relief. His voice sounded strained to his own ears when he spoke. "It's becoming a little close in here. Do you mind if I take off my coat?"

"Not at all," she said, wry amusement shading her voice.

"Is something funny?" His words were taut.

"Not exactly. Your request just . . . just sounded so formal and correct, when I have been parading around in front of you for the past hour with my clothes half torn from my back. And when we have been condemned to three days, perhaps more, of such . . . such close association as few people are called on to endure, even husband and wife." The humor left her voice, leaving it ragged. "Then it struck me that this was to have been my wedding night, and here I am with you, a man I never saw before in my life, and you—"

"I understand," he interrupted her. "There's no need to go on."

Elene was not sure he did understand; her own comprehension was none too good. In some strange fashion, she was glad to be sharing this enforced incarceration with Ryan Bayard instead of enduring being shut up alone in a bedchamber with Durant. How she had been dreading that moment, and also Durant's complacent and practiced possession of her body. She felt as if she had gained a reprieve, one that she might well have to pay for in some terrible fashion.

"Your bridegroom, was he killed?"

She could tell from the quiet rustling sounds that Ryan was removing his coat. She thought he folded it, or rolled it up, and placed it at the head of their pallet for use as a pillow. The further whisper and slide of cloth suggested that he was releasing his cravat, opening the neck of his shirt.

Her voice was compressed as she answered his question. "I don't know what became of Durant. I lost sight of him in the fighting."

"It's always possible he survived."

"Yes."

"I'm sure he fought bravely."

So was she. Durant might seem to have little purpose in life beyond the pursuit of pleasure and the wringing of the means to afford it from his sugar plantation, but there was no denying that he had courage.

She closed her eyes, repeating in a subdued tone, "Yes."

The man beside Elene reached to pick up his brandy glass. As he straightened, his sleeve brushed her arm where they sat with their backs against the wall. The cloth was warm with the heat of his body, and under it she felt the ridged layers of muscle. A tingling sensation ran from her shoulder to her fingertips and she flinched away from him, throwing a quick glance at his dark form. An instant later, she wondered at herself. She had been much closer than this in his carriage. Why shrink from him now?

The men she knew best, Durant and her father and their friends, had a gentleman's usual scorn for well-developed muscles, except perhaps in their sword arms. Such brawn was relegated to slaves and the lower classes who had to labor for their living. It was not only useless to a gentleman but prevented the perfect set of his coat across the shoulders. Elene had seen nothing whatever wrong with the set of Ryan's coat; still, she was disturbed by his evident strength. The nearest she could come to body structure resembling his was in slave blacksmiths on her father's plantation, or else the sailors and fishermen of Le Havre. No doubt while on board his ship he turned his own hands to the work of running it.

The thought of his ship reminded her of their host, and returned her attention to the place where they sat. "What is this place? Can it have been a tunnel?"

"The beginnings of one," Ryan answered. "I believe it was supposed to go through the rock all the way down to the beach, but Favier took fright when the French returned to the island and so stopped work."

"What of Favier? Dessalines, so far as I have heard, doesn't think a great deal more of mulattoes than he does of whites. Why should he spare him if there is a mass attack?"

"I would imagine because of the hefty amount in bribes Favier has paid. My hope is that he doesn't decide to curry favor and protect his own yellow hide by turning over two whites for Dessalines's delectation."

"Us? Is it possible he would?" Her voice was hushed in her shock.

"Very possible, if he's pressed. The only thing that will make him think twice is his fear that I will get to him before Dessalines gets to me," Ryan said.

"You are depending on that, on his fear, for our lives?"

"Sometimes a man's fears are more certain than his good intentions."

"Charming," she said, her voice scathing.

Ryan laughed without answering as he took another swallow of his brandy. It was good to hear the flash of spirit in her voice. He had been afraid he had frightened her again. Perhaps he should have kept quiet about his lack of trust of Favier, but he had wanted her to be warned, in case they had to move quickly.

"You seem to know the man well," she went on. "He must be an associate of long standing."

"Long enough."

"I've heard rumors of his activities. And, if I may say so, of yours."

"I'm flattered."

"You have no cause to be. The tales weren't complimentary."

There was a small silence, then he said, "I take it you have no liking for sea merchants like myself."

"Hardly. You call yourself a privateer, I think. Tell me, whose flag do you sail under?"

"My ship, like most in the trade, is registered in Cartagena," Ryan answered evenly. "I hold letters of marque from both France and England since they are at war with each other."

"You made your fortune in the past attacking Spanish and French shipping under a British letter of marque, and British shipping under one from France, and yet you live in a Spanish colony. You scoff at poor Favier for looking after his own interests, but so far as I can see, you're not a great deal better!"

"How do you know I have attacked Spanish shipping?" he said softly.

"Doesn't everyone? They are so rich, the Spanish, and so arrogant in their great clumsy crafts that they had become the quarry of every pirate."

"Privateer. There is a difference," Ryan corrected her.

"Don't tell me that you always trouble yourself with wars and treaties and letters of marque when there is booty to be had for the taking?"

"Doesn't it occur to you that robbing my own good King Carlos would be a perilous undertaking, not to mention a stupid one, since I live under his rule?"

"I see. To leave Spanish ships unmolested is a decision based solely on fear then, rather than loyalty?"

She was throwing his own words back into his face, after what he had done for her. Anger boiled up inside him. He would like to take her and—

Yes. He would like it a great deal too much. His anger subsided to a more manageable simmer. His voice short, he said, "You know nothing of the matter."

"I know you are a Frenchman who has stolen from his own countrymen."

"I'm not a Frenchman."

"Your speech—" Elene began.

"Oh, yes, my speech is French, and my blood is French, though liberally mixed with Irish from a follower of Alexander O'Reilly who sojourned in New Orleans and attracted my grandmother. Legally, however, I am Spanish, since Louis XV of France, to whom my great-grandfather swore his allegiance, gave my country to his cousin, the King of Spain, like getting rid of a troublesome and rather expensive mistress. One of my great-uncles, however, was shot in the Place d'Armes in New Orleans for rebelling against Spanish rule and threatening to set up a republic in the new world. The decrepit Spanish governor at New Orleans, Salcedo, along with Morales, the intendant, this past October canceled the right of deposit at New Orleans for the United States in direct violation of the treaty of 1793. Since the Americans can no longer store their goods at the port before transshipment, the result has been to strangle trade and threaten the livelihood of the city's merchants, not to mention angering the Americans to the point that they are ready to invade. Why should I love the Spanish? And what then am I?"

"You are French, as I'm sure you well know, since Carlos of Spain returned Louisiana to Napoleon over two years ago."

"Ah, but Carlos delays in signing the treaty to make it official, and Bonaparte busies himself elsewhere, neglecting to press the issue. Since France has not taken possession of us, the Spanish alcaldes still offer their arbitrary and sometimes expensive protection from crime in the colony, and a Spanish governor presides over the very dull and proper public assemblies. Therefore I am Spanish, at least officially."

"It doesn't matter in the least," Elene said with some heat. "You might have some consideration for the men and women of the land from which you sprang."

"Oh, I have that. I am a Louisianian, and I attack no ships consigned to merchants who are friends of mine."

"That isn't what I meant."

"You think I should sail against the enemies of France, perhaps? But I do, when they are laden with goods and gold."

With indignation swelling in her breast, Elene said, "You persist in turning my words. Tell me this, have you no decent feeling, no affection for France?"

"Which France might that be? The France that frolicked and gambled at Versailles while tossing a pittance to Louisiana now and again to prevent the starvation of the colonists sent out to discover riches for the coffers of a king? Or perhaps the France that spilled blood into the gutters of Paris until it sickened the very rats, and is now embarked on a vast and glorious military campaign that will fertilize the fields of Europe with the flower of French youth. No, spare me your homilies on loyalty. My best hope is that Napoleon will be so strapped for funds and so disgusted with shipping men off to the New World to die of disease as they have on Saint-Domingue that he will sell Louisiana to the representatives of the United States and make a republic of us after all."

"You must be mad! He would never do such a thing."

"Being too intelligent to throw away the best part of one of the most fertile continents in the world for the sake of being emperor of France? Then he hasn't seen Louisiana. Moreover, he has crowns in his eyes."

Elene sent Ryan a fulminating glance, one it was a pity he could not see. "Napoleon will not be so foolish as to try to set himself up as emperor. The French people will not allow it."

"Will they not? Even for glory? It's my impression they are tired of being ruled by pallid, arguing lawyers. They have a soft spot for monarchs who are adept at the grand gesture."

"What can you know of it," she said in derision, "plying between New Orleans and Cartagena, never leaving this millpond called the Caribbean?"

"The Caribbean is the most treacherous millpond ever constructed by a vengeful God, my girl, but I have also put into Le Havre and Marseilles. I have touched the stones of the Louvre palace and knelt in Notre Dame, crossed the Pont Neuf to the Left Bank and wenched among the twisting streets of Montmartre and in the salons of the wives of Napoleon's generals. How do you come by your opinions, my little provincial?"

"Not by wenching!" she returned with heat.

He gave a quiet laugh. "Hardly."

"You need not take that superior tone, you know! I was in France during the Terror, and afterward. I only returned less than two years ago."

"You what? What can your father have been thinking of?"

"His estates here mainly. That is—" She had not meant to say that, certainly not with such bitterness. It had just come out. How could she have been so disloyal when her father was dead, killed before her eyes. Her voice was tight, thick with tears, when she went on. "I didn't mean it, not that way."

"Didn't you?" he said, his voice grim. The distress in her voice made Ryan want to reach out and hold her, to remove her pain. He could not, nor could he think of any reason why the need should be so compelling. He downed the last of his brandy and set his glass on the stone floor beside the pallet with a sharp click. "Drink your brandy. And stop thinking of things you can't help."

"That's easy for you to say!" she flared, turning on him. "You've never watched your f—father d—die in front of you."

"Not my father, but a number of close friends. You have not been singled out for sorrow. It only seems that way."

"Thank you very much for that bit of philosophy. It helps immensely, of course!"

It was better for her to be angry at him instead of retreating into grief. "At least you're still alive to talk about it," Ryan said.

"You are the most unfeeling, unprincipled rogue it has ever been my misfortune to meet!" Elene whispered fiercely. "I cannot wait until we are released so that I may get as far away from you as possible!"

"I take that to mean you aren't going to New Orleans with me?" Ryan said calmly.

"I wouldn't dream of it."

"In that case, there's the little matter of two men I killed for your sake. I'm sure you intend to shed copious tears over their demise, but will naturally reward me in a suitable manner, afterward, for the service I performed in saving you from their clutches."

Alarm coursed along her veins. "What are you talking about?"

"You can't have forgotten so quickly. The two men in the woods?"

"Certainly I haven't forgotten!"

"Don't tell me you didn't appreciate being rescued from them?"

"Yes, but—"

"Have you no sense of gratitude then? No recognition of the debt? I thought surely someone of your high principles would have been mull-ing over ways of recognizing my efforts and planning suitable recompense."

"I haven't the faintest idea what you mean. You must know that I have nothing except the clothes I stand up in."

"Rather, in this case, the clothes you are sitting down in. Not that it matters. There is always your own sweet and fragrant person."

"Why, you—you— You can't expect me to to—"

"Words fail you, I see. Do you mean to say that I can't expect you to surrender to me the same privileges that you had expected to extend to your groom—or rather have him take by right—on this night? But of course I can. It's not such a great thing, after all."

Her gasp of outrage was perfectly audible. "Not to you, perhaps! No doubt such things palled for a libertine such as yourself long ago!"

"No, no, I assure you. I still find them infinitely pleasurable, as do the ladies I so honor. But it seems to me a deal of fuss is made over the initial act that could just as well be dispensed with. I am supposing, naturally, that the bridal night would have been an initiation. You will correct me if I'm wrong."

"I'll do no such thing!" she declared, her voice rising. "Let me inform you that your presumption, your sheer gall, passes all bounds. I owe you nothing, do you hear? Nothing! It will give me the greatest pleasure if you do not speak to me again."

He had, perhaps, gone a bit too far, Ryan thought, hearing the accents of loathing in her voice.

Their host apparently thought so too, for there came a thumping overhead, as if someone were stamping on the floor. A voice hissed: "Quiet down there!"

They fell silent.

It was astonishing to Elene that she could have become so involved in a quarrel with Ryan Bayard that she had forgotten their danger. There was no excuse she could make for it, except that he was a most infuriating man. Discovering her glass still in her hand, she took a deep swallow of brandy, then fought for breath. How very strong it was. Not that she was a connoisseur; ladies naturally did not drink such strong spirits. She actually felt a little dizzy. Most peculiar. Except that now she considered, she had eaten nothing since early morning, and even then only a roll and coffee. She had not felt able to take so much as a morsel at noon for the clench of apprehension in her stomach. Devota had offered her a bite of meat and roll this evening while she was dressing, but she had refused. There had been a grand feast planned for after the wedding. No doubt the victorious slaves had enjoyed the sumptuous viands that had been prepared over the past few days.

She really should not have any more of the brandy, but was afraid that she might spill what was left when she set the glass down. She drank it off quickly, then got to her knees, reaching to put the glass out of the way with the other things Devota had brought.

"What are you doing?" Ryan asked.

His voice, so near, startled Elene and she jerked away from him. She was thrown off balance in the dark. She could not catch herself with the glass in her hand. She came down on one elbow, a smothered cry of pain escaping her before she clamped her lips shut.

Warm, hard hands fastened on her arms, pulling her up. She was dragged across a taut thigh, cradled between strong legs. "Are you all right?"

"Perfectly," she said, though the words sounded breathless to her own ears. The realization was annoying. "If you will release me, I will be better still."

"By all means."

His grasp loosened. She pushed herself from him, put away her glass, and subsided once more at a fair distance with her back to the wall. Odious, interfering man. It would serve him right if she threw herself into his arms and persuaded him with wild and passionate art to make love to her in order to enslave him. He would then go slowly mad with desire for her because she would certainly not permit him to touch her again. How would he like that, him and his wenching in salons?

A soft laugh bubbled up inside her, and she clamped her hand over her mouth to prevent its escape. Goodness, but she must be more tipsy than she knew. Even if Devota's extravagant claims for the perfume were true and even if she could bring herself to lure Ryan to her, she knew very well that being the object of such a man's desire would not be a laughing matter.

"Are you crying?" Ryan asked, the words a fine balance between trepidation and impatience.

She took instant umbrage. "No, I'm not crying."

"What is the matter with you then?"

"Nothing. Nothing whatever! Why should there be anything the matter with me? I've merely seen dozens of people horribly killed, most of them my neighbors and friends, not to mention being forced to leave my dead father unburied, unmourned. I've escaped death by a hairbreadth myself, only to be nearly assaulted, and am now shut into a tomb with a strange man while in the house of a thoroughly untrustworthy individual who may or may not turn me over to a madman whose particular joy is torturing women. Why, I'm happy as a bride. Never better in my life. I give you my word!"

"All right, it was a stupid question."

"On that we are agreed."

"It might be best if you lie down, try to sleep," Ryan said softly.

"Thank you, no."

"Here I was thinking what a practical and sensible lady you were, not given to fainting or emotional displays, ready to do what was best for yourself. I should have known you were merely too stunned to make a fuss."

Elene swung her head to stare at his dark form. "What a pity for you that I show signs of reviving."

"Yes," he said, heaving a sigh.

Suspicion moved in her mind. She scowled. "You are teasing me."

"Am I?"

"The question is, why?"

"My frivolous nature."

"I don't think so," she said slowly. "I would guess, instead, that you thought it for my own good."

Ryan thought he would have to be careful with the clever Mademoiselle Elene Larpent. She was most acute. He answered her in dry accents, "You malign me."

"Do I indeed?" she said, the words thoughtful.

Silence, it seemed to Ryan, was the best answer. The minutes slipped past. There was no longer any noise from overhead, as if the household had gone to bed. Through the foundations of the house could be heard the faraway murmur of the sea and, now and then, the rustle of a night breeze through a clump of palm and sea grape trees that grew at the side of the house.

Elene tilted her head, listening to the distant sounds. Finally she asked, "Your ship that Favier is to contact, where is it?"

"Somewhere offshore."

"Somewhere—? You mean you don't know where it is. I should have known."

"Well, it didn't seem wise to drop anchor at Cap Française."

"I would imagine it wasn't wise to set foot on the island at all, but you're here," Elene said in quiet asperity.

"I had a cargo to deliver."

"Taken from some blameless French merchantman, I don't doubt."

"English, as it happens."

"In anticipations of the resumption of war between Britain and France."

"Correct."

"I suppose you just hove-to in some protected cove nearby and brought it in to Favier."

"Exactly so. The cove just before the house here, as a matter of fact," Ryan said.

"And then your ship stood out to sea again to wait for you while you arranged your business."

"What a privateer you would make!"

"You may stop jeering!" Elene hissed. "I'm only trying to think how Favier is to let your ship know that you require to be picked up again."

"A light from the headland will suffice."

"So I would imagine. That is, it will if your crew decides to put in near enough to check for one."

"Precisely."

"Therefore the three days, which is no doubt the time that will elapse before they begin to look for your signal."

"I congratulate you," Ryan said.

"It would have been more to the point if you had explained these matters to me."

"But you were so enjoying figuring it out for yourself."

"I would also enjoy watching you hanged as a pirate," Elene said with sweet reasonableness, "but it isn't necessary to my happiness."

"How fortunate for me. You are all such bloodthirsty creatures on this island," Ryan said in mock seriousness. "It must be something in the air."

"Abominable man." The words were tired, without heat.

"No doubt. If I allow you the last word, will you go to sleep?"

"How can I be sure it's safe?" she asked.

The tension in the air was sudden and severe. "Safe from me?" he asked, his voice quiet. "Oh, you can't, but it's a chance you will have to take, won't you?"

CHAPTER 4

ELENE was not herself. She had been annoyed with Ryan Bayard and so had deliberately insulted him. She usually had better manners. True, he had been provoking in the extreme, but she should have remembered what he had done for her this evening.

The trouble was, she had known perfectly well that she was safe with him. She had known also that the suggestion of doubt would disturb him. She had, in fact, credited him with the instincts of a gentleman. It was not what one would expect ordinarily of a privateer.

Not that she had any intention of apologizing. He had been equally insulting, and patronizing on top of it. She wished, however, that she had known how uncomfortable discord between them would be in such a confined space. If they were to spend the next three days sitting in strained silence, it would be unbearable.

Beside her, Ryan shifted. She looked toward him without moving her head. She thought he meant to speak and waited expectantly. When the seconds ticked past and he said nothing, she looked away again. Her chest rose and fell in a silent sigh.

Ryan could not remember when he had been so affected by a woman as he was by the one beside him. He wanted to strangle her for the aspersions she had cast upon his character, but at the same time he had a near uncontrollable urge to hold and comfort her, particularly to hold her. He had expected to be troubled by the restriction of movement in this hole and the prospect of hours of inactivity, but he was beginning to think they might be bearable simply because of Elene Larpent's presence. Her quick wits, sharp tongue, and unexpected gallantry fascinated him. More than that, her perfume was driving him slowly mad.

It was not that the fragrance was cloying, it wasn't that at all. If he felt the need for a breath of fresh sea air, it was not because it bothered him, but because he liked it much too well. He did not consider himself a fanciful man, but he thought he could easily become lost in it, and in the woman who wore it. Utter nonsense, of course. Maybe one of the Negroes this evening had fetched him a blow to the head he had not noticed at the time.

He stretched with what he recognized himself as more than a little ostentation. "I'm going to get some sleep," he said to the stiff form so near him. "You can do the same, or else, seeing we're a bit cramped, lend me your soft lap for a pillow."

"Certainly not!" To think she had been feeling remorse over what she had said to him!

"Certainly not which? You won't lie down, or won't be my pillow? It must be one or the other for the sake of room."

At the thought of his head weighting her thighs, pressing into them, Elene was aware of an odd heaviness in the lower part of her body. She had no illusions that he would not make use of her lap; she thought he might even enjoy it. In which case, he would not get the chance.

She removed herself from the pallet, allowing him room to stretch full length. Even then his head was nearly in their makeshift pantry, for she heard the clink of bottles and glasses as he brushed against them. He swore softly at their close quarters as he settled himself, then all was quiet.

Elene did not have to lie down beside Ryan on the piled quilts of the pallet. Instead, she could sit on the hard stone floor for the rest of the night. Pride was all very well, but she was suddenly weary beyond words, and she could see no reason to permit the privateer to have sole possession of the quilts Devota had provided for her comfort. Perhaps if her behavior was casual, matter-of-fact, it would not seem so daring of her to join him on them.

Moving without undue hesitation that might reveal her reluctance, Elene sat on the edge of the pallet. She removed her ruined satin slippers, feeling their split sides and the dirt embedded in them as she set them neatly side by side. Taking care not to touch the man beside her, she lowered herself to the soft surface until she could lie down with her back to him.

"Here, have this."

A hand was thrust under her neck, lifting her head, and a small pillow was pushed underneath. It was Ryan's folded coat. She put up her hand to grasp it. "It's yours, you keep it."

"For God's sake, don't argue," he said in goaded tones, "or I refuse to be responsible."

"What about you?"

"I never use a pillow."

She took a wrathful breath. "Then that threat—"

"No pillow," he said, a laugh vibrating in his chest, "only laps."

"Despicable." She pulled the coat back under her head with a sharp tug, though much of her anger was for the sharp leap of the senses she felt as she realized he might have wanted to press his face into her thighs.

"Oh, agreed," he answered.

She heard the bleak note in his voice, heard him stir, as if searching for a comfortable position on what was in truth a hard bed. She did the same. They were both still. Her eyes closed. She opened them again. She had already decided, hadn't she, that what had happened this evening was no excuse for lack of manners. Quietly, she said, "Thank you. For the pillow."

There was no answer. She slept.

Dark phantoms cavorted in the dusk. Hideous of visage, grinning, they attacked the innocents, rending, tearing. Elene tried to scream but could not make a sound, wanted to run forward but was unable to move, reached for a weapon only to have it slip from her hands. She was forced to stand watching the slaughter, powerless to intervene. And the phantoms knew. They tormented her, jeering at her over their shoulders. Until all their victims were dead and they turned to advance upon her. Still she had no defense, could not move or cry out.

She awoke with a strangled sound in her throat. Strong bonds held her immobile. She struck out with clenched fists.

"Hush, now. Be still." Ryan's voice was soft at her ear as he captured her flailing arms at the wrists, holding her close against him. "It was a dream, only a dream."

Elene ceased all movement, drawing in her breath with a harsh, smothered gasp. Then the hot, difficult tears came, burning the back of her nose, scalding as they squeezed under her tightly shut eyelids. They ran in stinging salty tracks down her face. Her chest heaved with her breathing and the effort to hide and control her grief. The horror of it could not be contained, and a sob caught, rasping, in her throat.

"Shh." Ryan rocked her, his clasp firm but gentle as he stared into the darkness above her head.

"There was . . . nothing I could do." The pained, constricted words seemed to be jerked out of her as she shuddered.

"No, of course not." Ryan drew back a little, frowning as he released her wrists.

"There were so many. It was over so fast."

"You're safe now. Don't cry."

She wiped futilely at her eyes with the heel of her hand. "I don't know why I should live when so many died. So many."

The guilt of the living for being alive, for having survived. He had known it himself. He might have guessed a woman like this one would feel it also. He cleared his throat of an unaccustomed tightness.

"There was nothing anyone could have done. Don't think of it any more."

"How can I not?" she cried, her voice rising. "That's all there is in my mind. It will always be there. Always!"

She must be quieted. He could try more brandy, but the half of a glassful she had drunk had apparently not been so effective, especially considering that she had been asleep for less than an hour.

"Hush. You will forget, I promise, if you let yourself."

"What do you know of it? You didn't s—see!" Another hiccuping sob wrenched through her.

There was a method that might silence her, from sheer rage if nothing else. Ryan cupped her chin in his long, hard fingers, turning her to face him. Bending his head, he placed his lips upon hers.

Elene choked on a raw, indrawn breath. Her every muscle went taut. Disbelief bloomed in her mind, along with a scorching anger that stopped the flow of tears. She tried to wrench her head away.

Ryan's grasp tightened. Somewhere in the back of his mind he remembered why he had begun this, but the reason was fast receding, routed by the feel of the warm and vibrant woman in his arms. He molded his lips to hers with infinite care, soothing their tender surfaces, offering comfort, surcease, an intimation of desire. He tasted the sensitive corners where they joined, and flicked the moist line of their meeting with his tongue in delicate, pensive pleasure.

Elene pressed her hands to his chest. She wanted to push him away, but seemed to have no strength as the tension ebbed from her body. Her mouth softened, beginning to throb. The privateer's kiss was not threatening, but offered instead a few minutes of practiced beguilement and forgetfulness. The last was the greatest enticement. What could it hurt if, hidden in the darkness, she allowed herself to be swayed? Only for a moment?

The beat of her heart quickened and she could feel the swift race of the blood in her veins. She permitted her lips to part infinitesimally. With a soft sound of surprise, Ryan took instant advantage of that capitulation. He probed the sweet and fragile lining of her mouth, tasting it, running his tongue along the smooth edges of her teeth. He ventured deeper, advancing and retreating in such tantalizing rhythm that excitement burgeoned inside Elene and she followed his lead, touching her tongue to his in her turn. He drew her nearer so that her breasts were pressed hard upon his chest and she could also feel the ridged muscles of his thighs against the smoothness of her own. She could also feel, through the bodice of her gown, the muffled thudding of his heart.

That evidence of his arousal affected her strangely. She had thought him armored inside himself, immune to the weaknesses of the flesh or to any appeal that did not concern money. She had misjudged him. The exposure of his vulnerability gave her a sense of affinity with him. There in that dark hole they were both at the mercy of the unkind fates and their own needs.

She spread the fingers and palm of one hand over his shoulder, enjoying the feel of the hard muscles beneath the fine linen of his shirt. The last vestiges of her nightmare terror eased away. In its place there grew a lassitude that spread, carrying warm acquiescence in its wake.

His mouth tasted of brandy and the sweetness of tempered passion. His tongue was gently nubbed, deliciously abrasive. Elene reveled in the awakening responses of her body, feeling her senses expanding until she was aware with every fiber of her being of the man who held her, the firmness and strength of his long form, the heated male scent of him, the thick crispness of the hair growing low on the back of his neck, the taut resilience of his skin. The play of the shoulder muscles under her hand was a fascination, until she realized he had moved his arm to place his hand on her breast.

A protest rose inside her, but was silenced by the rich rise of sensation as he closed his hand over the soft mound under her bodice and brushed its peak with his thumb. The rapture of it spiraled through her, sending a shiver of intense pleasure deep into the lower part of her body.

It was a pleasure the privateer tended with myriad caresses. He trailed a line of fiery kisses from the corner of her mouth to the turn of her jaw and down the curve of her neck to the hollow of her throat. He paused there, dipping into the small depression with the wet warmth of his tongue, tasting her skin with such consummate refinement that she was too charmed to notice the unfastening of her gown until she felt the waft of cool air on her bare skin.

Then his warm breath, his lips and tongue were upon the trembling globes of her breasts. Lost in rapture, she felt the rush of the blood in her veins, and with it the burgeoning of ardor and a wanton disregard for causes or consequences that she had not known she could feel. With swirling tongue and moist adhesion, he fed that ardor and its companion wantonness until the muscles of her abdomen convulsed in a thrill of purest delight.

To pretend disinterest would be futile. She opened her arms with languid and forthright grace, allowing him access to her body, aiding him as he slid the whispering silk of her gown and undergarments over her hips. She reached to tug his shirt from the waist of his breeches, smoothing her palm over the board hardness of his belly as he rid himself of his clothes and boots and turned to her once more.

The night was long and dark around them; there was no reason for haste. With eager mouths and questing fingertips, searing want and fierce restraint, they sought each other on the quilts. They traced the curves and hollows, the springing hardness and liquid softness of each other's bodies, learning the texture and tone of skin and hair, the shaping of the bones beneath, the sites of utmost response, the quivering limits of endurance. In these rites they never spoke aloud, only whispering a word, loosing a sigh or startled gasp. There was in it something of instinct augmented by carefully gathered signals, of generosity and the ultimate grace of concern. With these things they stretched the very fabric of mutual desire until it throbbed with unbearable tautness between them, refined and thinned so that there shone through it the illumination of some emotion so near to love it would do, this once, for a substitute.

Shuddering, gasping, they moved together then. He placed his knee between her smooth thighs, parting them, fitting his hardness to her softness in fevered, inevitable joining.

Elene felt an instant of burning pain, but it was gone almost before it could register in the glowing recesses of her mind, banished by vital, encompassing ecstasy. Striving, she soared, locked in the elemental dance of life, taking the shocks of Ryan's thrusts, feeling her interior being splintered and reform into a creature abandoned in her need. She wanted him deep, deep inside, and with the wish, rose against him in heated and trembling demand. He met it with unstinting effort, taking her higher, farther from herself, mounting to a plane unthought of, one from which there might be no return.

And there in that rarefied place they found, in defiance of the carnage of death that hovered beyond their refuge, the reverberating glory that in its abundance is the best, and perhaps the only real, affirmation of life.

They collapsed upon each other with heaving chests and racking breaths. The surface of their skin was heated and dewed with perspiration, their muscles quivered. Their hearts jarred against their ribs. They lay with eyes tightly closed and minds stunned to blankness. The closeness of the air in their hole was like a pall in which hung the vivid fragrance of roses and gardenias and something more that defied a name.

Ryan, his forehead resting between the firm twin hills of Elene's breasts, drew a breath that penetrated to the depths of his lungs. Exhaling on a soft, replete laugh, he said, "God, but you smell delicious."

What had she done?

Elene's eyes flew open and she stared fixedly into the darkness. Not once had she thought of the perfume. In fact, she had thought of remarkably little except the effect of Ryan's kisses and caresses. She had failed entirely to consider the effect she might be having on him.

Oh, but there was nothing to Devota's elaborate promises and warnings. Devota had only been trying to reassure her, to reconcile her to marriage with a man she did not love and of whom she was wary. Devota had meant merely to calm her bridal nerves. That was all. Surely that was all?

Elene had never attracted such a response from a man before. There had never been the opportunity, of course; she had never been with a man before in the same way. Still, Durant had never seemed in danger of being overcome with such desire for her, and hadn't there been something in the way Ryan Bayard had looked at her from the first, some extra intensity of interest? He had saved her life, which might account for it. And yet . . .

She didn't want to believe it, wouldn't believe it. Such things as Voudou spells and charms were mere superstition. They worked only because ignorant and gullible people expected them to work, and so let their minds be swayed by those who would manipulate them. She was neither ignorant nor gullible. What had taken place between Ryan and herself was the natural result of throwing a man and a woman together in a tight space under strained circumstances.

"What's it called?" Ryan's voice was deep, lazy.

"What?"

"Your perfume. Does it have a name?"

"I don't think so."

"Don't you know? I thought most women kept up with such things."

Reluctantly she said, "This one is . . . special."

"I thought I had never smelled it before. Did you have a perfumer make it up for you while you were in France?"

"Does it matter?"

He shifted his weight from her, turning to his back and pillowing his head upon her rib cage. "I was just curious. Perfumes make up a fair amount of the cargoes I come across from time to time."

"Particularly on French vessels?"

"As you say. Is it your private scent?"

His curiosity was excessive. Or perhaps it was simply that there was little else to think or talk about. Certainly she could bring to mind no other subject to distract him. "As a matter of fact, Devota made it for me."

"Did she?" He went on with a touch of wryness. "I don't suppose there's much chance of running across it again, then, is there?"

"It . . . isn't likely."

Her voice as she spoke was stiff, the words curt. Ryan turned his head, listening to the echoes. A frown pulled his brows together. "Is something wrong?" He rolled to his side, reaching out to touch her face. "Did I hurt you? I realize you were—"

"No, of course not." She had no wish to discuss her innocence with him.

"I would apologize in form, if it would help, only it seems a little late."

"Yes, please don't."

"In truth, I never really meant to go so far. I just—you were so sweet and felt so good, and your perfume seemed to go to my head."

"It was altogether my own fault, in fact. I understand."

"I didn't say that."

"No, I did." The bleakness of her tone came from the creeping realization that she should be lamenting her lost virginity. It had been wrong of her to give it so easily, wrong to enjoy the giving, or so she had been taught. Doubtless she would regret it in the morning. For now, it seemed right, beyond belief, but right.

"Well it isn't so," he said, his voice hardening. He sat up. "I wanted to comfort you, and I had to quiet you down."

"Thank you very much," she said in exaggerated courtesy. "You did an excellent job of both."

Ryan was silent a moment. When he spoke again the words were even, exact, and without heat. "I didn't mean that the way it sounds, any of it. I have no excuse. I wanted you from the first. When I found a reason to touch you, I wanted you more. That's all there is to it."

Such honesty, and chivalry, deserved a return. "Well, you needn't be such a martyr about it. I wanted you, too."

"Did you?" The slow grin curving his mouth crept, rich and humor-laden, into his tone. "And what about now?"

"You mean—"

"I mean," he answered, moving to recline once more beside her, pressing firmly against her thigh, "do you feel the same? Because you can certainly have any of me you want, and as much."

"Again?" She could not hide her surprise.

"And again, and again."

"Because I smell delicious?" The words were tentative.

"And taste delicious," he said, lowering his mouth to the peak of her breast, sliding his hand down her abdomen toward the apex of her legs, "and feel delicious. And the little sounds you make are delicious."

"So long," she said with a sudden catch in her voice, "as they are not too loud. The sounds?"

"I don't care how much noise you make," he whispered.

It was not the gray light of morning that woke them, though they saw it, coming apparently from some vent or crack in the foundation of the house, when they opened their eyes. What had roused them was a bumping, scraping noise from above them. Ryan raised his head. Elene, lying in his arms with her head nestled in the hollow of his shoulder, did the same. The noise came again.

"Devota," Elene said. If it was Dessalines and his army, the scraping and bumping would be a good deal more violent. Suddenly she sat upright. She was naked. So was Ryan. Shock brushed her, then she remembered. Heat surged to her face.

There came the sound of another chair being pulled back from the table above. The trapdoor would open at any moment. That Devota might see her unclothed mattered little, but there was nothing to say that she would be alone. Favier might be dithering around behind her, peering down at them, ready to attempt to persuade them to leave again.

Elene looked around wildly for her gown and petticoats—there was no time for undergarments. She flung the torn silk gown over her head, thrusting her arms into the sleeves and settling it over her breasts before whipping down the skirt. She could always pretend, if any comment was made, that she had removed her undergarments for coolness.

Beside her, Ryan was pushing his long legs into his breeches and doing up the buttons on each side of the front flap. He threw her a quick grin as he ran a hand through his hair, then reached for his shirt. He had it half on when he suddenly stopped, yanked it off, turned it right side out, then put it on again.

The trapdoor creaked as it was hauled upward. In spite of the faint lightening of the gloom around them with the coming of daylight, they blinked, squinting like moles at the brilliance of the morning sunlight that poured through the dining room windows. So bright was it that for long moments Devota was no more than a silhouette against it.

"Take this, please," she said. "Be careful, it's hot."

She was handing down a tinware pot of coffee. Ryan reached to catch the clothwrapped bail of the pot and set the full container on the floor. Devota then handed him a pair of coffee cups and a bowl of fruit, and after that a large can of hot water, a cake of soap, and a cloth. From her apron pocket she took out a small comb which she tossed to Elene.

Elene's thanks were fervent, and Ryan added his own. The woman waved them aside. "If there is anything else you need, tell me quickly."

Elene looked rather self-consciously at Ryan who shook his head. Devota, a shrewd expression in her eyes, gazed down for an instant at the two of them, taking inventory of their half-dressed state. A faint smile touched her mouth and was gone. She looked at Elene.

"I must go then. I will attend you this evening, *chère*, after everyone is abed. Take care."

"You also."

"Always."

The trapdoor closed. The chairs were replaced above them, then Devota's footsteps receded.

Elene hardly knew which she wanted more, the hot coffee to revive her spirits or the use of the hot water to freshen her body. Since tepid coffee was more objectionable than tepid water, however, she sat down first with Ryan to partake of a breakfast of the coffee and rolls along with a banana and a wing from the roast chicken brought the night before.

The combination of foods was ambrosial. Elene could not remember when anything had tasted so good or she had been so famished. Realizing it, she knew the rise of guilt. She should not be enjoying anything so much when her father and the others were dead. And yet, what good would it do for her to pine and starve herself. It would change nothing; certainly it would not bring them back.

She was subdued, however, as she dipped the cloth into the hot water and squeezed it out, then began to bathe her face. From the corner of her eye, she saw Ryan watching her. There was an absorbed expression on his features as he lounged back on the quilts with a cup of coffee still in his hand.

"What's the matter?" she asked. "Haven't you ever seen a woman at her morning toilette before?"

"Sometimes. Never one quite like you."

"My hair, you mean?" She raised the tangled gold curtain, passing her cloth across the back of her neck.

"The color is unusual, I will admit, but no. It's just that every move you make is graceful."

"What a tale," she said in disbelief. "You must want something."

"It depends," he said, a wicked look in his eyes, "on what you have to offer."

She allowed her mouth to fall open in pretended shock and outrage. "You're insatiable!"

"How can you say so? You know you satisfy me wonderfully."

A flush mounted to her face though she did her best to ignore it. "I hadn't noticed it, your satisfaction, that is."

"Can I help it if you also attract me wonderfully?"

Her movements slowed. She lowered her hands, holding the cloth between them as she wiped at her fingers. She and this man had made love three times more after the first, the last occasion just before dawn. Morning had brought the prickings of conscience, as well as tenderness between her thighs, but since neither problem could be helped, she was trying deliberately to ignore both, concentrating instead on her sense of well-being. Still, she had the distinct feeling that the activity she and Ryan had shared was excessive. She could not see her own face, but there appeared to be shadows under Ryan's eyes that had not been put there by sleeplessness alone.

Insatiable. That was the word Devota had used. *"He will be in thrall to you—his need for you will be insatiable."*

"Do I really attract you so much?" she asked, allowing her gaze to drop. "Or is it simply that you haven't had a woman in some time?"

He laughed as he drank off the last of his coffee and set his cup aside. He rose to one knee, leaning toward her. "Both, maybe. We could test it this morning, to be sure."

She warded him off with one hand. "It's daylight!"

"Does it matter?"

It occurred to her suddenly that the use of soap and hot water might have a considerable effect upon his ardor, if there was any chance that Devota had been telling the truth. "And besides, you haven't bathed."

"I don't know what difference that can make," he said, still grinning, "I only smell like you."

"The way my perfume might smell on a boar hog," she snapped, incensed by his lack of cooperation.

He grimaced. "Ah, well, in that case."

But undoubtedly it took more to remove the perfume than a quick swipe with a cloth for, when tested later, his lust for her was undiminished. If anything, it appeared to be even greater.

As a pastime, making love could hardly be bettered; still it was possible to beguile only so many hours in that fashion due to physical limitations. The day passed with dragging slowness. A dozen times, Ryan and Elene wished they had thought to ask Devota for a deck of cards, a chessboard, any kind of game with which to pass the time. The possibility of a book or two for the following day was discussed, but it was agreed there was just not enough light to see a printed page. They napped off and on, coming awake at every slightest noise. When they were not sleeping, they listened intently, speculating between themselves on what was taking place above them from the sounds they heard.

Most of all, they talked, developing a low pitch to their voices that was clear to each other, but would not penetrate beyond their hiding place. They told stories of their childhoods and of their schooling: Elene at her boarding school, Ryan with a pockmarked, vile-tempered, but brilliant tutor. They talked of books and plays and of pieces of music they enjoyed. They spoke of France and the man who had come to personify it these days, Napoleon Bonaparte; of his policies and his strength as First Consul for Life; his effect upon trade and in the social sphere, and also the scandals attached to his wife Josephine's name.

Mentally they walked the streets of Paris, pointing out to each other favorite views, favorite houses, favorite haunts. Ryan had not spent a great deal of time there, and neither had Elene, having only visited for a few days with her aunt, but it was enough.

"You will love New Orleans," Ryan said as the hours waned into the darkness of evening once more and they were waiting to see what Devota would bring them for a late supper.

Elene hesitated, unaccountably reluctant to say anything that might cause discord. There was no way to avoid it, however. "But I'm not going."

"Aren't you?" The question was mild enough, but even as it was spoken, Ryan felt the hardening of a resolve inside himself to see her on his ship if he had to carry her bodily. There was something about Elene Larpent that drew him irresistibly, something that fascinated him. She was sweet and warm and touchingly untutored in the ways of love, but there was more to it than that. It was as if she held some secret, as if there was some part of herself she would not give, except perhaps as a gift of inestimable value to one who proved worthy of it.

Elene made a brief, dismissive gesture. "I know nothing about the place, beyond the fact that the people speak French in spite of forty years of Spanish rule, that it's hot and incredibly muddy and crawls with snakes. That much my father told me in his letters while he was there."

"The snakes are bad only when it floods," Ryan answered. "Otherwise it's a pleasant town. The breezes from the water keep it fairly comfortable in summer, and the winters are just cool enough to be a change. It has the look, somehow, of both a French and a Spanish town. The reason is the fires during the Spanish regime that caused much of it to be rebuilt. The balconies, the wrought iron, and the courtyards give it a Spanish air, but the roof lines, the shapes and position of doors and windows, the rounded corners of the streets, will remind you of Paris."

"Papa said he was almost extinguished with boredom."

"He must have made no attempt to become known to people. There are always balls and dances, card parties and musical evenings and outings into the country, and for the gentlemen, cafés, cockfights, gambling dens, and drinking houses of all kinds serving everything from wine and absinthe to ale. Then everyone strolls in the square, the Place d'Armes, to take the evening air and see and be seen."

"You are fond of it, are you not?" Elene asked.

"It's my home," he answered, as if no other explanation were needed.

She looked away. She wished she had that sense of belonging. She must have felt something of it as a child for the island, but there had been so many years in France that it had faded. France itself, because there was always the possibility of being recalled to the island at a moment's notice, had never quite seemed like home.

Ryan waited for some comment. When none was forthcoming, he said, "New Orleans could be home to you, too."

Elene lifted her chin. "Saint-Domingue is where I was born."

"I assume you have thought of someone here who may help you then, some friend of your father's, or business acquaintance?"

"No one," she said, coolness entering her voice.

"Ah, well, I'm sure something will come to you." He stretched and relaxed, shifting to lie at full length on the pallet. "For instance, you can always throw yourself on the mercy of the officer in charge since the death of General Leclerc."

"General Rochambeau?"

"You think it would be useless to aim so high? You may be right. There is a fat colonel I met a few days ago who would, I expect, be the very man."

Suspicious of his cheery helpfulness, she asked, "How so?"

"He appeared to have a heart as soft as his brain, and a most lascivious eye. I'm sure you could persuade him to do anything you please. You might even marry him."

"Marry? Never!"

"Become his mistress?"

"What?" she cried in wrath.

"His laundress then? Though you should know that the women who go under that name are sometimes expected to perform other services when officers remove their uniforms."

"I know that," she said, goaded. "Anyway, I thought you were certain the French under Rochambeau will be defeated?"

"In that case, there will always be the beefy British officers removing their uniforms."

She snatched up his coat and flung it in the general direction of his head in the dimness.

The mock exasperated click of his tongue was muffled by the cloth of the coat over his face. "There's just no helping some people."

CHAPTER 5

"LIGHT the candle," Elene whispered.

Ryan came awake abruptly, which was not surprising since he had been jabbed in the ribs. "What is it?"

"There's something in here with us. Light the candle."

A pattering sound, slight, stopping then starting again, could be heard. It was followed by delicate scrabbling in the corner where their food supplies sat.

"It's a rat," Ryan said softly.

"I know that," came Elene's reply in a fierce undertone. "Light the candle!"

The creature had been attracted by the food, no doubt, and had made his way under the house's foundation and shimmied down into the hole with them. Nothing short of annihilation could keep it away from them now, and Elene had no intention of sharing their refuge or their food with it. Not only did such vermin carry fleas and disease, it just might become tangled in her hair as she slept.

Beside her, she heard the scrape of flint in the tinderbox as Ryan prepared to make a light. Stealthily, she reached out, feeling for one of his boots to use as a weapon.

She touched the rat's tail. It was hairless and cool and twitched under her fingers. She jerked her hand back, smothering a cry of repugnance.

"What is it?" There was concern in Ryan's voice.

"I touched it!" she said, shuddering with loathing.

She thought she heard the ghost of a laugh. A moment later, a yellow light flared as the tinder caught. Ryan reached for the candle and thrust the wick into the small flame, then as the candle caught, snapped the box closed to extinguish the lighted flint.

Elene pounced on the boot she had been seeking and raised it in her hand. She looked around for the rat. It was just whisking behind the water jug. She lunged after it, beating the floor as it jumped and dodged.

"Kill it," she said over her shoulder in passionate intensity, "kill it."

Ryan set the candle in a corner, took up a boot, and gave chase. He and Elene hammered and smacked the floor, leaping this way and that, dodging each other and the rat as it made frantic dashes from one side of the hole to the other. Their shadows swooped around the walls in a fantastic dance, colliding, separating, meshing, and springing apart.

The contest was never in doubt. The rat had got into the hole easily enough, but there was no easy way out, and there were two of them armed with unflagging determination as well as a boot each. Within seconds, it was over. Ryan removed the corpse to the dirt ledge just under the trapdoor, where it would be out of the way until Devota could dispose of it. The two of them sat down then to catch their breaths.

"Poor little beast," Ryan said in mournful tones, "all it wanted was a bite to eat."

"Yes, right out of your big toe, I expect," Elene said, unaffected by his spurious regret.

"What a hard-hearted female you are; I didn't know it was in you."

"I hate rats."

She refused to look at him. She was, if the truth were known, a little embarrassed by her own zeal, and sickened by the sound that had been made as Ryan dealt the rat the mortal blow.

"I thought you might," Ryan said, his voice dry.

She flung him a quick, frowning glance. "I didn't notice you being squeamish."

"No, indeed," he agreed promptly. "I certainly have no love for them. More than that, when a lovely lady requires my services, I give them gladly and to the utmost of my ability."

"Do you, now?"

"I do. Particularly when the lady is one who might, perhaps, be generous in her gratitude."

"You really expect me to reward you?" she asked in disbelief.

"Only if you feel it's due."

"Of all the insufferable, conceited—"

"Now how was I to know you would be upset? Here you were planning to give yourself into the keeping of a fat colonel merely for the sake of his patronage. Surely there's little difference?"

"I was planning no such thing! You're the one who made that vile suggestion."

"You had nothing else to propose, and it's as plain as the nose on your face that you will have to make an accommodation with a man in one way or another," Ryan said matter-of-factly.

"I don't see that at all," Elene said. She sniffed in protest.

"No? The fact is, only a man can protect you in these desperate times. On top of that is the fact that you are much too attractive, much too desirable, for the vultures to leave you alone."

"Vultures among whom you, naturally, don't count yourself."

"Oh, but I do. I'm chief among their number."

"At least you're honest," she said. It was meant to come out with cold sarcasm, but instead had a compressed sound.

"Such an admission! Now this is progress."

Ryan sat watching her, the way the candlelight made a warm pearl sheen on her skin and gathered itself in golden fire in her hair, the way it glorified the soiled splendor of her rag of a gown. It was foolish of him beyond measure, but he felt no real urge to leave this prison of theirs. If he was not careful, the end of their incarceration would be the end of their acquaintance, the end of something that was assuming the aspect in his mind of a subterranean idyll.

Elene sent a glance through her lashes at the man lounging at ease beside her. He was joking, she thought. He didn't really expect her to reward him for killing the rat by giving him her body. Or did he? He was a difficult man to know, or to trust. He gave so little of himself away. Despite the intimacy they had shared, the vast amount of talking they had done, she still could not feel she knew him. It was as if he guarded some essential part of himself. Not that she could blame him; she did the same.

Irritation flashed across Ryan's face and was gone. He gave a short laugh. "Don't make such hard work of it. I want nothing from you that you aren't ready to give. Lie down and go back to sleep."

Almost before he finished speaking, he leaned and pinched out the candle. The hole was plunged into darkness once more. Elene heard the rustle of his clothing as he prepared to lie down. She moved hastily to give him room, stretching herself out on the pallet. His arm touched hers and she drew away as if she had been scorched. They shifted a little, seeking comfort. Not finding it in any degree, they subsided in resignation.

The moments slipped past. Elene stared unblinkingly into the dark. She would like to discover some other option for safety than those Ryan had recounted for her: a relative overlooked until now, a government official who might be in her father's debt, a friend who would take her and Devota in or offer them passage elsewhere. There was nothing.

When she slept, the nightmare returned, but she conquered it silently and alone.

Elene and Ryan could always tell when someone was in the room above them. Footsteps sounded loud on the floor above their heads, making a hollow, rumbling echo in their enclosed space. Sometimes they could hear voices in snatches of conversation, a pair of servant girls or the querulous tones of an older woman who was without doubt Favier's mother admonishing, ordering this or that task done.

Dinner time was the worst to endure. Then the dirt that was embedded in the rug covering the trapdoor sifted down whenever a chair was moved. The smell of rich food and wine penetrated to them at a time when their own late evening meal might still be hours away, after the house was quiet for the night so that Devota could bring it. But most of all, the presence of Favier, with his mother and once even a pair of guests, forced Ryan and Elene to remain in absolute stillness for what seemed like countless eons. They learned to be intensely grateful that the members of the household took breakfast in bed and the noon meal somewhere outside, probably on a gallery.

The conversations they overheard during the course of various dinners proved illuminating, however. It appeared that while Dessalines himself was attempting to drive the French troops from the island, he had sent groups of his own men to encourage the rising of the slaves still on the plantations, urging them to the destruction of their masters for the purpose of eventually killing every white man, woman, and child on the island or else driving them from it. The list of houses burned and families massacred grew longer with each day. There were endless tales of people cornered in cane fields, found hiding in barns and stables, or caught as they tried to flee to Port-au-Prince or Cap Française. They all ended the same, with death, though only after the most savage assault and mutilation.

It sometimes seemed that Favier delighted in speaking of such things while he ate, talking overloud to be sure they could hear, as if in forcing them to listen he was paying back all the slights and insults that had been visited upon him by their kind over the years. However, his own position was none too good. It was always possible that a mob bent on blood might make a mistake, might choose the wrong house, accidentally or otherwise, under the cover of night.

It was somewhere near midmorning of the third day, as far as Elene could tell, when there came the sound of a pair of voices raised in altercation almost directly above them. They belonged to Devota and Favier's mother.

Ryan came as erect as was possible for him, crouching with his back to the stone wall, balanced and poised, as if ready to defend their sanctuary. Elene rose also. She listened intently, her gaze automatically lifted to the wooden barrier of the trapdoor overhead.

What had happened? Had Favier said something that made his mother think there might be something of interest hidden away down here? Or had the woman perhaps become curious about Devota's presence in the house and kept watch on her movements, discovering her interest in the dining room to be excessive?

It was always possible that she and Ryan had made some sound that had alerted the older woman, perhaps spoken an unguarded word at the wrong time. They had tried to limit discussion of any length to the late night hours, to listen always for footsteps before they spoke, and to remember even then to use the most muted of tones. Still, there had been times when they had forgotten.

After a few minutes, it became clear that Devota had been discovered trying to bring them their breakfast. The older woman was upbraiding her for sneaking food from the kitchen, demanding to know where she was going with it. Devota had apparently said she was going to the table to eat her meal, for the explanation brought on a shrill tirade about servant's getting above themselves, thinking they could use the master's furniture as they saw fit, lying abed until all hours, stuffing themselves with the best of everything from the master's pantry.

Devota's answer was insolent, there could be no other word for it. It also made Elene's eyes widen in shock. If the words Devota spoke were true, it appeared she had taken on the role of Favier's mistress.

It was an excellent excuse for being in the house instead of out in the slave cabins with the slaves, there could be no denying that, but was it only an excuse? Could Devota actually have given herself to Favier in order to safeguard Elene and Ryan?

Devota was ordered into the kitchen to eat. The voices receded. Only the smell of the coffee and bacon Devota had been bringing to them, maddeningly fragrant, remained.

Elene sank slowly back down onto the pallet. "Do you realize," she whispered, "that we are as trapped here in this place as the rat we killed?"

"The whole island is a trap, as I told you before. This is just another degree of it." Ryan let himself down to sit close beside her so they need speak no louder than a breath of sound.

"What will you do if we are discovered?"

"The only thing I can do. Fight, and hope there aren't too many of them."

"What if Favier's mother should find us? He seemed to think she will give us away."

"If she lifts that door up there, I think she will have to join us in here, willing or not," Ryan said. He clenched a fist.

"Yes," Elene said, almost to herself. It might be possible to do that. "Yes."

Devota did not come for the rest of the day. Nor did she come when dinner was over and the house grew still with the advance of night. Elene fretted over her maid's continued absence, not just because she was hungry, though they had had nothing except a chunk of bread since the night before, but because she was worried about the woman who was her aunt. What if Favier's mother had become suspicious, had shut Devota up somewhere, or decided to be rid of her son's troublesome new woman? What if Devota had left the house for some reason and been recognized and killed? The possibilities were many, each more horrible than the last.

Ryan was on edge also, cursing the fact that he could not stand up to his full height, that he could not tell what was taking place beyond the house walls, that he was unable to make things happen himself. Elene thought he did not trust their host, no matter how sanguine he pretended to be when she questioned him about it. This was the night when Ryan's ship could be expected to put in an appearance. If Favier did not bestir himself, if he should prove too cowardly to call attention to his house by going out and waving a lantern, then the two of them might have to stay in their hiding place another three days or longer. It did not bear thinking of, not when the danger of discovery increased every day, every hour.

Elene, in her bare feet, paced up and down the quilts in the small space available to her without stepping over Ryan's long legs with each turn. There was inside her a growing need to leave this dark place, to breathe fresh air and feel open space around her, to see the sun and the sky, trees and flowers and grass, to sit in a real chair and sleep in a real bed. The pressure of it was building inside her, until she was not sure how much longer she could contain it. More than that, like Ryan, she wanted to know what was happening above them. That need was so strong it seemed worth any risk to satisfy.

Ryan reached out to catch her skirt as she crossed in front of him once more in her striding. His voice rough, he said, "Sit down. You're driving me mad."

He was effectively prevented by the low ceiling from the free movement she was using to relieve her feelings. She made a rueful grimace that he could not see, then knelt to settle beside him.

"I'm sorry," she murmured.

"You can't continue like this, you know, living from day to day like a scared rabbit down a hole. You have to come with me to New Orleans."

"We have been through this before. I have no way to live."

"Is it any better here? But you do have a way. You can live with me." That had not come out the way Ryan had planned; still, it was close enough.

"I see. You rate yourself higher than a fat colonel."

"I want to take care of you. With me, you will not only be safe, you will have every comfort, every luxury."

"What a charming prospect. I am almost tempted, but you see I have been used to rather more respectability. I am assuming, of course, since you don't mention it, that marriage is not a part of your kind offer?"

"I have no wish to marry just yet," Ryan said. "It would not be fair to take a wife when I am so often away at sea."

"Fairness to a mistress not entering into the matter?" Elene had no more wish to be married than he, but to say so at the moment could only weaken her position.

"She would have no reason to complain," he returned, keeping his voice low with an obvious effort. "You don't understand what I'm saying at all, nor are you trying to."

"I understand you feel free to offer me this insult because in a moment of weakness I succumbed to your blandishments and my own need for consolation. I understand that you also have acquired a sense of responsibility for me—not enough to take me on for life, but enough to make you reluctant to leave me behind. I will even concede that you may have some degree of desire for me, if you like; I doubt that otherwise the invitation would include sharing your living quarters. Just don't try to make me think that your interest is based solely on concern for my welfare. I don't believe it, and won't believe it."

"Do you believe," he said pleasantly, "that I will put you on my ship with my own hands, no matter how much you kick and scream, if you don't agree to come with me?"

"Certainly," she said without hesitation. "I would put nothing past you."

He cursed under his breath for long, colorful moments. When he spoke again, his voice was strained, but calm. "The major cause of the problem here is that damnable perfume you wear. There might never have been any blandishments, as you call them, if it hadn't been so enticing. But never mind. Your stay in my house need be for the barest amount of time necessary to establish yourself elsewhere. I have no more use for a reluctant mistress, I thank you very much, than you have to be one."

"Indeed? How magnanimous! Especially since I have no means of establishing myself elsewhere." The words were merest bravado. She had managed to forget the role the perfume had played in her seduction.

"You can't have been using your head these last three days. You have only to make up a few batches of that scent, and your fortune's assured."

He was not serious, only clutching at straws to enforce his argument. Nevertheless, was the idea so farfetched? There was no denying that the fragrance was exquisite, with or without its supposedly unique property. If Devota were able to concoct it in New Orleans, if the ingredients, the precious oils and essences, were available, then it might sell. Naturally the incantations or the particular herb or oil that turned it into a powerful and long-lasting aphrodisiac must be left out, but that should not affect its smell.

"Oh, I'm sure that's just what New Orleans needs, a new scent." The words were jeering, yet inside Elene felt the slow rise of excitement.

"A sweet one, at any rate. All the perfumes of Araby could hardly cover the smells of the open gutters and back lot privies. There's also the overripe fish and soured fruit from the old French market, fermenting molasses from the warehouses, and the odors from the cemeteries where paupers are simply covered with quicklime in a mass grave. Nor is that saying anything of the mold and mildew that grows everywhere, or the effects on the human body of months of hot weather and, for some, scant bathing."

"You almost convince me that New Orleans is a wonderful place," she said in dry tones, "for a perfumer."

"It's the only place for you."

"Possibly so," she answered.

She allowed her words to stand for an agreement. It had, perhaps, been foolish of her to fight the idea. As a destination, a place of refuge, it had been apparent New Orleans was the best choice from the beginning. She would be among her own kind, people who spoke the same language, had the same customs. Even so, to go so far from all she knew, to make her home among strangers, arriving with not even a purse in her hand, much less anything to put in it, was not easy.

There was a part of her that was aghast at her acceptance of the prospect of living with a man, even for a brief period. She winced away from it. What she required was to gain control of her life. That was the only security, to arrange matters so she need not answer to father, husband, or even lover, but only to herself. If Ryan Bayard, or even her perfume, could be used to that end, then that was what she must do.

So busy was Elene with plans and ideas that it was more than a half hour later before she realized that her exact position in Ryan's house during the time she would spend there had not been determined. She opened her mouth, then closed it again without a sound.

Someone was coming.

They saw the glow of the candlelight first. It shone through the cracks between the floorboards above them, casting odd, moving streaks over the stone walls. The footfalls that accompanied it were light, almost creeping. There was a long pause, as if whoever was above them was standing listening, looking around with care.

The chairs began to slide, barely scraping, as they were quietly pulled back. Dust sifted as the rug was pulled aside. Ryan, on his feet, was still. Elene was the same, though she looked about her in the faint light for a weapon. Her hands slowly curled into fists. Tension sang along her veins and hovered around her like a tangible presence.

The iron ring used to lift the trapdoor rattled. There came a soft grunt of effort. With a creak of hinges, the heavy door began to lift. They saw a woman's skirt. Beside her sat a lantern of pierced tin, its rays wavering through the holes, making odd patterns in the darkness. There was no sign of a tray, no smell of food. The door was raised higher, higher still. It was laid back on its hinges.

It was Devota.

A small sound of relief escaped Elene. The maid gave her a quick smile of sympathy, but wasted no time on greetings or explanations. "Out, quickly," she said, her voice the merest husk of sound. "The ship is coming in."

They needed no further urging. Ryan took a running leap, put his hands on the edge of the hole, and with a powerful bunching of shoulder and chest muscles, hoisted himself up, catching the edge of the floor and pulling himself free of the hole. He turned, balancing on one knee as he extended his hand down for Elene. She stepped into her slippers, then caught his wrist. His firm fingers locked around her arm. She gave herself a boost, and was drawn upward until the floor edge was at her waist and she could scramble up onto the thick boards.

Ryan helped her to her feet, then bent to close the trapdoor. They threw the rug back in place and quickly replaced the chairs. Devota swung away then, picking up the lantern by its bail, whispering, "This way."

"Favier?" Ryan said softly.

"Hiding," Devota answered in disgust. "I waved the lantern myself."

"We are in your debt. But the light won't be needed again. Extinguish it."

Devota did as Ryan bid her, then set the lantern down in the middle of the floor and left it while she led them from the dining room.

They did not speak again. As quietly as ghosts, they moved through the house to the back doors, then through them out onto the gallery. A moment more, and they were on the open lawn that led to the lip of the headland.

The air was soft with moisture, warmly caressing, and so fresh with the breath of the night sea that it was like elixir. Elene felt her senses expand, swelling into the infinite space around her as if they had been cramped. A pale moon beamed down. It looked exactly like the one on the night she and Devota had run from her burning home, though now its light had the strength of a caress. Somewhere nearby sea grapes and palm trees rattled in the breeze, a constant, soothing sound.

They were halfway across the lawn, their shadows thrown by the moonlight racing ahead of them, when abruptly it seemed to Elene that there was too much space around them, that their position was too open, too exposed. It was, perhaps, the effect of confinement and her fears. That possibility held her quiet for another stride or two. Until she remembered her unease, before.

"Ryan?" she whispered.

"I know," he said. "Keep walking. Don't run, not yet."

They stretched their strides, taking another. Another.

A shout, shrill with anger, rang out behind them. It was taken up by what sounded like a hundred throats, becoming a deep and undulating roar.

"Now run!"

Elene picked up her skirts and sprinted as hard as she could go. There was no need to look back; she knew what she would see. The men, the machetes, the guns. Her eyes blurred with tears of effort, her chest felt raw with the gasps of her breathing. The thudding of her heart was a violent drumbeat. Stones and sharp pieces of shell embedded in the wild grasses cut her feet through her thin satin slippers, but she did not feel them. She could hear Devota pounding along on one side and Ryan on the other. It was her nightmares all over again, a race with howling death, one she could not win, not again.

A shot rang out. They heard the whine of the ball overhead. The yelling and blood-hungry cries behind them seemed closer. So was the lip of the headland. Another shot blasted the air. A path like a pale and sandy trench slanting down and to the right appeared before them. They swerved into it in a splatter of sand. Downward they leaped, sliding over the sand-covered rocks.

Below them was the moonlit crescent of a beach with the dark and sparkling waves slowly washing back and forth. The low shape of a boat lay at the water's edge. Beside it was two men who stood staring up at the headland with the muskets in their hands held at the ready. Beyond them, out on the breast of the waves, lay a twin-masted schooner with the graceful, raking lines of a ship built for speed. It rode at anchor within the enclosing arms of the cove, without a light or a hint of sound to indicate its presence.

The rampaging Negroes spilled over the edge of the promontory behind them, crashing through the growth that lined the edge. They yelled in piercing triumph as they spotted their quarry. The rocks they dislodged rattled down.

Another shot rang out, zinging past Elene's head. A lance, hurtled with incredible strength, impaled itself in the sand to the right. Two others fell just behind them, and one sailed above, arching to splash into the sea.

Ahead lay the flat stretch of the beach. Elene reached it first, hurtling herself along it with sand flying from under her feet. Ryan turned to look back. The dark forms were a surging mass on the slope of the headland. He swung back toward the boat and cupped his hands around his mouth. "Fire!" he shouted. "Fire!"

The double blast of both muskets going off at once smote the air. Cries of pain and panic rang out from the slope behind them. The pursuit slackened. The boatmen threw their muskets into the long craft and began to shove off, though holding it ready, afloat on the high tide.

Ten more yards, five, and then they were at the boat, clambering over the sides. Ryan snatched up a musket, took the powder and ball one of the boatmen tossed to him, and began to reload even as the two men sprang, wet and cursing, over the gunwales. They picked up the oars and began to row. Ryan swung his loaded musket and squeezed the trigger. The man in the lead of the Negroes streaming now along the shoreline threw up his hands and fell backward.

There was no time for more. The boat lunged over the waves in a hard, thrusting rhythm, leaving the beach behind. Another shot or two roared out, but the balls made harmless spouts in their wake. The stretch of water between boat and sandy shore widened, gently rolling, dancing in the moonlight. A few of the pursuers waded out, shouting, gesticulating with raised fists, but they could hardly be heard.

Elene turned to face the front of the boat. Though she held to the thwart on which she sat with both hands, she gave her attention to the ship that lay before them. Painted dark gray with a broad white stripe circling it just beneath the bowsprit, it appeared to have the carved figure of a woman in flowing robes for a figurehead. The black letters on the white stripe were etched in moonlight, spelling out her name, the *Sea Spirit*.

A rope ladder dangled down one side. There were a number of people gathered around it at the top. They had been shouting out encouragement, though with the distance and the wind on the water, Elene had thought the sounds to be some kind of bird cries. They reached out to give a helping hand as Elene reached the top of the swaying ladder. She accepted their support gratefully, though she turned at once to see to Devota who was none too happy over the perilous ascent.

In a moment, they were all on deck. Orders were given to bring the boat on board. A man stepped forward to shake Ryan's hand and congratulate him, a man with dark curly hair and laughing eyes whom Ryan addressed as Jean but introduced as the ship's captain. The others surged around them, men and women in what appeared to be evening dress, all of them exclaiming, laughing in excitement, asking questions in high voices.

Elene was suddenly so tired she could hardly see. The muscles in her legs were trembling in wrenching spasms. Afraid she would fall down, she reached out to catch Ryan's arm. He turned to look at her, felt the tremors running through her fingers, and slipped his arm around her waist to draw her against him.

"Let's get below," he said.

The way was miraculously cleared for them. The others trooped ahead, ducking through doorways, stepping over high thresholds until they reached what appeared to be a small common room, or officer's dining quarters. The men picked up drinks they had left standing here and there. The women took up sewing and embroidery, or a book. Yet they all waited expectantly as Ryan and Elene entered, as if they had been looking forward to meeting the famous privateer, Bayard, the man who was undoubtedly their host.

Where had they come from, all these people, Elene wondered in the dullness of exhaustion as she surveyed them by the light of a pair of lamps swinging in gimbals on the side walls. They had the look, in their clothing and their pale, sallow faces, of islanders, though it did not seem likely a privateer would carry passengers.

Even as the glimmering of an answer began to form, a man stepped from among their number. Of medium height, arrogant even with an angry red slash down his cheek and his white suit wrinkled and stained, he moved toward Elene with his hands held out, sure of his welcome.

"Elene, my love, my bride," Durant Gambier said in rich pleasure. "I thought I had lost you, but no. By the grace of *le bon Dieu* you have been returned to me."

CHAPTER 6

"BY the grace, rather, of Ryan Bayard," Elene said in brittle contradiction, then watched her fiancé come to a halt with the smile fading from his face.

Where the words had come from, she could not tell. There was a vague feeling in the back of her mind that they could prove dangerous, but that did not deter her. Her one aim had been to stop Durant from taking her into his arms, from claiming her once more. Ryan had been too obvious a shield to ignore. If there were consequences for using him, she would face them later.

The silence that fell had an avid quality, as though the little drama being enacted was a welcome distraction from problems the others who were gathered there would as soon escape. The dull red of rage began to rise in Durant's face. He put his hands on his hips, his gaze moving in frowning incredulity to Ryan's arm at Elene's waist before lifting to the face of the privateer. Ryan stared back with a faint smile curving his lips and one brow raised in enquiry.

Behind them, the ship's captain stepped into the room, moving around Devota who hovered just inside the door. It appeared he meant to ask something of Ryan, but sensing the stiff confrontation in progress, hesitated. Ryan turned to him. "Tell me, Jean," he said, his tone conversational, "who are all these people?"

The captain looked as uneasy as a small boy who has come home with more marbles than he had when he left. "Refugees, Ryan, people trying to get away from Saint-Domingue. They came out in small boats

—some yesterday evening, some two nights ago—whenever we came in sight of land. I couldn't turn them away."

"No, I don't suppose you could." Ryan turned to the group. "Forgive me, ladies and gentlemen, but Mademoiselle Larpent and I have had a trying time. We will make ourselves known in proper form later, but for the moment what we want is a bath, food, and a place to lay our heads. If you will excuse us?"

"Now see here—" Durant began.

"Later." There was the rasp of steel in that one word.

A woman stepped forward and placed her hand on Durant's arm. She moved with unconscious poise, as if she quite expected every eye to be upon her. She was not beautiful in the classic sense: her hair was a russet-red shade that was most unlikely to be natural, her skin was pale and rather sallow, and her features piquant. Regardless, her voice when she spoke had such lovely modulation, was so rich and sensual in timbre, that she was fascinating.

"Dear Durant," the woman said, "let them go if you have any kindness in your heart. Only think how desperate we were for the comforts of food and rest ourselves not long ago."

Ryan inclined his head to the red-haired woman, then began to move with Elene at his side toward a doorway on the opposite side of the room.

The ship's captain cleared his throat before calling after him. "Ryan? Our destination, what is it?"

"New Orleans," Ryan said over his shoulder, adding with delicate irony, "with all possible speed, if you can manage it. I don't suppose the committee who saw us off had a boat handy, but it might be a good idea to get underway, just in case."

The owner's cabin on board the schooner was by tradition the largest available. That was not saying a great deal. It contained a fairly wide bunk with a sea trunk at the foot, a drop-leaf table pushed against one wall with a pair of straight chairs drawn up to it, and a washstand with a china bowl sunken into the top. There was barely enough room left in the center of the floor for the bath tub when it was brought.

The tub, of English manufacture, was of painted tin and to Elene looked like nothing so much as a large baby's bootie. The bather climbed into the top and sat down with legs extended into the covered foot. The main advantage of the style aboard ship was that the water was unlikely to splash out of it. In addition, it took little of that precious fluid to fill it up and, when entered, the water rose to the shoulders for luxurious soaking.

Elene washed away the accumulated grime from her skin and hair, then sat for a long time, letting the tightly held fear and the tiredness seep from her bones. Her mind drifted as she refused to order her thoughts. Ryan had gone out again after ordering the bath and food, she thought, to give her privacy. It was considerate of him.

The motion of the ship changed, rising higher, falling deeper. They were not only moving, they had left the sheltered curve of the shoreline where the ship had been anchored. They were on their way to New Orleans.

How incredible it was. Who would have dreamed a week ago that she would be here on this ship tonight, with everything she owned gone from her, everything she knew dropping away behind her.

Except Durant.

Just for an instant when she had first seen him—the fiancé her father had chosen for her—he had represented everything that was normal and right and orderly. It had seemed that she must go to him, that she could not do otherwise. Then something inside her had revolted. Nothing was as it had been. Nothing compelled her to act now except her own desires, her own needs. Nor would she.

Where that left Durant, she was not sure. He must be made to understand that he could not take up where he had left off. She would not be pressed into a marriage she did not want. For now she needed time to look around her and see what this new life that had been thrust upon her had to offer; time to think, to plan, to discover what it was she really desired, what she needed.

How ironic that Durant should be on Ryan's ship. It had happened because the *Sea Spirit* was one of the few ships near Saint-Domingue at this time of upheaval when trade was nearly at a standstill. She could have wished, however, that he had chosen another vessel, any other vessel, to take him away from the island. If she had seen him weeks from now in New Orleans, when the past few days had had time to become no more than a terrible memory, she might have felt more like dealing with him, might have had a better idea of what to say and do. As it was, she would have to rely on luck and instinct.

She was still in the tub when a knock came on the door. Devota had just left the cabin to see what was taking so long to get something to eat. Elene struggled up, not without difficulty, and reached for the strip of

Turkish toweling. Wrapping it around her, she stepped from the tub and moved to the door.

"Who is it?"

"Hermine Bizet. I have a few things for you, since I understand you could bring nothing of your own and we are much the same size."

There was no mistaking the lovely voice of the red-haired woman. Elene opened the door. "It's very kind of you, but I wouldn't want to deprive you of what you were able to save."

"Don't give it a thought," the woman said, her smile roguish. "Theater people are used to leaving places at a moment's notice. They are always packed and ready."

"You're an actress?" That must be the secret of the intriguing quality of the other woman's voice.

"Not one of my recent admirers, I see. I'm with Morven Ghent." She paused expectantly.

"Oh, yes," Elene said. There had been discussion of the performances given by the brooding English tragedian of that name in Port-au-Prince the week before the wedding. Elene had been too involved with the last stitching on her trousseau to think of attending.

"Everyone remembers Morven, particularly the ladies," Hermine said with a wry grimace. "Well, I won't keep you standing at the door, or we'll have every sailor on the ship down here hoping for a peek. I'll see you in the morning."

Hermine pushed a bundle of clothing under Elene's arm that was not in use to hold her towel, then gave her a warm smile and turned away.

"Thank you," Elene called after her retreating back.

The actress merely waved and kept going.

The bundle, when unrolled, revealed a nightgown, also a pair of stockings, soft kid slippers with ribbon ties, and a day gown of tan poplin trimmed with gold-green braid. How very observant of the actress to notice her ruined shoes, though, on second thought, the blood-stained tracks she had left on the floor from her cuts must have been hard to miss. Walking was not really painful now, but would be worse by morning when the soreness set in. The new slippers would offer more protection.

Elene tossed her towel across the foot of the tub and pulled the nightgown on over her head. It was made of muslin in a simple design with small cap sleeve and a shoulder yoke edged with ruching from which fell the fullness of the floor-length skirt. It appeared to be missing a ribbon tie to hold it closed, however. The front gaped open nearly to her navel.

Elene looked up as the door opened to admit Devota bearing a cloth-covered tray. "Only see what the woman with the voice has brought."

"The actress?"

"You already know? I thought I would have something to tell you." Devota had an uncanny knack for collecting bits of information. She seldom asked a direct question, but she listened extremely well.

"There are two actresses," Devota answered, "and an actor who thinks himself something indeed. There is also a planter, amazingly fat, and his daughter who is as thin as a stick, along with the girl's maid who is a quadroon. We also have a petty official and his wife who is a woman with a tongue like a serpent, wicked and forever wagging. And there is Serephine."

Elene's gaze met that of her maid in a long look. Serephine was Durant's mistress, an octoroon, and quite lovely in a languid and care-less fashion. The arrangement was one of more than fifteen years' stand-ing; Serephine had been bought for Durant by his father when he was sixteen and the girl no more than fifteen. She had moved into the house, since Durant's mother was no longer alive to protest, and had served the function of housekeeper, and sometimes hostess, to the all-male gatherings of father and son, though not of course when there were ladies present. Serephine and Durant had a child, a son who was being educated in France.

"He could not have left her behind," Elene said. "In any case, it makes no difference."

"You are determined not to wed Durant?"

Elene gave an irritable shrug. "I don't care to marry anyone."

"That's all right then."

Devota was correct. It was all right. Elene had wondered often enough before the wedding what she was going to do about Serephine. She had been by no means sure that Durant meant to put his mistress aside. They had never discussed the situation; it was one most white women refused to acknowledge, much less bring into the open. There had always been the possibility that Durant would expect the two of them to reside under the same roof. Elene would not have consented, of course. The battle of wills would have been most unpleasant. Lacking real power, since there would have been no affection between Durant and herself, Elene knew she might have been reduced to such tactics as making matters so difficult for Serephine that she would be happy to remove to another establishment. It had not been a test to which she was looking forward.

Devota was setting out the food she had brought on the table. The portions of ham and beans, bread and fruit cobbler were more than adequate for two. Elene asked, "Will Ryan be returning to eat?"

"He said not to wait for him, that he would have something in the captain's cabin. Captain Jean detained him with questions, I think."

"Then sit down and tell me what else you learned about the others while we eat."

But Devota, as always, refused to step out of what she considered to be her place. "You forget, I had dinner tonight even if you didn't. I'll just rinse out your underclothing in the bath while I talk. Then it will be fresh for you in the morning."

By the time Elene had eaten, her eyelids were so heavy she could barely keep them open. She wanted to help Devota drag the tub from the room then tidy it up, but could not seem to summon the will. No bed had ever looked more inviting than the bunk against the wall with its tightly tucked sheets. The only thing that kept her from it was that she was not sure it was for her. No one had mentioned anyplace else, and yet if she took his bed, what was Ryan to do?

"Do you think," she said to Devota after slow consideration due to the fuzziness of her mind, "that I am to sleep here?"

Devota looked at her. "I would say so."

"What about you? The bunk there isn't very wide, but there's room for two if we sleep close."

"I've been provided with a place, don't you worry." There was affection and a curious amusement in the woman's voice. "Go on with you now. I'll douse the light."

"What about—" Elene stopped to yawn before going on, "—about Ryan?"

"I expect he can take care of himself."

"Yes."

Devota was standing beside the whale oil lamp in its gimbal, waiting to turn it out. In one hand she held Elene's wet underclothing, well wrung but still dripping a little. No doubt she would take them and hang them out somewhere, near a hatch, or even on deck where the sea wind could flap them dry. Devota was always busy, always thinking of her comfort, always—devoted. Elene rose to her feet with the help of both hands on the table edge. She hesitated a moment, her gaze on the familiar soft brown face of her maid, her aunt who, at thirty-four, was not so much older than herself. At last she said, "Would you tell me something, Devota?"

"Anything, *chère*."

"I overheard something at Favier's house. Is it true that you . . . went to bed with that man for my sake?"

Devota pursed her mouth, a roguish look in her eye. "Need it have been for your sake?"

"What do you mean?"

"I am a woman, he is a man. We were thrown together. These things happen."

Devota was not a simple person; she was perfectly capable of telling a cheerful lie to ease Elene's mind. "He can't have been much of a man. You still had to signal the ship."

"Ah, well, we were at least two of a kind. It doesn't happen often."

Two of a kind. Devota meant that she and Favier were both mulattoes, of mixed blood, neither black nor white. That knowledge lay in the maid's liquid brown eyes, a shimmer of rueful bitterness, slowly fading. Elene flinched from it. "I didn't mean to pry."

"It's your right, *chère*."

"No, not really."

Devota shook her head. "You worry too much. Here, I was nearly forgetting this."

The maid pushed her hand into her apron pocket and took out a small glass bottle. Stepping to Elene, she handed it to her, then moved once more to the lamp.

Elene looked down at the bottle. Her fingers tightened around it. The jade bottle of perfume Devota had made for her. Her maid must have been carrying it in her apron pocket all this time. Elene was reluctant to use it, but Devota had gone to such trouble to save it that she also hated to refuse. She would use only a little then, just a little.

She removed the stopper and quickly smoothed a few drops into the bends of her elbows, the hollow of her throat, and between her breasts. At once the mind-swimming fragrance surrounded her. She pushed the stopper back into place and set the bottle on the table.

"Lovely," she said, forcing a smile as she walked to the bed and sat down on it. "Good night."

"Good night," Devota said. The lamp made a soft popping sound as it went out. The door closed. Elene lay down and shut her eyes.

She came awake slowly. It was the brightness that had disturbed her. She considered it through slitted eyelids in a species of wonder. It was sunlight, pouring into the cabin, glowing with life, dancing in the brilliance of water reflections on the ceiling and walls. Beautiful. It seemed years since she had seen it. Never had she appreciated it as she should, until now.

Somewhere behind her, just above the bunk, the porthole must be open. The warm, soft breath of a sea breeze stirred her hair and gently fluttered the folds of the sheet that lay across her. She could hear the slap of waves and the steady swish of the boat's keel cutting through the water. As grace notes to these steady sounds was the hum of wind in the rigging far overhead, the occasional snapping flap of a sail, and the creaking of the wood of the hull as the ship rose and fell. That movement was soothing, and so soporific it seemed that if she just closed her eyes, she could go back to sleep again.

She easily might, except that there was something about her position there in the bunk that was disturbing. The pillow on which she rested her head was too firm and too warm to be the same one she had pulled beneath her neck the night before. Moreover, there was, just under where her hand lay, a steady throb, exactly like a heartbeat.

It was a heartbeat.

The fact should not have surprised her. She had awakened in a fashion not unlike this two of the past three mornings. Except for the fact that her left arm, on which she was lying, was numb, it was not uncomfortable. There was even an unexpected feeling of security in it. The muscles that lay under her cheek and her fingers, though relaxed in sleep, had a sense of quiescent power, and the thigh on which her bent knee lay supported her with easy strength.

She lifted her lashes in a slow sweep. Ryan's chest was bare, the sheet cutting across its bronzed expanse just above the waist. Fine dark hairs curled over it, a soft pelting that narrowed to a thin line as it disappeared under the light covering. A pulse beat in the hollow of his throat, throbbing in a vein that climbed the smooth column of his neck to his chin. His jaw and cheeks were only faintly shadowed with beard; sometime the night before he had found time not only to bathe but to shave away the three-day growth of beard he had accumulated while in hiding. The skin of his face was brown and smooth, the bones underneath well formed, rather prominent under the eyes. His nose, as she had noticed on that first night, had been broken, but was still a bold feature. His brows were heavy, as were his lashes. His mouth was deliberately defined, generous in its molding, with fine smile lines curving on either side. There were also lines radiating from the corners of his eyes, perhaps from laughing, but more likely from gazing through bright sun over endless reaches of blue water. His eyes were as blue as the deep sea far from shore.

He was watching her, suffering her slow inventory with humor and patience. As she met his gaze he said, "Don't tell me. You've forgotten what I look like."

"I'm not sure," she said with studied attention, "that I ever knew."

"I not only knew what you looked like, I held the memory well."

His voice was quiet, his gaze only a little teasing as he reached to pick up a pale gold tress from her shoulder and let it drift in shining filaments from his fingers. He did not think he would ever forget the way she had faced him, as regal as a queen in the moonlight, after her mauling by the brutish pair who had found her. It had taken the exercise of rare inner fortitude to overcome that shock so quickly and to submit to the incarceration that had followed. It was not to be expected that she had been too conscious of him as a man at the time.

She spoke carefully. "If you remember, why this morning visit? It can't have been curiosity."

"This isn't a visit, as you well know."

"Isn't it?"

The corner of his mouth quirked. "Elene, *ma chérie*, did you really think that after sharing your bed for three nights I would let you sleep alone now?"

She tried to shift away from him, but his grasp tightened, holding her where she was. Her temper flaring, she said, "You might have given me a choice!"

"I didn't think you would appreciate being awakened to make it."

"What you thought was, if you woke me I would refuse."

"And I was right, wasn't I?" He raised himself to one elbow, hovering over her, watching the silver dustlike flecks in her eyes flash with her anger.

"Indeed you were."

"Then aren't you glad I didn't?"

He whispered the words as he lowered his head to set his mouth to hers. His hand, while she was distracted, had closed gently upon her breast. The onslaught of sensations and the turbulent longing his touch engendered was strange in these surroundings, and yet so piercing and sweetly familiar that her defenses were breached before she knew.

How had it happened that she had become so enslaved to the desires he aroused in her? That was not the way it was supposed to be. The perfume. The perfume was to blame, both for Ryan's presence in her bed and her own response to him. Nothing else made sense. It was the perfume.

Oh, but the cause did not matter. Only the magic of soft caresses and the sweet mingling of breaths, the fervor of the joining and the storm and fury it brought to the blood had reason or existence. The plunging of the ship was a counterpoint of delight to their movements together. The fresh glory of the day, gilding their damp bodies with sunlight, added rich and new dimension. Ignoring time and puny prohibitions, they disported themselves in the joy of their renewed hope, and found not only bliss, but beatitude.

Lying on her stomach with eyes closed and her cheek against the rumpled sheet on the bunk sometime later Elene thought: If only things were always this simple, if only people could disclose themselves to each other as readily as they gave themselves, how easy it would be. The problem was, they kept their deepest wants and truest needs hidden away even from themselves. She knew, for she was the same.

The bunk mattresses canted for an instant as Ryan heaved himself up. She heard the pad of his bare feet on the floor, moving in the direction of the table, but before she could decide to move, he was returning. The sheet that covered her hips was flung aside.

She rolled to her side, but he caught her ankles, immediately turning her back on her stomach. She twisted to look over her shoulder. "What are you doing?"

"Nothing yet, but I'm going to do something about your feet. Be still."

"My feet? With what?" He was unscrewing the lid from what looked to be a most unsavory concoction. The smell of it, not unlike the odor of horse liniment, rose in the air.

"There's a man on board who studied the rudiments of healing for six whole months under a famous surgeon in Edinburgh. The men in the forecastle call him doc. He retaliates by tending their wounds from time to time. Since he doesn't kill any more of them than his medical colleagues on shore, he has a certain reputation. This salve is his."

Elene winced a little as the ointment touched the sole of one foot. She expected a tremendous stinging, but instead there was soothing warmth. Though she was still, Ryan closed his hand around her ankle, holding it firmly apart from her other foot. The pungent smell drifted around her, strong enough to overcome even the scent of her perfume. Her neck was becoming stiff. She faced forward once more, supporting herself on her elbows. Her tones skeptical, she said, "Are you sure this doc didn't study in a stable?"

"He would be grossly insulted. But I expect the muscles and hides of horses and people are much the same when they're sore."

He went down on one knee as he spoke. His view of her body, Elene realized in some discomfort, must be completely unimpeded. She did not move a muscle; there was no point in calling attention to her position. With a fine pretense at composure, she said, "I take back what I said. That really does feel better, thank you."

"Doc will be pleased."

His voice was soft, too soft, and the massaging pressure of his thumbs on the lacerated skin of her feet was hypnotic, addictive. "It . . . it must be late. I wonder where Devota is?"

"Having a well-earned rest, I would imagine. Besides, she has too much tact to come to you this early."

"Knowing you would be here, I suppose you mean?"

"She's an intelligent woman." He switched his ministrations to her other foot.

"I . . . wonder if the others are up."

"I wouldn't know," he answered shortly. "They are strangers."

"You don't like them being on your ship, do you?"

"We don't have time to coddle passengers."

"You could have left them behind."

"Short of throwing them overboard one at a time, I don't know how. Oh, I see. That's what you expected of me. Such notoriety as I must have gained. Gambier doesn't like it, either."

"Durant? You spoke to him." She shifted to look over her shoulder at him once more.

"It would be more accurate to say he spoke to me. He sought me out last night to demand an explanation of just why and how I happened to turn up with his bride-to-be."

"What did you tell him?"

"The truth."

"What!"

"Up to a point. I saw no reason to satisfy what seemed to be his chief concern."

"Which was?" she asked in some foreboding.

"Whether you are still a virgin."

She jerked upward, trying to push herself up to a sitting position, but he prevented it by clasping an ankle in each hand. "Let me go," she demanded.

"Not until you tell me why you're so upset."

"Why should I be upset? I positively dote on the idea of the two of you standing around discussing my virginity. What could be more flattering."

"I wasn't discussing it, Gambier was."

"Well, thank you, I'm sure. Would you care to tell me what kind of agreement was struck between you as to my favors after this manly conversation, or am I to guess at it from the fact that I found you in my bed this morning?" She kicked at him in annoyance at being held, but the movement was ineffective and he still would not release her.

He came erect in a smooth, powerful movement, and an instant later his weight was upon the length of her body, his pelvis pressing into the firm curves of her hips, his arms braced on either side like the bars of a prison. Against her ear, he said, "There was no agreement. Would you rather it was Durant here with you now?"

"Get off," she said through clenched teeth.

"Answer my question."

His position was a mistake; Ryan acknowledged it in grim control as he felt her movements under him as she tried to throw him off and the stirring in his loins in response. He would not relent until he had his answer, however. It's importance was too great.

"I told you how I felt about my arranged marriage. How can you ask such a thing? Or do you want to know for your own vanity?"

He rolled from her at once, sprawling beside her on the bunk. "Vanity?" he repeated in tones of disgust.

"What else could it be?"

What else indeed? He stared at her lying there with her hair spread around her, half concealing, half revealing the gleam of her shoulders and breasts, and lying in a shining swag in the indentation of her waist. He gazed at the pure clear light of her gray eyes, smelled the fragrance that was a part of her, and was struck by such intense yearning that he felt physically ill. His very heart hurt.

Deliberately he said, "I'm of no mind to give you up just because some precious sugar planter with a prior claim saved his skin by crawling aboard my ship. On the other hand, earlier last night you showed a great regard for respectability and I wouldn't want to be the cause of you missing the opportunity now that your bridegroom has returned from the grave."

"I understand," she said, the light in her eyes as cold and dangerous as a northern lake in a storm. "That's why you installed me in your cabin and spent the night with me, to make certain that Durant knows he would be getting soiled goods. Without you having to stoop to discuss it, of course."

"Oh, no," he said in quiet certitude, "I did that because I couldn't bear to have it any other way. Because I knew that morning was coming, and I wanted to be here, to see you naked in the sunlight."

She drew in her breath in surprise and sudden raw pain, as if she had received a mortal wound. She would not let it show. With a lift of her chin, she said, "Now that you have?"

"Now if Durant wants you, he will have to take you from me by force."

"It seems to me that choice should be mine."

"I rather thought you had made it."

"Just because I don't choose to be collected by Durant like some misplaced parcel doesn't mean I care to depend on you. You made it plain that would not be wise." Elene sat up, flipping her hair to one side and drawing her arms across her breast.

"Foolish of me."

"What does that mean?" she asked in suspicion.

"Nothing. Are you always this waspish before breakfast?"

His face was closed in, polite but totally unrevealing. There would be nothing more to be gained from questioning him. It was just as well. She was not sure she wanted to know more, why she was not sure.

They had missed breakfast. Ryan opened a door and shouted for the cabin boy, ordering coffee brought to them, but it was so near the noon meal that they decided to wait for anything more substantial. When the coffee came, Ryan drank his quickly, then threw on his clothes and left the cabin. He must have stopped to speak to Devota, for a few minutes later the woman arrived to help Elene dress.

When at last Elene stood gowned in the gold-green trimmed cotton poplin, with slippers on her feet and her hair neatly styled in a coronet of braids, she felt presentable for the first time in days, and also more herself. She was not given to conceit, but she hated to think of how bedraggled she must have looked the night before with her gown torn and soiled and wrinkled past saving, her slippers ragged and filthy, her hair straggling down her back in a tangled mass, and the dark shadows of exhaustion under her eyes. Perhaps she could redeem herself, in part at least, by her neatness today. She would not forget that it was the actress Hermine to whom she owed the opportunity.

She had been afraid that Ryan meant to leave her to make her way to the common room alone. She was perfectly capable of doing it, but after his maneuver with the cabin, effectively displaying their relationship to all and sundry, she saw no reason why she should have to face the others without support.

She need not have worried. Ryan appeared with the ringing of the bell that announced midday and the changing of the watch. He surveyed her with grave attention, then shook his head.

"I liked your costume this morning better," he said.

"But I didn't have—" she began, then stopped in annoyed comprehension.

"Exactly," he murmured, taking her arm and drawing it through his, admiring the color that had replaced the paleness of her face. "Shall we go?"

Once more, the others were waiting for them. The gentlemen came to their feet as Elene and Ryan entered, the ladies stared unabashedly. A young woman, the thin daughter of the planter, gave a nervous giggle. Durant, lounging against the wall, looked at them both, his eyes glittering and black with rage. It was the actor Morven Ghent who spoke, however, stepping forward with a glass of amber liquid in his hand and a flush on his broodingly handsome face.

"How honored we are," he said in sonorous tones more than a little flattened by drink. "What felicity is ours. This repast before us cannot but be improved in flavor by the company of our host, the privateer Bayard, and his beautiful blonde paramour!"

CHAPTER 7

"MORVEN," Hermine cried, "for pity's sake, mind your manners."

He looked at her, still holding his histrionic pose, his grin rueful. "Did I speak out of turn? Should I apologize?"

"At once!"

"My termagant speaks and I must obey, or be punished in various ways uncomfortable to my self-esteem." He turned to Ryan and bowed with the utmost grace. "I beseech that you and your lady will overlook the lapse. Or failing such magnanimity, if it please you, I will await your seconds with all due humility."

Ryan eyed the man without favor. "If you want to please me, Morven, you will save the play-acting for the stage."

"Spoilsport," the actor said. "The ladies were expecting to see our blood spilled on the floor before them. Will you deny them that small pleasure?"

"It pains me, it really does, but I don't want to hear the caterwauling you would make if I so much as nicked your arm, not to mention the death soliloquies you would inflict on us."

"What can you mean? I'm the bravest of fellows."

"You're a great humbug, like all actors."

Morven heaved a melancholy sigh. "You may be right, but how can we be sure if you won't indulge me?"

"Oh, I'll do that quickly enough," Ryan said softly, "the next time you malign the lady."

The actor's expressive brows arched high. "So that's the way it is? I am forewarned." He turned to Elene. "I am also contrite. In all truth, I am."

It was plain from their banter that the two men knew each other. It was also clear that Morven Ghent was right, that more than one of the ladies present were disappointed there was not to be a duel between the two men. For an instant, Elene had been ready to do the actor an injury herself, but that was before she had seen the devilish glint in his green eyes. As for his taunt, she supposed it was an attitude she must learn to accept.

Morven Ghent was outrageously handsome in a dark and poetic style. His hair had the blackness of ebony and was as fine as a woman's, his features were classically pure, his form elegant. His only fault was that he was well aware of how he looked, and enjoyed the effect it produced immensely.

She extended her hand. "M'sieur Ghent, I presume?"

"At your service, fair lady. I trust you are as recovered from your ordeal as you appear? I think all ladies should wish for such peril if it's going to leave them as lovely as you."

Florid compliments were the fashion in some circles, Elene knew, a meaningless courtesy. Still, they made pleasant hearing. "You are too generous."

A plump matron sitting just beside them spoke with judicious candor even as the actor made his denials. "M'sieur Ghent has been doing his utmost to keep up the spirits of all the ladies with compliments, so kind when we are not at our best. The truth is, *chère,* you look rather worn. Come and tell us about your ordeal."

Morven Ghent moved to one side. "Permit me to present Madame Françoise Tusard, the wife of a member of the officialdom of the island we are leaving behind us, though his position escapes me."

"He is, or was, assistant to the commissioner," the lady said, her large and rather splotchy face pink with irritation at the slighting reference. Her eyes were muddy blue and protuberant, her nose broad with a bulbous tip, her mouth small and tight and her thin hair turning gray unattractively. Her gown of black-dotted cherry muslin over an opaque chemise was somewhat the worse for wear, but still in the height of fashion. On her hands were soiled silk gloves the same cherry color as her gown, as if to maintain appearances even in the midst of chaos.

"Madame," Elene said in polite acknowledgment.

"This gentleman behind me is my husband, "M'sieur Claude Tusard," the assistant commissioner's wife said, indicating a rotund and mustachioed man in rumpled breeches, coat and waistcoat, and a shirt whose high collar would have made turning his head difficult if it had not been so wilted. The gentleman gave Elene an appraising stare and a bow. Before she could do more than curtsy in return, his wife went on, "Do come sit down and tell us everything."

"No, no," Morven said, "you must not monopolize the lady."

Madame Tusard seemed to swell. "That, I take it, is your privilege?"

"How can you suggest it with our host so near? Are you anxious to see the color of my blood after all? It's simply that there are others here whom she, and also Bayard, have yet to meet."

It appeared to Elene that she was witnessing one of those small struggles for dominance which take place any time a group of people are brought together. Morven Ghent had a natural tendency to assume center stage regardless of the occasion, while Madame Tusard appeared to be a woman of a managing nature who was used to relying on her husband's position to increase her status. For the moment, however, the official's wife was outmaneuvered.

Elene, with Morven at one elbow and Ryan at the other, was dutifully introduced. First there was the third member of the acting troupe, a young woman from Martinique who called herself Josephine Jocelyn and affected the rather torrid airs of Napoleon's wife from whom she had obviously taken a part of her stage name. Twisting a dark curl as she lounged in her chair, she fluttered her lashes and pouted full lips in Ryan's direction while ignoring Elene. "They call me Josie," she said to him. "I don't mind if you do the same."

The next girl, Flora Mazent, could not have been more different. She was so shy she could hardly keep her head up and her sallow, blue-veined skin took on a raspberry flush as she found herself the center of attention. Her lashes and brows were so fine as to be nearly nonexistent, and her figure rail-like and flat-chested. She spoke her greeting in a breathless voice, with only the briefest of glances from rather close-set hazel eyes.

"Speak up, Flora," her father, standing nearby, told her, but his words had a tired sound, as if he knew they would do no good.

M'sieur Mazent was a widower it seemed, a stout man in gray, with thinning hair, the same hazel eyes as his daughter, and a habit of standing with one hand pressed to his abdomen. He had been a planter, but, like Elene and her father, had been burned out. He had holdings in Louisiana also, he said, so had not been ruined completely.

"Now that is done," Madame Tusard said at the first pause, "perhaps we can eat. I see the food has arrived, and here is the captain to join us."

There were eleven of them to sit down to the meal, six men and five women taking their places at three tables. There was no particular order to the arrangement. Ryan and Elene were with Morven Ghent and Hermine. The ship's captain was seated with Josephine, along with M'sieur Mazent and his daughter Flora, while Durant was left with M'sieur and Madame Tusard. So close together were the tables in the small salon, however, that there was no difficulty in talking back and forth.

The fare was simple, a hearty seafood stew, or gumbo, rich with shrimp and sausage and served over rice. Their needs were tended by a steward who ladled the gumbo from a pot he carried by its bail, then returned with a bottle of wine and a stack of small crusty loaves of bread for each table. The man did not tarry, but went away and left them to it.

Elene wondered where Devota was eating. Applying to Ryan for the information, she was told her maid was dining with the Mazent girl's maid in a small room off the kitchen. Durant's mistress, Serephine, was also not present. It was doubtful the woman would care to eat with the servants, yet it was certain Madame Tusard would object strenuously if Durant's kept octoroon tried to take the vacant chair at her table. Such close quarters made for problems in these relationships where the woman was of neither one world nor the other. It was probable that Serephine was eating alone in whatever space had been found for her.

Not everyone was fortunate enough to have a cabin such as the one Elene shared with Ryan. Devota had told her that the other women were crowded into two rooms, while the men were bedded down with the crew. Captain Jean had gone to great lengths to prevent Madame Tusard from learning of the commodious cabin enjoyed by the ship's owner. He had been afraid she would try to commandeer it for herself and her husband.

The conversation at Ryan's table was lively. Hermine kept it going with quips and sallies. Her sense of the ridiculous was acute and she spared no one, especially herself. So unceremonious was she with Morven that it soon became apparent there was something more between them than an affection for the theater. Regardless, Morven did not hesitate to pay Elene the most extravagant court, with winks and languishing sighs, whenever Ryan's attention was directed elsewhere.

Hermine, catching Elene's quick, frowning glance between the actor and herself, gave a lovely, throaty laugh. "The trick is to learn to take no notice of Morven. It isn't that he's insincere, just that he has no control when it comes to women, especially those he knows he can't have."

Morven turned a wounded expression upon her. "Angel, how can you?"

"Easily, since it's true. I thought it best to warn Elene, my love, so that you don't get your face slapped quite so soon."

Morven shook his head, turning a soulful look on Elene. "She's a jealous vixen."

"Is she?" Elene could not help smiling at his nonsense.

"I don't know why I put up with her."

"I expect it's the other way around."

"*Et tu, Brute?* You would join my enemies in ridiculing me?"

"Women are so heartless," she mourned with him. "We can't help ourselves."

"I hate clever women."

"Oh, dear, have I ruined myself forever."

"Quite."

"Suppose I promise to come and see you perform in New Orleans—I trust you will be performing?"

"But of course! In that case, I will love you madly and forever."

"Clever indeed," Hermine said.

It was Ryan who answered. "Let us hope so. Elene, I believe Madame Tusard is trying to attract your attention."

The official's wife was leaning across the space between the tables. "Mademoiselle Larpent, I think I remember hearing that your father's house was one of the first burned some days ago. I was wondering how you survived until last night?"

The woman's question might have been directed at Elene, but her gaze moved with great suspicion back and forth between her and Ryan. Elene forced a smile. "I would not have survived at all without my maid. After a time, we were lucky enough to find someone to take us in."

"Lucky indeed. Who might that have been?"

Elene told her.

"An acquaintance of yours, M'sieur Bayard, I think?" the woman said.

"As it happens, yes."

"One concludes that this Favier must have hidden you both." Françoise Tusard's eyes were avid, her grip on her spoon so tight the ends of her fingers were white.

"Yes," Elene agreed, adding in an attempt to change the subject, "but what of you and your husband?"

"It's very nearly too dreadful to relate. We hid for hours in empty salt barrels in a storage shed. I was sure I would suffocate, but the savages moved on to burn and loot another place, thank God. Isn't that right, Claude?"

"Yes, *chère*," her husband croaked as soon as he had swallowed.

"Naturally, I don't mean thank God someone else was attacked, only that we were left unharmed, you understand. I could not wish for anyone to suffer as our next door neighbors did, poor souls. That was the widow Clemenceau and her three daughters. You would not believe what was done to them! Their bodies were found next morning, quite horribly used."

The details were ugly, and the woman did not hesitate to describe them. She ended with a shudder. "Of course, that was not the only such incident by any means. You yourself were not subjected to such abuse, one hopes?"

"It is not a subject I would care to speak of if I had been," Elene said, her voice cool.

"Very wise, I'm sure," the woman said, leaning closer so that she was in danger of falling from her chair, "but were you?"

"I was not."

"Fortunate, very fortunate." Madame Tusard sat back, her voice flat.

Elene glanced at Durant who had been following the exchange with taut interest, then to the others at the next table, where Captain Jean and the young actress Josephine Jocelyn were seated with the Mazents. She was in time to catch Josie leaning back in her chair, her breasts thrust forward in an impudent posture that outlined the nipples through the thin fabric of her cheap gown. M'sieur Tusard watched the actress with unblinking eyes, but it was at Ryan that Josie directed her smiles.

Hermine, following Elene's gaze, shook her head. "Josie has no control either."

Ryan ignored the younger actress's wiles as he tore a chunk of bread off the loaf beside his soup bowl. He looked at Elene, and amusement flashed bright in his blue eyes. She knew abruptly that he could have taken steps to dampen Morven's ardor and deflect the interest of Madame Tusard if he had wished. Instead, he had allowed her to fend for herself. No doubt he expected her to discover the true value of his protection with his removal of it.

It was possible he might discover something himself. Elene turned her head, leaning forward just enough to intercept the stare of the dark-haired actress. Catching Josie's eyes, she gave the girl a long, cold look as she slowly raised a brow. Josie straightened in her chair, then glanced away to the portholes along the wall before finding her bowl in front of her of great interest. Picking up her spoon, she began to eat.

Elene, her gray gaze limpid, turned back to Ryan with aplomb. "This gumbo is really quite delicious—"

The words nearly stuck in her throat. The look on Ryan's face carried such vivid understanding and smoldering need that she felt her heart leap within her.

It was M'sieur Mazent, sitting in the chair closest to her at the next table, who rescued her. "The gumbo's flavor is good, I'll admit, but it's a bit heavy on the spice, particularly the pepper. It'll play havoc with my stomach."

"Now, papa," his daughter murmured.

Captain Jean was all solicitude, offering to have an omelet made for the planter instead. It was refused with all politeness. As the young man tried to insist, Flora Mazent shook her head with an almost inaudible thank you, meeting his gaze for the merest second. When Captain Jean returned his attention to his own plate, however, she peeped at him from the corner of her eyes, and her pale lips curved in an oddly satisfied smile.

When the bread pudding that constituted dessert had been consumed to the last buttery crumb, they moved from the common room out onto the deck. There an awning made of a sail had been erected to protect the complexions of the ladies from the sun, and a few chairs brought out and placed beneath it. Straw pallets of the kind used by the sailors for their beds were strewn around the edges as additional seats.

To Elene, the sun was a wondrous thing. She could not get enough of it after her sojourn in underground darkness. She sat on a pallet of straw and watched its diamond dazzle on the waves, its silver sheen on the billowing white sails above them, its brilliant flashes on the ship's brass work and mahogany railings. She wished, in sudden wild longing, that she could throw off her clothes and stretch out full length in the glorious flood of light and heat. Instead, she sat sedately with her feet together and her hands clasping her knees to keep her skirts from billowing upward.

Madame Tusard was holding forth, telling a tale of a woman decapitated by the renegades, as if the horrible things that had taken place on Saint-Domingue had a fascination for her. "What I don't understand," she said when she had pronounced the last gory detail, "is why these things had to happen. Why did our Negroes turn on us with such savagery when they have never done so elsewhere?"

"The revolution in France," her husband said.

"Yes, perhaps it was the example of the Terror." It was Hermine who enlarged on the first suggestion.

"Or it might have been our own example," Elene said almost to herself.

Madame Tusard turned on her, her face stiff with affront. "Whatever do you mean?"

Elene wished she had not spoken, but since she had, she would not back down. "I remember as a child the whispers of some of the things the outlying planters did to their slaves, burying them alive for small crimes, cutting the tendons in the legs of runaways to make them cripples, forcing women into the fields less than an hour after childbirth, to say nothing of the whippings and brandings."

"There may have been a few madmen who did such things," the planter Mazent conceded, "but what fool would damage valuable slaves any more than a fine horse or good work mule?"

"Men who are afraid. The island has always been so isolated, so far from authority or help, and for every white person there were twenty slaves. It was plain a long time before the first uprising that if the slaves ever learned their strength they would be formidable. The planters thought they could keep them in subjection by fear." She had seen that attitude clearly in her own father. It had been one so ingrained he could not change it, not even for his own daughter.

"The slaves may have bought their freedom with blood, but what has it got them? More fighting, and more and more."

"Under Toussaint—"

Madame Tusard gave a sniff of contempt. "Don't speak to me of that man! Who ever heard of a black man governing? It's ridiculous."

"He didn't do so badly, under the conditions he inherited."

"He had to use the whip himself to make his precious followers go back into the fields to earn enough to keep themselves from starving. Isn't that right, Claude?"

"Yes, *chère.*"

Support for Elene came from an unexpected quarter. Ryan said, "If

Toussaint had been left alone, your husband might still have his position at this moment, the others might have their homes, their livelihoods, their lives. It was Napoleon, and his brother-in-law Leclerc, who brought on this last massacre when they reinstated slavery and took Toussaint away to die."

"It's all right for you to talk. You have no money tied up in Saint-Domingue. You have lost nothing except a few livres' worth of profit on your last cargo, if that much."

"Because of it, I can be objective as you cannot."

"Objective?" Madame Tusard cried in scorn. "Twenty-five years Claude and I spent on Saint-Domingue, with the exception of a year or two during the worst of the fighting. We lost two dear little boys that we buried in its sand. We have given it our youth, our hopes and dreams. Now what is left? Nothing. Not even the graves of our children."

The woman began to cry, rocking slowly back and forth. Her husband Claude patted her shoulder, speaking in low tones to which she replied with sobs. The rest were quiet, lost in their own thoughts.

They were joined on deck a short time later by Devota and the others who had finished their meal. They came in a chattering group led by Serephine who was saying something in rippling humor over her shoulder to Devota and Germaine, the Mazent's girl's woman.

The official's wife stared with red-rimmed eyes at the octoroon who was making her way toward where Durant sat to one side. A moment later, Madame Tusard rose to her feet with ponderous deliberation, obviously removing herself from the presence of the women of color. Her tone conspiratorial, she said, "Would any of you ladies care to join me in a promenade around the deck?"

Hermine and Josephine appeared not to hear. Flora Mazent was waving at her maid, calling out that she needed a ribbon to hold down her bonnet. Elene, troubled by guilt because she had been the cause of Madame Tusard's earlier distress, and also reluctant to remain and allow everyone to watch for her reaction as Durant greeted his mistress, forced herself to get up and accompany the official's wife.

She should have known it would be a mistake. They were hardly out of hearing before the woman was leaning close, whispering. "That Serephine is Gambier's kept woman, as I'm sure you know. The very idea of imposing her presence upon us for this voyage! She would have been in no danger if left behind."

"She might have been, she is very nearly white," Elene pointed out in mild contradiction.

"And gives herself airs because of it. I don't know how you can bear it, seeing them together, knowing what they were to one another even when your marriage was being planned. You have my admiration for the cool way you are taking it. A woman must hold her head high and pretend she doesn't care about these things."

"I really don't, you know."

Françoise Tusard went on as if Elene had not spoken. "On the other hand, taking another man into your bed is revenge indeed, though I wonder at you flaunting it. Such things are all right for Paris, but attitudes are stricter in the islands, and even more so, I'm told, in the Louisiana colony under Spain. You may find that you have given Durant Gambier cause to withdraw his suit. That cannot be what you want."

"Can't it?"

"Well, I admit there is much to be said for Ryan Bayard as a man— even I see his appeal at my age—but he cannot compare to a wealthy planter such as Gambier, now can he?"

"Durant is no longer so wealthy."

"I'm happy to see that you are being realistic, but I urge you to move with care or you may find it's too late to change when we reach New Orleans. A white woman can soon descend to a position such as that of this Serephine, or even that Germaine with the Mazents. She is Mazent's mistress, you know, has been for years."

"Is she?"

"You find it hard to credit? Scandalous, isn't it, with his daughter present, poor thing. But I assure you it's the truth. This Germaine of his is amazingly haughty, too. She is a free woman of color, and has been since before the first revolt, as she will tell you if you dare to call her a slave. I would advise having nothing to with her, myself. She was most impolite when I only asked her how long she had been with young Flora and her father."

"Indeed."

The lack of encouragement did nothing to stem the flow of ill comment. From Serephine and Germaine, Madame Tusard went on to criticize the color of Hermine's hair and the sound of her voice which she considered to have tones reserved for the bedchamber. The way Josie walked came under attack, as well as the way she smiled at the gentlemen.

"Why, I even caught her making eyes at my Claude! But what can you expect from an actress?"

Elene, reaching the prow of the ship, paused. When the other woman would have walked on, she made no move.

"Aren't you coming?" Françoise Tusard said impatiently. "If you stand there the wind will ruin your coiffure and you will soon have every common seaman on the ship ogling you."

Elene touched her braided coronet put up with pins Devota had found for her. "I think I will chance it."

"Oh, very well, I will send Durant to you. That should help matters."

"No!" Elene cried, but it was too late. The woman was striding away.

Elene considered taking refuge in Ryan's cabin, but such a retreat seemed the coward's way out. She did not care to have Durant think she was either afraid of him or wanted to avoid him. It might even be best to speak to him here in some degree of privacy in order to make it clear that he no longer had a claim upon her.

She was standing with her face lifted to the sun and wind and her gaze resting on the far horizon when she heard Durant's footsteps behind her. The nebulous peace she had begun to sense fled, and the tightness in her chest became an ache.

"It was wise of you to send for me," he said at her shoulder. "A little longer, and I might have been forced to say things in front of the others that you might find embarrassing."

"I didn't send for you." She answered without turning.

He stepped to her side, facing her with his back to the rail. The wind blew his hair forward onto his forehead and flapped the ends of his cravat. He narrowed his eyes against it, eyes that were dark with anger. "I don't understand you, Elene. Four days ago we were to be married. A few minutes more, and it would have been done. How can you just ignore that? Have you no concern, no interest, in what happened to me?"

How like him it was to expect her to be absorbed in his adventures. She glanced at the slash across his face. "You were injured, I can see that. Since you are here, I assume you fought your way free. What else is there?"

"I was struck from behind, felled in my tracks, as I received this." He touched his face with his fingertips. "If I had been wearing rings, I might have been minus a few fingers. As it was, I was stripped and left for dead under a pile of corpses. I might still be there if it had not been for Serephine."

"Serephine," she said, her tone dry.

"She came to search for me. You did nothing, so far as I can see, to discover if I was alive or dead."

"I did not see how you could be alive," she said in protest. "Besides, I was in no position to see about anyone."

"You might have shown more joy at finding me among the living last night."

"I hardly knew where I was or what I was doing."

"What was your excuse this morning? I don't call your greeting that of a fond fiancée!"

"I am no longer the girl I was, no longer your bride-to-be," she cried, facing him. "Everything is different now, can't you see?"

"Oh, I see all right." His voice rasped with pent rage. "You mean to ignore our betrothal. You have found something more to your taste and, just like that, you no longer want to be married."

"The wedding was never my choice, you know that."

"Maidenly dithering. It would have been different on our wedding night."

She gave him a level look. "You are so sure of yourself, aren't you? Why shouldn't you be? I don't suppose Serephine ever complains."

His face went blank. "Serephine has nothing to do with this."

"Not now, no."

"She never did. She will make no difference to the respect and love my wife will receive from me."

"But you have no intention of putting her aside, nor did you ever intend it."

"Where would she go? How would she live? I have a responsibility to her."

"How very convenient."

His dark brows drew together. "I don't intend to discuss it with you. Such an arrangement is not the concern of the wife; she should not know it exists, much less presume to comment."

"You mean the wife should not admit she knows, another convenience."

"I am not at fault here, Elene, nor is the way I live. You are the one who has formed an improper alliance. You should be happy that I will even consider marrying you after the way you have behaved."

"Well, I'm not," she declared, lifting her chin. "I don't want to be married. I particularly don't want to be married to you."

A murderous light appeared in his black eyes. "How unfortunate, since you signed the marriage contract."

"A minor thing. I spoke no vows, made no pledges in church."

"Minor to you, perhaps, but it gives me the right to defend your honor as my own. I wonder how you will like seeing your rescuer spitted on my sword?"

She stared at him in consternation. "You wouldn't!"

"You doubt me?" he asked in heavy irony.

"It would be the most flagrant ingratitude, since Ryan is providing the means of your escape from the island."

"The injury he has done me is greater than the favor."

"Impossible," she said hotly. "I don't know why you still want to marry me. I'm well aware you have no affection for me, that you never did."

"Are you so sure? That is not the issue, however. It's a question of honor, as you must realize. Maybe the actor has a point, maybe what you really want is to see two men fighting over you, ready to spill their blood for your sake."

"No such thing! The thought sickens me."

"Too bad. I have a great need to teach Bayard that it is a dangerous business, deflowering other men's brides."

"He saved my life."

"I see you don't deny the deflowering. I thought not."

She stared at him in despair at the futility of trying to make him understand. "It wasn't like that. It wasn't."

"It's possible the fault may not lie with him, but that is something I will have to look into when I have taught him a few of the finer points of being a gentleman. It may be I will join you in his cabin then. I believe persuading you to give me the answers I seek could turn out to be—pleasurable."

He meant to frighten her. It was a mistake. She had known real terror in the past few days, and survived it. Her eyes narrowing to a gray glitter, she said, "You will need to take care. You have a reputation as a swordsman, but then so does Ryan Bayard."

He made a disparaging gesture. "Cut-and-slash fighting like a common pirate. There's no skill in that."

"There is strength and endurance, and a certain facility for staying alive."

He started to reply, but his words were lost in a hail from the crow's nest above the sails.

"Sail away! Off the port bow!"

Durant and Elene swung to look. Durant's gaze widened, then a slow smile edged with malice curved his lips. "Maybe I won't have to trouble myself with Bayard after all."

"What are you saying?"

"It appears he intends to engage another foe."

Elene guessed his meaning almost before he spoke, alerted by the sudden flurry of motion aboard the *Sea Spirit* as orders were shouted and men scurried here and there. To the port side was a fat-sailed merchantman with the stubby shape of an English vessel. The *Sea Spirit* came around, preparing to intercept. Along the deck, where the women were seated, Madame Tusard began to scream in sudden hysteria.

"He can't do this, not with all of us on board," Elene said under her breath.

"Can't he now? He's a privateer and the ship yonder is a prize. Why should he not take her? Prizes, of one sort or another, fair or not, seem to be his greatest interest."

She threw him a flashing glance. "If you are suggesting that he views me as a captured booty, I find it insulting."

"I would hate to think that you surrendered to him," Durant said softly.

The sound of his voice sent a shiver along the back of her neck, but she refused to be intimidated by it. She picked up her skirts and stepped away from him. "Think what you please!"

He thrust out his hand, catching her arm, halting her where she stood. "Oh, I will. And if I prove it, not only your privateer is going to be sorry."

CHAPTER 8

RYAN took the quarter deck as the gap between the two ships closed. She should have known he would, Elene told herself; he was Bayard the privateer, not just the ship's owner. Somehow she had managed to avoid considering what that meant on the sea. She had expected that Captain Jean would continue to order the setting of the sails and the actions of the crew as he had done all morning. To see Ryan striding across the deck without coat or cravat, with his shirt sleeves rolled to the elbows for action and his sword bright at his side, gave her a tight feeling in the pit of her stomach.

She had known Ryan was a decisive man, one capable of sudden movement and violent acts. Still, watching him direct the *Sea Spirit* toward her target with single-minded precision was chilling, even frightening. The lumbering vessel they were steadily bearing down upon seemed at too great a disadvantage. She knew an errant need to warn those aboard the merchantman of their danger, like shooing away a bird from the path of a stalking cat.

Orders had been given for the *Sea Spirit*'s passengers to go below. Morven and M'sieur Tusard lingered, but the women, for the most part, had departed with scarcely a backward look. Elene hesitated. If there should be gun fire, she could not bear to think of being trapped below decks, helpless to know where the next shot might land, unable to get out if the ship should begin to sink.

The danger was slight, she realized that. Most merchantmen were built to carry the greatest amount of cargo with the least amount of crew, and with little space allotted for heavy armament. Few such ships carried guns at all. In any case, the merchandise stacked in the ship's hold belonged to men with money to invest who remained safely on shore. The captain and crew were not likely to risk their lives to save the profits of others. Still, there were captains who invested in the cargoes they transported, men who fitted their vessels with bow guns loaded with grapeshot that could cut a boarding party to pieces.

Ryan's voice rang out in a hard order. One of the *Sea Spirit*'s guns that had been run out of her gun ports boomed in a thundering report. The shot arched across the bow of the merchantman, not so near as to be a danger, but not so far away as to give hope of mercy. The crew of Ryan's ship fell silent as they waited for some sign of flight or surrender from the English ship.

Elene looked once more toward where Ryan stood balancing with the rise and fall of the ship in easy grace with his hands on his hips. The wind fluttered the sleeves of his shirt and ruffled the polished walnut darkness of his hair. He was familiar, and yet remote, a figure of authority and implacable intent with little regard for anything other than the task at hand.

What had this privateer to do with her, or she with him?

The destruction of the life she had known had been so sudden, so complete. She felt cast adrift. She had no idea whether she had done the right thing in trusting Ryan Bayard, sailing for New Orleans, or even in denying Durant's claim upon her. Of only one thing was she certain: she had no wish to see Durant challenge Ryan over her. Whatever else the privateer might have done, he had without doubt saved her life. He deserved a better recompense.

A ragged cry went up around her. The English ship was losing way, striking her colors. It seemed the prize had been gained without the loss of a single life, without even a fight.

Bayard went aboard the captured vessel to meet with its captain. He returned with a number of trunks and boxes, then dispatched a prize crew to take the merchantman to Cartagena. There in that haven for privateers and pirates it would be sold for Ryan's profit.

In an amazingly short time, the English ship was disappearing over the horizon. The *Sea Spirit* resumed its course, under full sail as it glided over the water.

There was a feeling of anticlimax in the air. It was not that anyone was disappointed that there had not been a desperate fight between the schooner and the merchantman. Still, they had all braced themselves,

and the effects of that useless expenditure of effort were felt in varying
degrees. Hermine was euphoric, ready to dance and sing and open the
wine, while spots of the high color of frantic excitement lingered on
Josie's cheeks. Madame Tusard was as irritable as if she had dressed for
a ball that had been canceled, and her husband, perhaps as a consequence of her mood, was glum. The planter Mazent seemed to have
gained vitality, being greatly reminded of an incident in his youth,
which he insisted on telling to anyone who would listen, concerning a
pirate attack he had helped prevent. His daughter Flora tried to discourage her father's reminiscences one moment, then the next turned to
listen with rapt attention as Morven, dress sword in hand, demonstrated with dialogue and fierce action the way he had played the role of
a courageous sea captain defending his ship in some melodrama.

Josie, watching also, clapped her hands with a flirtatious shake of her
dark cloud of curls. "Isn't Morven a wonder?"

"Yes, isn't he?" Hermine said, her tone droll. To Morven's wounded
look in her direction, she merely returned a moue.

Josie's attention shifted to Ryan as he approached. "Here is our bold
privateer! Tell me, sir, what did you get? What was the English ship
carrying? Jewels, perhaps? Or was it chests of silver and gold?"

"Nothing so fine," Ryan said easily, his air of hard authority banished as if it had never been. "The days of the Spanish treasure ships
laden with gold are gone, worse luck."

"What, then? Do tell us!"

"A cargo of rum and sugar from Jamaica in the main, with the
addition of some rosewood and mahogany from South America bound
for a cabinetmaker's shop."

"Oh, but that doesn't account for the trunks and boxes you brought
on board."

"Books, *chère*. Still interested?"

Josie gave a pettish shrug. "How boring."

"Isn't it?" Ryan said with sympathy, though there was the gleam of
suppressed amusement in his eyes as he glanced toward Elene.

Durant, standing beside Elene's chair under the awning where they
were all gathered, spoke up. "One can easily see why the English captain did not choose to die for his cargo. What a boon for you, Bayard,
that he was a coward."

"The man was a realist." There was a sudden alertness in Ryan's
gaze, but his words were without heat. His glance dropped to Durant's

fingertips, where they rested on Elene's shoulder, and the corners of his eyes tightened.

"I wonder would you have attacked so quickly if he had been a man of stronger principles, and his ship better armed."

A perceptible tension vibrated between the two men. Elene, feeling it, fearing what it meant, snatched Durant's hand from her shoulder. Before she released it, she met her former fiancé's gaze. Her voice low, she said, "Please, don't."

Ryan heard that plea. It gave him a hollow feeling inside that was more disturbing than the entire incident with the merchantman. Deliberately he said, "It's difficult to know how a ship, or a man, is armed until you lay down your challenge."

"Still, it's always possible to withdraw in haste if the quarry proves too strong for you."

"Sometimes events move too fast, go too far."

If there was a warning in Ryan's words, Durant would not heed it, any more than he would heed Elene's gaze upon his face. "All in all, I think you prefer a helpless quarry, don't you, Bayard? They give you less trouble, rather like a defenseless woman."

The others, grouped around them, had fallen silent. Now there was a faint gasp from among the women at this pointed insult.

"Is it my character or my lack of courage for which you wish to call me to account, Gambier? Or something else entirely?"

The hard rasp of Ryan's voice scraped along Elene's nerves. The threat it held was not directed at Durant alone. There was the promise of a reckoning in the privateer's gaze as it raked over her. Her eyes widened as she felt its impact, realized its cause. He thought that she had been complaining of his conduct toward her to Durant, that she had brought this quarrel upon him. She wanted to protest, to assure him it was not so, but could think of no way to say it that would not inflame Durant further, make him all the more set upon the course he was following.

Durant drew himself up as he made his answer. "Whichever you prefer."

"I would not want to disappoint you," Ryan said softly. "Do I take it the weapon is swords?"

There was a sharp cry and the sound of running feet behind them. Elene turned her head in time to see Durant's mistress, Serephine, leaving the gathering in a flurry of skirts and with her head down to hide her face. Devota rose at once and went after her.

In the brief moment it had taken to follow that small contretemps, Durant and Ryan had drawn their swords and matched them as to length. Now the chairs and the awning sail were whipped out of the way, and everyone moved aside to give as much room as possible. The two men faced each other, Durant removing his coat and cravat while Ryan, who had not yet donned his again, pushed his sleeves higher as he stood waiting.

At last Durant was ready. He swept his sword up in a salute, his smile tight with pleasurable anticipation. Ryan, his features expressionless, repeated the gesture. "*En gardé*," he said.

Durant attacked in a vicious display of skill. He obviously expected to make short work of the contest, to pierce Ryan's defenses with sudden and devastating expertise.

It did not work that way.

Ryan seemed barely to move his wrist, but the blade of the other man was turned aside smoothly, easily, again and again. For long moments, Durant forced Ryan, endlessly parrying, back step by step, then in an abrupt and brilliant riposte, the privateer gained the initiative so that Durant had to parry *en seconde* at speed to protect himself. The two men drew apart for the space of a breath, their sword tips barely touching.

Ryan lifted a brow as he met Durant's rage-filled black eyes. There was in his face the knowledge not only that Durant had expected to best him in a few easy moves, but that he was not overly concerned with what injury he inflicted in the process. Durant's face hardened. They engaged once more.

The pace of the fight slowed, taking on an even, searching cadence as each tested the other's strength and will, their knowledge of swordplay and experience at facing an opponent. Their concentration narrowed, closing out the onlookers, the movement of the ship, and the strain and pull of muscles. Perspiration broke out on their brows and glistened on their forearms. Their breathing deepened, rasping in the quiet, broken only by the noises of the ship riding over the waves and the quick shuffle of their feet on the deck as they shifted back and forth. Between them emerged a sense of respect that had been missing before, though there was no less anger, no less determination.

Elene stood in taut stillness against the railing. Beside her was Hermine. "Magnificent," the actress murmured, her gaze lingering on the broad shoulders and muscles of the two men.

Elene was not blind to the superb male forms before her, but her attention was on the weapons of death in their hands. She wanted to look away from the blades that flashed and slithered like silver ribbons in the sun, but could not. Her teeth were tightly clenched, and her heart battered against her ribs with its every beat. In her mind was both rage at being made the cause of this meeting between the two men, and despair that she could do nothing to stop it. Wild impulses rioted through her. She wanted to scream at them for being a pair of fools, or else fling herself between them. The only thing that stopped her was the certain knowledge that, however much they might pretend to be fighting over her, the issue was in fact their honor, their ridiculous male pride. For that there was no curative that she could offer, and no salve except blood.

Durant feinted, lunging. Ryan parried *en quatre* as he stepped back, then seemed to overbalance with the rise of the ship. Durant overextended in haste in his attempt to take advantage of that moment of misfortune. Ryan recovered in an effortless recoil of taut muscles, striking with swift precision. There was a brief whirling of the blades, a teeth-jarring scrape of steel on steel. Abruptly Durant's sword fell to the deck and he stood with blood seeping through fingers that were clamped to his upper arm.

Ryan stepped back at once to stand at ease, his chest rising and falling with his deep breathing. Durant looked down at the blood on his hand, then up at the other man, and his eyes were wide with disbelief. Ryan met his gaze squarely, without triumph but also without pity.

It was Morven who strolled forward to step between them. "Well, then," he said in brisk pragmatic tones, "is honor satisfied?"

Ryan inclined his head in a small, graceful gesture. For the space of a long breath, Durant said nothing. At last he gave a slow nod. "I do believe it must be."

The sighs of relief around Elene were short and sudden, like the expelling of held breaths. She closed her eyes and leaned back in unexpected weakness against the railing.

"Poor M'sieur Gambier," Hermine, standing nearby, said in low, melodic tones, "someone should see to his arm."

Elene looked around for Devota who had considerable skill at tending wounds and illnesses, but the maid was not to be seen. No doubt she was still with Serephine. Elene pushed from the railing and moved toward the duelists. She had helped Devota attend to injuries among the slaves a number of times in the past months since her return from France. There might be something she could do.

Abruptly her way was barred by a shining, red-stained blade. She swung her head to stare at the man who held it. Ryan spoke with soft inflexibility. "No."

She did not pretend to misunderstand. "He needs help."

"Not from you."

The concern Ryan saw in her face for the other man was galling. He had been aware of it even as he fought. It roused in him an emotion he scarcely recognized and would have denied if he could. It was jealousy, and it did not incline him to be reasonable.

Blood was reddening Durant's sleeve, running down his fingers. It must be stopped at once, Elene knew. "Who do you suggest? You?"

"Doc will see to him," Ryan said. "We have matters to discuss, you and I."

Doc was the sailor who had sent the ointment for Elene's feet. Already the wizened little man was coming forward with a box that must contain the tools of his adopted trade. The others of their small group were gathering around also, the two actresses exclaiming in sympathy as they ran their fingers over Durant's shoulders while Flora Mazent picked up his sword as if holding a sacred relic.

Elene held her ground. "I . . . I think I should see that the bandaging is done properly. I feel responsible."

"It may be you are indeed responsible," Ryan said, his voice grating. "That is one of the things we will talk about."

He dropped the point of his sword and caught her arm with his free hand, turning her toward the entrance to his cabin. She pulled back against his hold. "I have nothing to talk to you about."

"Your mistake, *chère*. Will you come, or shall I carry you off over my shoulder?"

"You think the others will let you?"

"I think they may, as long as I have this." He hefted his sword.

Elene looked from the dark hardness of his face to the blade he held. "How enchanting," she said in forced sarcasm, "the conqueror claiming his spoils. Again."

"If you like."

It was not his threat that decided her. It was, rather, the somber expression on his face as he accepted her strictures. He had been forced into a fight for his life because of her. It was possible that she owed him an explanation. With a last scathing glance, she swung from him, moving in the direction he indicated.

She was supremely conscious of him behind her, of his height and size and raw male strength that had so recently been on display. Her footsteps were swift as she made her way into the common room and beyond it to the cabin they shared. In that small, enclosed space, she waded among the boxes and trunks of his captured booty before she turned to face him. He kicked the door shut, then walked to fling his sword down on the table where it landed with a dissonant clang. Turning, he folded his hands across his chest and braced one hip on the table as he stared at her.

"Just how does it come about," he asked in tones deceptive in their quietness, "that I am accused of taking advantage of a defenseless woman?"

She controlled a shiver, and forced herself to meet his cold blue eyes. "That was Durant's charge, not mine."

"He must have got the idea somehow, from someone. Who else but you?"

"From himself. He finds it inconceivable that I could go from being his bride-to-be to becoming your mistress in a matter of days without coercion. So do I, for that matter."

"You would prefer to be his bride again, all pure and unsullied?"

"You needn't jeer!"

"That isn't an answer. Did he suggest that the wedding proceed after all?"

She looked away over his shoulder. "What if he did? It's impossible; I can see that. Things would never be the same."

"But you would like for them to be." The accusation was like a whiplash. He had sensed something secretive about her, something that grew day by day. This was the explanation, he was convinced of it.

She would not give him the satisfaction of hearing her deny it. "I would like to be secure. No more, no less."

"The only people who are truly secure are the dead."

Annoyance flared up in her. "What do you know of it?" she demanded. "You're a man, able to make your own way, a terrible and fearsome privateer who frightens women and children and shopkeepers. You're strong enough to take what you want and dare anyone to stop you!"

A hard light appeared in his eyes. "Are you by any chance accusing me of stealing?"

"What do you call all this," she asked, waving at the boxes around her, "if not stolen goods?"

"Merchandise." That single word had the weight of a stone.

"Books, I suppose? If you expect me to be taken in like poor Josie, you will have to try harder."

"I am a merchant. I buy, sell, and trade. In New Orleans, I have a warehouse—"

"Full of stolen goods!"

"Filled with goods taken under letters of marque, along with furs and wheat from the Illinois country," he said in contained fury. "There would be more of the last, and less privateering, if the Spanish would cease interfering in honest trade. No matter. The English ship was fair game."

"What if it had been a French ship? Would you have taken it?"

His silence was her answer.

"You see? You have no loyalties."

"I am loyal to my own, to my friends and my land—"

"Land? You? Hah!"

"My land, yes; I am also a planter, if I must prove my respectability. But I was speaking of the only land to which I acknowledge duty or fidelity, and that is Louisiana."

"Yes, yes, and I'm sure that will impress the Spanish when you take the wrong ship and they decide to hang you."

"The Spanish at New Orleans have no interest in the welfare of their colony of Louisiana, no interest in anything except what may benefit Spain a world away."

"All that doesn't matter if you're dead!"

He stood watching her, admiring the color indignation had brought to her face and the way her breasts rose and fell under her gown, hearing the echoes of her words in his mind. A smile tugged at the corners of his mouth for the picture she made and the concern she had expressed without realizing it. "I'm not dead yet. I'm very much alive. More alive than is comfortable at this moment."

She could see, in the smooth fit of his breeches decreed by fashion, precisely what he meant. She looked away from that proof to his damp shirt that clung to his shoulders and the muscles of his upper arms, the corded strength of his forearms where his sleeves were rolled back, the dew of perspiration that gilded his skin. The sheer virility of him, the sense of force inside him, a force she had seen amply demonstrated so short a time ago, was all at once overpowering in the small cabin.

"I want you," he said, the words quiet, wondering.

They set off a heated response that began somewhere in Elene's chest and spread quickly downward, though at the same time spiraling in dizzy swirls upward into her brain. She met his gaze, and was snared in its relentless blue light.

He swung from her in an abrupt movement, and knelt to release the lid of a trunk. "Would you like to see my misbegotten gains? Shall I drape you in their richness and sparkle before I ravish you?"

"That will not be necessary—" she began in cold hauteur, then stopped.

The trunk was filled with books of all sizes from the tiniest fat volume to fit a pocket to great folios containing curious illustrations. They were packed one against the other as closely as they would fit, a collection of fascinating age and variety, the gleanings from a marvelous library. Some connoisseur of such works was going to be sorely disappointed when they failed to arrive.

Elene gestured at the others boxes and trunks around her. "All these are books?"

"They are in short supply in New Orleans."

"A need you mean to fill?"

"When I have taken my choice."

She moved to the bunk and dropped down upon it. She watched him, the way he picked up a book of poems then set it back down, with care, with appreciation, with a certain reluctance. It was borne in upon her once more with stunning effect how little she knew him, how impossible it was to judge him.

He closed the trunk lid and moved to take a place beside her. "Would you have preferred ropes of pearls and sapphires the size of robin's eggs?"

Would she in truth? She shook her head without looking at him.

"I would," he whispered, reaching for her. "I'd like to see you wearing nothing else, and search for your sweetness and heat among the cold and tasteless gems. But I also desire you unadorned."

It was a ravishment indeed, though only of the senses. Her body responded to him in wild fervor that had nothing to do with her will. The undulations of pleasure that rippled over her at his touch were both a delight and a scourge. Mindlessly she gave herself, and took the joy and the surpassing strength, the rampaging ardor and quicksilver glory he had to give, and was amazed, in the outer reaches of her mind when she had leisure to notice, that the exchange seemed weighted in her favor.

CHAPTER 9

THEY came in sight of the coast of Louisiana, a low, blue shape on the horizon that turned slowly brown and green, the best part of a week later. It had been a tedious passage beset by calms, particularly during the long stretch while they skirted the island of Cuba. They did not try for an immediate landfall, however, but turned more westerly. They sailed past the myriad of outlets for the Mississippi River where the muddy yellow water poured into the green gulf to turn it brown, including the east pass which led to the inspection post of La Balise, and from there over a hundred miles up the main river channel to New Orleans.

It appeared that Ryan, for all his talk of being a respectable merchant, did not boldly drop anchor before the Spanish city at the end of his voyages. It was his habit instead, he said, to make his landfall in a secluded inlet known as Barataria Bay. From there, he moved through the intricate systems of bayous and waterways of the delta country to the back door of New Orleans. His cargoes were stored in a makeshift warehouse on the beach until he could send after them or else sell them to his business associates who would see to their transport into the city themselves. The maneuver, so he claimed, was to avoid the endless delays of Spanish bureaucracy, not to mention the bribes demanded by the corrupt port officials. He refused to submit himself to either on principle, because of the attempt of Governor Salcedo to strangle trade with the Americans.

Ryan pointed out that he was not alone in his use of the bay. It had become an informal entry port for other so-called privateers. There was no formal organization among them, however. They came and went as they pleased, and respected each other's property partially because it was the way of the sea, partially because to do otherwise could be exceedingly dangerous.

The refugees from Saint-Domingue lined the rail of the *Sea Spirit* to watch the land grow closer. They were jubilant over the end of the voyage, and yet also subdued. There was no way of knowing what awaited them on shore; where they would live, how they would occupy themselves or, for some, what they would have to do to maintain life. The time spent sailing across the Caribbean and in the Gulf of Mexico had, until now, been a hiatus, a journey suspended between their rescue and their future. They had thought of little beyond some means of making the endless sun-filled days and starlit nights pass. Now the future was upon them.

Elene was aware of trepidation, but also recognized within herself slow-growing elation. Ahead was a new country, a fresh start. Everything would be different, the sights, the smells, the customs, the people. What she would make of it would be up to her alone.

Overhead circled great flocks of gulls, their wings white against the bank of gray clouds that lay in the southwest. Their piercing cries sounded like a cross between irate scolding and desperate pleas. Nearer in toward shore, a large brown pelican flapped in ponderous dignity on a parallel course with the narrow beach. The low-lying land exuded the smells of mud, decaying marsh plants and fish, a rich and fecund miasma that beckoned even as it repelled.

"Faugh!" Hermine, standing beside Elene, exclaimed with a comical grimace. "What an odor."

"It isn't so bad."

The smell of the land came and went on the changing gusts of the rising wind. Overhead, the ship's sails flapped and billowed in fitful bursts. The gowns of the two women were flattened against their bodies while their skirt hems fluttered behind them.

Hermine reached up to hold the knot of her hennaed hair in place at her nape. "I'd rather smell stale face paint, cheap rooms, and the dung of horses on the streets any day. This wilderness terrifies me as well as offending my sensitive nose."

"Nonsense," Elene teased, "that isn't wilderness you smell, it's our dinner cooking in the galley."

"Don't let Cook hear you or he'll feed us fish every meal until we step off the ship. Since I must breathe, let me stand close enough to smell your perfume. I've been meaning to tell you how lovely it is for days."

Elene thanked her. It was not the first comment she had received on her perfume, but was perhaps the most frank. Hearing it spoken of still made her self-conscious, as if she had been caught in some misdeed.

"I would love to have some like it, if you don't mind telling me what it's called and where to get it."

"I'm afraid it isn't available."

Hermine shrugged. "Ah, well, if you would rather not say, that's your right."

"It isn't that." Elene's tone was apologetic.

"Then if you would just tell me which perfumer in Paris makes it, when next I'm there I will—"

"It doesn't come from Paris."

"Are you sure?" Hermine said, frowning. "It has the same richness, the same true essence."

"I'm very sure," Elene answered, and went on to tell the actress how she came to have it. On impulse she added, "I am thinking of making it, with Devota's help of course, when I'm established in New Orleans."

"Are you? How marvelous! Will you open a *parfumerie*? If so, I shall be your first customer."

Elene gave a light laugh at the instant enthusiasm. "You almost make me feel the venture will be a success."

"Naturally it will be. With such a fragrance, how can it fail?"

Elene sent the other woman a quick look, but there was nothing in her piquant face to indicate she meant anything more than a compliment to the scent. She relaxed. "The first bottle I make is yours."

The actress turned toward Flora Mazent who was sitting nearby with her maid Germaine beside her. "Did you hear? Elene is going to make her perfume!"

"That's nice." Flora looked up with a brief smile. She stared at them with indecision in her face, as if she was thinking of joining them there by the railing. After a moment, she lowered her lashes, returning her attention to the needlework in her lap.

Hermine looked at Elene with a raised brow and a shake of her head. There was something in Flora's attitude that was near aloofness, as if she preferred her own company, even considered it superior, instead of being merely shy. It almost seemed she looked down on Hermine and Josie and even, perhaps, Elene. Since she spurned the overtures of Madame Tusard also it was difficult to be sure. However, no amount of coaxing could draw her out of her self-imposed solitude, and most of the passengers had ceased to try.

The refugees had come to know each other well. Thrown together under perilous circumstances and then left with time on their hands, they had turned to each other for distraction as well as comfort. There had been talk and talk and more talk. They all knew the details of M'sieur Mazent's gastric disturbances and his daughter Flora's terrible experiences at a boarding school on Martinique where she was forced to kneel on peas for hours and have her hands slapped with a ruler for failing to speak above a whisper. Madame Tusard had entertained them with vivid descriptions of her female ailments, and they had all expressed their amazement over an incident a few years earlier when M'sieur Tusard had been suspected, unfairly of course, of falsifying records and embezzling funds. Josie had made her dissatisfaction with her ingenue parts on the stage well known, and they had been privy on several occasions to the flaring quarrels, followed by private reconciliations, between Hermine and Morven.

None of these matters took precedence in interest over the ongoing drama of Elene's relationship with Bayard. There had been much speculation about it, Elene knew; she could tell by the avid interest aroused whenever Durant and the two of them happened to be in the same room together. Durant had deflected it somewhat, however, by avoiding all appearance of interest in Elene. He either concentrated on Serephine who had nursed him during the first days of his injury, or else sought the company of the gentlemen of the group. As his arm, as well as the slash on his face, healed in the salubrious sea air, he had made a particular friend of Mazent who, as a fellow planter, could be assumed to have much in common. It was not at all unusual to see the two of them walking the decks in close conversation while Flora trailed along behind, snatching glances at Durant, flushing a splotchy red and quietly preening whenever he happened to notice her existence.

Relations among the group were not always cordial. Morven and Madame Tusard carried on verbal warfare over everything from who would lead them all in to dinner to what songs would be sung under the stars. Josie took offense at some remark of the island official's wife and, for her own sake as well as to champion Morven, kept up a running dispute with Madame Tusard over the placement of their individual chairs under the awning. Madame Tusard was jealous of the attention her Claude paid Josie and any other woman, not excluding Serephine, and the shrill registration of her distress had reverberated throughout the ship on more than one occasion. Devota and the Mazent's woman, Germaine, had words over the use of the English bathing tub and also the sole smoothing iron on the ship, one that belonged to Hermine. Flora bothered no one, but did become upset one afternoon when the sailor whom she had been watching for some time dared to wink at her.

Such contretemps were no more than to be expected, perhaps, given the close quarters and strained tempers of them all. The camaraderie of shared misfortune, shared terror, was stronger and more lasting. As the ship neared the bay where they would leave it, there were many vows to keep in touch, to gather together again soon. They were sincere at the time, however unlikely it might be that they would be kept.

They scudded into Barataria Bay on the edge of the storm that threatened. Dropping anchor, they stripped their yards of canvas, cleared the decks, and battened the hatches to sit it out.

The schooner pitched and tossed with the wind and waves. Overhead the thunder grumbled, sounding ten times more menacing because they were closed in below decks. Lightning crackled, striking into the water. The anchor chains sang with the tension against them. The ship's timbers groaned like something being torn apart while still alive. The rain, when it came, was in wind-driven sheets that lashed the decks like huge wet whips.

Elene and the others had eaten early and retired to their bunks. So violent was the motion of the ship that lying in that impromptu cradle was the safest place to be. Ryan moved about the ship, checking for damage, soothing fears, returning now and then to check on Elene. As the worst of the wind eased off, however, he pronounced himself satisfied with the way the *Sea Spirit* was holding in her sheltered anchorage. In the cabin once more, he pulled off his wet clothes and flung them into the corner. Then he climbed into the bunk with Elene.

He was chilled, his skin rough with gooseflesh. Elene, in a welling of sympathy and tenderness, held him close, drawing up her nightgown to drape one leg over his. Shivering in reaction to her warmth, he dropped a light kiss on her forehead before relaxing against her. She rested her temple against his chin, staring blindly into the dark that glowed now and again with the blue-white flashes of lightning through the porthole. The rain drummed overhead, running from the decks to fall in splattering rivulets into the waters of the bay.

In the days since Ryan had crossed swords with Durant, Elene and the privateer had shared this cabin and the bunk in which they lay. They slept together, ate together, walked and talked and made love together, but they had not talked again about New Orleans except in the most general terms. Elene assumed that he still meant her to live with him in the same way in New Orleans. Certainly his desire for her showed no sign of abating.

He was an interesting companion when he wished to be. The two of them had spent many evenings reading from his purloined library and discussing the ideas they had come across. They had sometimes played at cards, staking pieces of their clothing, and he only cheated when the prize was rich enough to be irresistible. In bed, he was a strong and considerate lover, vocal in his encouragement, his appreciation, and his praise. He never failed to be protective of her before the others, nor did he neglect her for his responsibilities aboard the ship. He soothed her nightmares and checked her healing feet. He was still fond of her perfume and responsive to it. Yet he never spoke of love.

Elene did not really expect it of him. For all that they had endured together, they were strangers. He owed her no avowals, no promises, nothing; if anything, she was in his debt. The warm rapport between them was of the flesh alone, without the complications of sentiment.

She wondered if Ryan would be the same once they reached New Orleans. There among his friends and past companions he might discover that she was a hindrance, a reminder of a period of time he would as soon forget. He might find another woman and cast her and Devota out, so they would be forced to make their own way, without his help.

At least if he did that, she would know once and for all whether it was the perfume that held him. She could, of course, put it to the test at any time by ceasing to use it. The results would not be conclusive, however, as long as they were on the ship. There was nowhere else for her to sleep if he did not want her beside him, and sheer propinquity might cause him to turn to her. In any case, she did not quite dare chance it. She was in no position to risk losing his aid just now.

Ryan, sensing her tense contemplation, smoothed his hands over her back as he tested her stillness. He bent his head, his warm breath stirring her hair. "What is it, *chérie*? Is something wrong?"

She sighed without sound. "No, nothing."

A frown creased Ryan's brow, but he did not persist. He held her, he thought, by the most tenuous thread. To put strain of any kind upon it might be to have it break in his hands. It would be time enough to force the issue between them when they reached New Orleans and he could show her what she would be losing if she did not stay with him. Until then, he would wait.

For the moment, she was warm and pliant and incredibly seductive beneath the cotton of her nightgown. The movement of the ship rocked her gently against him, and the thunder of the storm was in his blood. He kissed her eyelids in the darkness to seal them shut. He found her lips, teasing them until they opened for him, until he tasted the honeyed sweetness of her response and felt beneath his hand the echoing thunder of her heartbeat. It sufficed, for the moment.

Barataria Bay, as the sun rose clear, bright, and hot next morning, was seen to be a large body of water like a brackish lake surrounded by marshland. The thin beach was edged with spiny, waving grass and palmetto and littered with water-blackened logs in grotesque shapes and the decomposing body of a dead porpoise. Birds called, wheeling and diving, their cries carrying in shrill thinness on the air. Frogs croaked, mosquitoes whined in maddening persistence, and now and then there came the bass roar of an alligator. The men and women of the *Sea Spirit* lined the rail, pointing out the log-like shapes of the primitive beasts that now and then floated into view, watching them in their desultory search for a meal of fish.

While they passed the time with such sport, Ryan was busy overseeing the unloading of the ship. The longboat made a number of trips to the ramshackle warehouse that sat back from the water's edge. There were a few other makeshift shacks nearby built of driftwood, palmetto fronds, and pieces of woven jute. A tail of smoke rose from just outside one such shack to stain the morning sky, but there was no sign of movement for some time.

Finally, as the unloading was nearing completion, a man emerged from the largest of the scruffy dwellings. He stood stretching and scratching at himself as he turned slowly to survey the ship at anchor. He shouted something. An Indian woman ducked through a doorway covered by a hanging animal skin. She looked at the ship, at her man, then turned and went back inside. It was as total a dismissal as any Elene had ever seen.

The occupants of the shacks, it seemed, were fugitives from the law, thieves and murderers and sometime-pirates. Barataria was remote from New Orleans, separated from it by endless miles of water and mud and soggy marsh. Men came in the late fall and winter to hunt the ducks and geese that flew in from the north in massed waves one behind the other, and sometimes they came to fish, but the bay was usually deserted in the heat of summer.

The men knew Ryan well; that was plain from the way they came to greet him when he had himself rowed ashore. They were more than willing to let him have the use of their pirogues to haul his passengers to New Orleans, though for a small fee, of course. If they felt any sympathy for those on board as refugees, however, they failed to show it, but sat around watching them climb into the boats, looking for a glimpse of ankle and shapely calf while they jeered and laughed and made crude jokes. It was no more than a sensible precaution that Captain Jean was left on the *Sea Spirit*, along with a skeleton crew, to protect the ship.

The trip through the maze of waterways to New Orleans was not one Elene wanted to remember. As they left the waters of the bay, the wind died away and the hot sun of mid-June and wide reaches of water combined to form a steamy heat that brought streams of perspiration and made it difficult to breathe. Mosquitoes and gnats rose from the grass and weeds in a black fog, biting, stinging until every inch of exposed skin was covered with red welts and smeared with the black stickiness of dead insects and sweat they had wiped across their faces. Not a great deal of skin was left uncovered, of course, not only because of bites and stings, but for protection from the burning rays of the sun.

Hour after hour they rode the waterways, trending ever to the northeast with the men wielding the paddles dipping and pulling with hardly a splash. Snakes made arrow-shaped wakes in the water as they darted around the boat. Alligators lay half buried in the mud, watching them pass with unblinking indulgence. At intervals in the morning someone would break into song to match the rhythm of the paddles and pass the time, but as the hours lengthened the silence of endurance fell over them.

Now and then they stopped to rest and refresh themselves, though they avoided wading far into the water for its coolness because of the leeches that might like a taste of their blood. They spent a night hiding from the mosquitoes and starting awake at the roar of alligators and, once, the scream of a hunting swamp panther. With dawn they were in the pirogues once more. Finally they came to the gates of New Orleans.

Elene, seeing the sentries on duty, expected trouble. There was none. Ryan slapped the men on the back and inquired after their families or their women. There was the glint of gold passing from one hand to the other and the unloading of a keg of rum. The gate opened and they were inside.

It was, in large part, a new town. There had been three fires in the past fifteen years, two of them disastrous. The last, only nine years before, had destroyed more than two hundred buildings, creating losses that totaled well over eight million piastres. Because of the danger, as well as the huge cost of these fires, a building code had been passed requiring that any structure of more than one story be built of brick or adobe and roofed with tile, and that roofs replaced on existing structures must be of tile. The result was a town that, in the central area, had many predominantly Spanish features, including inner courtyards, balconies, windows and doors covered with gratings, and porte cochères, or openings under the second story through which carriages and pedestrians could pass to the inside courtyards. The local bricks were so soft that it had been necessary to cover them with plaster. This plaster was lime-washed in white or yellow, but the action of sun and rain in leeching color from the brick clay, and in encouraging the growth of mosses, molds, and mildews, had created a hundred shades of green and gray, rust and gold and peach.

New Orleans was not a large town, holding no more than ten thousand people. The earthen embankment with its six-foot-high palisade that surrounded it enclosed an area a half mile long and a little over a quarter mile wide. There was a fort at each of the four corners of the palisade, plus another on the back wall, and batteries and guarded gates set into the sections in between them. For added protection, there was also, outside the palisade, a ditch twenty feet wide and four feet deep. These fortifications had been brought to their present strength in 1796, when the colonists of Louisiana had feared that their slaves, many of them imported from Saint-Domingue, might imitate their island brothers and stage an uprising. The walls were not intended to hold off the army of a major power, for which they were clearly inadequate, but to offer protection in case of an insurrection.

Inside the walls, the streets were mere dirt lanes between the houses, though fairly wide and straight, and with a gutter down the center. Drainage ditches, clogged with weeds and refuse, had been dug around each block of houses, turning the sections in wet weather into islands. These ditches and street gutters drained into the Carondelet Canal to the rear of the city. Regardless, the streets were ankle deep in mud.

The houses nearest the palisade were the most neglected. Here were the one-story wooden dwellings from the French days that had escaped the fires, many of them succumbing to the ravages of the damp climate, too far gone to warrant, or with an owner too tightfisted to bear, the expense of repairs with brick and tile.

The town bore a decided stench, though not more than most tropical ports. Horse and mule dung was churned into the mud of the streets.

Kitchen refuse from vegetable peelings to fish heads, also bits of rags and rotted leather and an occasional dead animal, either floated in the green-scummed water in the gutters or lay piled outside the back doors of houses. All of it was steadily ripening in the heat of the sun.

Some of the women among the refugees made faces and covered their noses. Elene breathed with shallow care and thought of perfume.

Ryan lived on Royal Street, which was both the main commercial artery and most favored residential thoroughfare of the city. Lined with houses of two and even three stories, most with balconies railed with lace-like wrought iron, the thoroughfare was important enough to warrant street lanterns slung diagonally from house corner to house corner on ropes. The residences and shops were intermingled in the European fashion, with the business establishments occupying the ground floor and the owners either living in the space above or else leasing it to other individuals as private quarters.

The ground floor of Ryan's house was shuttered and locked, but carried no hanging sign advertising wine or candles, cloth or hats. The rooms, he said, were used instead for storage most of the time, but for the moment were empty. As evening was drawing near, he offered the weary group of travelers the hospitality of his home.

The offer was accepted with gratitude. Together, they all piled from the wagon Ryan had borrowed from a farmer on Bayou Saint John outside the city where the boats had landed. They trooped through the porte cochere and into the stone-paved courtyard, skirting a fountain surrounded by ferns and geraniums, and headed toward a flight of stairs that led up to a gallery that ran around three sides of the court. Before they reached it, a Negro man stepped forward with grace and dignity to meet them.

The manservant, blue-brown of skin and with white in his curling dark hair, might have been anywhere between thirty-five and fifty years of age. His name was Benedict and he served as Ryan's majordomo. Effortlessly, he took them in charge, clapping his hands to bring maids and footmen running, offering refreshment, parceling out rooms. He missed nothing. Not only did he place the Mazents and Germaine in a set of adjoining chambers, but he also, by some strange means of communication with his master, appointed a maid to lead Elene and Devota to what was without doubt the master suite.

There was no uncertainty about whom the room belonged to because Ryan's small sea trunk was delivered by a footman moments after Elene and her maid entered. It was placed on the floor beside a marble-topped table with gold-leaf encrusted legs upon which sat a silver tray piled with cards of invitation addressed to Ryan Bayard. Prominent among them was one requesting his presence at a dinner to be given that evening by Pierre Clement de Laussat, colonial prefect of France, the man who would be governor when France regained Louisiana once more.

By sunset, the passengers from the *Sea Spirit* were comfortable. They had bathed and donned the changes of clothing that had been found for them, their insect bites and sunburned skin had been seen to, and food and drink set before them. Their host excused himself for the evening. He felt that the dinner with the future governor, a man who had only just arrived in New Orleans when Ryan had left it for the Caribbean, would be too good an opportunity to catch up on the latest news to be refused. He would not be back before morning. The city gates were locked at nine o'clock, and the house taken by Laussat was located just outside the gates. Ryan would find a bed with friends who lived nearby.

Elene wondered where Ryan found the stamina to go off visiting after the two days just past. She was weary to the bone, and wanted nothing more than to crawl into bed, close out the damnable mosquitoes with a nice thick *baire*, and sleep for a week. The others seemed of the same inclination. It was not long before Elene said her good-nights and sought the room she had been given.

Devota was not there. As much as Elene loved her maid, the privacy was welcome. She stood for a moment looking around the room, at the dark oak armoire of English manufacture, four-square and heavy, the washstand not unlike that on the ship except it was made to fit into a corner, and also the shaving stand of French design and a Flemish carpet that harmonized with the tapestries on the walls. It was a large chamber, extending across the width of the house, with a set of glass-paned doors at one end opening onto the gallery overlooking the courtyard, and another set at the opposite end giving onto the balcony that faced the street.

Elene's gaze came to rest on the bed that was the focus of the room. Raised on a platform for coolness, its carved headboard and footboard were touched with gold leaf. Above it hung a draping of white mosquito netting, while ecru-colored linen sheets covered the mattress stuffed with Spanish moss and the pillows fat with goose down. She thought of lying in that bed with Ryan, and then looked quickly away, moving toward one of the French doors which stood open to the evening air.

The door gave onto the balcony that looked down on the street. It was cooler out there in the open, where the breeze off the river wafted over the tiled rooftops. The light of evening was going, gradually fading to a dull and melancholy purple, the color of half mourning. Elene thought of her father lying near the ruins of Larpent House, the place he had loved so well. It was fitting, somehow, that his bones would be scattered among the ashes. A hard lump formed under her breast bone, pressing against it with aching force, but she refused to cry. She had discovered in France, when her father had left her behind, that crying did not help.

She thought of Ryan instead, and of his absence for the evening. Was it true that the gates would be closed? Surely, if the guards had turned their heads once for money, they would do so again. It was possible the curfew was no more than an excuse to be away for the evening. Perhaps there was a woman he must see, someone to whom he wanted to explain the presence of his new mistress. She herself had no right to complain if he chose to stay the night. None at all.

Up and down the street, other people were enjoying the respite from the warmth of the day. Older couples, courting couples, families that included grandparents, mother and father and children in ages from early teens to babes in arms, lined the railings of balconies decked with ferns and sword-like yucca in clay pots, or else sat in chairs on the front stoops. They called back and forth to each other, exchanging greetings and gossip and friendly waves. Somewhere nearby a suitor played a sweet air on his guitar. A young girl laughed in pleasure and excitement. Friends and neighbors, they all belonged.

Elene did not. She wondered how long it would be before she would cease to feel disoriented, uprooted. She was a stranger in a strange place. She had nothing except her own intelligence and strength of will. There might be those who would help, Devota and perhaps even Ryan between his own concerns, but the only one she could depend on to make her way was herself. But she would make it. She would.

Behind her, she heard a movement. It was Devota, turning down the bed. Elene lingered another moment more, then moved back into the room.

Devota looked up from where she was lighting a candle against the gathering darkness. Elene met her gaze for a moment, then said abruptly, "Well, what do you think? Should we stay?"

"Where else would we go?"

"I don't mean tonight. But what about tomorrow?"

"There is a small matter of money."

"I have my earrings Durant gave me, and my mother's necklace. We should get something for them."

"Yes, but would it be wise to risk losing them? Is it wise to go, when here you have what you need, food, a bed, safety."

"And a position as Ryan's mistress. What good is that?"

"Women have used such positions before to gain money and power."

"Women such as La Pompadour, and Josephine before the First Consul persuaded her to marry him? Maybe, but they have also been called parasites. And worse."

Devota frowned. "Yes, though why a man is allowed to sell his strength while women may not sell their power to solace is more than I understand. Still, it would be foolish to scorn what you have here for the sake of pride."

"There's nothing wrong with pride," Elene protested.

"By no means, but you must think. Ryan can introduce you to people, and he has the means to procure the precious oils and essences that go into perfume, either by bringing them to you or asking his friends among the other privateers and ship's captains to do it. Here you will have leisure and space, and who knows, even a shop if M'sieur Bayard can be persuaded to forgo a part of his storeroom downstairs."

"Why should he do anything of the sort? He has no interest in me beyond my presence in his bed."

"You underestimate him, I think."

"Do I? I expect he prefers to keep me dependent on him. It's what Papa would have wished in his place, or Durant."

"All men are not alike."

"No, indeed," Elene said in irony. "Only you must think about what I am expected to do to live under his protection here in New Orleans."

"Is it such a hardship? Is it entirely his fault? The truth, *chère*."

Elene swung away without answering. After a moment, she said almost to herself, "I dislike using Ryan."

"It is a complicated question just who is using whom."

"Yes." Again Elene fell silent. Putting her hands to her hair, she began to remove the pins that held it.

"We stay then?" Devota asked softly.

Elene's movements stilled. She gave a soft sigh. Over her shoulder, she said, "We stay."

It was sometime later when Elene woke from a deep sleep. The room was dark, with only a faint glow from the street lantern along the way coming through the open door. The night breeze lifted the soft muslin curtain that was pulled back from the glass panes, stirring the hem gently, as if someone had just passed. Elene lay still, waiting with every nerve tightly drawn to see what had roused her.

There came a soft, sliding sound of cloth on cloth. A floorboard creaked. She whipped over in bed. There beyond the mosquito netting was a dark shape, the form of a man. She drew in her breath to scream.

The netting was batted aside. The man threw himself across her, clamping a hand to her mouth, catching her in the hard circle of his arm. His chest was bare and warm against her breast, the smell of him, mixed with wine, was familiar, pleasantly so. As his hand closed over her breast, cupping its fullness, she knew.

"Ryan—"

His hand that had muffled the word was lifted. He laughed, a rich, satisfied sound, then swooped to press his lips to hers in a quick, hard greeting that changed in midkiss to something deeper, more searching, infinitely promising. They both breathed in swift heaves of their chests when he released her lips.

"I thought you could not come back." The thudding of her heart made Elene's voice shake. He had not visited another woman. He had returned, to her.

"There are always ways."

"Bribing a guard, I suppose."

He shook his head, a faint movement in the dark. "They were too sound asleep to hear the offer."

"Then how—"

"The palisade isn't in the best condition, particularly along the back rampart. I crawled through it."

"You might have been caught!"

"I thought of you here all soft and warm in my bed and decided it was worth the risk of a night or two in the calabozo."

"Very flattering," she said, trying, not too successfully, for the sound of disbelief.

"And what else?" he asked as with tantalizing slowness he began to peel away the open neckline of her nightgown from over the globe of her breast.

"Frightening. You frightened me," she gasped.

"Forgive me. And what else?" His warm breath feathered over her naked skin, raising gooseflesh in its wake, causing the peak of her breast to tighten into a succulent berry.

"Disturbing. I was asleep." She fought the urge to lift her breast toward his lips. Dear God, how wanton she was.

"*Pauvre petite*. I will soothe you back to sleep. And what else?"

She caught her breath as the heated and wet suction of his mouth closed over her nipple. "I . . . refuse to gratify you further by . . . saying."

"Then I will gratify you by word and deed and with every wile I possess until you are persuaded," he murmured against her skin. "Until you learn exactly how glad you are that I am here. Though it can never equal my joy."

CHAPTER 10

THE men of their group dispersed immediately after breakfast the next morning, including Ryan who had to set about picking up the threads of his business affairs neglected during his time at sea. The women lingered until their men should find a place for them to stay. They gathered on the gallery overlooking the courtyard, talking in fits and starts about the surprising luxury of Ryan's house. They spoke of the amenities that New Orleans might have for their comfort and amusement, and about the steps they must take, from learning the name of a good physician to finding a source for lip rouge, before they could settle into this new life. In spite of their familiarity, there was a feeling of constraint among them, one not unlike that of guests left waiting on the doorstep for their carriage when the party is over.

By noon they were all gone, however, the Mazents to the best inn New Orleans had to offer, where Durant would also be staying; Morven's troupe to a room over a tavern on the north end of Bourbon Street; and the Tusards to the home of a friend of M'sieur Tusard's who was a former member of the French colonial service gone into retirement in New Orleans.

Elene was left alone. She sat on the shady side of the gallery, watching the splash of the water in the fountain and the play of sunlight through the leaves of the big live oak on the flagstones of the courtyard below. There was a soft footstep behind her. She looked around to see Ryan's majordomo approaching. The man bowed with deference.

"Your pardon if I disturb you, mam'zelle. M'sieur Ryan left orders that you are to be treated as the lady of the house. If there is anything you wish done, any preference you have as to your bedchamber or for luncheon, you have only to tell me."

It was a most artful speech, informative, couched in tones of respect, and yet it gave unmistakable notice that, while willing to follow his master's orders, Benedict considered himself in charge. The direction of the household, if she wished to burden herself with a pretense of the undertaking, would be carried out through him, as no doubt it had been for some years. He would naturally temper that direction as he saw fit.

Devota emerged from the bedchamber just behind where Elene sat at the sound of the majordomo's voice. She bristled as the implication of his words reached her. "Mam'zelle Elene," the maid said with terrible clarity, "has had the ordering of an establishment far more grand than this hovel since well before she put up her hair. She had no need of anyone to carry her orders. Nor does she require suggestions as to what those orders might be, I do assure you!"

The battle lines were drawn between the two servants at that moment. Elene knew it and rose to her feet, cutting short any answer Benedict might have made. She faced the majordomo and her maid who were staring at each other with set mouths and hard eyes. With a warning glance at Devota, she turned to Benedict. Her voice calm, as if she saw nothing wrong whatever, she said, "I am a stranger to New Orleans, to your ways here, and to what might be available in the market in the way of foodstuffs for meals. I will leave all that in your hands for the moment, Benedict. It would give me pleasure to have you show me over the house, however, and perhaps tell me something of how you manage things."

The maid and the manservant gave each other triumphant looks, Devota because her mistress had quietly assumed her proper position by issuing an order to the majordomo couched as a request, Benedict because his position and its importance had been reaffirmed. Elene turned from them and stood waiting for the majordomo to join her.

He glanced at her, obviously reluctant to leave so promising a quarrel. "Now, mam'zelle?"

"If you please." The answer was pleasant but firm.

They started in the salon, the largest and most formal room of the house. Though enveloped in dimness at this time of day, while the shutters were closed to keep the lingering coolness of the night in and the sun's hot rays out, it was a room of some elegance. Like the main bedchamber, it was furnished with the best of English settees and secretaries, but with French tables, mirrors, chandelier, and wall fabric, the last a lively white and red *toile de jouy*. The dining room that adjoined it, as well as the various other bedchambers in the main building and the wings of *garçonnières* which enclosed the courtyard on both sides, were set out in similar style.

There were, by Elene's count, thirty rooms in the house and its *garçonnières*, the side buildings usually used for young boys in large families. Beyond the salon, the dining room plus butler's pantry, and Ryan's bedchamber which were on the upper floor of the main building, there were six other bedchambers in the upstairs portions of each of the *garçonnières*. Downstairs, there were the storerooms facing the street and, around the courtyard, the kitchen, laundry, billiard room, and quarters for house servants. All of the rooms on each floor opened into each other on the inside, while outside they were connected by the gallery which acted as a hallway. The courtyard in the center offered coolness and quiet, an oasis away from the busy street outside. The arrangement, sharing many features with the houses of the islands that had been constructed to temper a tropical climate, did much to make living in a city pleasant.

Because Elene showed no sign of taking a high hand, the majordomo grew more forthcoming as the tour progressed, explaining the times and arrangements for meals and shopping, for cleaning and for repairs. He assembled the house's complement of maids and footmen in the courtyard for introduction by name, though the cook, being a person of major importance as well as extremely busy with luncheon, was visited in her kitchen. Elene was shown the linens and napery and the stocks of soap and tooth powder and hair pomade. The storerooms were opened for inspection, even though they were empty. With great pride, Benedict listed for her the items Ryan sometimes stockpiled for his own use and that of others, the boxes of candles, kegs of Malaga, Bordeaux, and Madeira wine and the liqueurs, the clay bottles of olive oil, brandied fruit, boxes of raisins and prunes, the vinegars and nuts and cheese; the barrels of flour and unground corn, the hogsheads of tobacco and tea, coffee and cocoa, plus the bundles of muslin and rough broadcloth for household use.

Elene showed a suitable interest, but her attention was caught by a small room at one end of the main building, one that fronted on the street. Long and narrow, it had a low wooden counter on one side and shelves ranged on the other wall, while at the back was a small alcove.

Though it was redolent of tea and coffee at the moment, it would make an excellent perfume shop.

Ryan returned to the house to take the midday meal with her. They ate on the gallery where a small table was placed for them in the shade beside a wrought iron post on which was twined a lush yellow jasmine vine. Its blooms, appearing in February, were long gone, but the foliage was the home of a pair of chameleons that watched the progress of Elene and Ryan's meal with avid beady eyes while waiting for their own to appear on the wing.

At breakfast earlier, Ryan had relayed the news of the city gathered the night before at the colonial prefect's dinner. It seemed that the American president, Jefferson, along with the congress and their countrymen, had expressed such wrath over the rescinding of the right of deposit at New Orleans and the resulting embarrassment to American commerce that the Spanish cabinet at Madrid had taken fright. Fearing that the United States would march on New Orleans and seize the city, they had given the order for the city's reestablishment as a duty-free storage port for American shippers. A proclamation stating that fact had been posted in New Orleans while Ryan was away. There was now no bar to trade, a great relief. Ryan could return to his principal occupation, being a merchant rather than a privateer.

There had also been confirmation of the rumors of the outbreak of hostilities once more between Britain and France. Britain had declared war the month before, so that the ship Ryan had seized during their voyage to New Orleans was confirmed as his legal prize of war.

The other great stir in the city in his absence had been caused by the arrival of a vessel in early June, just over a week before, bringing rumors that Napoleon had ceded Louisiana to the United States for some fabulous sum. Colonial Prefect Laussat had scoffed at the idea, declaring that he had received no hint of such a transaction.

Elene and Ryan ate in silence for a few moments, enjoying a savory dish made with rice and herbs with bits of seafood and ham. At last Elene said, "Did you hear anything more this morning about the cession of the colony?"

"Nothing definite, though the Americans are already celebrating it as a fact. I understand they have been holding parties with pyrotechnics and toasts to the newest piece of America. They certainly swagger down the streets as if they owned them. A pair of drunken Kentuckians nearly forced me off the *banquette*."

The *banquette* was the planking, like a raised walkway, that extended alongside the streets to keep the pedestrians out of the mud. Elene could imagine that Ryan would be difficult to dislodge. She wondered if the other two men had wound up in the muddy street, but did not care to ask. "I thought you were pleased at the possibility of becoming a good American."

He grimaced. "It would be a great deal better if it could be done without the *Kaintucks*."

She knew what he meant. She had seen a pair of these men from the Kentucky country that morning from the balcony over the street. Huge men, dressed in cured skins and with long, unkempt hair covered by brimless hats that still had animal hair on them and animal tails hanging down the back, they had been drunk and rowdy, falling over themselves, singing profane ditties, and calling up insults couched as compliments when they caught sight of her. She had gone inside the house and shut the door.

"Surely they aren't all like that in the United States?"

"No. Some are gentlemen in appearance and speech, but extremely sharp traders, too sharp. There are some of more noble sentiments among them—there has to be since the country has produced men such as Washington and Jefferson, but few of them are attracted to New Orleans. No matter. Whatever the Americans may be, they are better than the Spanish."

"I still can't believe Napoleon would sell."

"The reason, so he has said, is to provide the British with a future enemy by making a giant of the young United States."

"That's rather a long-term bit of planning, isn't it?" Elene made no secret of her skepticism.

"Napoleon is a man who thinks far ahead. But the truth is probably that he saw no way to hold it, given the distance involved, the loss of so many of his soldiers in Saint-Domingue, and the outrageous expense incurred there. It's more likely that instead of merely creating an enemy for Britain, he hoped to sway the United States to become an ally for France, as France allied themselves with the Americans against Britain in their revolution."

"I wonder how the Spanish will react?" Elene said.

"No doubt there will be protests, if it's true. To cede Louisiana was expressly prohibited in the Treaty of San Ildefonso. The Spanish ministers thought to keep it as a huge land buffer between the United States and their holdings in Mexico and Central America while ridding themselves of the expense of governing it. Napoleon, I fear, has also made problems for Spain."

"How can that be if it's prohibited?"

"The First Consul of France doesn't take much notice of prohibitions."

"You speak as if you believe the cession is a fact. Surely Colonial Prefect Laussat would know if it were so?"

"Not necessarily. The notice will have to be official before it can be recognized, and officialdom moves very slowly. There would be much legal work to be done, many papers to be studied and copied, shifted and signed. It takes time."

"In the meantime we all sit here, guessing, not knowing. It's so frustrating!"

Ryan agreed, then changed the subject by asking what she had done during the morning. She told him, making a droll tale of the friction between Devota and Benedict, and the exhausting thoroughness of the majordomo's presentation of the house.

Ryan sat watching her. He had brought a copy of the latest issue of *La Moniteur de la Louisiane*, the newsletter published in New Orleans, but it lay forgotten beside his plate. There was such grace in the movements of the woman before him, in the way she lifted her fork, the way she moved her head. The fragility of her blue-veined wrists caused an odd pain inside him. The amusement that came and went in her eyes was fascinating, as was the way the light reflecting from the courtyard below lay across her cheek and glowed with a soft gold sheen in the wing of hair at her temple.

The color brought to mind the glint of gold coins. He took a purse from the pocket of his coat and dropped it in front of her. Fat and heavy, it made a clanking sound as it subsided on the tabletop.

"Money? You are offering me money?"

"Since you apparently have none, and must be in need of a round of visits to the seamstresses and milliners."

"I will not be a charge on you for my clothes."

Ryan strove for patience, though he could not be surprised at her objection. "In what way is allowing me to pay for what you wear different from paying for what you eat or where you sleep?"

"It just is, and you know it." She pressed her lips together with a mutinous frown and a look of disdain for the purse.

"That dress that Hermine gave you is charming, but I'm a little tired of seeing it. And though the nightgown you wore last night had allure, I don't think you want to wear it outside the house. Come, be sensible. Take the money."

"I can't."

Ryan leaned back in his chair, his gaze intent upon Elene. The light from the courtyard caught the underside of her jaw line as she lifted her chin, making the skin appear translucent, like fine silk. It also glinted on the chain that lay along her neck with a fine cameo hanging from it. He stared at the necklace, and an idea came to him.

"Let us make this a matter of trade then. You will give me a suitable guarantee to be held, and I will extend you a sum of money."

In flat tones she asked, "What might you have in mind?"

"Not your delectable body, unless that is what you prefer?"

Elene stared at him, her expression suspended, thoughtful.

He shrugged. "Then perhaps the bauble around your neck?"

"My mother's cameo?" She put up her hand to clasp it in a protective gesture.

"I would only keep it until you could redeem it. This is a loan, remember?"

She remembered, but she also saw that he never expected to be repaid. The arrangement was an excuse to dress her in finery that he had bought. He was going to be surprised. She would pay him back. She would do it with the money she would make selling her perfume. She had considered parting with the necklace for the money to begin with, as much as she had hated the idea. It would be much better to allow Ryan to hold it. He might not be at all pleased at the use she meant to make of his loan, but that was something she would face later.

"Very well." She bent her neck, drawing the chain off over her head.

Ryan had expected more of an argument. Watching her, he tried to work out in his mind why she had capitulated so easily. He did not flatter himself that he had fooled her; he had expected they would reach one of those sophisticated arrangements where each might pretend to be acting from the purest of motives. He should have known she would not play the game the way it was written among men and women of the world. So wrapped in his own thoughts was he that when she held out the chain and pendant to him, he accepted it by rote. His immediate instinct was to hand it back, but something stopped him, some dignity in her manner, something firm in her eyes. The necklace in his hand was warm from her skin, smooth from rubbing against it. It gave him a peculiar sensation inside, but did not help his uneasiness.

Elene and Devota went shopping. They discovered, not without surprise, that there was no lack of the items required for elegant dressing in New Orleans. The shops were filled with *mousselines*, laces, silks, velvets, taffetas, and embroidered stuffs. Also on the shelves were plumes and aigrettes, ornamental beads and buttons, ribbons, point-lace veils, and a surfeit of jewelry. There was, in addition, a wide variety of creams, powders, and face paints, and a fair quantity of perfume, most of it imported from France. Devota, eyeing the last with some disfavor, pronounced it dark with age, past its fresh prime.

Nor were the streets empty. They rubbed shoulders with well-dressed matrons with mantillas over their hair and young girls in chip straw bonnets, and nodded as sauntering young bucks with dress swords at their sides and perfumed handkerchiefs in their sleeves stopped to bow. Nuns in black habits and white wimples smiled as they passed. Spanish soldiers in red uniforms with white cockades in their bicorne hats turned to stare after them.

Elene and Devota bought lengths of figured and striped India *mousseline* for a few morning dresses, and a rose mull silk for an evening costume on the chance that such a thing might be needed. They also bought fine lawn for underclothing and some ribbons and laces for trimming. Stockings were essential, as were slippers and shoes, gloves and a bonnet or two against the sun. They spent nothing on seamstresses and little on milliners, however. With Devota's help, Elene was quite capable of sewing her own clothing in the present simple mode, and also of trimming her own bonnets and hats.

There was a fair amount of the money in her purse left, then, by the time the last purchase had been made and dispatched to Ryan's house by the shopkeeper's assistant. It would be as well to begin work on the perfume without delay, for there was only a drop of two left in the bottle Devota had given her. By the time the new was made, the old would be gone. Elene and Devota asked the direction of the nearest perfume shop and set out to find it.

It was located on a muddy side street where the houses were of the French regime. It was far from impressive, being not an establishment in itself, but only a few shelves located in a back corner of an apothecary's shop. The apothecary was a simple pill-roller. The man from whom he had bought the shop the year before had happened to have a stock of the pure flower, wood, and leaf essences in oils and pulverized powders, and so he had kept the shelves supplied. Though he also had alcohol, he had made no attempt to blend perfume.

Elene walked up to the shelves, staring at the various amber, marigold, and clear liquids. There they stood, the floral and herbal, wood and animal ingredients in their flasks and bottles and vials and boxes, the scents that would give her security.

She and Devota weighed the merits of the ambergris and civet binders, the Far Eastern waxes of myrrh and frankincense, and the chips of cedar and sandalwood. They sniffed the oil of jasmine and attar of roses and frangipani, the ground roots of parma violets, the crushed rind of lemons and oranges, the powders of mint, anise seed, rosemary, and cinnamon, and the oils of cloves and daffodils and geraniums. They bought what they could get in the quantities that were available, though there were one or two things that Devota wanted that the apothecary did not have. The man behind the counter put their purchases into the basket the maid had brought since Devota did not want to trust them to a delivery boy. The maid took the clanking burden over her arm, and she and Elene left the shop.

The sky was gray toward the southwest as they emerged, and the air was hot and still. A man hurried past them, and across the street a woman with a bundle of clothing on her hip dragged a whining child along by one arm in great haste while casting worried glances skyward. There came a grumble of thunder and a puff of wind. Elene glanced at Devota. It was going to rain. A shower in the afternoon was commonplace in New Orleans during the summer months, or so they had been told. They increased their pace. Ahead of them could be seen a two-story house with its projecting balcony that would offer some protection.

Once more thunder made a muffled thudding, as if the air were too thick to carry a harsher sound. A fat drop of rain, incredibly warm, struck Elene's face. Three more fell with full, splatting noises in front of her, wetting the ground in spots the size of a demitasse cup. A handful landed in scattered and uncoordinated rhythm. Elene began to run. Devota was on her heels, the stoppered bottles and vials in her basket making a delicate clinking sound.

Abruptly the smut-colored sky disintegrated and the rain came pouring down. The last wild dash to shelter was made through what seemed an ever thickening wall of water.

Then they were under the balcony, laughing, wiping water from their faces with their hands. A gust of wind sent a wavering curtain of water from the overhang above, splaying inward toward them. They stepped back, taking refuge in the open doorway of a milliner's shop.

A small girl, who had been watching the rain, turned at their entrance and ran back to her nurse and two older sisters, and also her mother who was talking to the lady proprietor of the hat shop. As the child clasped her mother around the knees, the woman looked down.

"Now, Zoe, don't be shy," she said in soft, elegant tones as she gave her a gentle push back toward her nurse.

Elene smiled at the child before moving a bit farther into the shop. She looked with interest at the mother once more. The woman was in the full bloom of lovely maturity and carried about her a charming air of confidence. Her manner toward the milliner at her elbow was a little distant without being at all condescending. She was attired in pale blue linen with a fichu of finest muslin edged in heirloom lace, a gown of such impeccable lines and quality that it could only have come from Paris.

The milliner held a hat of fine leghorn straw dyed the same pale blue as the customer's morning dress in her hands. She reached to pick up a sprig of daisies with white silk petals and yellow velvet centers from a basket of posies on the nearby counter. "Perhaps these marguerites, Madame Laussat?" she suggested, placing them on the hat's crown. "They will lend such freshness."

"I think not," the wife of the colonial prefect answered, tipping her head to one side. "I have no wish to appear to ape poor Marie Antoinette, turning myself into a milkmaid with daisy chains."

"For such a straw head covering, madame, one requires simplicity." The milliner seemed inclined to bristle, as if she resented the slur upon her daisies or the failure of the customer to take her advice. She put down the daisies and began to smooth the straw of the hat with trembling fingers.

"Simplicity, yes, that I like," Madame Laussat said with great diplomacy. "Sweet peas, perhaps? Or else a circlet of leaves about the crown." She turned to Elene. "What do you think, mademoiselle?"

Elene moved forward. "The hat is for casual wear?"

"For driving with my husband in an open carriage. He has a passion for exploring the countryside, and I find one must have more protection than a bonnet from this Louisiana sun."

"Then possibly, since your fichu is white, a trimming of wide ribbon will suffice? Nothing appears so cool as white, and you might have long streamers on your ribbons to wave in the breeze of your passage."

"Not to speak of their usefulness to tie it on. How very suitable, and chic. I am indebted for the suggestion, Mademoiselle . . ."

As the other woman paused suggestively, Elene gave her name. At the same time, she received a malignant stare from the milliner for her interference.

"Ah, yes, Mademoiselle Larpent." Madame Laussat introduced herself, adding with a wave toward the children, "And these are my daughters, Zoe, Sophie, and Camille. Your curtsies, girls?"

Elene exchanged solemn bows with the children before their mother went on. "I have heard of your trials on Saint-Domingue, mademoiselle. Please accept my condolences on the death of your father."

"Thank you," Elene said, at a loss. "It's very kind of you to concern yourself, but I don't see how—"

"How I came to know of it? From M'sieur Bayard, of course. What men they have here, do you not agree? So gallant in action and handsome in deed."

"Yes, I suppose," Elene said, her tone a shade dry.

"Such an unfortunate thing this revolt; Saint-Domingue is a terrible place these days. My husband and I stopped there for two days in February, on our voyage here. Matters were so volatile that we did not leave the ship."

"It has been . . . very bad," Elene agreed.

"Indeed. I feel for you most strongly, but it's much easier to sympathize, you understand, when such a man as M'sieur Bayard tells the story of a woman's sad trials and valiant recovery."

Elene was given no chance to answer, even if she could have found something to say. At that moment, the milliner spoke. "These refugees from Saint-Domingue are many, very many," she said with boredom and contempt in her tone. "They are none of them valiant that I have seen. They do nothing but gamble. The women are worse, flaunting themselves in bright colors in defiance of fashion, wearing decolletages cut shockingly low. And so dependent are they on the slaves who tried to murder them that they can not now do one little thing for themselves."

Such an attack could not be allowed to pass without challenge. Elene gave the milliner a level stare. Her voice even, she said, "I'm sure the women of my island are much like those anywhere else, no better—and no worse."

"Indeed, and what of those who bring their slaves with them, proud creatures who wear the kerchief tied around their heads that they call a tignon, and pollute the minds of our servants with their worship of the terrible serpent god of the Voudou and their death wishes."

"They, too, are the same, as you will see if you look at my maid Devota here beside me."

The proprietor of the hat shop stepped back in haste. She closed her lips and did not open them again as she attended to the purchase of the colonial prefect's wife.

The rain stopped as suddenly as it had begun. The sun came out as bright and as hot as before so that steam rose in slow eddies from the tile rooftops with their dripping eaves.

Elene and Devota took their leave of Madame Laussat and her daughters. As they made their way back toward Ryan's house, Elene thought of the instinctive way she had sprung to the defense of those from Saint-Domingue. She had felt as if it were the island itself she was defending, as well as the way of life they had all lived there. Was it possible that she, like Ryan, considered herself more a citizen of her birthplace than of her adoptive country of France after all?

Before work could begin on the perfume, the substances the apothecary did not carry would have to be found. When they reached the house, Devota consulted with Benedict, a delicate proceeding conducted with hauteur on one side and bare civility on the other. Afterward, she took a basket and went out. She did not say where she was going, and Elene did not ask, but the maid walked away in the direction of the river levee where the ships were docked, more than a hundred of them, with their masts making a cross-hatching pattern against the sky.

It was over a week before all the essences were gathered for the perfume. Much of that time Elene spent sewing, making up the evening gown, the morning dresses, walking ensembles, and other items to fill in the deficiencies of her wardrobe. She and Devota also made a few things for the maid. Regardless, there was time left over to clean the storeroom chosen to be their workroom. Utensils were gathered, a large glass bottle in which to mix the various oils and powders in a base of alcohol, a china measuring container marked off in increments, a score of small bottles of dark blue glass to hold the finished scent, a tiny funnel with which to fill them, and minute cork stoppers to seal the fluid in them. While they worked, she and Devota tried names for the perfume on each other, but they all seemed too tame or too crudely erotic; nothing was quite right.

The morning came when everything was assembled. Elene and Devota waited until Ryan left for his warehouses for the day and Benedict made his regular morning visit to the market for food. When the time was right, they repaired to the workroom.

Elene brought paper, pen, and ink with which to record the ingredients and their quantities as they were added, for the only place the formula resided for the moment was in Devota's head. The two of them threw back the shutters to allow the morning light to enter. They moved to the counter. Devota picked up the first vial. Elene took up her pen and wrote down *jasmine*, with the measurement beside it, then after that, *bergamot*.

Step by step, one after the other, the precious fluids were mixed and poured together until the last vial was tipped for a bare few drops of frangipani. Devota lifted the large bottle of combined scents and gently swirled the amber contents. She put it down. She stepped back with a brief gesture toward Elene.

Elene hesitated, then put down her pen and paper and picked up a fresh linen cloth that lay ready. She tipped the bottle to dampen the cloth with a few drops. She set it down, then waited a moment while she shook the cloth gently. Finally, she passed the cloth under her nose as she inhaled.

She frowned, then took another cautious sniff. She turned to face Devota with disappointment in her eyes. "It isn't right."

"What?"

Devota took the cloth from Elene's hand and breathed deeply. She put down the cloth and tipped the bottle to spill a drop on her wrist, waited for the alcohol to evaporate, then sniffed the skin-warmed smell. She made a sound of exasperation. Almost to herself, she said, "What can be wrong?"

"Maybe the flowers aren't the same here," Elene ventured.

"It isn't that."

"You are sure you have everything you used in Saint-Domingue?"

"Almost everything."

They stared at each other for long moments. Elene could guess what was missing. It was the vital ingredient that, according to Devota, gave the perfume its power over men. What that element could be, she had no idea. It might be one of the liquids or powders sitting so innocently on the counter in front of her, some subtle change in the way they were mixed together, or even the time and place of the blending. The perfume was different without it; that much was undeniable.

"The fragrance is still good," Elene said slowly. "Perhaps it will do?"

"It might," Devota agreed, lifting her wrist to smell it once more.

A knock came on the workroom door. So great was their concentration that they both jumped, startled. They turned as the majordomo entered.

"Yes, Benedict?" Elene's voice was sharper than she intended.

"A visitor, mam'zelle," the man intoned with stiff dignity. "Mademoiselle Bizet."

"Hermine? Now?" Elene snatched off the apron she had donned for the mixing and ran a hand over her hair. To Devota she said, "We'll decide later on the scent, when we have had time to think about it."

Benedict moved ahead of Elene toward the stairs that led to the upper gallery. He made a smooth gesture in that direction before standing aside. "I put your guest there. Shall I bring a pot of chocolate and a cake or two?"

"Please," Elene said, her voice warm to make up for her earlier sharpness. "That is, bring chocolate for the lady, but I prefer coffee."

Benedict bowed with a faint smile. Elene turned away to move up the stairs.

"Elene, *chère!* I had to come see how you are and to give you all the news." Hermine rose to meet her, giving her a quick, light embrace. Elene made the actress welcome, waving her back into her seat as she took a chair across from her. They exchanged the usual pleasantries.

Her face alight with amusement, Hermine went on, "You will never believe it. There is not a professional theater in New Orleans. Not one!"

"You can't mean it."

"I do indeed. Oh, there is an occasional amateur production at a makeshift theater called the *Spectacle de la Rue Pierre*, and another place known as *La Salle de Comédie*—or perhaps they are the same, I don't know. Anyway, they hardly count. What can have possessed the Spanish to do without?"

"An excess of piety? Or perhaps they just have had no talented professionals such as your troupe to inspire them."

"I like the last reason," Hermine said with a twinkle in her eyes. "But you will be happy to know the situation is about to change. Morven has found us a place."

"A theater where there is none?" Elene did her best to show proper interest, despite the distraction of the problem with the perfume.

"Nothing so miraculous. It's a vauxhall."

"A what!"

A vauxhall, Elene knew, was a pleasure garden in imitation of the famous attraction of that name in London. Such places frequently included a stage for light entertainment on the order of juggling and acrobatics, a few comic skits, the singing of light airs, and music for dancing. The audience usually sat in boxes having supper, drinking, laughing, and talking, giving only cursory attention to the entertainers unless they were either sufficiently comical or risqué to catch their attention.

"Don't look so shocked, my love. We've performed in worse places, I assure you. It happens that our patroness has a major financial interest in the vauxhall outside the city, at the end of the canal."

"I see."

Hermine grinned. "I doubt it. This patroness is a middle-aged widow, one not only rich and amorous, but completely charmed with Morven. Widows are rather a specialty of his."

"You mean that he—"

"That he takes advantage? He can't help himself, poor dear. And the widows appreciate it so. It gives them memories to make them smile when they are old."

"Don't you mind?" Elene asked in perplexity.

Hermine gave a light shrug. "Only a little. It doesn't mean anything to him, and we have to live."

"I suppose." To Elene's ear, however, the actress's explanation was far too airy and offhand. It did not match the desolation in her eyes. Hermine, for all her sophisticated understanding, did mind. She minded a great deal.

"Anyway, we will have a performance at the end of the week, and you and Ryan must come. Not only shall we love to see you in the audience, we need the applause!"

Elene agreed. She did not think Ryan would mind since Morven was an old friend.

The chocolate and coffee arrived in separate pots, both of delicate Sevres porcelain painted with roses. Benedict poured the beverages for them, then withdrew as quietly as he had come.

Hermine sipped, pronounced her chocolate delicious, then tilted her head to one side inquisitively. "Have you heard from the others of our group? M'sieur Mazent has driven out to inspect the plantation he had the foresight to purchase here some years ago. It was converted to sugar production shortly after he bought it, and now he finds himself still a wealthy man in spite of having lost a fortune on Saint-Domingue. He considers building a fine new house on his lands, but hesitates because Flora prefers the delights of town."

"And the Tusards?"

"When I saw Madame Tusard, she was bitter. M'sieur Claude spends all his time at the Café des Réfugiés on St. Philip Street with the other gentlemen from Saint-Domingue, drinking absinthe and talking about the time when they were figures of importance. The friends with whom they have been staying are already casting out hints that they find a place elsewhere. Madame fears she will be reduced to some paltry cottage and a pittance from the French government—if even that small pension can be pried from the First Consul. Napoleon, it seems, is bored with the importuning and the horror tales from the survivors of the island. As are the people of New Orleans."

"I know what you mean. I've noticed something of it myself," Elene said, thinking of the milliner's tirade against the women of Saint-Domingue.

"Madame Tusard is to be pitied, but she can be tiresome. She came to see me yesterday. She seemed convinced for some reason that her Claude might be with me instead of at the café. She seems to think that I am the actress who apparently led her husband astray years ago, causing him to absent himself temporarily with government funds."

"I didn't know there was an actress involved in the scandal. I don't think she was mentioned on the ship."

"Nor do I. In any case, I was glad to be able to disabuse the lady of the idea that I had anything to do with it. It is too absurd; I was in Paris at the time, I swear it! But I think the tragedies the woman has endured has made her see enemies everywhere."

Elene nodded. "It can happen."

"And I suppose you have heard from Durant?"

"No, nothing." Elene could not think why the other woman would assume she had, unless she thought Durant would be visiting her while she was ensconced as the mistress of another man. He had, in fact, ignored her as if she didn't exist, which was just as well. Ryan had been very busy with his affairs in the past few days, but she did not think he would approve of Durant making himself free of his house when he was not present.

The actress drank the last of her chocolate and set her cup aside, then went on in her melodious tones. "Durant appears to have had resources he did not mention while on board the ship. He has not only togged himself out splendidly at the most expensive tailor in town since his arrival, but has purchased the flashiest carriage you ever saw, a phaeton of black lacquer with bright blue trim and pulled by a pair of chestnuts that have no equal in the colony."

"Durant always did enjoy owning the best."

"Which reminds me that his mistress has been provided with a gown the same shade of blue as the carriage, and a blue bonnet with black plumes. For Serephine's sake, he has taken the upper floor of a house, also, one located at quite a fashionable address. It happened that the proprietor of the inn where Durant and the Mazents were staying objected to his mistress sharing his rooms and eating in the common room with the other guests. Durant removed her and has been flaunting her about ever since."

"It sounds like him."

"I assume that was the whole purpose of the carriage, to show himself and his mistress abroad, tooling up and down the levee road. It isn't as if he has estates to inspect or relatives to visit out of town, which is the only reason most people here buy a vehicle. It seems excessive."

"Durant enjoys that also."

"I thought he might, though it's always possible he misses you to excess instead, and is busily showing everyone he doesn't."

Elene shook her head with a wry smile. "Doubtful indeed."

"How disappointing. I had every hope that being thwarted in love might be the making of Durant!"

They talked of other things until finally Hermine rose to go. Elene walked with her down the stairs and through the courtyard to the opening of the porte cochère. Just inside the shadowy underpass, the actress paused.

"We, the troupe, that is, have left the boardinghouse we found, you know, and moved in with the widow to rehearse in her garden. You must come to see us when you have nothing else to do."

"The widow won't mind?"

"No, no. She adores visitors."

The actress gave Elene careful directions to the house. Elene was repeating them when the door to the small room she and Devota had taken for a workroom swung open just along the wall behind her.

Devota emerged. "I've done it, *chère!*" she cried as she caught sight of Elene. "Now it's right."

"You finished without me?" Elene did not try to hide her disappointment.

"It came to me what was missing. Only smell now—" Devota pressed the bottle she held into Elene's hand along with the square of linen. Only then did she catch sight of the actress. "Mam'zelle Hermine, I didn't see you there. My eyes—it's so bright out here when I've just come from the workroom."

"Good morning, Devota," the actress said easily. "Don't tell me you have made more of the famous perfume already?"

Devota gave a reluctant nod.

"What a fascination it is, the making of a good scent. To smell it is to breathe the distilled memories of flowers, to wear it is to create memories of one's own." Hermine's gaze moved to the blue bottle in Elene's hand. She watched intently as the stopper was removed and the ritual of inhaling the fragrance was performed.

"Well?" the actress demanded.

"Well?" the maid questioned.

Elene divided a slow, wide smile between the two women. "Beautiful," she said. "Perfect."

Hermine sighed. "Wonderful. You will permit me one little sniff? I can't wait to see if it's truly the same as yours. Such a marvelous fragrance."

Elene was aware of a moment of reluctance, of dislike of the idea of handing over her perfume. It was because the triumph of getting it right was so new, she told herself. There was no call to be so absurd. She relinquished the sample of perfume and waited for the reaction of the actress.

"Ah, wonderful," Hermine sighed in bliss. "Nothing, but nothing could be so heavenly. It's a breath of paradise, nothing less. Tell me this little bit isn't all you have made, I beg of you. I must have some of it. I really must!"

A promise had been made. There was nothing to be done now except keep it. Elene forced a smile and passed the tiny stopper for the bottle to the actress. "Take this, the very first bottle. It's yours, just as we agreed —and since you have given us the perfect name for it. I think we will call it, simply, Paradise."

Devota made a small gesture, as if she would retrieve the bottle, then quickly drew her hand back. That movement was lost as Hermine threw her arms around Elene, crying her thanks. When the actress had gone, taking her perfume with her, Elene looked around. Devota was gone, slipping away back into the workroom.

CHAPTER 11

ELENE stood in an invisible cloud of perfume. Its aura hovered around her, redolent of tropical nights with exotic flowers pale in the moonlight, of warm breezes laden with the scent of spice, of sun-kissed white sand beaches and rolling turquoise waves, of arching palm trees and moist fern bowers. Oblivious of the intangible aura she had created, she stood carefully measuring minute quantities of perfume into tiny blue bottles with green and lavender ribbons tied around the necks. Each bottle was firmly fitted with a stopper and set to one side.

Ryan stood watching her with his shoulder braced on the door frame. The gold of her hair seemed to glow in the dim room lighted only by the fading gleams of the setting sun beyond the windows. Her face was absorbed, almost stern, and yet the curves of her mouth were gentle and soft with pleasure. She moved with quick competence, her fingers nimble among the small bottles. There was nothing in what she was doing that was the least enticing; nevertheless, he wanted her with a sudden, almost frightening, intensity.

He had gone about his business much as usual in the past few days, but his heart wasn't in it. His thoughts had a way of returning to Elene here in his house at the most inconvenient times. He made love to her nightly, held her in his arms while she slept, sat across from her as she presided over his table, and kissed her good-bye each morning as he left her. Still she eluded him.

Obsessed. He was becoming obsessed with her. It was all he could do not to return to the house a dozen times a day to see if she was still there. His desire for her, instead of being slaked by constant appease-ment, seemed only to grow. She lingered in his mind just as the scent of her perfume lingered on his body and haunted the corners of his house. His life was permeated with her, while it seemed that she was hardly conscious he existed, except when she was in his arms. It was intolera-ble. Just as it was intolerable that she should go on working without knowing he was there.

He pushed away from the door frame and stepped into the room. Moving in behind her, he circled her waist with his arms to draw her against him.

Elene stiffened in alarm. The empty bottle she held clattered to the tabletop. She whipped around, stepping back.

"What are you doing here?" The words were taut, and her face flushed with guilty chagrin.

"I live here, you will remember."

"But you left—"

"I took a wild notion to return, in the main because Benedict hinted this morning it might be of interest."

"Benedict," she said, her voice hollow.

"You will have to forgive him. It's his job to look after my welfare." He braced one fist on his hip, waving with the other hand toward the bottles arrayed behind her. "You didn't expect, surely, to keep this from me for long. The smell alone is enough to give you away." Nor had he needed Benedict's hint. Her eagerness to be rid of him and her preoccu-pation of late had been enough to arouse his suspicions.

"We have been opening the doors and windows and working only an hour or two at a time." She lifted her chin. "We haven't done any harm to your house or your storeroom."

"I never thought you had." A frown drew his brows together at her defensive gesture. "My concern is for why you thought it necessary to do it behind my back."

"To avoid just such a scene as this, the outrage of the master of the house because a mere female wanted to do something on her own. Why should I come begging for your permission? To give you the pleasure of refusing?"

That she could so misjudge him brought the rise of real anger. "What in the name of all the gods do I care what you do in here? It's nothing to me if you want to spend your time dabbling in perfume. I even made the suggestion, if you remember. But you might have trusted me enough to discuss going ahead with it."

"Dabbling! It's a joke to you, just as when you first mentioned it. You don't take it seriously at all." She glared at him, an infuriated golden angel in the dim room.

"Don't put words in my mouth. You have no way of knowing what I think, what I want, or what I will do."

"Fine talk, but you would still have refused to allow me this, just as my father always denied his permission, to prove your power over me."

"I'm not your father. I don't have to prove anything!"

Elene's attention was snared by the hard conviction in his tone. She stared at him, at the dark shadows in his eyes and the grim planes of his face, while his words sank slowly into her mind. Before she could speak, he went on.

"I will tell you this about me. You may do what you like, in here or elsewhere, but don't ever try to make me your dupe again. That I will not tolerate."

"You . . . don't really mind this?" Her question was tentative as she indicated the storeroom around them, as if she still could not quite believe him.

"Why should I? I'm not using the room."

"But you might need it later."

He held to his temper, giving her a perplexed frown. "Do you want it or not?"

"Yes, I want it!"

"Then take it."

He was right, she didn't know him. A part of the reason was his own armored defenses, but another was her need for self-protection. If she did not allow herself to come too close, she could not be hurt when they went their separate ways. There was also her guilt over using the perfume against him. Discomfort of conscience did not encourage intimacy.

Now there was this added apprehension. If he was so incensed at being deceived over the use of his storeroom, what would he feel when he learned of the perfume?

She lifted her chin to meet his gaze squarely. "I'm sorry. On second thought, it might be better if I didn't use it. In fact, it might be as well if I left your house."

"No." The word was rough as he reached to catch her arms. "I won't let you go."

"You can't keep me against my will."

"Try me."

There was in his grasp the firmness of restrained strength. It would be difficult, if not impossible, to break free. She did not try. Her gaze clear, she said, "And give you the opportunity to prove your power after all?"

He acknowledged her riposte with a twist of his lips. "Why should I release you? So you can go to another man?"

"So you would be left in peace."

"Peace isn't what I want, nor is it a house without you, without your damnable perfume."

She tilted her head, her eyes shadowed. "It's the perfume that attracts you then?"

"You know it isn't."

"Do I?"

"I could show you," he said in grim amusement. "Have you ever had passionate love made to you on a hard floor?"

"You are well aware—"

"Yes, I am, one of my favorite memories. You know, sometimes I long for that black hole under Favier's house."

She stared at him at a loss. "But why?"

The reason, Ryan knew, was because there in that dark space he had not been able to see the reserve in her eyes. Because then there had been a strong probability that her bridegroom, Durant Gambier, was dead. Because for those brief days Elene Larpent had been wholly his, unable to evade him.

"Marry me," he said.

The breath stopped in Elene's throat. She wished with abrupt raw longing that she had never heard of perfume. She had not believed in its power at first, had not wanted to believe. But every day she sensed the growing force of Ryan's need for her, and it seemed that something so virulent could not be brought about otherwise than by Devota's aid. It would not be fair to him to accept his proposal that might well be made under most peculiar duress. The question of her own will in the matter was of no concern. She did not want a husband who had been compelled to make his offer.

"Why?"

Her voice was so quiet he had to lean close to hear. There was in it, inexplicably, the sound of a warning. "Call it an impulse."

"What is wrong with the way we are?"

His grasp slackened. "You may be satisfied, but I want more."

"What more is there, for us?"

"A shared future. Children." His voice was low, with a warm note of urgency. The blue of his eyes was dark but clear.

There was a constriction around Elene's heart, slowly squeezing until it hurt to breathe. How easy it would be to say yes, to take what he offered and never look back. But what if he should discover what she had done to him so unwittingly? Marriage was a bond that lasted forever, and forever was a long time to be tied to a man who despised her.

That his words could affect her to such a degree was a betrayal, one that brought a saving resentment. "I can't give you that. Please don't ask it."

He saw the angry desolation in her face and it made no sense—unless the thing she mourned was the loss of her future with Gambier. He cursed the day that Jean had taken the planter aboard the *Sea Spirit*. Why could the man not have been left behind to take his chances? Still, there was something here he did not understand. He could have sworn she was not indifferent to him or the things he had said.

"It's my turn now to ask why."

She gave a slight shake of her head. "You don't mean it. It's only a whim that will pass, one brought on by being thrown together with me, and by my perfume."

"To hell with your perfume!" he said in exasperation. "I know what I—"

"It's important you understand that it's special," she interrupted him, driven by a compelling impulse to unburden her mind, to tell him everything. "It affects men in strange and powerful ways. You don't know—"

"I know as much about it as care I to," he said, in grating impatience. "What interests me at this moment is why you won't give me the answer I want."

She had tried to tell him. Perhaps it was as well he would not listen. She looked away from his intent gaze, searching her mind for something to say to appease him. "It was supposed to be a temporary arrangement, our being together, nothing more."

"And that's the way you like it."

"I have to make my own way, control my own coming and going, instead of letting someone else do it for me."

"I don't want to control you, Elene. I only want to keep you safe beside me."

"Yes, that's what you say, but you will leave me when you can, if you can."

She had not meant to say the last. It had come from inside her, the result, she knew with sudden clarity, of her father's sending her away to France, then leaving her there among the dangers of the revolution, and even, perhaps, because he had deserted her once more, like her mother, in death. She could not risk being left again.

Maybe that was why she had found it so hard to stop using the perfume, even to test it. It was necessary to her to keep the security she had gained with Ryan, to prevent him from leaving her before she was ready.

A crooked smile curved Ryan's mouth. "I will leave you only if you force me. Don't let it distress you, any of it. As you say, to marry was a passing suggestion. Forget it, forget leaving, and I will give you another. We are invited to attend the vauxhall performance of Morven's troupe in three day's time with the Mazents. M'sieur Mazent has hired a box and a boat and wants to form a party of those who escaped Saint-Domingue together. What do you think?"

His words were light, but Elene could sense the coolness, the withdrawal, and the waiting behind them. He had even removed his arms to stand braced with one hand upon the table beside her. To accept what he offered, she understood, would be to return their relationship to its former footing. It was best this way, without promises or deep emotions, retaining their secrets. Surely it was best. She swallowed on the drain of tears in the back of her throat. Her voice too bright, she said, "Why not?"

"Why not indeed," Ryan said, and wondered if somehow she knew already that Gambier would be one of the party.

The vauxhall was located among an assemblage of taverns, gaming houses, inns, and dance halls that had been built where the canal constructed by Spanish Governor Carondelet joined Bayou St. John. This canal began at the outer ramparts of the city and flowed into Lake Pontchartrain to drain the city during flooding. The party organized by Mazent was able to step into the barge-like boat arranged for them very nearly at the back gate of the palisade.

They left just after the sun had set, joining a line of other barges wending their way toward the bayou. A breeze had sprung up from the lake, cooling the air and fanning their faces. The man who poled their barge sang as he bent to his work. The flat-bottomed boat was necessary, for the canal, once a well-kept waterway, had not been cleaned out for several years so that it had filled in with silt to a depth of almost three feet in places. Willows and cypresses crowded the edges, hanging over the water, pale green and cool. The seeds of the cypresses, like carved green stones, hung heavy among the fragile, lacy leaves. When the willows were brushed, mosquitoes rose in clouds. Gnats and other flying insects danced ahead of them over the water, while waterborne bugs skated away as if racing against their clumsy craft. The pink and lavender afterglow in the western sky was reflected in the water, turning it to liquid opaline.

It should have been peaceful, but was not. Ryan was in a strange mood. He was polite but distant, with little to say to Elene though he spoke often enough to the others. He had not been the same since she had failed to agree to marry him. It was not that he was surly or inclined to sulk, but rather as if he had something on his mind.

He had not approached her for the past three nights, however. It was also true that in that time she had not used the original perfume, from the bottle brought from Saint-Domingue by Devota, for it was gone. In fact, she had used none at all. If proof of its effectiveness was needed, she seemed to have it, no matter how painful it was to realize how much Ryan's attraction to her depended on it. To try the matter further, she had anointed herself liberally with the new scent while she dressed this evening. So far, it had made no impression whatever on Ryan, or none she could see. She should have been glad of it. She did try to be.

Flaring torches lit the box area and the garden paths of the vauxhall, not merely to provide light, but to discourage the mosquitoes from preying on the patrons. The smoke from the flambeaux drifted through the orange trees that lined the white, shell-strewn paths, its acrid tang blending with the sweet fragrance of the orange blossoms. The night was balmy after the heat of the day, and made even more pleasant by the breeze from the lake that lifted the tendrils of the ladies hair and fluttered the hems of their gowns, and also did its part to hold the mosquitoes at bay. It brought the aroma of food cooking somewhere, and also the milky richness of the pralines and the *tout chard calas*, or hot rice cakes, of the *marchandes*, or sellers of wares, the free women of color in their white aprons who carried their wares in flat baskets perched on their wide hips. The citrus tartness of the oranges and the rich fragrance of the pink-purple roses and the creamy white of wild gardenias being hawked by pert young girls could be caught now and again, as well as a whiff of the honeysuckle that twined among the shrubbery.

The Mazent party strolled through the grounds, taking the air, enjoying the breeze while they waited for dinner to be served and the performances to begin. Elene's gown of blue *mousseline* was made with long streamers of grosgrain ribbon falling from a love knot set at the high waist under her breasts. The ribbons flew about so in the evening breeze that at last she caught them in her hands, threading them through her fingers as she walked.

She was not the only one in new finery. Madame Tusard wore a gown of lavender silk overlaid with black sarcenet, and carried a sarcenet reticule to match. Flora Mazent was much more elegant in pale yellow silk. The color did nothing for her sallow complexion, however, and the layers of ruffles and flounces placed about the shoulders and around the level of her knees to compensate for her thinness made her look like nothing so much as an animated corn shock.

The young Mazent girl walked beside Durant. There were spots of color in her cheeks brought on by the excitement of her position, and her grasp on Durant's arm made the ends of her fingers white. An orange seller strolled by, and the girl eyed the round fruits hungrily.

"May I have one, M'sieur Durant?" she asked, a hint of a demand in her tone as she stared up at him.

It was Madame Tusard who answered at her most patronizing. "It would be most unwise, my dear. You will get the juice on your lovely new gown."

"I don't care for that."

"But silk is so very dear here in New Orleans."

"I don't care," Flora said again with a look of fright for her own boldness. "Papa, please may I have an orange?"

"What my puss wants, she must have," M'sieur Mazent said to the older woman, his voice apologetic and yet tinged with pride. He drew out his purse and motioned the orange seller, a grinning young Negro girl of no more than thirteen, forward. Being a man of expansive habits, he offered to buy everyone else an orange also. They refused. Because Flora looked a little uncomfortable at being the only one indulging in the wares being offered around them, Elene asked for a praline. So spontaneous was her praise of the creamy confection made of milk and sugar and pecans that Madame Tusard suddenly developed a craving to taste one, and sent her Claude puffing after the seller.

Durant, his expression somewhat testy but resigned, produced his penknife to peel Flora's orange, then his handkerchief to wipe the juice from his hands as well as hers. M'sieur Mazent watched the two of them with a fond eye, though he declined a portion of the orange, and also the candy everyone was nibbling. The acid and sugar would upset him, he said, one hand going unconsciously to his abdomen; what he needed was his dinner.

The evening meal was announced shortly. They all settled around the table in their box, a very good one located directly opposite the center of the raised, open stage. The fare was surprisingly palatable if uninspired, a coq au vin served with an array of vegetables seasoned with honey, and hot loaves of bread. The butter was separating from the heat and the wine only mediocre, but the dessert that followed, a creme caramel topped with fresh blackberries, was delicious.

The entertainment was of equal quality, being a mixture of the good and the only passable. The pair of comics who began the show were hilarious and the tumblers who followed them excellent, even amazing. The skit, a farce of some daring which involved a bedroom equipped with four doors through which three men, two ladies, and a maidservant went in and out in rapid succession, lacked taste, but that only caused the appearance of Morven's troupe to be greeted with that much more enthusiasm.

No one applauded louder than the woman in the box to the left of Mazent's. A lady of perhaps forty years of age, with masses of silken black curls untainted by silver, she wore a gown of Parma violet silk with an astonishingly low-cut bodice that was filled in by a magnificent diamond necklace. Matching earrings and bracelets added their sparkle, but the ultimate glitter was achieved by a huge amethyst encircled with diamonds that hung from a fillet at the center of her forehead. Watching her enthusiasm, and also the rapacious look she turned on Morven as he inclined toward the woman in a special bow, Elene was forced to wonder if this was not the patroness of whom Hermine had spoken. Such thoughts were banished as Morven moved down stage and began his first soliloquy.

In contrast to the light vein of the other acts, Morven had chosen a tragedy for his troupe's first appearance in New Orleans. It was a tale he had written himself about a nobleman in love with two women, one young and voluptuous who caters to his bodily desires, the other more mature and intelligent who supplies his mental needs. Unable to choose between them, he forces them to choose for him. The effect on the women is to increase their essential traits. The result is tragedy as the woman of superior mental powers, finding him unworthy due to his lack of mental strength, removes herself from the competition with a dagger to her heart, because she can't stop loving a man she can no longer respect. The nobleman, realizing that he has caused the death of the woman he truly loves, stabs himself with the same dagger.

Morven was spectacular as the nobleman tormented by love and remorse, while Hermine played the intelligent woman to perfection, giving her a fine, slicing wit and yet an agonizing empathy with the moods and passions and ultimate requirements of the man she loves. Josie, though hers was the lesser part of the overtly promiscuous female, was more than adequate, seeming to radiate careless, sensual energy.

The applause rolled toward the stage in waves when the final curtain fell. Flowers were thrown at all three, but particularly at Morven and the suggestively dressed Josie. The trio took four bows, then ran from the stage, giving it up to a return of the comedians.

Still in costume, Morven and the two women made their way first to the box of the woman decked in diamonds. There was a brief exchange of compliments, then the troupe, with their patroness among them, moved toward the Mazent box.

The woman was introduced as Madame Rachel Pitot. On closer inspection, she looked as if she too might have had some familiarity with the stage at one time in her life; she moved with control and a certain arch self-consciousness, and her face paint was excessive. She welcomed them to the vauxhall as befitted her financial interest in the place, though it was perfectly obvious that she cared not at all what they thought of it or of her, so long as Morven was at her side.

M'sieur Mazent, in a hospitable gesture, insisted that Madame Pitot and the others must join his party. Agreement was immediate, as if the troupe had expected nothing less. Madame Pitot lifted a hand and a waiter came at once to take the order of the actors for their dinner, since they had not eaten before the performance. Chairs were shifted to make room and others added. At the same time, several men and women from the audience left their boxes to come crowding around to shake hands and offer congratulations, preventing the troupe from sitting down. There was a period of mass confusion as people reached across those who were seated in their attempt to touch the actors. Finally, the well-wishers trailed away back to their own seats and order was restored.

Elene, able to speak to Hermine and the others at last, leaned across the table. "A most impressive play! You were all wonderful. I was thrilled."

A chorus of agreement followed her words. Morven, flushed with triumph and the euphoria following a performance, bowed. "I flatter myself it wasn't a bad debut for us here."

"You certainly do flatter yourself," Hermine said. "You stepped on my toe during the last scene."

"You weren't showing enough anguish," Morven replied, his smile smug.

"You did it on purpose!"

In the face of her wrath, Morven threw up his hands, "No, no, my sweet. I'm a clumsy oaf."

Madame Pitot disagreed in husky, caressing accents. "You are the most deft of men, *cher* Morven. You could not be clumsy if you tried."

Hermine stared at them, then looked away, her face grim.

Flora, who had been silent until then, said in breathless tones, "You really were very good. I cried when you killed yourself, Hermine. But you are pale as death, all of you."

"It's the paint we use," Hermine said, and wiped a hand along her face before displaying the whitened tips of her fingers. "Or more accurately, it's the flour. A great many actors and actresses use white lead powder, but it's most unhealthy, besides making your skin erupt into sores."

"I use white lead and I have no sores," Josie said, a bit vehement in her protest, perhaps because she felt left out of Flora's compliments.

"You will, in time," Hermine told her, then gave a rueful shake of her head as the other actress merely shrugged.

Flora knitted her brow. "You have such pale skin already, Hermine, that I don't see why you need flour or anything else."

"It's the lanterns with their reflectors at stage front. They are so bright one looks like a gray ghost with nothing on the face. As for my skin, I confess I am not so wise there. I come from Breton fishermen stock, and tend to look like a sailor who has been out in the north wind if I don't take care, entirely too red-faced. I sometimes drink a cordial laced with a grain of arsenic to take away the high color."

"A fool thing to do, too," Morven said, "as I've told you often."

"So you have." Hermine did not look at the actor as she spoke, but went on with a warm smile for the younger girl. "I'm sure we ladies all have our little beauty secrets like this."

"I have none," Flora said.

Since this was perfectly clear from her plain and featureless face, there was a small silence. Elene broke it. "My mother used to paint quite openly, but it's becoming less and less the thing to do. Beauty must be natural now."

"Or seem so," Hermine agreed with a twist of her lips.

"I, for one, am glad of it," Madame Tusard said, her gaze upon the actress just a little malicious in its condemnation. "If men may go about with naked faces, why should we women not do the same?"

"My dear," Claude Tusard said, touching his mustache in a conscious gesture, "hardly naked. Shaven in part, yes, and without artifice, but hardly naked."

"Naked, Claude. Please don't dispute with me."

"Yes, *chère*."

Josie chuckled. "I don't see why we shouldn't all go completely naked. What good are clothes, after all?"

"They cut down on the area where mosquitoes can land," Ryan said, slapping at an insect on his face.

"That's true," Josie said as if presented with a new and arresting observation. "What vicious little creatures they are!"

"Permit me," Claude Tusard said to the younger actress and, reaching out, crushed an insect that was sitting on her bare shoulder.

Josie gave him an arch smile. "Thank you, m'sieur."

A smile twitched the mustache that decorated M'sieur Tusard's upper lip. A gleam rose in his eye.

Madame Tusard drew a seething breath. "Claude!"

"Yes, *chère*." The gleam was extinguished, leaving Madame Tusard's husband with a morose expression on his lined face.

Flora, ignoring the byplay, had turned her attention to the box on their right where two men, Americans, judging from the square cut of their coats and simple cravats, were finishing their meal. Their voices were somewhat loud and they leaned back in their chairs, looking around as if they owned all they surveyed. Elene saw the young girl give an exaggerated shudder as she leaned toward Durant.

"Those men, one of them is staring at me," she said in an undertone.

"Don't be alarmed," Durant said with a scant flick of his eyes in the direction Flora indicated. "Those two will stare at anything and everything, like bumpkins from the country."

"I don't like it. They give me shivers."

"Then don't look at them."

"How can I not? Oh, do make them stop!" In her agitation the girl clutched at his arm.

Durant removed her fingers from where they were wrinkling his sleeve. "Calm yourself, mademoiselle."

"Calm yourself, indeed!" Madame Tusard said, her breast swelling as she joined forces with Flora. "I hate being stared at also. It's so vulgar, and possibly dangerous. What if those two ruffians should follow us on our homeward way and attack us?"

Flora gave a little squeal of dismay. Ryan, leaning back in his chair and picking up his wine glass, glanced from Flora to Madame Tusard, then at the Americans. "They may be vulgar, but look quite harmless to me."

"One even looks rather sweet," Josie said. "I think he threw me a posy just now. It wouldn't surprise me if it wasn't you he was watching at all, Flora." The actress in her low-cut costume patted the curves of her breasts with a most self-satisfied air without looking to see the effect her words had on her audience.

"Slut!" Flora Mazent gasped. Picking up her wine glass, she dashed the contents directly into the cleavage of Josie's gown.

Josie screamed and jumped up. With an oath straight from the back streets of Paris, she lunged for the other girl. Flora gave a small, frightened cry and leaped from her chair to back away. M'sieur Tusard and Ryan caught Josie before she could go after Flora. M'sieur Mazent got to his feet, wringing his hands. "Now, now," he said, "now, now."

Hermine gave a peal of laughter. Elene met the other woman's gaze. Her lips twitched, then a moment later, she joined the actress. Around them, the audience roared.

For an instant, Flora blanched. Elene, seeing her distress, quieted at once. As the laughter rumbled on, she saw the realization strike Flora that the general merriment was for the action of the comedians on the stage. A sigh left the other girl. Trembling, she allowed Durant to lead her back to her chair, but only after Josie had resumed her seat.

Hermine caught Elene's eye with one brow arched in comical dismay. The amusement of the actress died away, however, as she glanced toward where Morven and his patroness, the widow, had their heads together in whispering oblivion of what was taking place around them.

The waiter came to a halt at their table, holding a tray of food high above his head. Elene, sitting nearest to the box entrance, leaned forward in her chair so that the man could step up in the box and pass behind her. Her gaze met that of Durant, still standing behind Flora's chair. He was staring at her with a taut, brooding expression in his black eyes that carried what seemed to be an accusation. He was exquisitely turned out by his tailor, as Hermine had told her, but the black of his evening wear gave him a severe look that was somehow threatening. The slash on his cheek, though perfectly healed, was livid.

Beside her, there was a scraping sound as Ryan got to his feet. Elene's nerves leaped under the skin as he leaned to speak near her ear. His voice was no more than a murmur as he spoke, however. "Shall we walk while Morven and the ladies are eating?"

She agreed with alacrity. She had a sudden and imperative need to get away from the unsettling crosscurrents of emotion that eddied around the group. They would all doubtless make other friends here in New Orleans in time, but for the moment it seemed that they were drawn together, not only by the ordeal through which they had passed and the attitude of the people of New Orleans toward them as the latest, and least wanted, refugees, but also by a set of emotional relationships that grew more complicated each day.

They strolled in silence, with Elene's hand tucked under Ryan's elbow. They had plenty of company on the paths nearest the stage as others also walked off the effects of the meal. The farther they moved from that center, however, the fewer people they met and the more the noise of clattering silverware, laughter, and raised voices receded.

The darkness of full night had fallen while they ate. Many of the torches that lighted the paths had burned out. Now and then there was a giggle or a soft murmur from some twisting byway or vine-covered bower set among the trees as lovers took advantage of the darkness and seclusion. In the distance, from the stage, came the sound of music as the dancing started.

Elene glanced at the man beside her. "Was there something you wanted to talk to me about?"

"Not really. Need there be before you will walk with me?"

"Of course not." Elene was disturbed by the taut undertone of stringent control in his voice.

"Gambier has watched you this evening like a cat with its eye on a dish of cream that's out of reach." Ryan had not meant to say such a thing. It was as if he were driven.

"He may be concerned for my welfare. Our families have been friends for years."

He wondered if she really believed that, or if it was something to say to placate him. "Next you will be saying he loves you."

Did Durant love her? Elene had no reason to think so. But then, neither had he given her cause to think he did not. "It doesn't matter, since we are not to be married."

"Much to your regret."

"I have no regrets at all," she said sharply.

Ryan stopped, turning on her. "You won't marry me and you don't want to marry Gambier, or so you say. What is it you want?"

"Must I want something?"

"It's usual."

She wanted to sell her perfume, to have the money to pay her own way and that of Devota. She wanted the discomfort between Ryan and herself ended so that she could rest easy. She would like to recover the fortune her father had invested over the years in the property on Saint-Domingue, though she didn't expect to ever see it. What else was there?

There was one thing more.

She wanted Ryan to desire her for herself, not because he was compelled by some Voudou magic. The thought sent a surge of purest exhilaration along her veins. She felt the heat of a flush rise to her hairline, and was fervently glad he could not see. Her heart throbbed, filling her chest, threatening to choke her.

"What is it?" he asked. She was so still, and yet he had heard the soft catch of her breath as if in sudden pain, or sudden pleasure. He put out his hand to touch her arm.

Her skin was soft, yet firm and resilient over the slender bones. Ryan felt an abrupt urge to hold her, to protect her, to take her there in the orange blossom-scented darkness. It had been so long. Three days and three nights without her. Pride, that had been the reason. He had thought she might refuse him her body as she had refused her hand. Wary of another rejection, he had waited for some sign of her wishes. There had been none, and he would not force himself on any woman.

Now he could feel the trembling inside her and it hurt him somewhere deep, deep where he lived. He had not meant to cause her pain.

"Elene—*chérie*," he whispered.

She drew a deep breath. "What I want," she said, a distinct tremor in her tones that were so low they could scarcely be heard, "is for you to want me."

He felt the words like a blow to the heart. Before their sound had died away, he swept her into his arms, holding her close. Against the silk of her hair, he said, "Always."

She spread her hands over his muscle-clad chest and lifted her mouth in delicate invitation. The quickness of his response gave her a heady, joyous sensation. He did want her. She had drawn him to her, and without the magic of the original perfume.

His mouth upon hers was warm and sweet, infinitely tender, softly stroking, yet firm in its possession. He brushed the curves of her lips with his tongue, delicately abrading their smoothness, tasting, seeking entry. She gave it to him, and on a swift, indrawn breath, he caught her closer.

She slid her hands upward along the strong column of his neck to the thick curls that grew low on his nape. She twined her fingers through them, clasping, increasing the pressure of her mouth on his as with a wordless murmur she flattened her breasts against his chest. She could feel the buttons of his coat and waistcoat digging into her flesh, sense the rise of his desire for her. Rich languor poured along her bloodstream. She twined her tongue with his in frolicking play, flicking the hard and smooth edges of his teeth, retreating with refined enticements which he accepted at once. His movements, the heated feel of his invasion as he thrust against the moist and fragile warmth of her inner mouth, sent her spinning into a dark vortex of desire. Her breathing quickened. The layers of clothing that separated them were unbearable. She needed to feel him naked against her, inside her, with a longing too strong to be denied.

There came the scrape of footsteps. Ryan cursed softly, and swung to shield Elene with his body while she recovered her equilibrium. The intruders, a young couple walking arm in arm, passed by them with hardly a glance.

Ryan gave a short laugh. "It's a good thing they came along."

"Is it?" Elene patted her hair into place with trembling hands.

Ryan heard the shadow of frustration in her tone and felt its echo within himself. "It is indeed. The shells on the paths are too sharp for your tender skin, and the ground that's not covered by them is too muddy for your finery. Besides, there's a serious lack of privacy. Let's go home."

"The others—" she began, though the protest was weak.

Ryan's smile sounded in his voice as he answered deliberately, "The others can't come."

M'sieur Mazent was ready to return to the city also, had been waiting, in fact, only for Elene and Ryan to get back from their walk so they could embark.

The homeward journey was completed in near silence. Other than a few desultory remarks concerning the entertainment, no one seemed inclined to talk. The bargeman was not only fresh out of songs, but must have been anxious for his bed, for he poled with such diligence that they were soon at the city gate.

The party separated then, everyone going in a different direction, calling out their last good-nights and promises to get together again as they picked their way across the mud. Within a few short minutes, Elene and Ryan were entering the porte cochere of his house where at the other end hung the lantern welcoming them home.

When they emerged into the courtyard, they heard voices raised in light, flowing laughter. They stopped abruptly. From the gallery above them, Devota called, "Is that you, *chère?*"

Elene answered. A moment later, Devota came down the stairs with the shadowy figures of two other women behind her. As she came into the lantern light, they were revealed as Serephine and Germaine.

"Evening, mam'zelle, m'sieur," Serephine said in her soft and faintly slumberous tones. The Mazent's woman, Germaine, hung back, offering only a nod by way of greeting.

"Good evening." Elene kept her voice even, pleasant. She had never felt rancor toward the girl who was Durant's mistress, and there was even less cause to do so now.

Serephine turned to Devota, giving her a swift hug, apparently in appreciation for the small blue bottle she held in her hand. Germaine clutched one also. The three women of color exchanged a few words. Then Serephine and Germaine turned quickly and passed into the porte cochere where they were soon lost to sight in the darkness.

Elene looked at Devota. The maid gave a slight shrug. "Serephine came about the perfume. She heard we were making it. Germaine she met on the way."

There was something about the remembered laughter of the three women, as if they shared a secret life and a rapport of the blood unknown to white people, that sent small prickles of disturbance over Elene. She wondered if Serephine and Germaine, like Devota, were followers of the Voudou. It was impossible to know, however, or to find a reason for questioning Devota about it that did not sound as if she was suspicious of the presence of the other two women or else held resentment against her former fiancé's mistress.

"I'm very tired," she said finally with a quick glance, half-smiling, at Ryan. "I think I will go to bed."

"I'll join you in a moment," he said.

Devota spoke. "Is there anything you need, m'sieur?"

"Benedict will see to it."

The majordomo had come from his rooms downstairs under the *garçonnière* to stand silently waiting at the edge of the lantern light. Now he bowed, partly in greeting, partly in acquiescence. He suggested in soft tones, "Perhaps a cognac?"

Ryan agreed. Elene turned away, trailing up the stairs. She had thought perhaps Ryan would come with her, that they might undress each other and fall into bed. Privacy seemed no easier to come by here than at the vauxhall.

It was Devota who undressed Elene and put her in a nightgown of fine lawn decorated with tucks and a small crocheted edging at the neckline and around the cap sleeves. The maid poured warm water for her to bathe herself quickly in the basin and, afterward, brushed her hair into a shining gold curtain. She put away Elene's evening gown and other accessories, then gathered up her underclothing to be laundered. Extinguishing the candles that burned in their candelabra, leaving only a single candle in a silver holder on a table beside the bed, Devota moved to the door.

The maid turned. "We sold our first perfume, *chère*."

"So we did." A slow smile curved Elene's mouth, lighting her eyes. "That is, you did."

"There will be others to buy, many others."

"I'm sure of it."

Devota nodded as if satisfied, her gaze steady on Elene's face. Wishing her a good night, the maid went away.

Elene thought of the perfume and the identity of their first customer as she waited for Ryan. Who would have thought it would be Serephine? What reason could she have for wishing to use the same scent as the woman who would have been Durant's wife? It made no sense. But then, what did it matter? The perfume was sold, the money was in hand. And there would be more.

She would have to be careful in the future how much of the perfume she used herself. It wouldn't do to deplete the stock. Smiling a little, she reached out to pick up her own bottle of the new perfume and renew the fragrance she had applied earlier in the evening.

Where was Ryan? Surely he would have seen Devota put out the light and know that the maid had gone. He would come any moment. Just in case, Elene got up from the dressing table stool and moved to push the French door onto the gallery wider.

She stood with her hand on the handle, listening for some sound, watching for a movement. There was nothing except the soft rustle of the breeze in the top limbs of the oak, the faint shift of the shadows cast by its great dark limbs on the pavement stones of the courtyard.

"Ryan?" she called.

The word seemed to fall into a soft and deadening pool of silence.

A bereft feeling gathered inside her. He wasn't coming. He might even have gone out. Anger, fed by unappeased need, rippled through her and trailed away into dismal resentment. It forced her from the bedchamber and out onto the gallery. The hour was late. The quarter moon had set, leaving only the stars to light the night sky that arched above the rooftop. She stood for a moment, trying to penetrate the shadows in the courtyard, wondering if Ryan had drunk too much cognac on top of the wine at the vauxhall and gone to sleep. It was unlikely. She had never seen him the worse for drink.

There was a glow of light coming from under the gallery on which she stood. She thought at first that it might be reflecting from one of the servant's rooms along the lower side of the courtyard square, but they were dark, even those of Devota and Benedict. The light was coming from the storerooms, from her workroom where the perfume sat on the counter in its fragile bottles.

She turned toward the stairs. At the head, she paused, then began to creep down the treads in her bare feet. She reached the bottom and rounded the newel post.

The light in the workroom went out, plunging the courtyard into utter darkness. Elene went rigid where she stood as a frisson of fear ran down her spine. There came the scrape of a footstep, a soft, stealthy sound.

The man came at her from under the open staircase, moving with lightning swiftness. One hard arm caught her around the waist and the other at the bend of her knees. She was lifted high against a chest like a breastplate of molded steel, held so close she could not move. Her mind congealed in the confusion of terror, though at the same time she was assailed by scents and sensations that brought the euphoria of relief and joy. Her senses whirled dizzily as the man swung with her, carrying her in a few long strides into the darkest depths of the courtyard, under the spreading arms of the great oak.

He stopped. She could feel the powerful thudding of his heart against her side. Overhead, the wind whispered among the leaves of the oak that shifted above them in the starshine, like vast schools of fish fleeing through deep blue-black water. When the wind stilled, the only sound was the musical tinkle of the water in the center fountain. Around them, the night gathered thick and protective.

Elene uncurled the fingers of her hand that had clutched a coat collar. Her voice a mere breath of sound, she said, "Ryan?"

"There are no sharp shells, no mud, here."

"No," she agreed with caution as his meaning began to creep in upon her, "but what of the others, your servants, Benedict?"

"Benedict is on watch for us at my order, though anyone would have to have the eyes of a cat to see."

"That may be, but—"

"I have been thinking of making love to you under the night sky for what seems like hours, since the vauxhall garden. Will you deny me?"

How could she when he asked it so simply, and with such vibrant desire in his voice? The answer was, she could not.

She said softly, "Not I."

CHAPTER 12

HE lowered her to her feet and brushed his lips across her forehead. He quickly shrugged from his coat, then spread it on the flagstones and went to one knee on its silk lining. Taking her hand, he drew her down to kneel before him. He lifted her other hand also, and pressed both to his lips in turn. His warm breath feathered the sensitive skin of their backs as he said quietly, *"Je t'adore.* I adore you, not just because you are more generous than any woman I have ever known, but because you are more honest."

Elene's chest swelled with pent breath and pain. It was so nearly a declaration, but one made for the wrong reason. She was not honest, had never been, even from the first. But she could not tell him, not now when they were so close within the sheltering shadows of the soft summer night. She could offer an apology hidden in a caress, however, one to soothe her misgivings even if it could not relieve them.

Gently she released her hands. With fingers that were unsteady, she touched his chest, smoothing over the linen that covered its muscular hardness. His cravat had been loosened and she slipped it free and let it fall. Finding the stud that held the collar of his shirt, she worked it from its hole, aware at the same time of his hands upon her back, tracing her shape underneath her nightgown. She set the stud aside and opened his collar to spread the placket of his shirt wide, exposing his chest to below his breastbone.

Ryan drew in his breath as she lowered her head to brush the dark, curling growth of hair about his paps with her tongue. Her hair spilled across her shoulders, falling in a pale swath to rest on his hard thigh where he could feel its warm weight. Caught in enchantment, he reached to tangle his fingers among the shimmering filaments that caught the starlight with a silver-gold sheen.

An odd exultation moved like wine along Elene's veins. He wanted her, needed her, felt for her some degree of emotion, however fleeting, that he called adoration. There was no compulsion for him this time. In that knowledge there was for her a sense of glorious freedom, as if some restraint had been removed. She could give joy as well as receive it, and that realization made her bold.

She flicked her tongue over the hard, tight bud of his nipple. Feeling the shudder of pleasure that rippled over his skin, she smiled to herself in rising gladness. At the same time, she slid her hands in slow exploration down the taut, muscle-padded stretch of his rib cage to his waist and began to tug his shirt from his breeches.

He accommodated her, stripping his shirt free and drawing it off over his head in a single, sure movement. The crisp linen made a soft, whispering sound as it landed behind him. He reached for her then, cupping her shoulders in the palms of his hands while his thumbs caressed the fragile lengths of her collar bones under the skin. Gently he eased the cap sleeve of her nightgown from her shoulder and, bending his head, pressed his lips to that smooth and rounded surface. He trailed a line of fiery kisses to the curve of her neck and delicate hollow under her ear, at the same time easing the nightgown lower and lower still until it was caught on the upper curves of her breasts.

Elene made a movement, as if she would reach to untie the ribbon closure. He was there before her, slipping the bow free, drawing the opening wider until the soft batiste slid over the peaks of her breasts and dropped in soft folds about her waist.

"Sweet, sweet," he whispered as he tasted the twin mounds he had uncovered with the grainy surface of his tongue, lapping their sensitive nipples with careful attention as he fitted their weight in his cupped hands.

Exquisite, blooming sensations rippled through Elene in vivid waves, vibrating downward to the lower part of her body. She drew breath in such rich delight that it lifted her breasts in a voluptuous gesture of encouragement. Her nightgown, dislodged by the movement, drifted lower until it pooled about her knees.

Ryan released her to put a hand to the waistband of his breeches. She forestalled him, brushing his fingers aside to loosen the fastening and also that of his underdrawers. She inserted her fingers in the opening and spread them wide over the iron-hard surface of his belly, enjoying the roughness against her palms of the narrow line of hair that grew there. She touched the heated resilience of his manhood that thrust against the crotch of his breeches, capturing it with a thumb on either side. As she heard the soft hiss of his breath through his teeth, there burgeoned within her a sense of power and glorious, wanton rapture.

With a sudden, wrenching movement, she slid his breeches and undergarments from his hips. He moved to help her, levering off his low evening boots before sliding out of the last of his clothing.

Elene drew her nightgown from under her knees to spread its fullness with Ryan's coat. She lowered herself to her side on that thin, makeshift pallet. Ryan joined her there, stroking along the turn of her leg, skimming the curve of her hip with his lips and tongue before stretching full length and pulling her against him. He held her close as, heart to heart, they reveled in the tactile sensations of skin against warm skin, with curves and hollows, firmness and softness perfectly matched, so nearly complete. Yet not quite.

The mounting pressure of desire shuddered through them. They stirred, their caresses becoming more heated, less controlled. Elene's heart jarred against her ribs, sending her blood in a swirling mill race along her veins. Her skin glowed with rising internal heat that brought a moist sheen to its surface so that Ryan's seeking hands glided upon her as he sought the intricate opening of the recess that led to the core of her being. Finding it, he brought more moisture still. Lost in infinite bliss, she returned his caresses.

Dipping, bending in the ancient dance that leads to love, like relentless marauders they used their hands and mouths to drive the aching ecstasy higher and higher still, until both were slippery with the dew of their exertion and drenched in the scent of a perfume that evoked haunting visions of elusive paradise. Together, they gave each other joy, until the effort to hold the ultimate release at bay was so great the torment was more rending than the pleasure.

Heaving to his back, Ryan drew her over to lie upon him, urging her with firm hands to take him inside her. She needed no second bidding. Her taut moan of gratification came from deep within as she encompassed him. The muscles of her thighs trembled as she pressed down further and further upon him so that he filled her to the utmost depth. She began then to move in exquisite, rocking rhythm, plunging toward a bright and beckoning fulfillment. So near, so incredibly near. It spiraled through her, gathering brightness, spreading, growing, until as it burst upon her she cried out and went still.

Ryan gathered her to him so that their foreheads rested together and their breathing mingled as their chests rose and fell. A mosquito whined around their heads. He muttered a soft curse. Brushing along her back and hips with his hands as if to dislodge any biting insects, he then pressed her knee down to straighten her left leg and, with a powerful surge of coiled muscles, swung her over and to her back with the long strands of her hair flailing, twisting around them. At the same time, he raised himself above her to cover her body protectively with his. Once more, he pressed into her resilient softness, driving deep. And once more the splendor gathered around her.

Her senses stretched, soaring. Her muscles convulsed, the tendons strung with tightness. The darkness around her expanded into a limitless universe in which nothing mattered except this wondrous joining. She lifted her hands to clench them on the effort-ridged muscles of his arms and shoulders, using that hold to move with him, lunge against him, to absorb the hard shocks of his thrusts that propelled her higher and higher still in the frenzied urge toward the fulfillment.

It burst upon her in furious grandeur, a wild yet silent explosion of the innermost self. Magical, amazing, that internal violence convulsed her being around the man who held her so that movement, thought, all sense of self was lost in the wondrous flowering. She gasped his name. Hearing that soft sound like a plaudit and a plea, feeling the velvet grasp of her heated tissues, Ryan locked her in his arms and plunged in final, wrenching exertion to his own instant of glory.

The wind rifled through the leaves of the oak. The shadows in the corners of the courtyard shifted as the starshine flickered among the tree branches. Somewhere a cricket chirped with monotonous regularity. The fountain chuckled to itself. A pair of mosquitoes sang in a circling pattern, then were ominously still.

Ryan stirred. Resting his weight still on his elbows, he brushed the fine mesh of hair from across Elene's face. He kissed her gently, thoroughly in a warm salute of appreciation and pleasure. Then gathering himself in what seemed to be a species of reluctance, he rolled from her and pushed to his knees.

"As agreeable as this is," he said in replete humor, "it would be foolish to sacrifice more blood than we have already for the sake of it."

Elene made no move to rise. "I was beginning to think you enjoyed being eaten alive."

"That wasn't my greatest pleasure."

"No? Possibly it was the dark and the hard bed. You seem to have a regard for those, also."

"What I have a regard for is your delectable body, as well you know. Now, will you come inside before I leave it, with deepest regret and only slightly wavering determination, to the mosquitoes?"

"I'm right behind you," she said on a gasp as the whining of a mosquito came again and she felt a sting on her ankle.

"Of all the positions I can think of for you, that is the least satisfactory." Ryan reached to scoop her into his arms. Lifting her high against his chest, he surged to his feet and strode with her toward the stairs.

At the foot of the flight of steps, the form of the majordomo melted away in the darkness. Beyond him, near the workroom door, was a second guard. Devota.

Elene's grasp on Ryan's shoulders tightened and she set her teeth in her bottom lip. As the two of them reached the gallery, she said in stifled tones, "I don't know what they think of us."

Ryan gave a breathless laugh. "Don't you?"

"Make a joke of it then," she snapped. "I don't know why you didn't just sell tickets while you were about it."

He pushed through the opening of the French door and stepped into his bedchamber. Knocking aside the mosquito netting with one shoulder, he deposited Elene none too gently on the cool surface of the moss-filled mattress. Looming above her in the dim golden glow of a single candle, he said, "I might have, if I hadn't been too involved at the time to think of it."

"Humph," she said, flouncing over in the bed, "and I suppose the whole household will get to snicker in the morning when they find our clothes."

"Benedict and Devota will take care of them, and of us, as always. What is the matter with you? Was it so bad as all that?"

She looked away from him. The trouble was, it hadn't been bad at all. She was afraid she had revealed too much, given too much of herself into his keeping. If that was so, she didn't know how she would survive if he should ever leave her.

But there was more to it than that. Honest, he had called her. What would he think if he knew the truth? She should tell him. She should confess in full now, this moment, make him understand how she had tricked him, enthralled him. Not deliberately, no, but the results had been the same.

She could not do it. It would be the end; she had no doubt of it. He had said himself he would not tolerate being tricked. Never would he permit the woman who had done so to continue to live under his roof, to lie in his bed, at his side.

"Elene," he said, his voice questioning as he joined her on the bed. He reached out to put his hand on her shoulder, turning her toward him.

She looked into the dark blue of his eyes with their soft sheen of concern that contrasted with the hawk-like severity of his features, and she knew she could not tell him. Surely there was no need. He had come to her without the coercion of Voudou sorcery, had he not? And easily might again.

She forced her lips to form a smile, though her throat hurt and her voice was husky with unshed tears as she spoke. "You know very well it was not bad at all, that it was incredible."

"Do I?"

She flung herself against him, hiding her face against the strong column of his neck as his arms closed around her. "You should, since you paid for it in mosquito bites."

"A few itches is a small price," he said as he stroked her hair. There was a frown between his thick brows, however, as he stared at the carving on the headboard of the bed. He could feel Elene trembling against him, sense the disturbance that made her grip him so close. He could not begin to fathom its cause. He wished he understood her, but at the same time feared to know too much. It was not a situation he enjoyed, or one that was at all familiar. He did not like it. In fact, he despised it, and despised also the cowardice that prevented him from forcing the issue and discovering the truth.

Morning came too soon. The knock that heralded the arrival of Benedict with coffee and rolls sent Elene burrowing under the sheet. The majordomo was discretion itself, however; he spoke no greeting, but placed the tray on a side table and went out again with a near silent tread, closing the door softly behind him.

The aroma of hot, yeasty brioches and the coffee and hot milk for café au lait wafted on the air. Elene ignored it, keeping her eyes firmly closed as she held tight to the last vestiges of sleep. If she did not let go, she need not face the problems that waited.

Beside her, Ryan shifted. His hair-roughened leg touched hers and his arm snaked around her waist to draw her securely against him with her hips nestled against his belly and something else that was just as rigid and much warmer. He blew on the nape of her neck so that a shiver ran over her. Softly against her ear, he said, "Are there any itches you might have this morning that I can scratch for you?"

She flung over to her back to stare up at him as he lay propped on one elbow. "You're impossible!"

"Almost, but not quite."

"I was not referring to your prowess in bed."

He gave her a look of mock innocence. "Who said that I was?"

There was such a teasing light in his eyes that her heart swelled inside her, throbbing with pain. The dark stubble of a beard shadowed the bronze planes of his face, giving him a ruffianly appearance that was oddly endearing. She cleared her throat. "Humbug. Your coffee will get cold."

"No great matter."

"It's daylight."

"So it is," he said after a brief survey of the window.

"The servants will tell everyone we do nothing else."

"It's a harmless diversion."

"The gossip? Or—"

"Or what?"

"Or the dalliance in bed," she said, refusing to be cowed.

He kissed her shoulder without taking his eyes from the delicate color in her face. "Is that what this is?"

"You know very well—"

"So I do. Now that we have begun, we might as well continue."

"We haven't begun!"

"What a shame." He reached to catch the top hem of the sheet, slowly peeling it downward to expose the apricot-tinted peak of one breast.

"Something you apparently have none of whatever," she declared, though the words were not so incensed as she could have wished due to her interest in the warm circles he began to make with his tongue on her uncovered skin.

"Shame? No, none, not when it comes to you. You could teach me, of course."

She might indeed, she thought, but she did not say so. Instead she shook her head as she reached to push her fingers through the whorls of glossy, walnut-colored hair that grew low on his neck. "I have better things to do."

They ate their breakfast cold. Afterward, Ryan threw back the covers and slid from the bed. There was a ship due up from Balise that morning with cargo aboard in which he had an interest, and he needed to see to its unloading and storage.

Elene lay and watched while Ryan, stalking about in splendid nakedness, shaved himself and dressed for the day. He did not ring for the aid of his majordomo, though that was not unusual. He had no use for a valet on board ship, he said, and the fact that he was on land did not make him suddenly helpless.

He came to stand beside the bed when he was ready to go. Leaning over her, he pressed his warm lips to her forehead, then quickly to her mouth. He smelled of the freshness of soap and starched linen and leather polish from his boots, with a faint hint of spice from a preparation he used as a septic for shaving nicks and also his own male essence.

He did not move away at once, but stood with his hat in one hand, his gaze searching her face. His voice low, he asked, "Are you all right?"

"I'm fine," she answered, her smile deliberately slumberous with sated desire. "When will you be back?"

His mouth twitched at one corner. "Before you have time to miss me."

"Ah, well, then that can't be long."

"Noon, at the latest." With a look that held more than a hint of amorous threat, he swung away and walked from the room.

Elene's smile faded. Ryan's continued passion for her should be gratifying. She would have liked to enjoy it, would have liked for the banter between them to be real and unforced. Somehow, it could not be. Wasn't there something unnatural still in his constant need of her? Could it be possible for any man to be so physically enamored of a woman that the slightest touch could incite immediate need for possession?

Something was wrong; she knew it.

She suspected what it was, though she did not want to believe it. There had, for a short time, been a chance for hope. If what she thought was true, then that hope was false. And this time she was the dupe as well as Ryan.

There was only one way to be sure. Elene was reluctant to take it, not only because of the betrayal it might reveal, but because so long as the answer was in doubt she could hold to the illusion that Ryan felt something for her of his own will. There was comfort in illusion.

There was no conscious decision made to sleep on the problem. Elene simply closed her eyes, and worry and weariness did the rest. The heat of late afternoon was in the bedchamber when she awoke. The room had not been disturbed; the breakfast tray still sat on the side table and the French doors, instead of being closed to retain the morning coolness, stood open to the hot air gathering in the courtyard.

It was a knock that had awakened her. Hard upon it, Devota swept into the room and closed the door behind her. She carried a brass can of hot water. Crossing to the corner basin, she filled it from the can and began to lay out fresh toweling.

The maid glanced over her shoulder. "M'sieur Ryan is on his way from the levee and a meal is being reheated for him in the kitchen. I thought you might want to share it."

Elene pushed herself to a sitting position, thrusting her fingers through her hair to free it of some of the tangles and drag it out of the way behind her shoulders. Her voice groggy, she said, "What time is it?"

"Late enough, not that it matters. There was a message earlier that m'sieur could not return at noon after all. I saw no reason to wake you for that."

"No," Elene said slowly.

"It was possible you would not care to get up even now."

The acerbic tone of the other woman finally reached Elene. She stared at her. "What do you mean?"

"If you refuse a proposal from a man, most people assume you lack interest in him."

"Do they? And who told you I had refused a proposal?"

"Benedict had the story, one direct from his master, or so he gave me to understand."

"You are speaking to him now?"

"It was necessary to say something last night while we waited."

While they waited for the tryst in the courtyard between master and mistress to end. Elene cleared her throat. "I see. As it happens, Benedict is correct."

Devota set the water can down with a bang and turned to face Elene. "I could not believe it. I thought it must be a mistake. How could you refuse him when you are alone here in this place, this New Orleans, with nothing? How could you?"

"You of all people should understand my reasons."

"I don't see at all! What would be wrong with marrying Ryan Bayard? He is young and handsome and wealthy, and he desires you at the head of his table and in his bed. What more can you ask?"

"You felt the same about Durant."

"Well?"

"Does it make no difference who becomes my husband?' Will just any man do?"

"Bayard is not just any man," Devota said with a stubborn tilt to her chin.

"No, but what of love?"

"He loves you."

"Because he wants me when he can't help himself? That isn't love!"

"There is more than that between you."

The words would have carried more conviction, Elene thought, if Devota had not looked away as she said them. "Is there? Is there really? What is it then, tell me that?"

Devota did not answer. Her soft brown face slowly suffused with grief. "I'm sorry, *chère.* I did not mean to make you doubt yourself. That was never the purpose at all."

Did she have doubts? Of course she did, though at the moment it hardly mattered. Elene made an impatient gesture. "That isn't the point."

"Yes, it is. Because the perfume aided you in the beginning does not mean that your man can feel nothing for you without it."

"No? What if he doesn't? What if his infatuation fades even as I fall in love?"

"Ah, *chère,* is there some danger that will happen?"

"What does it matter?" she cried, sitting forward in the bed. "What I want to know is—"

They were interrupted as the door swung open. Ryan stepped through. He glanced from Elene's flushed face to Devota. Of the maid he asked, "You told her?"

Devota frowned. "Told her what, m'sieur?"

"I thought the news might have arrived before me, though I came as soon as I heard."

Elene answered him. "I've heard nothing. What is it?"

"A message came just now from Morven." He stopped, as if reluctant to go on.

"Yes? What did he say?"

"It's Hermine. She's . . . dead."

Shock rippled over Elene. She stared at him, the thought running through her mind of Hermine with her wry quips in her inimitable voice, her rich understanding of others and the current of vibrant life that was so apparent in everything she did. It was impossible that she could be dead. She whispered, "No."

Ryan shook his head, his face grave. "It doesn't seem so, but it is."

"But . . . what happened?"

"They don't know much just yet since she was found less than an hour ago. Morven thinks it must have been an accident. The doctor who was called in has declared it a suicide."

"Suicide!"

"From an overdose of arsenic."

Morven Ghent, for all the magnificent despair with which he played his tragic nobleman in performance at the vauxhall, was not the man to die for love. That was not to say that he did not grieve for Hermine. His eyes were red-rimmed, and now and then he would stop what he was saying and stare into space with a look of such ineffable sorrow on his strong, classic features that every woman in sight longed to comfort him. In the times in between, however, he talked with ease and assurance of his thoughts on the chances of success for a theater in New Orleans and the plays which might contribute to a satisfactory first season; of where he would go when he left New Orleans and what he thought was the future of the theater in France under Napoleon.

The reception, if such it could be termed, following Hermine's funeral was held at the home of Rachel Pitot, a large house in the West Indies style located just outside the city gates. Ordinarily, a call of condolence would not be expected for over a week, but Hermine had been in the city so short a time, and the troupe of actors had so few acquaintances, that it had seemed best to lend Morven and Josie the support of the company of their friends. The other members of the group who had come together on the ship from Saint-Domingue must have felt the same, for they were all present.

If feminine support was what Morven required, there was plenty available. On one side of the actor sat Josie attired in black relieved with a white collar and cuffs, rather like a maid's uniform from some play, while on the other was the widow Pitot in lavender-gray satin with a pelisse of black lace and, rather tastelessly, a necklace around her throat of silver with an amulet of a striking cobra.

As Elene approached to speak to him, the actor rose to his feet. He took the hand she held out to him, his green eyes dark as he smiled down at her, then he drew her into his arms. The embrace was close, molding her to his long length. He brushed her cheek with his lips, and would have taken her mouth if she had not turned her head in quick prevention.

Caught by surprise, Elene waited for some reaction to his touch. There was nothing except irritation for the advantage he was taking. To repulse him would seem to indicate a lack of compassion for his loss. Still, as his arms tightened, it was only the comment Hermine had made weeks before on the ship that prevented Elene from using an elbow to break his hold. *"He has no control where women are concerned,"* the actress had said in droll acceptance, and perhaps she was right.

Behind Elene, Ryan cleared his throat with a soft, warning rasp. Morven let her go without haste. His gaze as he looked at his friend was unrepentant. "You don't begrudge a hug, do you, old man? Some condolences are more effective than others."

"They can also be more dangerous," Ryan answered, and there was warning in the coolness of his smile.

Ryan had attended the service, as had Messieurs Mazent and Tusard, and also Durant. Women did not put in an appearance at such ceremonies in New Orleans, the experience being considered too harrowing. This one was more so than usual since Hermine could not, of course, be buried in consecrated ground.

As the evening wore on, Morven inveighed bitterly against that decree. Hermine had not had the least reason or intention of killing herself, he declared again and again. The church was adamant, however; the doctors called it a suicide and lacking proof, it must be treated as such.

"What I say," Madame Tusard whispered to Elene, leaning to breathe hotly in her ear as she spoke, "is that Morven Ghent would like us to believe that poor Hermine's death was an accident. Otherwise, that strutting cock of an actor might have to admit that if she had reason for taking her life, then it was he who gave it to her!"

"You can't really believe Hermine would do such a thing?" Elene protested.

"She might if she were losing Morven, say, to that female there." The former official's wife nodded at Rachel Pitot. "Hermine was no match for such a black widow as I hear that one can be."

"Hermine may not have been happy over his flirtation with Madame Pitot, but it was nothing unusual."

Madame Tusard shook her head in decided disagreement. "They say the woman practices the black arts. Some even suggest that her husband died in a mysterious fashion."

"Oh, really!" Elene could not hide her irritation with such malicious and unfounded chatter.

"You may not believe it, but such things happen." Madame Tusard insisted, her expression taking on an injured cast.

"I'm surprised," Elene said slowly, "that you would defend Hermine. I was under the impression that you had words with her a few days ago."

The other woman gave her a fierce frown. "Are you suggesting that anything I might have said or done gave this cheap actress cause for swallowing poison? I assure you it isn't so!"

"I thought I had made it clear that I can't conceive of Hermine ever giving up her life willingly, not even for Morven."

"Then just what are you saying?" Madame Tusard asked, her small dark eyes narrowed to slits.

There was something so cold and inimical between the two of them for an instant that Elene was startled. The impression was banished, however, as Josie came flouncing over to join them, casting herself down on the edge of the chair near the settee on which Elene and Madame Tusard were seated.

The girl eyed them with bright interest. "What are you two talking about over here? Something juicy, I'll bet. Did you know that I'm to have Hermine's parts on stage from now on? Morven has promised. We will look for someone else to play the ingenue, someone young and silly who will not ask for much except the chance to strut about in costumes."

Madame Tusard turned her ire on the newcomer. "Some of Hermine's parts were quite demanding."

Josie shrugged. "I will give them my own style, or Morven can change them. You have no idea how tired I was of playing silly females, and of feeling left out when Hermine and Morven talked about how to act their roles with depth, whatever that may mean."

"Madame Pitot may have something to say about who plays what on her stage at the vauxhall," the older woman said.

Josie's eyes darkened as she frowned. "As far as I'm concerned, the sooner we leave New Orleans and Madame Pitot, the better."

Elene glanced across the room to where Rachel Pitot was holding Morven's arm, leaning against him. "She does seem rather possessive."

"She's terrible! Do you know, she prowls in and out of our rooms here in the house as if we have no right at all to privacy, as if we were no more than her slaves."

"That's what happens when you allow others to support you," Madame Tusard pointed out with condescension.

"We have paid for her support, believe me," Josie said darkly. "Morven more than any, of course. But—you remember the perfume you gave Hermine, Elene? The widow took a sniff of it and decided she had to have it. Hermine tried to tell her it was special, but she wouldn't listen. There was nothing to be done except give it to her."

Hermine's perfume. Elene felt a stirring of anger herself that the actress had not been permitted to keep it. It would not have been so bad if she could be given another bottle, but it was too late. Too late. Hermine was gone, and with her, her wonderful ability to laugh at herself and the world, and also the rich, hypnotic sound of her voice. Gone.

Madame Tusard changed the subject, speaking of the rumor in the streets of a pair of sailors from a ship just in from Havana dying at the charity hospital of yellow fever. The disease was a constant threat in the islands and a summer scourge in New Orleans. It seemed to strike the newest residents, as if it preferred fresh blood, or rather as if long acquaintance with it was a protection.

Even as the official's wife spoke, however, Madame Tusard glanced busily about her for other topics of conversation. When Flora Mazent came into the room, followed closely by her maid Germaine, she called out to her.

"Oh, Flora, come and talk to us. How nice you look this evening. Tell me, is it true that there is to be an announcement of interest from your father in the near future?"

The girl colored a painful red, whether with embarrassment or annoyance was impossible to tell. "Wherever did you hear that?"

"One hears things. But is it true?"

"It isn't decided." The answer was carefully chosen.

"It is true then. Is he handsome, this prospective fiancé?"

The girl sent them a quick, almost coy glance from under her short, colorless lashes. "Some people think so."

"Who is he?"

Germaine leaned to whisper something in the girl's ear. Flora nodded. Her voice barely audible, she told the others, "I would rather not say. Excuse me, now, I think my father wants me."

Josie stared after the other girl with a look in her eyes both baffled and unbelieving. "How could someone like her have attracted a husband, and so quickly?"

Madame Tusard gave a harsh laugh. "You would be amazed how potent a weapon of seduction wealth can be."

"That's the way it is then?"

"So one assumes."

Elene felt, suddenly, a suffocating sensation inside her. She got to her feet in haste and walked away, away from the heartless chatter, away from those who always assumed the worst, from those who seemed incapable, ever, of assuming the best.

CHAPTER 13

IT was strange how one day a person could be alive, laughing, talking, eating, breathing, and the next be dead. It was so final, and yet, nothing changed. They were missed, there was loss and its pain, but the process of living went on as before. The sun rose and set, the rain fell, the seasons advanced as they always had. The death of a single human being hardly mattered. It was, perhaps, egoism to think that it should, and yet it seemed there should be some sign of the event besides a stone marker in a muddy field.

The fabric of the refugees' lives in New Orleans closed over the death of Hermine without a rent or wrinkle. The authorities made no attempt to look into the matter. By their lights, the actress was a transient, no part of the community they were sworn to protect. Moreover, she was a woman who acted on the stage, which in their view placed her on the same level as the females who sold their bodies near the ramparts. Such women were forever killing themselves by design or being killed by accident or the intent of their lovers. The death of one more was not a matter for great concern.

The days crept past, the summer advanced. Elene learned her way around the city so that she moved up and down the streets with confidence with either Devota or Benedict at her heels carrying her shopping basket. She learned which merchants gave short measure and which gave lagniappe, that small amount of something extra to sweeten a sale. She discovered which hours were best to shop the stalls of the market on the levee for fresh vegetables and meat, and which to avoid because of the swarms of gnats, house flies, and blue-bottle flies around the overripe bananas, stinking piles of fish, and hanging sides of meat. She perfected the art of bargaining with spirit and firmness and sudden smiles, or with confusing requests for a little more of this or that so that the totals had to be recalculated. And she learned how to avoid the glances of the men on the street so that they had no chance to stop her for conversation, or to return their bows with a single cool nod that gave them no encouragement to follow her.

She began to realize, also, that the milliner was right in part about the women of Saint-Domingue. They were instantly recognizable on the street or sitting on the balconies of the houses. There was verve in the way they tilted their sunshades or draped their shawls around their shoulders. They seldom wore hats or bonnets, but when they did, it was with a certain dashing impudence. The shades and hues of colors they chose made the paler tones of the ladies of New Orleans appear, if not drab, then at least rather faded. And these were the respectable ladies.

The quadroons and octoroons were even more noticeable. They tied their hair up in tignons of brilliant silk shot with gold or silver, painted their eyes with kohl, and hung sparkling jewelry in their ears. The bodices of their gowns, both morning and evening, were cut so low that the increasing summer heat could hardly have been a problem, and if it had been, the dampening of their petticoats to make their skirts cling to their voluptuous forms furnished the remedy. They walked about with a maid trailing them, sometimes carrying a lap dog or perhaps a pomander against the smells of the streets, a fan or a sunshade or a fly whisk of peacock feathers done up with tassels and ribbon. They were, it almost seemed, a breed apart and thoroughly enjoyed their special status.

Now and again, Elene saw women she knew from Saint-Domingue, or else remembered from her childhood. She made no effort to approach them, nor did they go out of their way to speak to her, though she thought she sometimes saw a flicker of recognition in their eyes. Her position was not respectable, and it seemed that commodity was of increasing importance in New Orleans.

One evening, Ryan planned a dinner at his house. At his special request, Elene was to act as his hostess to welcome a number of the merchants from up and down the street on which he lived, with the addition of one or two planters from outlying areas. Among the latter would be Etienne de Bore, a charming little man who had perfected the granulating of sugar in Louisiana, and also handsome and wealthy young Bernard de Marigny de Mandeville, who at just eighteen was already a bon vivant famous for bringing the game of Craps to the city from Paris the past spring and for helping his father entertain the royal princes of the house of Bourbon during their exile to the colony five years before. Marigny was also an aide to the illustrious colonial prefect and representative of France, Laussat. Laussat himself was to be the guest of honor.

Elene was nervous. She did not know why she should be, since she would have little to do during the evening. She had discussed with Benedict, Devota, and the cook the food that was to be served, from the turtle soup followed by red fish poached in a white sauce flavored with shrimp, crab, scallions, and red pepper, to the roast pork with new potatoes and green beans cooked with sausage and the dessert of fresh peach tarts. Still, though she herself would signal the removal of the courses, the responsibility for seeing that the various dishes were brought to the table in their proper order and proper form would not be hers alone. She might introduce a topic or two if the conversation should lag, but it was Ryan and his servants on whom the smooth progression of the evening would depend.

It was her part, she thought, primarily to provide a calming influence in case words should become heated, and also to serve as an ornament for Ryan's house. Whether she could do either was questionable.

She took a great deal of care with her appearance, donning the most formal of her gowns, the only one that could be called a true evening gown. Of deep rose silk, it was intricately draped and folded over the breasts, while just underneath them fell the deep inverted pleat of a full skirt that in turn elongated into a small train in the back. Her gloves and slippers were of pale pink, and she wore several pink rosebuds nestled among the curls of her high-piled hair. For confidence, she also wore her perfume, an item that had now become such second nature to her that she felt naked without it.

The guests arrived rather earlier than the normal dinner hour. The men who lived outside the city could not tarry long or they would find themselves locked up until morning. None seemed overly concerned at the possibility, unless it was Laussat who could not be expected to take so cavalier an attitude toward the prospect of bribing the Spanish guards as the others. It would not do to start an international incident, especially with matters so unsettled.

Bernard Marigny was late and, when he arrived, brought with him a companion for whom he entreated a place. Hospitality was elastic in the colony; there was always room and a welcome for another guest. With the division of the sexes already standing at eleven men to one woman, there was no question of unbalancing a carefully constructed seating arrangement.

While a servant took the hat and cane of Marigny's companion, Elene turned to signal to the majordomo to lay another place at the table. At Benedict's quick, annoyed bow, as if there was no need for her guidance, she turned back. Running through her mind was the knowledge that they would now sit down thirteen to dinner, but it could not matter. She was not superstitious herself, though she had discovered that many were here in New Orleans.

A moment later, she was not so sanguine. The thirteenth guest was Durant Gambier. His smile was ironic as he bent over her hand, murmuring apologies. Gathering her composure around her, she made him welcome on Ryan's behalf and turned away to speak to M'sieur de Bore.

The discussion around the table was lively, even heated on occasion. The question of where matters stood on the cession of the colony was uppermost in everyone's mind. Was it, or was it not, a fact? The Americans were laying in stocks of wine with which to toast the event on their holiday of the Fourth of July. The people on the streets rumbled with discontent, contending that if there was a chance that such a thing was to come to pass, they should surely be asked for their opinion. Laussat was worried, but had still received no official notification of such a transaction, so that his public posture must be one of disbelief.

A man of no small attraction, perhaps in his late forties, Colonial Prefect Laussat had a luxuriant shock of hair, heavy-lidded and somewhat world-weary eyes, a firm mouth, and a cleft in his chin. He took great interest in his food, particularly those dishes containing ingredients native to the colony. He seemed reluctant to speak of his position, perhaps from the typical politician's fear of saying something that might be misconstrued.

He did make one small comment, however. Waving a negligent hand, he said, "Rumors of the cession are gaining ground, this I can certainly realize. The fluctuations of the political thermometer in this respect are indicated by the greater or lesser eagerness with which people seek me out. When I first came, that eagerness was great. Now it is on the decline."

"From what I gather," Durant said as a respectful lull fell following the prefect's remarks, "there will be great changes brought about if the cession is a fact. The prospect of trade will be considerably increased, and also the likelihood of profits for the men involved in that business."

The sneer in his voice made it obvious that he considered such trade beneath his dignity as a gentleman. It was also plain the slur was directed at Ryan.

"Free access to the oceans of the world will stimulate trade, regardless of who is in power," Ryan said.

"But isn't it true that you feel the chances are better under the United States than under Spain—or France?" The smile Durant directed at Ryan held a challenge. He knew Ryan's views on the subject very well. What he meant to do, under the guise of polite comment, was to force Ryan to commit himself to a position that would annoy the colonial prefect at present and prove extremely embarrassing later should the cession be revealed as a hoax.

Ryan leaned back in his chair, his smile urbane and his manner careless. "The greatest profit will always be generated by the country with the best access to those profits. I'm sure Napoleon could turn the Mississippi into a stream of purest gold—if the vast lands and wide rivers that empty into it were only located a bit nearer to Paris."

The colonial prefect nodded. "Distance can be a formidable object. But if France loses these lands, she loses a colony with a beautiful future. An area so large must become emancipated in time, but while it is ours it will be a source of wealth and a rich outlet for the mother country. Here we can form a new France. I have many plans to double agriculture and triple or quadruple trade, thus leaving behind a lasting and honorable monument to my time here. If this is not to be, if I cannot produce such good here, I will leave with profound regret."

Durant was silenced. There was some discussion of the Bowles incident, a furor created by a dynamic American soldier of fortune, William Augustus Bowles, who had thrown in his lot with the Creek Indians for the purpose of ousting the Spanish from the Americas, then fallen afoul of the Spanish government. Arrested, shipped from Mobile to Havana, and from Havana to the Philippines and on to Africa like some unwanted package, he had finally escaped and returned to the Creeks, only to be betrayed by his Indian friends for the sum of four thousand piastres. He had recently been through New Orleans on his way to prison in Havana.

From Bowles, the conversation moved to the varieties of wild birds, from plovers to warblers to partridges, which could be eaten in Louisiana, and from there to the incredible heat that made poultry a bad buy in the markets. The prefect himself admitted he had started a poultry yard below his gallery with chickens, geese, ducks, and peacocks for his table. In addition, he had a menagerie of a few sheep, one or two tame deer and a half dozen raccoons.

As the meal progressed, no little interest was directed at Elene, though none of it overt under Ryan's watchful eye. If the gentlemen felt curiosity about her presence or her purpose, they did not voice it. She received a few languishing glances and a pretty compliment or two from young Bernard Marigny, who was known as a gallant, but there was nothing in it to which even a duenna could have objected.

It was Durant who made her most uncomfortable. He stared at her as he had not since they were on the ship, as if he were a starving man and she a meal shut away from him behind bars. It made her extremely uncomfortable.

In truth, she did not feel like flirtation. Whether from the strain of being constantly pleasant and keeping abreast of the crosscurrents of the discussion going on around her, or from the frequent refilling of the wine glasses, she grew aware of a sense of unreality. Her head began to ache, and the voices of the men seemed to rise and fall in waves. She was hot and her face felt flushed, but at the same time there seemed to be a faint tremor, almost like a chill, running along her skin.

It was an abnormally hot night with a still quality to the air in which the whine of the mosquitoes ghosting through the open doors and feasting on their ankles under the tables had a harsh, threatening sound. Now and then there came the distant boom of what seemed to be thunder. Looking around the table, Elene saw that one or two of the men there were also flushed, particularly Laussat who had no experience of such debilitating heat.

It was a relief when, as the meal ended, Laussat declared that he did not feel quite well and would like to get home before the rain that threatened began to fall. Several others followed the prefect's example, among them Bernard Marigny and Durant. Elene was forced to stand beside Ryan at the door, accepting the salutes of her hand and the effusive compliments upon the evening as most of the others departed one by one.

Finally only three or four men remained, among them Mazent, who claimed to have a proposition to discuss with Ryan for their mutual benefit. Madeira and a plate of sweetmeats was ordered brought to the salon where the men who remained were gathered. Ryan brushed Elene's cheek with his lips and suggested that she go to bed, since he had no idea how long their meeting would last. She was glad enough to comply.

Devota was not in the bedchamber when Elene reached it. To ring for her seemed too great an effort for the moment. Her head was bursting. She was so hot. She pulled the roses from her hair and looked around for a place to put them. The table was so far away. She closed her eyes, swaying. The roses dropped from her fingers. The bed. So soft. Cool on the moss mattress. Must reach it.

Her knees would not work. Falling, falling.

Funny it did not hurt to strike the floor.

It was later, much later, when she heard Devota exclaiming, felt the maids hands removing her clothing. A cloth was placed against her face, and she shuddered away from the pain of it. Why was Devota crying?

Strong arms lifting her. Floating. She remembered a dark courtyard and smiled. No. Another time.

The bed at last. So soft. So hot. Darkness and the sound of rain. Light and the sound of rain. Soothing. Someone holding her, always holding her.

Cloths moved over her body, cooling while steam rose from her hot skin. Something bitter, bitter on her tongue. She gagged and there was black liquid pouring from her mouth. She had not meant to vomit, so embarrassing. She knew that sight from Saint-Domingue. Black blood. Yellow fever. Somewhere a maid was screaming. Stupid girl.

A hard voice rapped out order. Ryan. Darling Ryan. Quiet, blessed quiet inside her head. Still someone held her.

Time expanded, then collapsed. There was no night or day, only the aching, bone-cracking grasp of the fever and the faces that came and went above her. She tried to respond, to help them, but finally could do nothing more except retreat somewhere deep inside herself where everything was gray and still and no more effort was required. There she lingered, as a child playing hide-and-seek might remain hidden until it could catch its breath or the pursuit came near. And the grayness stretched around her, covering her in layers that grew deeper and deeper.

From a pool of darkness and silence, Elene rose by slow degrees, floating up toward the sound of voices raised in supplication and in anger. On her tongue was the taste of one of Devota's many infusions of herbs, a taste she recognized from her childhood. It was unpleasant, yet comforting. She opened her eyes.

Around her bed, candles burned and there was a ring of white sand poured on the rug. Beside her stood Devota. The maid murmured a soft incantation while sprinkling her form under the linen sheet with some liquid from a calabash gourd she held in her hand.

At the same time, a dapper man with a receding hairline and a pince-nez perched on his nose strode up and down in agitation, railing in the accents of academic Paris against such heathen ceremony when it was the science of chemistry and solutions of *quinquina* which must save the poor demoiselle. He, Dr. Blanquet Ducaila, professor of chemistry, had been given the honor of treating the colonial prefect for this terrible malady of the yellow fever, and had brought him through his crisis. He would do the same for Mademoiselle Larpent, if he were permitted. He had tried, truly he had tried. But never had he seen such ignorance as among the medical professionals here with their purgatives and emetics and bleedings, and now he must contend with this superstition of a savageness unimaginable. He was amazed! He was shocked! When he told his colleagues of it on his return to France, he would not be believed. If mademoiselle died, it was this creature of the Voudou who must answer to M'sieur Bayard. He would not care to face the merchant-privateer if it came to pass, not he!

From under her lashes, Elene looked at her hands. They were yellow with jaundice and thin, so thin. She was damp with the sprinklings from Devota's calabash, and a wet heat suffused her. She was so hot that her hair felt on fire against her neck and the weight of the sheet over her was nearly insupportable. There was no air in the room for every door and window was closed. The candle flames seemed like giant, roaring fires. She could hear them burning, feel their scorching heat. And the voices of the two who hovered around her went on and on, drumming in her head, filling it, rattling and rumbling, until the sense of the words was lost and the sound was only noise, maddening, inescapable noise.

The door swung open. Ryan stepped into the room. He wore a dressing robe and his hair was tousled, as if he had risen from another bed somewhere. There were dark shadows under his eyes and the stubble of the beard on his chin seemed to shine with glints of silver, as if turning gray. He looked at Devota and the doctor in frowning annoyance as he demanded, "What is this noise?"

They began to explain, both speaking together. Their voices roared in Elene's ears. She closed her eyes with a soft moan in the back of her throat.

"Enough!" Ryan said.

The voices stopped. Ryan's footsteps approached the bed with slow caution. "*Chère?*"

She opened her eyes as if lifting weights of incalculable heaviness. She fastened her gaze on that of the man above her. "So hot," she whispered.

"I know. Don't try to talk."

Ryan stared down at her with his heart twisting inside him. She was dying, he knew it, dying because he had brought her to New Orleans. If he had left her on Saint-Domingue . . . But thinking of that didn't help. How he wished he could give her his strength, could take her pain upon himself. Why did it have to be her? Why?

She should have been ugly with the jaundice of her skin and the fever that had burned away the little excess flesh on her bones. Instead, she looked refined and exalted as she lay with the candlelight shimmering in the waves of her hair and her eyes huge and bright with fever, like some saint caught in the throes of religious passion. No doubt it was blasphemy to think so when he should be praying for her, but he could not help himself.

Dear God, but he felt helpless. Maybe he should allow her to be bled; everyone said it was a spontaneous nose bleed two days ago that had saved Laussat. But it had also come close to killing him. The prefect had lain in a stupor for hours before the professor of chemistry he had brought with him from France had pronounced him out of danger.

Perhaps they should sponge Elene off again; that seemed to help as much as anything. Ryan looked to Devota, on the verge of making the suggestion, but the woman stood with her eyes closed and her lips moving in her pagan incantation. The professor pulled at his lip, his eyes filled with doubt as he looked at the woman on the bed. Ryan looked back to Elene.

She was staring at him with a plea in her eyes. Her voice was no more than a breath of sound as she spoke. "Outside?"

"I don't recommend it," Doctor Ducaila said with decision. "The night air, you know. Quite noxious."

Devota opened her eyes. "You must not break the spell. Inside the ring of sand she is protected."

Elene's hand twitched, inched toward him. He needed nothing more. He stepped to the bed and flung the sheet back to the foot in a single sweep.

"I warn you, m'sieur," the doctor said, "you run the risk of contagion yourself if you suffer more than the briefest touch of her skin."

Ryan gave the man a look of contempt. Pushing his hands under Elene, he scooped her up against him and swung toward the door that led to the gallery.

Devota stepped in front of him. Ryan's blue eyes were hard as they clashed with those of the maid, though his voice was soft in deference to the woman in his arms. "Open it," he said.

The maid searched his face for long moments. What she saw there seemed to decide her. She stepped back abruptly and turned to throw the door wide.

Ryan pushed through the opening and strode along the gallery. The night was so deep and warm that nothing stirred there. He continued along to the steps, descending them to the courtyard. He stood for a moment, then moved toward the black shade of the oak tree.

There were footsteps behind him. It was Devota, bringing a wooden bench which she placed against the tree. Ryan sank down upon it, using the tree trunk for a backrest as he settled Elene comfortably in his lap. He reached to brush back her hair, straightening the long strands that had become entangled with the braiding on his dressing gown. He felt her cheek, and knew despair at its unrelenting heat. Bending his head, he pressed his lips to her forehead.

The relief at being in the open and the pleasure of the gentle caress against her skin was so great that Elene sighed and curled closer against the man who held her. She had lain like this she knew for countless hours in the last few days. She did not care if she ever moved.

From her heated skin rose the fragrance that seemed a part of her, smoothed into her skin by Devota even in her illness. The air around Ryan was permeated with it, a rapturous blending that caught at the spirit with intimations of a thousand half-forgotten memories, a thousand fervently remembered desires.

"Elene, my love, I love you," he said, the words a whisper almost lost in the rustle of a stray breeze in the leaves overhead.

But she heard them, and marveled that he could be so ready with the words she most needed to hear, even if he did not mean them. She sighed and closed her eyes.

Perhaps an hour later, while she slept, her skin was dewed with perspiration as the fever broke. The perspiration, mingling with her perfume, soaked through the thin gown she wore and Ryan's dressing gown until he was bathed in the essence of her. Feeling that sweet, moist warmth, he was suffused with wonder and a strange, inevitable joy.

The dog days of summer, the fever time, dragged on. The daily rains, appearing punctually every afternoon, continued until the curtains were spotted with gray mildew and any piece of leather left shut away from the air was instantly covered with mold. Elene's convalescence was slow due to the unremitting heat and dampness. July had passed away and August was upon them before Ryan considered that she was strong enough for visitors.

The first to come was Madame Tusard. Ryan did not leave the woman alone with her, but stood guard as if he had nothing in the world better to do. Elene tried to suggest that he go about his business that she was sure he must be neglecting, but he would not hear of it. The reason may have been that he knew already the news that Madame Tusard was bursting to impart.

There was first the courtesies to be observed, the inquiries after Elene's health, the expressions of regret for her absence from among the group. Mention was made of the returning health of the colonial prefect who was slowly recovering also, but still not making appointments. They also discussed the progress of the fever epidemic that had so far sent several score of people into flight upriver to stay with friends and relatives until the danger had passed.

Madame Tusard and her husband had thought of going, but the expense would be prohibitive and the traveling inconvenient since, inns being practically nonexistent, they would be forced to rely on the hospitality of landowners along the way. Too bad about Mazent; people were saying he and his daughter had spoken of leaving town before his death.

It was a moment before the woman's words, so casually spoken, made sense. Elene said, "You mean—M'sieur Mazent is dead? Flora's father?"

"I fear so. Such a tragedy."

"He died of the fever?"

"No, no. I did not mean to mislead you. The medical men were quite sure it was yellow fever at first, or else a colic due to his stomach disorders. But then this doctor of chemistry brought from France by the colonial prefect chanced to view the body. He said at once that the cause of death was neither fever nor colic. It was one you will never guess!"

As Madame Tusard paused expectantly, Elene shook her head. "I'm sure I won't. What was it?"

"Arsenic, *chère*. Can you believe it?"

Arsenic. First Hermine, now Mazent. A chill moved over Elene. "Oh, but how? Why?"

"No one knows. There seems to be no reason, though some suspect the maid Germaine. Flora is prostrate, of course, poor child. Also, her betrothal was just about to be announced. One supposes that will be postponed until after the mourning period."

"This doesn't seem possible. Are you sure?" A second death from poison would be too bizarre. What connection could there be between the two, that of an actress and a middle-aged planter?

"There is disagreement between Mazent's physician and Laussat's man. The doctor from Paris is said to have mentioned a smell of garlic as pointing toward the poison, though garlic is a common seasoning in food here."

"Then it may have been a natural death, after all," Elene said in relief.

"It may be. Of course, there are always those who will snicker and claim, when a man Mazent's age keeps a mistress, that he expired from what is known as an excess of physical excitement." The woman's eyes glittered as she made her suggestion.

"You mean—"

"Precisely."

"M'sieur Mazent and Germaine, after all this time. It seems unlikely."

"I assure you these things do happen."

Elene sought for a way to deflect Madame Tusard's thoughts. "Flora will be lost without her father."

"Indeed. The wealth she will inherit will not make up for her loss, though I suppose the fiancé will come forward to support her; certainly he could not be so foolish as to be backward in that regard. No doubt the man was the choice of her father. Flora need not have him now, of course, though I cannot picture her doing otherwise."

"Not really," Elene answered, though her mind was not on Flora's reaction to her marital prospects. "Who do you think this fiancé could be?"

An expression of annoyance crossed Madame Tusard's face. "The chit does not say; in fact, she is being most stubborn about keeping the name of the paragon a secret. Why, one can only imagine, unless there was some disagreement between her and her father—which is why I wonder if she will have her father's choice now." The glint of a shrewd smile crossed the woman's black eyes. "One is privileged to guess the man's identity, regardless, and I can't help remembering that it was Durant Gambier who escorted Flora on the night we attended the vauxhall."

It was precisely what Elene had been thinking. Almost to herself, she said, "I cannot quite see the two of them together."

Madame Tusard laughed, a sound shocking in its bitter irony. "Nor can I, but stranger matches have been made when money calls the tune."

Elene thought of the money Durant had been spending and the death of Mazent that had made his daughter an heiress, and a shiver moved over her.

From the corner of her eye, she saw Ryan start forward. His features set in a hard mask, he said, "That will be enough for now, I think. I'm sure Elene is grateful for your visit, Madame, but she must not tire herself."

"Oh, but I have so much more to tell—"

"Another time."

The brusque words were a dismissal. Madame Tusard made her good-bys, though not without a number of resentful glances in his direction. Ryan paid no attention whatever, but removed the pillows from behind Elene's back where she was propped against them and settled her in her bed for an hour of rest. It might have been her imagination, but Elene did not think his hands were as gentle as they usually were, nor his admonition that she sleep quite as concerned. Moreover, while she rested, he left the house for the first time in weeks.

Josie came the next morning while Ryan was out. She was dressed in a fashion more than a little reminiscent of Hermine's, being less fluffy than was her usual wont. It gave her a certain flair, and even a modicum more dignity. She could not imitate Hermine's voice, however, along with her manner of acting and her clothes, and though she was entertaining in her chatter of plays and fashions and bits of scandal, she could not duplicate Hermine's caustic wit.

"How is Morven?" Elene asked.

"Much as usual. He holds the widow captivated while flirting with all and sundry. I don't know what the fuss is about. He deigned to give me a tumble one evening while the widow was out, and frankly he wasn't that much as a lover."

Elene nearly choked on her coffee. "You mean you and he—"

"Over before I knew it. I was never so disappointed in my life. Men are so funny. It's the ones you would never expect who are best."

"Speaking from your vast experience?"

Josie grinned. "I've had a few, more than you, I don't doubt. Now, my new man isn't much to look at, but he knows how to use what he has, and the dear is so grateful for being allowed the privilege. He is also more generous than you would believe. Nothing could be more perfect."

"You mean to marry him?"

"Why should you think so? No, no, I have no wish to be tied to any man. Besides, he's married."

"I see."

"Do you now?" Josie asked, preening a little, arching her back to push out her chest as she looked at Elene askance. "I don't see you jumping into wedlock with Ryan. I have it from Madame Tusard that he is most attentive, guarding your health and comfort with the devotion of a knight-protector."

"She exaggerates," Elene said with an attempt at a light laugh.

"Does she? When he has not left your side for weeks? This is dedication beyond most lovers—beyond most husbands, for that matter. You would do well to capture him while you can."

"Would I indeed?"

"You needn't jeer; you don't have a profession to fall back on."

"I have my perfume," Elene said with a shading of stubbornness.

"So you do, which reminds me that I must have a bottle. I've spoken of it to—to my lover, and he has given me the money. He dotes on giving me what I want."

Elene looked around for Devota to send after the bottle of scent, but at some time during the conversation the maid had slipped from the room. Josie rattled on about other things, jumping from the death of Mazent, and Flora's subsequent expedition for mourning clothes that had enriched several dress shops, to a boating party given by Bernard Marigny for a few of his male friends and two or three carefully selected women, one of whom had been Flora. Somehow, the perfume was forgotten.

Elene thought of it perhaps a half hour after Josie had left. She turned at once to Devota, telling her the problem. "Why don't you deliver a bottle to Josie?"

Devota paused in her task of stacking the coffee cups Elene and her guest had used on a tray along with their crumb-filled cake plates. It was only a brief hesitation; still, it took on significance as Elene stared at the maid's stern features, noting the way she avoided meeting her eyes.

"Is something wrong?"

"Nothing, *chère*. How could there be now that you are growing stronger?"

"It's the perfume, isn't it?"

There coursed through Elene's mind a sudden spate of memories, of Devota bringing the new perfume to her while she talked to Hermine. Of the three days Ryan had refrained from touching her in their bed while she went without scent, and the way he had returned to her as magnet to steel when she had used the newly made perfume. Josie's words so short a time before echoed in her ears. *Devotion. Has not left your side for weeks. Dedication.*

Devota's silence was an assent.

"It's the same. You replaced the missing ingredient."

"It was not right otherwise."

"It isn't right now! You can't go around giving people such power!"

"I thought you did not believe in it?"

"How can I not?" Elene said, the words a cry of despair.

"The power is greatest where there is belief, and knowledge."

"But that doesn't mean it won't work. Does it?"

"No, *chère*."

"Do the others, Serephine and Germaine, know what they bought?" Elene asked slowly.

"They know."

Of course they would, being from Saint-Domingue. Most likely they were members of the Voudou cult, familiar with its mysteries. Hermine had not known, and Hermine was dead.

Aloud, she said, "You told them, but not me."

"It was to safeguard your future! You should have married Ryan, then this would not matter."

Elene stared at her maid, her eyes dark with the knowledge of her betrayal. She had thought Ryan's devotion, Ryan's love was for herself. "It would matter."

"It was for you, only for you." The maid's words, though soft-spoken, hovered in the air.

Elene closed her eyes, suddenly tired beyond measure. After a time she heard the quiet rattle of crockery and Devota's soft footsteps as she went away.

Elene lay still, trying to grapple with what it meant that the perfume was not as she had thought, trying to think how many people had the perfume and how they might be affected by it.

She could not avoid thinking of how it affected her, also. Once she had been fascinated by the capacity of the scent to enthrall, to captivate. Now she felt as if she was its most certain slave, for none was more dependent on its power than she who had none without it.

CHAPTER 14

ON the first day that Elene felt strong enough, finally, to exchange her nightgown and wrapper for a morning gown of yellow batiste embroidered with green leaves and vines and to leave her cushions and settee, she descended the stairs to the ground floor workroom. She moved with care, not only because of the lingering weakness of her illness, but because she did not want to attract Devota's attention. The maid would not approve of what she meant to do. It would be best if it was accomplished before she learned of it.

Elene found an empty olive oil jar, a pottery vessel shaped like a huge snail. She would have preferred a pail, but since none was available, she would make do. Placing the jar on the workbench, she took down the bottle that contained the last of the perfume Devota had made. Removing the stopper, she poured the contents into the olive oil jar. Setting the empty bottle aside, she reached to gather the small, ribbon-tied blue bottles that she had made up for sale. She held one in her hand, feeling its slight weight, smoothing her thumb over the glass.

She thought of the pride and hope that had gone into its filling, of the dreams of independence, and the certainty she had felt that she was doing something to secure her future. There was so much diligent effort contained inside, Devota's as well as her own, so many plans, so much anticipation of success. Useless, all of it had been useless.

Tears welled up, burning in her throat, spilling over her lashes. Her fingers tightened around the small bottle until they were white.

Power, that was the main thing the perfume she held represented, the ability to control men, and therefore the pleasures and elegancies of life. Power, not just for herself, but for countless other women. What a boon it could be to them, providing the means to order their existence as they wished, without regard for the dictates of men. It was a breathtaking thought.

It was also a power it would be base to use, and possibly dangerous. She could not do it, could not allow it.

With a sudden movement, she wrenched the stopper from the bottle-neck, and tipped the small amount of perfume into the olive oil jar. The smell of the liquid rose into the air, cloying in its richness, stifling in the failed promises and subjection it had come to represent. Elene allowed the last drop to fall, then set that bottle aside. The perfume dripped over her fingers and onto the crisp lavender and green ribbons at the bottle's neck, but she ignored it. She reached for another bottle, and another.

"What are you doing!"

It was Devota who cried out the question, her voice as near a scream as Elene could ever remember hearing it. Elene did not look up as she answered, "Removing an unfair advantage."

"This is madness!"

"Funny, it seems the only reasonable thing to me." Elene set down the bottle she held and brushed away tears with an impatient gesture before picking up another. There were three left.

Devota's gaze moved from the bottles that were left to the pottery jar. "What will you do with it?"

"Destroy it."

"By pouring it in the street? Isn't that a risk?"

"That someone will roll in the mud or scoop it up, dirt and all? I hardly think so. But I mean to pour it into the river. That should weaken it."

"I can't let you do it."

"You can't stop me." Elene's voice was rough with determination.

"Think of your mother's necklace. How will you regain it if you destroy what was bought with it? You will lose it."

"I can't help that."

As Elene reached to take another bottle, Devota shot out her hand and grabbed up the two that were left, holding them to her bosom. "These I claim as my part, for my labor."

Elene did not think, just now, that she would be able to wrestle the bottles from Devota, even if she felt it necessary. She did not. There was more than one way to neutralize the perfume's effect.

She met the maid's brown concerned gaze, her own implacable. "Wear the scent yourself if you wish, but you must not sell it."

"No, *chère*."

"I have your promise?"

Devota made a brief gesture as binding as any Christian oath to those who would recognize it.

"Very well then. Is there anyone else you sold or gave it to that I don't know of, anyone other than Hermine and Germaine and Serephine?"

"No one."

"Good. It should be easier then."

Devota watched her, her dark eyes opaque with hidden thoughts. "What do you mean to do?"

"Get back the perfume that was sold."

"That may not be easy."

Elene knew it well enough, but she could not let it deter her. It was something that must be done before she could feel free in her mind. She must try at least.

She began with Madame Rachel Pitot. She had no particular reason except that it seemed the woman might be easier to persuade to give her bottle up since she could have little idea of exactly what it represented. By way of persuasion, Elene prepared a story of a bad ingredient in the perfume which could cause a rash, and planned to carry what money she had with her to offer so that replacement perfume could be bought. She hoped the last would not be necessary, since Madame Pitot was a woman of wealth and had not, in any case, paid for the perfume originally. However, she knew that the wealthy were notoriously tightfisted when it came to small things.

For some reason she felt on her mettle where her appearance was concerned on this visit. Her walking costume of blue poplin was eminently suitable for the visit, and her small straw hat with its veil as protection from the sun was stylish as well as practical. But she took the time to pinch color into her cheeks that were still pale from her illness and even had recourse to a bit of carmine for her lips. As she viewed the results in the mirror when she was ready, she also vowed to stuff herself until she was as round as a barrel at every meal, for though she had regained some of the weight she had lost, she was still too thin.

She had no conveyance to take her to the house of the widow. The way was not long; still, she was forced to stop twice to rest, pausing to sit on one of the benches that were placed outside many shops and houses for convenience in taking the evening air, or else as a resting place for elderly shoppers. The sun grew hot as it rose higher in the morning sky, so that heat shimmered in waves above the dirt of the road outside the palisade, and dried the fresh footsteps made in the mud almost before the eyes. Elene could feel perspiration creeping down the back of her bodice, and she kept her handkerchief in her hand to slip under her veil and blot the beads of sweat from her skin.

At last the widow's house was before her. As Elene climbed the steps and passed under the coolness of the gallery, she realized she should have sent word that she was coming. The lady might well have a visiting day when she was at home to callers, while all other mornings were spent in paying visits to others.

The door of the house stood open, however, in the effort to entice any faint breeze, of which there were few, into the house. At Elene's light knock, a manservant appeared and bowed her inside, begging her to be seated in the salon while he went to see if his mistress was at home to callers.

Rachel Pitot received Elene in her boudoir, a room hung with watered silk in a flattering peach tone and liberally set about with the satin-covered gilt chairs of a more opulent age. She looked for all the world as if she had just that moment risen from her bed. Her hair straggled down her back, and her nightgown and wrapper were wrinkled in a pattern to indicate she had been lying about in them. She reclined on a chaise longue liberally strewn with lace pillows and with a plate of bonbons and a pot of chocolate on a small table beside her. It was as well that Elene did not care for the brew, for none was offered to her. The smell of the chocolate turning cool in a delicate china cup hung in the air along with a hint of blowsy decadence, but there was nothing else, not even a whiff of perfume.

Rachel Pitot stretched out a negligent hand and picked up a bonbon. "So brave of you to come when I hear you have been ill, Mademoiselle Larpent. I trust it will not prove too much for you."

"I'm sure it won't," Elene said, her voice dry as she watched the woman pop the bonbon she held in her mouth. If the widow Pitot had any concern, she would have offered refreshment. Otherwise, her words were mere pretense.

"Perhaps you came to see Morven? I believe he is amusing himself by rehearsing with a young new actress in the summer house in the rear garden. I can ring for a servant to fetch him, if you wish, though I doubt he will be overjoyed; the girl is so impressionable."

"No!" Elene said, then added more quietly, "I didn't come to see Morven."

"Josephine, then? She went early to town, before the heat grows too severe she said, though I don't expect her back from whatever assignation she is actually keeping until evening."

Elene let the comment pass. "I saw Josie just two days ago, and though I would not mind saying hello, my business is not with her."

"I'm sure that when you catch your breath, then, you will tell me why you have ventured here."

In the woman's acid words, her slovenly appearance, and her cool reception of Elene there was a deliberate insolence, as if she considered her inferior in station, on the same level as a milliner or seamstress come to offer a hat or gown. Elene felt it even if she could find no reason for it. Still, it could not affect her unless she permitted it.

"Yes, indeed," she said, her tone brisk and her back as straight as an applewood slat. "I have come about the perfume."

Rachel Pitot listened with a slight frown between her brows that she reached up to rub now and then with a forefinger against wrinkles. When Elene had finished, she said, "I had the perfume, yes, but it's gone now so there's no need to worry."

"Gone?" The word was blank. Elene had expected many things, but not this.

"Quite frankly, I believe it was stolen. If I had to suggest a culprit, I would say it was Josephine, though she denied the theft when I taxed her with it. She had the impudence to hint that my maid had taken it."

"Is there any possibility that could be true?"

"None whatever. My servants would not dare, since they know I would have the skin off their backs for it."

"A strong deterrent."

"I've found it effective. But I confess I'm amazed that you would go to so much trouble over a possible rash. Some women are susceptible to such annoyances, others are not. In any case, no one is likely to connect such a thing with your perfume."

"Perhaps, but I would know."

"Oh, come, I am not so naive! I believe this has something to do with a whisper among the quadroons and free women of color about a perfume with strange properties. I had thought it mere superstition, but it seems I should have guarded the scent with more care."

"I can't think what you might have heard, but surely you can't believe—"

The other woman paid no attention to Elene's attempt at denial. "There are things we don't understand, things that in our subjection of the Africans we have forced them to hide from us. I have seen them myself, in the rites the slaves hold in the swamps. Such demonstrations can be most stimulating. Still, if it's true, what they say, then it's easy to see what Josephine wanted with the perfume."

Elene's protests died on her lips. "What do you mean?"

"Why, Josephine had a great passion for Morven, didn't you know? And when it proved disappointing, there was another man she had been keeping on a string for some time whom she felt the need to captivate."

"Her lover."

"If you want to call him that, though I would not. M'sieur Tusard is hardly any woman's idea of a *beau ideal*."

"Tusard?" Elene's voice was blank.

"Surprised? He has a weakness, so they say, for actresses. Even Hermine—"

Elene, sickened by the woman's casual and heartless revelation of things better left unknown, sprang to her feet. "Excuse me, but I must go. It was good of you to see me, and I do appreciate your—candor. It was most helpful. Good day."

"Do come again," Madame Pitot said, but Elene had the feeling the words were no more sincere than the woman's concern for her health.

Elene made haste to leave the widow's house as far behind her as possible. One reason was her dislike of the woman, but another was the fear that Morven might return and find her there, forcing her to repeat the lies about the perfume, a performance she had no wish to make again any time soon. She was no actress.

Nor was she as strong as she had thought, though a part of her gasping weariness was from trying to outrun her thoughts. She slowed and looked around her, then left the road back to the city, whose rooftops and palisade walls lay not far ahead of her, to sit down under the shade of a beech tree. She leaned her head against its solid support, removing her hat so as not to crush it. Closing her eyes, she waited patiently for her heartbeat to slow and the heat flush to die away out of her face.

Josie and M'sieur Tusard. Their affair had a strange kind of logic, given the man's penchant for women on the stage. Was it possible that the rapture of the former official with his paramour was caused by the perfume? Had Josie stolen it as Rachel Pitot said?

And what of before? While the fragrance had been in Rachel Pitot's possession, Morven had been enamored of her, but now had apparently, from the widow's tart remarks, turned his considerable charm to the seduction of his new ingenue. What a muddle it was.

But there was one possibility slowly emerging which Elene did not like, one that had lain slowly festering in the back of her mind since she had learned that Hermine had given away the perfume. The bottle of scent that Elene had given to Hermine had been used by the widow to win the affections of Morven, however temporarily. It had been during that period of his infatuation with the woman that Hermine had died. Could it be that the woman who had loved Morven best had so despaired over the unusual strength of his new attachment that she had taken her own life with an overdose of arsenic?

Was it possible that she, Elene Larpent, had caused Hermine's death?

Surely the cause was not as she suspected, and yet the doctors had called it suicide and Elene had seen herself the unhappiness Morven's defection had caused. It made no sense that a woman like Hermine, one who had been taking arsenic for years for her skin, would be so careless as to take too much. Yet, if neither of those explanations was true, what else was there?

There was murder. If the dead woman had been Josie instead of Hermine, and the death had occurred two weeks later, then one could always say the wronged wife, Madame Tusard, had done it. Poison was known as the weapon of women, after all, and husbands and wives were traditionally the first to be suspected in murder involving a lovers' triangle. On the other hand, Hermine had known M'sieur Tusard no better than Elene herself. Admittedly there had been that peculiar accusation made by Madame Tusard that Hermine was the actress her husband had known years ago, but that little misconception had been straightened out quite satisfactorily.

No matter the cause of Hermine's death, there appeared to be no connection between it and that of M'sieur Mazent. How could there be? Still, there had been a bottle of perfume in the Mazent household also, that belonging to Germaine. Suppose the death of Mazent had not been from stomach colic or fever or poison, but rather from apoplexy due to overexcitement from the effects of the perfume on the body of his mistress, as Madame Tusard had suggested?

No, no, that was too morbidly fanciful. She was giving too much credit to the perfume, or else taking too much blame upon herself. The fault could not be hers in the death of Mazent, surely it could not.

If there was a merciful heaven, she would find that she had gone to sleep here in this place and dreamed this whole nightmare. On waking she would discover that the perfume had no magical effect at all. She would come miraculously to understand that she had no part in these deaths around her, that there was some evil abroad that chose its victims at random. As much as she longed for the comfort of either explanation, however, she could not accept them. Unable to rest, Elene pushed to her feet and began to trudge once more toward the city gates.

So exhausting was her expedition to see the widow that it was more than three days before she could find the energy to emerge from Ryan's house once more. Even then, she was driven not so much by duty as by fear of what might happen if she did not retrieve the perfume.

Regardless, she was not sanguine about her chances of success. It was just as well.

There was no way she could see Germaine without Flora being present, since the girl was in the parlor of the set of inn rooms when the door was opened to her. Flora Mazent took it for granted Elene had come to see her. She seemed delighted to be able to entertain a visitor, bustling about with a red splotch from excitement on her pale cheeks and her black skirts swinging around her.

"Would you care for chocolate—no, that will not do for you, will it? I was forgetting. I'll order coffee and cakes, then. Shall I?"

"Please don't go to any trouble."

"It's no trouble at all, I assure you."

The order was given to Germaine who was busy in the connecting bedchamber, though she must have left on her way to the inn kitchen from another outside door, for she did not come through the parlor. After a moment, however, Flora returned.

Elene, grasping at a reason to explain her presence while she sought for a way to speak to the girl's maid, rushed into speech. "I'm sorry I was unable to make my visit of condolence on the loss of your father."

Flora sobered, settling deeper into the dull and heavy settee that was typical of most inn parlors. "Thank you, but I do understand. You are quite well now?"

Elene answered, and they spoke of the progress of the fever through the city, of the heat and the daily rains that made it doubly hard to bear. They discussed also the arrival of a ship from France, regrettably without the news of the cession that everyone awaited. All in all, Elene was impressed with the way Flora conducted herself. On reflection, she could never remember her having so much to say, probably because in the past she had tended to rely on her father to answer most questions for her.

Still, no opportunity presented itself for an exchange of words with Germaine, though the woman brought the coffee and poured it for them, then retreated once more into the bedchamber of the set of rooms. There was nothing to be done except bring the subject out into the open.

"Oh, dear, I had almost forgotten," Elene said to Flora. "My maid asked me to deliver a message to your woman, if you don't object?"

"Why, not at all." Flora called out, and within seconds Germaine reappeared to stand in front of them. There was nothing servile in her manner, only a quiet, waiting stillness.

She said, "You needed something, *chère*?"

Flora indicated Elene, who launched into her prepared speech about the rash. She ended with a direct question concerning the whereabouts of the perfume supposed to cause it.

"My perfume?" Germaine asked, her smooth, cream-colored face as expressionless as the great sphinx unearthed from its centuries of sand by Napoleon's soldiers in his Egyptian campaign. "Oh, it was spilled a few days ago."

It was a lie, of that there could be no doubt. That Flora knew it also was apparent by the change of color under her fair skin. What reason the woman had for telling it made little difference, whether it was the kind of soothing tale told to keep a white person from fretting, for her own protection until she knew there was no danger for herself, or if it was simply because she had no intention of giving up such a powerful weapon. The fact was the perfume could not be pried from her.

Unless Flora could be induced to supply the lever.

Directing her words at the young girl while pretending to speak to Germaine, Elene said, "You know, I suppose, that people are spreading scandal concerning the death of M'sieur Mazent, saying that he—so to speak—died in your arms?"

"No, mademoiselle, I did not know that."

"I assure you, it's true. I fear that if rumors of this perfume should begin to spread, I may be blamed. There could be an unsavory scandal, something I'm sure we all want to avoid."

"I would help you if I could," Germaine said, and her dignity was such that she made Elene ashamed of the innuendos she had dragged forth.

Elene turned instead to Flora. "This is a delicate matter for you. It would be unfortunate if your future fiancé should conceive a dislike for the arrangement between you because of the idle gossip of a few. I have no wish to be involved in it myself, which is why I am anxious to remove any hint that my perfume was associated with the tragedy."

"I see," Flora said slowly, her face clouded, "though I don't know how I can help you. My father died of a stomach disorder that had plagued him for some time, almost as long as I can remember. There can be no question of this no matter what idle gossips are saying. As for the perfume, Germaine has told you it is gone. I'm afraid I can add nothing to that, as much as I hate the idea of people saying horrible things about my father."

Elene was left with no more to say, nor did it appear there was anything further to be gained by talking to Flora Mazent and her maid. Elene took her leave.

She had not much hope of regaining the perfume Serephine had bought after her lack of success with the other bottles. It was just as well. Serephine made no excuses, told no tale of lost of stolen scent. She was not rude, but she made it plain that she valued the perfume and its supposed benefits highly, and was suspicious of any attempt to wrest the little she had left from her. Quite simply, she refused to part with it. Nor was Elene inclined to pursue the matter when Serephine told her the cause. Durant, the quadroon said, loved for her to wear it. The reason was because it made his mistress smell like Elene.

Ryan was waiting for Elene when she reached the house once more. He rose from a chair on the gallery, walking to the head of the stairs to meet her as she ascended the steps from the courtyard. He took one look at her pale face and the shadows of exhaustion like bruises under her eyes, and the planes of his face hardened into grimness. Taking her by the arm, he propelled her into the nearest chair.

"What in the name of living hell have you been doing to yourself?"

"Nothing. That is—"

"You've been gone all morning, and without so much as a word to Benedict or Devota. Why?"

He loomed over her with a hand braced on either arm of her chair. The implacability of his voice and the hard glint of his eyes affected her with a peculiar combination of annoyance and extreme weariness, distress, and guilt. The worst thing was the knowledge that his wrath was fueled by an anxiety and concern that had its roots in his abnormal desire for her. How different everything would be if she could think that what he felt was for herself alone, without artificial aid. It was not.

There was no point in wishing for what could not be. Therefore, she must answer him somehow without telling him precisely what she had been about.

Or must she?

She was so tired of this lie she was living. It was like a burden carried inside her, one that grew heavier the longer she sustained it. She recognized that it might be the weakness left from her bout with fever and the depression of spirit caused by her lack of success in retrieving the perfume that made ridding herself of her guilt so seductive an impulse. Still, it was irresistible.

"If you will sit down," she said quietly, "I will tell you about it."

Ryan stared at her for a long moment. There was something in her voice, in her face, he did not like. It gave him a peculiar feeling under his breastbone. There was another chair not far away, but he did not take it. Instead, he straightened and backed slowly away to the gallery railing. Leaning against it, he crossed his arms over his chest and waited.

Elene drew a deep breath and let it out slowly. She had tried to make him understand before and failed. It was unlikely he would be so distracted this time that he would not take it in. She wished she had more time to think about it, to decide if it was really the right thing; to plan exactly what she was going to say and how she was going to put it. Devota would not understand, that much was certain. But the problem was not Devota's. It was hers alone, and it had become, finally, unbearable.

There was a tremor in her voice as she began to speak. She tried to explain what the perfume was and why it had been made in the beginning, though she was not sure she was making sense. The look on Ryan's face was suspended, closed in. Regardless, she pressed on, explaining that first night in hiding on Saint-Domingue and how little she had thought of the effect of the scent she wore, how little she had believed in its efficacy, detailing all that came after. She did not stop until he knew everything.

When at last she was silent, the look on Ryan's face was perplexed. Holding her gaze with his, he said with slow care, "You mean you think I'm keeping you here with me because of your perfume?"

"I don't think it, I know. I didn't want to accept it, but the evidence is too strong to deny."

"Because I make love to you when you're wearing it and don't when you're not."

She swallowed, looking beyond him over the railing to the leaves of the oak. "Something like that."

"And I can never leave you?"

"No."

A smile dawned on his face, rising to his eyes in bright, shining mirth. "That's ridiculous!"

"No, it isn't." The words were earnest as she sat forward in her chair.

"You make it sound as if I have no free will."

"You don't."

His grin grew wider. "I don't believe in Voudou."

"That doesn't matter! I don't believe in it either, but I've seen what it can do over and over: make people well, make them ill, even cause death. It's no laughing matter!"

He tried to compose his features in a sober mien, but it didn't work. "I'm sorry. I keep thinking of you in that hole under Favier's house. All the time I was taking unprincipled advantage of you, you thought you were doing the same with me."

"I was!"

"Then I hope you will do it more, and often."

She rose to her feet in agitation with her skirts swirling about her ankles. "You don't understand, won't understand."

He pushed away from the railing and moved to put his hands on her shoulders. "I understand all right. I'm just telling you that there's nothing to what you're saying, no matter what Devota may have told you."

"What about Rachel Pitot and Morven? Or Morven and Josie? Or Josie and M'sieur Tusard? What about Hermine's death, and that of M'sieur Mazent? Doesn't all that show you anything?"

"Coincidence, nothing more. Just as it was a coincidence that I didn't touch you while you weren't wearing that damnable scent. It certainly wasn't because I didn't want you in all that time. I just thought—never mind what I thought. Just believe me when I say you have nothing to feel guilty about. This whole thing is a farce."

"It isn't! I can't live like this anymore. I won't do it!"

"If I understand what you're saying, all you have to do is stop using the perfume. Stop, and you'll see."

She jerked out of his grasp, backing away from him. "You're the one who'll see! That is, unless you shower me with affection just to prove me wrong!"

Impatience hardened his voice. "Then wear the stuff and forget it. It doesn't matter. It really doesn't matter!"

"What if it harms you somehow? What if somebody else dies because of it, even you?"

"It won't happen. Anyway, there's nothing you can do about it now!" His voice was rising, the tone grating.

The door to the bedchamber was open behind her. She turned toward it. "Yes, there is. I can leave here. I can leave you!"

He watched the door where she had disappeared for a stunned moment. She wasn't rational on the subject of this perfume. It had to be her illness making her talk like this; there was no other explanation. With his fist clenched, he strode into the bedchamber after her.

She was opening the armoire to take out her clothes. He put his hand on the door, slamming it shut again. "You aren't going anywhere."

"Yes, I am."

"You aren't strong enough yet. What would you do? Where would you stay?"

"I'll do something, find somewhere." She tried to open the armoire door again and he held it shut with one stiff arm. She turned to glare at him.

He looked at her, and something black and implacable rose inside him. "You are going nowhere," he said, the words sharp with the obsidian edge of danger. "I won't let you. You will stay here with me until hell is cool and this tiny earth goes spinning into the last pit of infinite darkness. Nothing will change my mind. Nothing will pry you from me, not some puny scent or lack of it, not a horde of quadroons panting for love, not death itself. I will never let you go."

Her eyes widened and her lips parted as she stared at him. Ryan, seeing the bewilderment and the wonder in the depths of her eyes, heard in his mind the echo of what he had just said. And suddenly, disconcertingly, he knew the first unfamiliar flicker of doubt.

CHAPTER 15

NAPOLEON'S cession of the colony of Louisiana to the United States was confirmed on August 18 in the form of a letter to Laussat from the French chargé d'affaires, M'sieur Pichon, at the young nation's capital of Washington City. The transfer had been made at a cost of seventy-five million francs or fifteen million dollars. French and Spanish merchant ships were granted the advantages of most favored nations status, but that was the only concession to former ownership. It was also noted that King Carlos IV of Spain had at last, that past May, put his name to the document officially granting Louisiana to France. Matters were finally beginning to take on a semblance of solidity.

The official transfers of governmental power, both that from Spain to France and from France to the United States, could not be made, however, until the actual dispatches authorizing them were received from Paris by way of Washington City. Life proceeded, therefore, at the same slow pace as before, with the Spanish exercising nominal power and the French colonial prefect chafing at his forced inactivity.

Laussat, according to Ryan, was somewhat bitter at the time and effort he had wasted in this fruitless trip to Louisiana. He had thought to build a rich colony for France, had been full of plans and ideas, but now they were for nothing. Great sums of money had been expended in closing his home in France and moving his family to what was supposed to be a prestigious and influential post. He had endangered his health, not to mention that of his family, and also his future career for what had proven to be a useless cause. Now he was held here while the wheels of the petty bureaucracy ground out the necessary papers, in all their many laboriously copied versions with appended seals and ribbons, that would make everything correct and legal. He was growing impatient. A part of his testiness could be attributed to the summer heat, but another was because his wife had proven the claim made by local residents concerning the fecundity of the waters of the Mississippi. Madame Laussat was pregnant. The prefect and his wife had three, perhaps four, months of grace before a sea voyage would become too dangerous; then they must leave the colony if they were not to be stuck there until after the lady's confinement.

It was sometime near the beginning of September that Ryan broached the possibility of his traveling to Washington City. The suggestion had been made by Laussat. He had expected the all-important dispatches permitting the double transfer to follow soon after the letter confirming the sale of the colony. Their failure to appear made him fear there had been an accident somewhere along the dangerous overland trail between Washington City and New Orleans. The list of things that might have befallen the messenger bearing the dispatches was endless, from attack by Indians or wild animals, to being swept away during one of the numerous river crossings. One of the first reforms of the United States, so the Americans claimed, was going to be the stationing of outposts along this trail with changes of horses so that the whereabouts of the post riders would be known at all times. The time usually required for the journey, forty days one way, would be cut to something more reasonable, such as twenty or twenty-five.

But why should Laussat expect you to go?" Elene asked. "You are no post rider."

Ryan leaned back in his chair as they sat over their dessert and coffee after a light dinner. His smile was rueful as he replied. "Laussat seems to think I have a knack for staying alive."

What he meant, of course, was that Laussat needed a man of daring and enterprise who could not only handle a weapon, be it knife, sword, or pistol, but who also knew something about getting out of tight positions. "Yes, but why you? He must know you have favored the cession from the beginning."

"All the more reason to suppose that I will do everything in my power to return with the dispatches."

"You have agreed, then?"

Ryan shrugged. "It seems a worthwhile jaunt."

"It's no jaunt," Elene said, her voice low and intense as her fingers curled around the arms of her chair. "You could be killed."

"That would, of course, be inconvenient."

"It's no joking matter!"

"Why, *chère*, one would almost think you cared." His voice was light, but the look in his eyes was somber as he watched her.

She looked away from him. "I have no wish to see you dead."

"I'm comforted. I've thought once or twice lately that it might be otherwise."

"What are you talking about?" she asked, sending him a quick frown.

It was a moment before he spoke, then he only said, "You don't seem very happy."

"I'm . . . not unhappy. It's just that so much has happened. It's taken so long for me to regain my strength, and in the meantime I'm a charge upon you."

"Have I complained?"

Her lips tightened. "No, but I don't like it."

"It seems a natural enough arrangement."

"That doesn't mean it's right. I prefer to make my own way."

Ryan knew that very well, and respected her for it. He had prevented her from leaving him on the evening she told him about the perfume by main force, logic, and caresses; still, he knew he could not hold her forever by such tactics. He wished sometimes that she was like other women, full of tears and helpless appeal, but then she would not be his Elene.

They had been close since her illness, closer than he had ever come to a woman. And yet there was a wariness between them. It was caused in part by her refusal to resign herself to her role as his mistress, but also by something he recognized within himself as a growing distrust.

He did not trust himself where she was concerned.

When she had first told him of the perfume, he had laughed. The more he thought about it, the less comical it seemed. He had always known his desire for her was excessive, beyond anything he had ever experienced. It came upon him at the most inappropriate times, while he was discussing business or inspecting his warehouses. It took less than nothing to make him ready for her when they were together: the trill of a laugh, the shift of her hair as she turned her head, a whiff of her fragrance.

Her fragrance, that was the problem. Its appeal to him was not reasonable. He tried to tell himself that it was because she had been drenched in it on the night they first made love, but that fact should not make him turn homeward two or three times a day just to discover if she was still there. It should not make his heart jar against his backbone when he found her bedchamber empty. It should not bring to mind a picture of her face whenever he saw a fetching bonnet on a woman on the street, or when he heard a snatch of lovely melody. He had thought, for a time, that he was only falling in love, but the sensations were so consuming he could not help wondering if there was not some magic to it, some bewitchment.

Elene sensed the withdrawal in Ryan. The cause was not hard to guess. According to Devota, she was a fool for telling him of the perfume. That was entirely possible. He had, it seemed, begun to question his feelings for her. She should be glad; she had been so uncomfortable with the knowledge that whatever affection he might have felt for her was caused by something outside himself. What she had not taken into account was the possibility that without the perfume he might feel nothing more than the compassion he would accord any female in need of a place to stay.

Oh, he still turned to her in the night with desire, even since she had ceased to use the perfume. She was there, after all, a convenient outlet for his male needs. Why should he not make use of her since he was paying for the food she ate and the roof over her head. But there had been no more words of love, no more trysts in the darkened courtyard. It was as if she had removed a protective garment with her perfume, and was now vulnerable to pain and loss. The idea that he might find another woman, take another mistress, haunted her. If that should happen, she did not know what she would do, where she would go. Her choices were so few.

She had cudgeled her brain for a way to find more money to buy perfume ingredients, this time for a scent that was truly no more than a delicious smell. She was sure there was profit in it even yet, and all the benefits that went with it. Moreover, she had discovered within herself great satisfaction in working with essences, measuring and mixing and sampling the results, breathing perpetually fragrant air. So far, however, the means to continue eluded her. She might sell her gold earrings, but they would bring little in a market already flooded with the jewelry of the refugees still pouring in from Saint-Domingue as the British and French with their various Negro factions fought back and forth over the island. This state of affairs also made the prospect of ever gaining a penny from her father's estate appear dimmer every day. The only possibility she could see was to ask Ryan for the money, and this she refused to do.

"Anyway," Ryan said finally, "it's likely the papers Laussat expects will arrive any day and there will be no need for a special courier. He's a good enough man in his way, but too much of a European to realize the distance, or the difficulties, involved in traveling across this vast land. We must all be patient."

They were patient indeed, but still there was no sign of the courier from Washington. The hot, wet days continued. The fever raged through the city so that public entertainments were canceled and there were few parties or visits for fear of the contagion. Funeral corteges became regular sights as they wound their way through the streets with coffins on carts followed by hatless male mourners. Black became the most common color seen on the streets as people in the intricately interrelated families went into mourning for aunts and uncles and cousins of several degrees, as well as for closer kin. The scarlet uniforms of the Spanish soldiers, as faded and worn as most were, became jarring notes of color among such melancholy vestments.

Elene seldom left the house. The daily shopping for food had become Benedict's responsibility once more, though sometimes Devota went with him to make some special purchase for Elene's use or to tempt her appetite. Now and again, however, Elene and Ryan would join the few hardy souls who braved the threat of illness to stroll along the river levee in the coolness of the evening.

On an evening toward the middle of the month, the two of them circled once around the promenade of the Place d'Armes, then turned toward the river. The day had not been so terribly hot; it seemed that the grip of summer might be loosening. There were more people moving about than had been seen in some time.

The breeze off the water was pleasantly refreshing. The surface of the river made a rippling, opalescent mirror for the sunset that faded from orange and blue and gold to pink and lavender-purple. There was a quality of stillness about the long twilight that caused movements to slow and voices to hush to quiet murmurs. Buzzards drifted in slow sweeping circles overhead and pigeons from the pigeoniers around the city wheeled in precisely aligned flocks before dropping to the ground like a handful of carelessly thrown pebbles. Now and then a dog barked or a horse neighed. The sound of the southward flowing water was like soft music, an intriguing and soothing refrain.

Ahead of them, coming from the opposite direction, Elene saw Flora

Mazent with Germaine, like a gray shadow, behind her. The girl nodded and spoke without quite meeting Elene's eyes as they came abreast; certainly she showed no sign of stopping. She and her maid moved on out of hearing distance.

Ryan sent a glance over his shoulder after them. The pain of the rebuff rose up inside Elene along with something waspish. "What is it?" she asked. "Aren't you used to being slighted by a woman?"

Lifting a brow as he gave her his attention, Ryan said, "It's happened a few times. I thought the Mazent girl looked upset."

"The strain of being forced to acknowledge me, no doubt."

He was silent a long, considering moment. "Does it hurt so much, being a fallen woman?"

"I am not a fallen woman!" she snapped.

"Being my woman then, or however you want to put it." The impatience was plain in his voice.

"I don't regard it."

"Yes, if you fail to regard it any more, you're going to give yourself another fever."

She gave him a cold look. "It's just that I dislike discourtesy. If it wasn't for you and your ship, that girl would most likely be dead."

"That doesn't mean she has to like me, or that I care a fiddler's damn whether she does or not."

"It's a question of manners, of suitable gratitude."

"I don't want her gratitude."

"Neither do I," she said in exasperation, "but that doesn't mean she shouldn't feel some obligation to be civil, perhaps to pass the time of day."

Elene didn't know why she was allowing herself to become overwrought. It wasn't as if any of it mattered. It was simply that she was on edge of late, her usual calm worn thin by the things that had taken place along with the debilitating effects of her fever.

"I agree," Ryan said.

Elene, ready to defend her position further, stopped and stared at him. "You do?"

"Naturally. She should have been more cordial. But since she was not, there is nothing to be gained by blaming yourself for it. For whatever reason, it was her discourtesy, therefore it reflects on her. It's nothing to do with you."

She narrowed her eyes. "Don't patronize me. I know it wasn't my fault, but that doesn't mean I can ignore it."

"By no means," he countered in abrupt anger. "Pay attention to this, too. Since nothing I say can please you, I will leave you to your own company."

She watched his straight back, the swing of his broad shoulders and narrow hips, as he walked away. Desolation crowded in upon her. She opened her mouth to call him back, then shut it again. What good would it do? There was nothing she had said for which she wanted or needed to apologize. If he could not understand how trying she found her position with him, then there was no possible way she could explain it.

Elene swung around, walking back along the levee the way she and Ryan had come. Despite the aspect given by the tall embankment, she looked neither toward the river, at the houses of New Orleans within the palisade that was open on the levee side, nor even along the thoroughfare that led toward Bayou St. John and the Marigny plantations. Her gaze was on the dried mud and sun-bleached grass of the track on which she walked, while her thoughts ran in circles.

"Elene? Mademoiselle Larpent? Could I please speak to you?"

She looked up, startled. It was Flora Mazent who stood in front of her. The girl's pale, red-rimmed eyes were anxious and she looked over her shoulder like a hunted rabbit before turning back to Elene.

"Is something wrong?" Elene said.

"I only have a moment. I sent Germaine on an errand, but she will soon be back."

"Perhaps you would like to come to the house?"

"No, no. Germaine would scold; you know how maids are. She thinks I should not be talking to you at all."

Elene knew indeed how maids could be from her years with Devota. So closely did they identify with the affairs of those they served that they sometimes tended to forget who was mistress and who was maid. When the relationship was one of long duration, it could be difficult to reestablish authority without unpleasantness.

"What may I do for you?" she asked.

"It's about the perfume. I wonder if I could get some."

Elene blinked. What she had expected, she could not have said, but after her attempt to retrieve the scent that had belonged to Germaine, it was certainly not this. Still, her voice carried equal parts of warmth and reason as she replied. "I don't think you know what you're asking."

"I know very well. I must have the perfume, I must!"

"I'm not making it any more, as I think I told you the other day. There was something that caused a rash—"

"Oh, don't tell me that! I know what it can do, and that's what I need. I'll pay whatever you ask, anything at all. But I have to have it. I have to have it now!"

"It's impossible—"

The girl's face twisted and she clenched her fingers together that she clasped before her. "Don't say that! You don't know how important it is."

Elene put her hand on the girl's arm. "Please calm yourself, Flora. I don't know what you think the perfume can do, but I assure you, there is no more to be had."

"You have some of your own, you must have, or you wouldn't still be with Bayard!"

Elene drew in her breath at the sudden pain the words caused, then lifted her chin as she let it out again. "I'm sorry."

"Don't say that. Don't say that to me because you aren't sorry at all. If you don't give me the perfume, the man I love isn't going to marry me. He said he would, before my father died, but now he's trying to get out of it. I can't bear it if he refuses me. Really I can't."

"I'm not sure the perfume would help."

"I know it would. I wore it before, but now it's all gone and my fiancé doesn't want me anymore."

Flora had worn the scent, not Germaine. How odd. "I would help you if I could, really I would."

"I don't believe you. I know you have more of the perfume. I know it."

"No, really."

"You're lying. You're—" Flora Mazent's words stumbled to a halt as she glanced beyond Elene. Her face changed. She turned to look back down the levee to where Germaine had detached herself from the crowd around a seller of candied violets. Abruptly she said, "Never mind. Forget I spoke to you. Forget all of it. I . . . I'm a trifle upset. The shock, you know, on top of Papa's . . . Just forget it."

Whirling around, she walked quickly away. Elene stared after her until the girl caught up with her maid and the two women descended from the levee to disappear among the streets.

Ryan spoke from just behind Elene. "What was the matter with her?"

Elene had no wish to hear him laugh about her perfume again.

"Nothing," she answered distractedly. "She was just a little upset. Her father, you know."

There was more to it than that, Ryan knew, but he did not question her. He must realize that he did not own her, could not control her, had no right to make demands. If he wanted to keep her with him, he was going to have to remember these things. The problem was that the need to possess was new to him, something he had never felt for any other woman. It might also be, he was aware, a symptom of the spell she had cast around him.

Perfume or no, he was under a spell. He had thought to leave her there on the levee to make her way back to the house alone. That had been until it occurred to him that she might choose not to return. The idea was insupportable. Because of it, here he was, Bayard the privateer, playing escort to a female, allowing himself to be led like a prize ship in tow instead of capturing his prey and making away with it. His only consolation was that she did not seem to know her own power, or at least had the scruples not to use it. For that mercy he was not sure whether to be glad or sorry.

Madame Tusard was one of those women who counted the calls she made on her friends and acquaintances and balanced them against those made to her in return. If the two were unequal, she was piqued and hurt. If the balance failed to be redressed for any length of time, her miffed feelings turned to outrage, and she was prone to retaliate with none too subtle slander against the culprit that she passed out on her visits to those who were still on terms with her.

Elene owed Madame Tusard a visit. She could not quite like her, but she did pity her for her lost children and vanished dreams, for her altered circumstances and limited social circle in New Orleans. She could also sympathize with her plight as the wronged wife, whether Madame Tusard knew of her betrayal or not. Moreover, because Elene had been Josie's confidante concerning the adultery, she felt a shadow of guilt herself for keeping it secret. And Elene did not have so many social contacts herself that she could afford to despise friendship of any kind. For these reasons, she set out some days after the meeting with Flora to pay Madame Tusard a visit.

She found the woman with her head tied up in a turban and a duster in her hand as she cleaned the small room that passed as a salon in the cottage she and her husband had taken on Dumaine Street. The woman started at Elene's knock and turned to where the front door leading directly into the salon stood open to catch the morning breeze. She met

Elene's gaze for no more than an instant, then tore off her turban and flung her duster down upon a table. Her manner flustered and her cheeks scarlet, she came to the door.

"Forgive my dirt," she said, her voice unnaturally high. "I had sent my girl to the market this morning before I noticed the layer of dust she has permitted to accumulate in this room. Such a careless creature! I don't know why I keep her."

Elene murmured something soothing in reply as she stepped inside. She wished she had not come, but it was too late to retreat now. It was plain there was no girl. Françoise Tusard had been served by slaves for so many years in her husband's island post that to be forced to do her own work was a greater humiliation to her than the loss of their livelihood.

Madame Tusard moved to seat herself on a chair which, though covered in rich blue velvet and edged with gold fringe, had crocodile feet for legs and arms made of the reptile's head and tail. Elene subsided into a matching chair on the other side of a small table near the room's single window. An exchange of compliments and pleasant nothings followed. Elene responded with only half her attention while she looked around her.

The cottage had six rooms, all opening into each other. The walls, set directly on the ground, were of *bousillage*, a plaster of mud and moss or deer hair filling in the interstices between a framework of log timbers. The windows were closed with shutters, the floors were of rough planking on which had been laid carpets of faded colors and dubious quality. The interior walls and ceilings were plastered and washed white with lime.

Nevertheless, there was a chandelier of crystal and brass filled with expensive beeswax candles hanging in the salon, figurines of Sevres china on the mantle, and a mirror over the fireplace of rococo design covered in gold leaf. The other furniture, in keeping with the chairs in which they were seated, was of the latest style inspired by Napoleon's Egyptian campaign. It was possible to guess that Madame Tusard's preoccupation with appearances had dictated the attempt at modish furnishings here in this public room. It seemed likely, however, that it did not extend to their private quarters.

The decided air in the house of making do with the least possible expenditure did not sit well with Josie's claim that M'sieur Tusard was her present lover and protector. It was not to be expected that Josie would rush to the man's embraces for the sake of his *beaux yeux*; it must be assumed that he was expending fair sums of money for the pleasure of her company. It also made no sense that Madame Tusard would permit her Claude to spend money on a mistress while she herself did her own cleaning and cooking. There was the possibility that M'sieur Tusard had means of which his wife was unaware, but if so, what could they be? And how had he managed to keep the fact hidden?

Aloud, she said, "Your husband, I hope he is well?"

"Splendid. He has a new position, you know, with the colonial prefect. It is regrettable that it cannot be permanent—word of the cession was naturally a blow to us. We have hopes, however, that Claude will be able to go with Prefect Laussat when he is assigned to his next post."

"That would be something indeed."

"It can't happen soon enough for me. I despise this place."

"Do you? I rather like it myself."

"How you can after your dreadful bout with the fever I cannot imagine. I live in terror that either Claude or I will fall ill with it. I would not care to be buried here. They say the gravediggers cut holes in the coffins with an ax so they will not float out of the graves, or else the coffins are sealed up in brick walls until they disintegrate, at which time the bones are removed and another coffin takes the place of the first. Horrible, quite horrible. I do grieve for poor Flora Mazent that she has to think of her father's remains being placed in such conditions."

To change the subject, Elene said, "Flora doesn't look well lately."

"No. One hears that the betrothal has come to nothing, too. I'm by no means certain that it isn't just a vicious rumor started by some incorrigible gossip though, for I saw Flora at the dressmaker's shop just yesterday looking at the sort of linen and batiste that's most suitable for a trousseau."

Relief touched Elene. "Perhaps the problem, if there was one, has been solved. Have you heard yet who the lucky man is to be?"

Madame Tusard looked conscious. "I rather thought it might be Gambier, you know, but he was seen no more than three days ago with that harlot of an actress, Josephine Jocelyn, on his arm. Then my Claude let fall an interesting tidbit about a meeting he witnessed between Mazent and another man before the death of Flora's father."

"You mean a meeting to discuss the terms of the nuptial agreement?"

"Claude would not tell me! You know what men are when they think they have revealed too much. Still, one assumes that was the purpose."

"Who was the man?"

"My dear, I hesitate to say, since you seem to have no inkling of it."

There did seem to be a certain apprehension in the woman's small eyes, but mingled with it was avid anticipation. The closeness with which Madame Tusard watched her, the heavy-handed tact with which she spoke, were signals for alertness. Elene remembered suddenly the meeting between Ryan and Mazent on the night of the party. There had been something of a private nature between them all right, but surely it could not be what Madame Tusard was hinting at so strongly?

"Inkling of what?" she asked bluntly.

"Why, that Mazent was bent on persuading Bayard to wed his daughter."

"I don't believe it."

"As you please, *chère*, but Claude certainly heard it being discussed. I am sorry if it distressed you; that was not at all my intention. Regardless, I could not let it pass without giving you a warning. Men can be so unkind to females in your position."

The sympathy was so perfunctory that it crossed Elene's mind to wonder if the disturbing possibility Françoise Tusard had handed her was not a form of revenge. Elene had embarrassed the woman, and she had struck at Elene where she was most vulnerable in retaliation.

Surely she could not be so petty? Elene's gaffe had been purest accident, after all. Oh, but human beings were capable of being very petty indeed when it came to matters of pride.

They could also be stubborn. Elene did not get up and leave at once as she most fervently desired. In order to prove that she was not in the least disturbed, she sat talking for a good half hour longer. She stayed, in fact, until it became a near social solecism that she had not been offered refreshment, a lack all too obviously caused by the want of a servant to prepare and bring it. Only when Madame Tusard in desperation offered to pour her a glass of orange flower water and cut her a slice of cake with her own hands did Elene, with all graciousness, decline and depart.

That small victory did nothing for her spirits. Her footsteps dragged as she made her way back to Ryan's house. She went over and over the evening when Mazent and Ryan had been closeted together, but could come to no conclusion. That had been the night she had come down with fever, and nothing about it was clear.

She could ask Ryan, of course. She might have, if there was not so much distance between them. But what was the point? At the time of the discussion, supposing it had taken place, she had been wearing her perfume, and it was impossible that he could have agreed then to a marriage. Soon after, Mazent had died. If the option had still been open, which she doubted, Ryan would have mentioned it had he decided to take it.

Or would he?

Ryan and Flora.

No, it could not be. There had been nothing whatever to indicate such a thing. Nothing, except, perhaps, that he felt sorry for the girl, except that he had a liking for easily obtained riches, and Flora was apparently quite an heiress.

Surely Flora would not have importuned Elene for perfume to entice the very man with whom she was living. That would take effrontery beyond imagining, or else a colossal ego, so that no one's feelings and needs mattered except her own.

No. It just was not possible. It was not.

In late September, there came a gale. The sky grew yellow and roiling. The wind high among the clouds sent them chasing along. The trees thrashed and groaned. The seabirds appeared from the marshlands to the south, but did not tarry on their way inland. The river rose and also the lake. The wind veered to come from the north, chasing away the heavy heat that had smothered them all summer, turning the day unnaturally cool. Slowly the sky grew dark, and darker still.

The rain began as a fine mist that tasted of salt. With every hour, it grew harder, drumming on the roofs, pelting from the eaves, gathering in the streets until they were full from banquette to banquette. Still it fell.

The wind rose, whipping the sheets of water, snapping them into curling spray like wash on a line. Shutters rattled under the impact, and roofing shingles and tiles were torn free and sent tumbling to the ground yards away. Bits of bark and leaves filled the air. Tree limbs smashed into the sides of houses or fell with thundering crashes into courtyards. The rain grew harder, falling as heavy and thick as warm lead from a sky the color of steel.

In the height of the storm's fury, Elene lay in Ryan's arms, replete with loving that had somehow partaken of the wild and elemental nature of the gale. She listened to the rain and to the heartbeat under her cheek, and felt safe, content. Ryan stroked her hair and the curves of her shoulders, cupped her breasts to taste them one after the other, and clasped her hips in his hands to draw her against his reviving male hardness. Secure in the return of his desire and her own, awash with sated and insatiable love, she was aghast that she had ever doubted him.

Toward midnight of an endless day, worn out with loving and discarded fears, soothed by the endless song of the rain, she slept in Ryan's arms.

When she awoke, the storm was over.

And Serephine was dead.

CHAPTER 16

THE gathering was noisy, overly bright with the extravagant use of candles, too warm with the crowding of too many guests in too small a place with too few windows, and totally unorganized. The dinner that preceded the dancing had featured an excess number of heavy dishes served without elegance. The wine, though plentiful, was cheap, and the orange flower water and tafia that accompanied it were both too weak and too sweet. The music was much louder than necessary. The floor had not been waxed so that the grit tracked in on the shoes of the dancers made a scraping sound that rasped on the nerves. The clothing of the men was too somber and far too heavy for the climate, while that of the ladies lacked refinement, style, or, in some cases, even decency.

The party was American, in celebration of the confirmation of the cession of Louisiana, even though the transfer was still delayed. Doubtless the arrangements would have seemed elegant in another place, under other circumstances, but Elene was in no mood to be pleased.

Elene had not wanted to come, but Ryan had insisted. The host was a business acquaintance of his originally from Boston in the United States, a man of wealth and influence who was also a friend. There was nothing to be gained by ignoring such men, he said, except a reputation for clannish snobbery and discourtesy. The Americans were here to stay, and soon there would be more of them. It was a fact of life, one they must learn to live with whether they wished it or not. A new era was beginning, one that promised prosperity. The French could become a part of it, or be left behind. The choice was simple.

It was a choice Ryan had made without regret, or so it appeared. He moved with ease among the Americans, the Spanish, and the French alike, a man respected by all. Whatever he might have been in the past, it was plain that he was a man of standing here in New Orleans now. The city, once a provincial backwater, was on the edge of a new frontier and a vast new future. What was required to make it prosper were men of vision and daring. Ryan, it seemed, was just such a man.

The gathering was graced by the presence of the colonial prefect and his lovely wife, who was barely showing her delicate condition in the current forgiving fashion in gowns with high waistlines. Also present were Bernard Marigny and Etienne de Bore, the latter rumored to be Laussat's choice as mayor of New Orleans if the French regime ever came into being, plus a number of other prominent men of business from the French community. In one corner sat Madame Tusard, whispering to her husband while her sharp gaze darted about the room. Claude Tusard nodded dutifully as he sipped his wine, but had a gloomy, trapped expression on his face. Nearby stood Rachel Pitot, dressed in black satin daringly trimmed with ruby-red silk, thought to be the color of the devil, and with a red-dyed aigrette in her high-piled hair. She had a retinue of young men about her, though she still searched the crowd with avid eyes for others.

The only other member of their group from Saint-Domingue who was in evidence was Durant. He leaned his shoulder against the wall on the far side of the room from where Elene stood, an elegant and remote figure in white knee breeches, gray satin waistcoat embroidered in black, and a gray satin coat. There was a drawn look about his face, however, that was as much a reminder of his recent loss as the black arm band on his coat sleeve.

As if he could feel her scrutiny, Durant turned to look in Elene's direction. For an instant their eyes met, a clash of gray and black. There was weariness in his expression, and pain, and a fleeting glimpse of longing. A moment later, he turned away.

Elene danced with Ryan and with their host, and then with Ryan again. It was good to discover that her strength was equal to the exertion, particularly as the hour was growing late. She had been telling Ryan for days, since the weather had turned cooler after the storm, that she was completely recovered from her fever; perhaps now he would believe her.

The American's house was in a much coveted location, being one of those near the levee that looked out over the river. The breeze from the water blew through its rooms and there was a fine view of the wide crescent turn of the Mississippi just before the city. As the dancing began to pall near midnight, the guests were invited to step outside for a special treat.

A buzz of anticipation ran around the room. People began to crowd toward the long windows that opened out onto the railed gallery. If the American had thought to surprise his guests, however, he should have made other arrangements, for as they moved outside whispers of "pyrotechnics" ran among them. They were all craning their necks expectantly when the first explosion of fireworks went off.

The fireballs soared out over the water from somewhere below the house, glowing puff-balls of blue and green, yellow and red that chased each other into the dark, star-sprinkled sky. The colors lit the night, staining the up-turned faces of those who watched, and were reflected in the gliding surface of the river. The popping, thudding, whizzing noises filled the air, while the thundering bursts of the rocket explosions echoed back from the far shore. Set pieces, anchored on barges in the river, were set alight, great spluttering and sparkling fountains and trees, dragons and catherine wheels of fire. Hardly had the last such fiery piece died away to the sound of wonder and applause before more rockets went up, climbing higher, bursting louder, showering down more fiery sparks.

Elene, standing near the front railing, felt the movement at her side before Durant spoke. "A vulgar display, but impressive."

"Yes."

"One assumes that's the way it will be now. The Americans have much energy but little finesse." When she made no answer, he said abruptly, "You might have paid a condolence call."

She sent him a quick glance. The light of a blue and gold fireball made his face look bruised. "I'm sorry about Serephine, truly I am. I would have called if I had thought it would help, but the situation was rather . . . awkward."

He drew breath, then let it out in a sigh. "I suppose so."

"It must have been quite a shock."

"Yes."

An uncomfortable silence fell. Elene was tempted to make some excuse and leave him, perhaps to join Ryan who was with his host a few feet away. There was something about Durant, an air of dejection, an intimation of despair, that prevented it.

Reaching up to touch the arm band he wore, she said, "This is a lovely gesture."

"Under the circumstances, you mean? Because Serephine was no more than my mistress, and a quadroon at that?"

"I'm sorry," she said, withdrawing her hand.

"No, please, I know you didn't mean it like that. I don't know what's wrong with me."

"You loved her, that's all."

He gave a hollow laugh. "You understand that, don't you? It's funny, but I think you must be the only person I know in all the world who does."

"You need not speak of it if you prefer, but we've heard so little about her death. Was she ill long?"

"Ill? She wasn't ill at all."

She met his gaze. "You mean—it wasn't the fever?"

"By no means. The police have not concerned themselves greatly in the matter, Serephine being what she was, but they seem to think I may have killed her."

"You?"

Around them, people turned to stare. Ryan swung to look in their direction, and a frown drew his brows together. Durant said hurriedly, "I can't explain here. But I would like to talk about it, if you will permit me to call."

What could she say? The past that lay between them would have demanded that she give him a hearing, even if compassion and curiosity had not. Elene agreed, and together they turned to watch the pyrotechnics, their shoulders touching in a way that was almost companionable.

On the following morning, Durant presented himself after Ryan had left the house, but before Elene was dressed. It might be the custom for certain ladies, such as Napoleon's sister Pauline, to admit men into their boudoirs while they bathed and donned their clothes, but Elene had no intention of following their lead. It was bad enough to receive a man without Ryan being present; there was no point in exacerbating the situation unduly. Instructing Benedict to serve Durant coffee and cakes in the salon, she sent a message also that she would join him there at length.

It was a gray day, with a misting rain falling beyond the windows and an unseasonable coolness in the air. Elene wore a paisley shawl over her morning gown of yellow muslin, though she was sure that she would have to discard it immediately if the sun came out. She held the shawl's fringe back with one hand and gave the other to Durant as he rose to greet her. As he kissed the smooth backs of her fingers, then stood holding them while he looked down at her, she felt a moment of uncomfortable familiarity. They had met like this many times in the days of his courtship. It was possible this visit was going to be a mistake.

They seated themselves across from each other. Durant smiled at her as he leaned back with one elbow propped on the arm of the settee and his chin between his thumb and forefinger. "I always forget how beautiful you are when I'm away from you. I used to think my life was perfect, you know, all those acres of cane beside the sea and a gracious home, servants to do my bidding, the amusement of the town when the country palled, a compliant mistress, and the prospect of a beautiful and intelligent wife."

"I see I came last," she said in an attempt at lightness.

"Only because you were to be the final and most perfect addition."

Flirtation or truth? It was impossible to tell, and in any case, it did not matter. She gave him a straight look. "Fate decreed otherwise."

"Yes, and now it's gone, all of it."

She allowed a moment of respect for his very real losses before she spoke again. "I don't at all understand about Serephine. Why should the authorities think you killed her?"

"I suppose they don't actually, or I would be in the calabozo kicking my heels and listening to the gallows being built outside. It was merely a possibility that held their attention for a time. They seemed to think I might have wished to be rid of her and decided poisoning her was easier than providing for her."

"Poison," Elene said slowly. "Not . . . arsenic?"

"Exactly."

Questions crowded in upon her, too numerous to be sorted into coherent thought. Frowning in concentration, she fastened on a portion of what he had said. "Why should anyone think you wanted to be rid of her?"

"I have no idea." He made a quick gesture with one hand without looking at her.

"Don't you really?"

"All right, we had quarreled, a rather noisy quarrel over a trunkful of new gowns she had ordered. But that was no reason to kill her."

Elene could not picture Serephine quarreling with Durant. She had always been so—what was the word he had used? Compliant. That was it. Serephine had always smiled and agreed, smiled and obeyed. People did not always behave in private as they did in public; still, the quarrel did not ring true. It was more likely that Durant had been abusive, berating his mistress for her extravagance.

Aloud, she said, "I thought you had brought enough wealth with you from the islands that you had no need to worry over a few gowns."

"So a great many people thought," he said with a shrug. "One can only borrow so long."

"Borrow?"

"Tailors and carriage makers have an uncomfortable habit of demanding to be paid. Borrowing is one way to satisfy them."

She assumed he meant he had borrowed against his estates on the island; it was possible there was a lender willing to gamble on their return. It would be ill mannered to pry further. "Was Serephine upset? I mean, was she distraught enough to—"

"You mean, did I drive her to take the poison herself? I don't know."

His words were hard, to cover his pain and the guilt that rode him. That was why he was so haggard. It was the guilt.

"I don't believe it."

The hope that sprang into his face was distressing to see. "Don't you?"

"She enjoyed living, enjoyed loving too much. She may not have thought about tomorrow and its problems; her concern was for the present and its pleasures. That kind of person doesn't take her own life."

There was in Elene's mind a disturbing echo. She had said much the same thing about Hermine, hadn't she?

Durant gave a hard nod. "I know that's what she was like, but I can't seem to convince anybody else. If they don't have the sensational murder of a mistress by her paramour on their hands, they aren't interested. The clerks write down everything carefully, then go away and push the papers into a drawer somewhere and forget them. They look at me, and I can see they think that if I didn't kill her myself with an arsenic draught, then I did it with words, words that threw her into such despair she couldn't bear to live."

"There was a rumor," Elene said carefully, "that you were about to contract an advantageous marriage."

He stared at her. "Where did you hear that? Not that it matters. It isn't true. I promise you it isn't true at all."

They went on to speak of this and that, of Morven who was rumored to be conducting a discreet affair at the moment with the wife of a prominent Spanish official, in spite of residing still with his widow and new ingenue, and of M'sieur Tusard who was seen often, according to Durant, in the gaming halls beyond the city walls. There came the time, finally, when Durant could prolong the call no longer without encroaching on the noon meal. Elene walked with him to the door of the salon where Benedict appeared with his hat and cane.

With these accoutrements in his hand, Durant bowed once more. "This has been most pleasant. It was good of you to receive me; I didn't expect it."

"I don't have so many friends and acquaintances in New Orleans that I can afford to ignore one of them."

"That puts me in my place along with everyone else," he said with a wry smile. "I hope it also means you will allow me to come again?"

"Of course. Though not too often when Ryan isn't here."

He smiled again without replying, then released her hand and turned to go. After two steps, he turned back. "I don't like to disturb you, Elene, but I can't leave without asking—"

"What is it?" she asked as he came to a halt.

"I have been wondering, are you sure your own illness was yellow fever?"

"Reasonably sure. Why?"

"Nothing," he said, with a shake of his head. "Nothing at all." Turning again, he walked away down the stairs.

Yellow fever or poison?

That question and a thousand others haunted Elene for days.

She thought she had had yellow fever, had been told that was her illness, but was it so in truth? It must be. The symptoms had been there, the fever, the red lips, the black bile pouring from her throat, and then the yellow skin. What else could it be?

Except that arsenic, administered in small doses, could cause many of the same symptoms.

No, it was impossible. Her skin had been as yellow as sunflowers.

But there were other substances that could be given a person to bring jaundice to the skin.

She would not believe it. The colonial prefect and a hundred others had been stricken with yellow fever at the same time. It had been epidemic, as it was to a greater or lesser extent every summer in most southern ports. She had had the same doctor as Laussat, a chemist from Paris who must know arsenic poisoning when he saw it, and could certainly compare two cases of yellow fever. Like the colonial prefect,

she had survived the tropical malady, which made her one of the lucky
ones. Instead of raising specters for herself, she should be thinking of
who might have killed Serephine.

The problem was, there was no one. Serephine had had no enemies,
had not been a threat to a soul. Even if Durant had wished to be
married, which he denied, Serephine had been no impediment. She had
been totally harmless, a lovely and generous plaything who lived only to
provide happiness for Durant. The only possible reason she might have
been killed, and it was grasping at straws indeed, was for revenge
against Durant.

There was, of course, the similarity between Serephine and Hermine.
The actress had lived to give joy to many on the stage and to Morven in
private, but had been a danger to no one. Everyone had liked her.

And yet, was that strictly true? Madame Tusard had accused her of
leading her husband astray. It had been a mistake, but the accusation
had been made. Josie, as subsequent events had shown, had coveted the
roles the more experienced actress played and also the caresses of
Morven. Rachel Pitot might even have felt that Hermine stood in the
way of her final possession of the handsome actor.

Poison, they did say, was a woman's weapon.

But what possible connection could there be between Hermine and
Serephine? The answer appeared to be none. They hardly knew one
another, had scarcely spoken. They had been chance passengers on the
same ship, nothing more. Nothing.

So had M'sieur Mazent been on that ship, and he was also dead of
arsenic. And yet, even if there could be found some tenuous link between the two women, it seemed highly unlikely that they could both be
found to have anything in common with the middle-aged planter.

Yet, there had to be something. There had to be.

There was.

It was perfume.

Hermine had owned a small blue bottle of Paradise, as had Serephine.
Mazent had never owned one himself, but his mistress Germaine had,
and had shared it with his daughter.

Was it possible there was something in the perfume that could kill?
Perhaps the same thing that could enslave?

No, no, it didn't make sense. Elene herself had used it longer than
any, and she was not dead.

She had been ill.

Fever, she had had yellow fever.

Suppose it wasn't? Suppose it was simply that some people were weaker or more susceptible to the deadly ingredient than others? Or that some of the bottles had more of it, whatever it might be?

Suppose that the perfume Devota had made for her in Saint-Domingue was different from that they had made together in New Orleans? There had been that extra something Devota had added to the perfume mixture while she herself was gone from the room.

She was being foolish. Hermine and Mazent and Serephine had been killed by arsenic, not some secret Voudou concoction. Everyone agreed that was the cause of death.

What if they were wrong?

What if there was poison in the perfume, a decoction of arsenic that was absorbed through the skin to kill like the white lead of the face powder used by actresses? If that was possible, there might be other deaths. Unless Germaine had told the truth about the breaking of the perfume bottle, she could be the next to die. Or else whoever it was that had stolen Madame Pitot's bottle.

If that were possible, then the full weight of responsibility for so many deaths must lie on Elene's shoulders, for she was the one who had insisted on making the ill-fated scent.

Oh, but what possible reason could Devota have for putting such a thing into the perfume? With her knowledge of plants and herbs, it could hardly be an accident.

It might be possible that some container, either at the apothecary's shop or wherever Devota had gotten the extra scents she needed, had been labeled wrong; that could happen to anyone. Devota had no cause to set out to kill anyone, least of all Elene herself.

Was that really true?

There had been many mulattoes in the slave quarters on Saint-Domingue who had risen to kill those related to them by blood in the big houses. Devota was half-white, half-black, something that could not be forgotten, however much they both might try. Because of her blood, she was forever relegated to the life of a servant. No, not a servant; that was a polite euphemism. Devota was Elene's slave.

If Elene died, Devota would be without a mistress. Elene had no heirs to receive her property, had no legal document stating its dispensation, and with the colony of Louisiana in such a ferment of change, the government might well forget to take possession of her estate, which consisted entirely of one slave, Devota. Thousands had been killed on Saint-Domingue to ensure freedom for those enslaved.

Still, what earthly purpose could she have had for killing Hermine? Or Mazent, for that matter?

Did there have to be a purpose beyond the color of their skin? Could it have been that random? Serephine, however, was her own kind. Surely she would not have harmed her.

Such terrible suspicions to be forced to entertain, and all because of a memorable perfume. It was enough, almost, to make her wish never to smell it again.

There was a decision to be made. Elene could do nothing, and hope that she was wrong, that the deaths which had occurred had nothing whatever to do with her or her perfume. Or she could try to discover what Devota had put in the mixture they had made, to test the extent of Devota's guilt and her own responsibility. She was horribly tempted to do the first. If she had caused the death of innocent people, she did not think she could bear knowing it. Nonetheless, she must know. The chance that she might save others demanded it.

Elene moved along the gallery in search of Devota. She could hear her humming somewhere, a rich, tuneful melody tinged with melancholy. She followed it to the dressing room off Ryan's bedchamber.

The maid sat on a stool mending a small three-corner tear in the sleeve of one of Ryan's shirts. Her head was bent over her work as her needle flashed in and out, and the expression on her soft brown face was absorbed, intent on the job at hand. Her tignon was snowy white, but shot with blue silk thread, and her dress of blue chambray had been carefully starched and ironed. Neat, competent, industrious, she was the picture of the perfect servant.

"Devota?"

The woman looked up, startled. "*Chère*! You will give me a heart attack, sneaking up on me like that. Why didn't you call if you wanted me, or send that no-good Benedict?"

"There was something I wanted to ask you, in private."

The smile faded from Devota's face as she surveyed Elene's features. She knotted her thread and snapped if off, then shook out the shirt she held before laying it aside. She got to her feet. "Yes, *chère*?"

"It's about the perfume." A tight knot formed in Elene's throat, clogging speech. She looked at this woman she had known all her life, and the question she was about to ask seemed so wounding an insult she could not bring herself to give it voice.

Devota gave a slow nod. "I have been waiting, wondering when you would ask."

"Have you? Then it can't be true, you can't have put anything in it that would kill. I knew you couldn't have."

The maid's eyes widened with shock. "Kill!"

"I thought you were expecting—"

"Never! Never did I think you would ask such a thing!"

"It had to be done. People are dying, people who have had contact with our perfume. I can't ignore that."

"You think I killed them? I? Why should I do that? Tell me why!"

Never could Elene remember Devota being so belligerent. Never had she heard her raise her voice so high or seen such wrath in her black eyes. Evasively, she said, "I don't know why."

"I think you do. I think that like all whites these days, you look at the color of my skin and you see an enemy. You forget what has gone before, all the years of love. All you see is black, black, black!"

"Three people are dead! What I want is to know how it happened and who did it. Don't you understand? If it was something in the perfume, I have to know. I have to, because if it was, I'm to blame. I helped to kill them."

Devota stared at her, her face calming. "Oh, God, *chère*. Oh, my dearest God."

So intent were they on each other that they did not hear the quiet footsteps as Benedict entered the room. The clearing of his throat had the sound of thunder. He said, "There was nothing in the perfume."

Elene swung on him with jangling nerves. "What do you know of it?"

"Nothing whatever, except that I have smelled this scent in the house night and day. I know this woman of yours is not such a person as could kill others by stealth, at random, the guilty and innocent alike. She has no such hate in her. She might kill in anger, but not otherwise."

Devota looked at the tall, thin man with his impassive face through narrowed eyes. "I thank you, I'm sure."

"I rather thought you would," Benedict said, and bowed.

For an instant there was something vital, almost tangibly alive, in the air between the two servants. Then Devota turned to Elene.

"I will bring you what is left of the perfume. You will do with it as you will. Test it. Taste it. Use it. Pour it away. I don't care. It was made for you, for your aid and pleasure. It has nothing to do with me."

Devota left the room. Benedict melted away in silence behind her. Elene also moved from the dressing room, though she was hardly aware of what she was doing.

In the center of the connecting bedchamber, she stopped. She stood staring down at the mille-fleur pattern of the Flemish carpet in red and blue and gold with blank concentration. It did not help. Beyond Devota, there was Madame Tusard to suspect of these terrible deeds, and after her, no one.

Devota swept into the bedchamber with the remaining bottles of perfume in her hands. She set them down on the table nearest Elene, next to the bed, then turned away.

"Wait," Elene said. "I mean no insult, no slight, but there is one more thing I must know."

"Yes?" The word was stiff with hurt feelings.

"Is there no way, by accident or design, that anything harmful could have been put in the perfume without you knowing?"

"Perfume is all odor, a collection of pure essences both weak and strong. To those who have the nose to smell, any least thing added or subtracted changes the ultimate bouquet in greater or lesser measure. There can be no arsenic in this scent, for it smells of garlic and would overpower all other scents. So it is with most other things I know that might cause harm. Therefore, it cannot be. Cease torturing yourself, *chère*; you have no blame."

"What is this? What's going on?"

It was Ryan who asked, pushing into the room in time to hear Devota's last words. Elene's head came up as she turned to face him. "It was nothing."

"I don't think so. What is it about the perfume now? Has it suddenly gained the power to make the bureaucrats in Paris move faster? Or has it persuaded Salcedo and Morales to love the Americans so much they are offering apologies for abuses?"

His tone was bantering, but hard with impatience. It was also annoying. "Nothing so beneficial," Elene said in caustic tones. "I was attempting to ease my mind on its role in these murders."

Ryan made a curt, dismissive gesture toward Devota who went out and closed the door. Moving toward Elene, he passed her and went to lean against the end of the high mattress of the bed with his arms crossed over his chest and his booted feet crossed at the ankle. With deliberation, he said, "I believe I had better hear more of this."

She explained as succinctly as possible, though as she spoke, she grew more and more attuned to how utterly beyond rational thought were the things she was saying. Still, she had to go on to the end in spite of her faltering logic, in spite of the flush of mortification that rose to her cheekbones as she saw the disbelief in his hawk-like face.

"You think," he said slowly when she was done, "that this perfume of yours can not only make men behave in ways entirely contrary to their natures, but also cause disease and even death?"

"Not just the perfume itself, but something in it. There have always been whispers that poison was behind the ability of the priests and priestesses of the Voudou to wish death on a person. I know it sounds crazy, but I thought Devota could have—that is, that she might have wanted revenge or else been paid to cause those deaths. I don't know exactly what I thought, if you must have the truth. It just seemed a possibility that could not be ignored."

"Because, if it were so, you were at fault."

She made a quick, embarrassed gesture, looking away from him toward the mosquito netting that draped the head of the bed. "Something like that."

"You would be at fault because Devota was your slave."

"Yes, and my responsibility."

He pushed away from the bed, coming erect, and caught her arms in his hands. He drew her so close that she had to press her hands against his chest to prevent herself from falling against him.

"Once and for all," he said quietly, "your perfume has no magic powers, for good or ill. It's a nice smell, that's all."

She lifted her head to meet the clear blue of his eyes without evasion. "How can you know?"

"I know. The need I have for you comes from inside me, not from a few drops of liquid out of a bottle. It's in my heart and mind and the part of me that longs to sink, hot and firm, inside you. Your perfume is no threat to me. I am no woman's slave, not even yours, though I want you enough now, this minute, to give up my best hope of freedom in exchange for an hour in your arms. But I can walk away from you if need be. I can leave you, not without regret, but certainly without endangering my life or mangling my soul beyond repair. I don't need you to live."

His words dropped like acid into her mind, burning, eating away at her pride. The confidence in his tone brought the rise of rage. Her gray eyes dark with a mixture of pain and disdain, she said, "If you are so sure, then why don't you go?"

"I will."

"What?" She was so close to him she could feel the heat of his need, the taut muscles of his thighs. Underneath her hands spread over his chest, his heart thudded in mute denial of his calm words.

"I will prove that I can go. I leave for Washington City as soon as I can make ready, to bring back the official authorization for the double transfer of Louisiana. I go at Laussat's request, to hasten this long, drawn-out process of change from one country to another, but also to convince you that I can."

"All right, go then!"

She tried to wrench away from his grasp, but it was useless. He pulled her closer, encircling her in his hard embrace so that her breasts were flattened against his chest. He smoothed one hand down her back to clasp the curve of her hip while he lowered his gaze to the pink and moist surface of her lips that were parted with her quickened breathing.

"Ah, no, not without a last whiff of perfume and a proper and passionate farewell. Where would be the glory in riding away without that? Where would be the victory?"

It was a challenge, one Elene was loath to accept, but one her heart could not refuse. She flung herself against him as he pulled her closer, straining on tip-toe to meet the hard force of his kiss. Her lips trembled as they conformed to his firm demand, but she would not lessen the hard pressure of her own that bruised them both. She slid her hands up behind his head, tangling her fingers in his hair, clasping the corded strength of his neck. She thrust her breasts against him until they ached, and writhed her hips in slow and agonizing need so that the heated softness of her cradled the hard form of his maleness.

He caught a harsh breath. With hands that had lost their usual dexterity, he slipped the buttons of her gown from their holes and drew it from her shoulders along with her wide-necked camisole. She aided him, sliding the garments to her waist, loosening the tape of her pantaloons and single petticoat, letting them fall. Then moving close to him once more, she pulled his shirt from his breeches and unbuttoned their front flap while he dragged his shirt off over his head in swift divestment. As he levered off his boots, she kicked out of her own slippers. Then she hoisted herself onto the bed, where she began to unfasten her garters.

Ryan stopped her with a swift gesture as he stripped his breeches free and slung them aside. In magnificent nakedness, he moved to stand between her knees, spreading them wider as he released her garters one after the other, then peeled the silk of her stockings down over her knees and calves. He knelt to press his lips to the ticklish and smooth turns of her knees, then trailed moist fire along the sensitive inner surface of her thighs to their juncture. He toppled her backward onto the mattress with a deliberate push as he directed his attention there, and Elene, suffused with lovely wanton pleasure, let herself fall.

She should protest, should do something to regain the initiative, but she was lost in delight and difficult, painful fatalism. If this was the last time, and it might well be, then let it be special, a loving to remember.

His touch fired the blood in her veins to hot and thunderous desire. Like a scalding cataract, it poured through her, coalescing in the core of her being to form a whirlpool with an aching emptiness at its center. Nothing mattered except to have him fill it.

When he stood up, she reached for him, but he did not join her. Instead, he stepped to the side table and picked up one of the perfume bottles that sat there. Removing the stopper, he turned toward the bed.

Elene's eyes widened. She sat up, turning to her side and lifting her legs onto the bed. Her voice husky, she said, "What are you doing?"

"The test would not be complete without this, now would it?" He hefted the bottle so that a few droplets of the scented liquid splattered over the lip. It dripped onto his fingers and fell to the sheet, releasing its familiar fragrance on the air.

It was disturbing that he was so detached while desire pulsed heated and uncontrolled under her skin. She moistened her lips. "I suppose not."

"Then lie back down."

She did as he directed while he placed a knee on the mattress, raising himself up on to the bed. The moment she lay flat, he sprinkled the perfume over her, beginning between her breasts and ending at her knees. Quickly, before the trickling rivulets could escape, he massaged the precious liquid into her skin with sweeping strokes, kneading the scent into the white mounds of her breasts, the narrow sides of her waist and the flat surface of her abdomen; into the fine-spun triangle of gold at the apex of her legs, and over the slender flair of her hips and the delicate white skin of her inner thighs. A shiver of reaction ran over Elene, and he smiled with bright and tender resolution before he lowered his body to cover hers.

His weight pressing her into the softness of the moss-filled mattress was welcome, gratifying in some manner to her sensitized skin. Their contours meshed, hardness and softness, in a perfect, if not quite complete, union. The odor of the perfume rose around them, heated by their bodies to a cloying richness. It blended with their own scents, male and female, to produce a mind-drugging ambience. He moved upon her, spreading the delicate oils that dewed her body over his own, absorbing it even as his prickling body hair, the hard contours of his chest and ridged thighs, sent frissons of delight spiraling through her. They glided together, titillating each other with gentle nudges, enthralled by the burgeoning, engulfing grandeur. Elene could feel the jarring of his heart, the taut strength of the control he imposed upon himself. She endured it, revering him for it, until on a crest of joy, she eased her thighs apart and took him inside her in a sweet, liquid slide.

The shock of fevered excitement rippled through her. She was suffused with it, so that a strangled cry caught in her throat and she arched her back to rise against him. He met her need, striving, driving deep and deeper still with infinite strength and inflexible will. She absorbed the jolting force of his strokes as her senses expanded. Her breath was ragged, gasping in her ears. Her heartbeat thudded in a wild rhythm. Still, she was held, firm and secure in his arms.

It came from inside, spreading in vivid, fiery wonder, the crimson tide of surcease. Elene, on a sob, let it wash over her. Ryan felt its surge in her silken depths, and surrendered to it. Held in its fearsome grasp, lost in its rapturous wonder, they were still. And opening their eyes, they stared at each other in silent, useless glory.

A moment later he rolled to his side, taking her with him, still fused, inseparable. He rocked with her back and forth in an agony of tenderness, inhaling the fragrance of her hair, imprinting the shape and feel of her upon his body. He sought her lips, kissing her hard once, twice. Then, moving as if his muscles were cramped with reluctance, he placed her on her back and rolled away from her.

Rising, he walked to the washstand where he used cold water and a cake of soap to wash away the stench of perfume. Drying himself with vigor, he tossed the toweling across a chair and moved to the armoire where he took out a pair of leather riding breeches and a rough coat of similar quality.

Short minutes later, he was dressed, except for a shallow-brimmed hat that he held in one hand along with a strapped roll of extra clothing. He stepped toward the door and put one hand on the knob, then turned back. His gaze traveled over her as she lay there, her skin gleaming palely in the shuttered dimness. With a quiet oath, he left the door, to move swiftly toward her. He swooped to taste the proud nipple of one rounded breast, then snatched a hard kiss from her lips.

Straightening abruptly, he went to the door once more and pulled it open. Turning back, with bleak pain in his eyes, he said, "If this is victory, I prefer defeat."

The door closed behind him.

CHAPTER 17

HE was gone.

Elene lay staring up into the soft drapings of mosquito netting looped up for the day until Ryan's footsteps faded away along the gallery and down the stairs. She did not move until the silence and lack of stir indicated that, like a storm passing, he was no longer in the house. She rolled slowly to her stomach then, burying her face in the pillow.

She did not cry. Her chest was tight and her breathing came in short, hard gasps, but the tears were locked inside. He had left her. In spite of the perfume. In spite of the union of their bodies. It was not supposed to be possible, but it had happened.

It had happened because she loved him. She had known it, felt the caring growing inside her. Devota had warned her. To fall in love would be to lose control of the relationship between her and her man. She had said something more, something about a loving heart, but Elene could not quite bring it to mind.

Ryan thought he had vanquished the spell the perfume had over him, or at least proven to her that he was unaffected by it. Perhaps he had; she no longer knew what to believe. But why had he gone so far away?

It was not necessary to put his life in danger to prove that she could not hold him. He could be killed on the long ride to Washington City. He was a privateer, not a courier. It was nothing more than male pride that forced him to that long, grueling trek through the wilderness.

No, that was not true. She must be fair. The mission he was on had nothing to do with her. He was a man concerned with the fate of

Louisiana, his native land. The great events stirring in the colony were of vital importance to him, and he had been drawn into their vortex. It was a part of his life in which she had no place.

There was nothing to say that she had a place in his life of any kind. He had spoken to her of wants and needs and of adoration, the last an intense response that must have been perfume induced. Simple, perfect love he had not mentioned, except when she was ill with fever, when he had thought she needed to hear it to go on living.

Devota had not promised her love, of course. Desire, yes. A surpassing devotion of the flesh. Enthrallment. The enslavement of her mate. All these things. She had had them in full measure and they had brought excitement, even rapture. But how fleeting they were, and how empty, without love.

How could it be that two people could share such intimacy, such mutual and total possession and untrammeled joy, and only one of them succumb to love? Was it possible that in duping him, albeit unwittingly, with her perfume, she had traded the chance that he might love her for an ephemeral attachment of the senses? If during those three nights in the dark hole under Favier's house she had not worn scent, what would have happened between them? Would they have discovered a slower growing but deeper and more abiding attraction, or would they have each sat in their separate corners, making polite conversation, never touching? Which would she have preferred? To have had the passion they had shared, or to have had nothing at all?

When Devota came into the room sometime later, Elene closed her eyes and breathed in a deep and even rhythm. The woman went silently away again. When evening came, the maid brought a tray with a light supper of baked chicken, crusty bread, and wine, with a crème caramel for dessert. Elene forced down a few bites, but could do no more. She sent Devota away, blew out the candle, and pulled up the covers.

When morning came, she was heavy and drugged with sleep, but unrested and disinclined to leave her bed. She held the cup of her morning café au lait, but watched Devota with a dull gaze as she bustled about, throwing back the draperies and picking up the scattered clothing. She permitted herself to be bathed and the bed linens to be changed, though more because the smell of the stale perfume was abhorrent to her than because she had any desire for freshness. She wanted nothing, in fact, except a quiet, dim room and the oblivion of sleep.

"*Chère*? Are you going to stay in that bed forever?" Devota made her demand with her hands on her hips.

Elene pushed the hair back from her face and pressed her hand to her eyes. Finally she answered, "I don't know."

"You've got to get up. You frighten me, *chère*. This isn't like you."

"Get up and do what?"

"Something. Anything. M'sieur Ryan left money for the shopping. You can go to the market."

"Benedict can go."

"He worries himself about you, too, Benedict does. M'sieur Ryan will blame him if you are ill when he returns."

"Will he indeed?"

"Benedict thinks so."

"He's wrong. I doubt very much that Ryan will care."

"What do you mean? Of course he will care!"

Elene sat up in bed. Her voice hard, she said, "He left me, Devota!" Then more softly she repeated, "He left me."

"He will return."

"You said—you told me he would be enslaved to me, that he would only wish to please me."

"Is that what you want in a man, a slave?"

Elene swallowed tears as she shook her head in a quick negative. "But I never thought he would want to go away from me. I didn't think he could."

"This is why you eat little and lie in bed all day?"

Elene shook her head, unable to speak for the knot of grief in her throat. Tears filled her eyes and spilled over to run in wet tracks down her cheeks. Finally she whispered, "If I get up, I'll have to leave."

A frown gathered on Devota's soft brown face. "Leave?"

"Leave this house, find a place elsewhere."

"But—why?"

Elene looked at her in despair for the necessity of explaining the unexplainable. "I can't stay with a man who doesn't love me."

"How can you say—"

"He doesn't. I trapped him, and now he's set himself free. I will not be a mere convenience for a privateer."

"You know he is much more than that," Devota said sternly.

"The principle is the same."

"This is foolish! You needed him before and you need him now. That much hasn't changed."

"Nor will I use him for my convenience."

"Even if he wishes it? Even if the convenience is equal?"

"Even so. I know the situation is the same; I see that. But I am different. I love him, but there is more to it than that. With this perfume of ours, I first took advantage of him, and now may have embroiled him in something far worse. I can't stay and let him reap the result of it, whatever it may be."

"You mean the murders. That was no fault of mine or yours, I swear it. Can't you believe me?"

"I can't take that chance."

"These principles you have so many of, you cannot eat them. How will we live? Where will we go?"

"I don't know. I have been trying to think, but nothing seems to come."

"Then maybe nothing will come before M'sieur Ryan returns," the woman said with mingled irony and hope.

Devota went away. Elene sat drinking her coffee and chewing slowly on a bite of one of the feather-light beignets that was her breakfast. She felt better, now that the decision she had felt weighing upon her had been put into words. However, the problem of what she was going to do remained.

She had no money, no means to take a place of her own. That meant she must rely on her acquaintances, at least for a short time. If Hermine were alive, her problem would be solved, she thought; the actress would have found a place for her somewhere, a pallet to sleep on and a small job of some kind to do. Josie was not so inventive or so sympathetic. Morven might be helpful, but she was afraid that, with Ryan's protective presence removed, his aid could well have a price. He had never made a secret of his attraction to her, though there was no great honor in that. There were few, apparently, who repelled him. In any case, the troupe's accommodations belonged to the widow Pitot, and Elene was not sure she would be too welcoming.

It was unlikely that M'sieur and Madame Tusard would take her in. There was the problem of Madame's pride that would not permit anyone to know she had no servant, but the couple was also somewhat pinched for funds. In addition was the fact that Françoise Tusard was a woman of bourgeois attitudes. While she had lowered herself enough to visit with a woman who was being kept by a man, she might be less than overjoyed to have that same woman for a house guest.

Respectability, Elene suspected, was most important to Flora Mazent also. In addition, she had disappointed and angered the girl over the perfume she had wanted. Flora could hardly be expected, then, to welcome her with open arms, even if there were accommodations for her. Moreover, it would be unacceptable behavior in her to intrude upon the girl's period of mourning over her father. That Elene had lost her own father should have meant that the two would be able to comfort each other, but Elene doubted Flora would consider their situation to be at all similar.

That left only Durant out of those who had come from Saint-Domingue.

Her ruminations were interrupted by the entry of Devota. The woman advanced into the room with her hands twisted in her apron and a look of doubt overlaid by distress in her eyes. She came to a halt. "There is something I must tell you."

"Yes, what is it?" Elene dropped her beignet back onto her plate and set her coffee cup down.

Devota hesitated, her lower lip caught between her teeth. She drew a deep sigh. At last she said in a rush, "It's about the perfume. It has no power."

"What are you saying?"

"Just that. The perfume I made is only a nice scent, nothing more."

Elene stared at her. "What are you saying?"

"I told you otherwise to give you confidence and courage for your marriage to Durant. I told you it would make any man who held you desire you because I know that desire is a thing of the mind, that a woman who thinks she is desirable, is desirable indeed. One who thinks she can enslave men, often can."

"Oh, Devota," Elene whispered, her eyes wide as the implications began to seep into her mind.

"So you see, the perfume can have nothing to do with the way M'sieur Ryan took you to him, nothing to do with poison and death."

Silence fell. Elene closed her eyes tightly, then opened them again. "How can I believe you?"

Devota drew herself up. "Because I tell you."

"You told me wrong before, or so you say. Against your word I have Ryan's actions. He loved me while I wore the perfume, and when I left it off he did not touch me."

"Always?"

Elene thought of the last few weeks since most of the perfume had been destroyed. "Not always, but often enough. Anyway, if what you say is true, why did you not tell me before?"

Devota gave a slow shake of her head. "At first, because I thought you still had need of the power in the idea of it, and later because I knew you would not accept it. As now, you would want to believe, need to believe, too much to allow yourself the relief of it."

Was it possible? Could it be true, what Devota said? If so, then Ryan had made love to her, had brought her to his home for his own pleasure, from his own need. More than that, he had asked her to be his wife because he wanted her near him.

Where was the relief in that knowledge? She could find only pain, pain that she had thrown it all back into his face.

There was, however, the release from fear concerning the deaths of the three from Saint-Domingue. She was in no way responsible for them if the perfume had no effect, nor, by extension, could Devota be involved.

Elene moistened her lips. "It strikes me that this confession is very convenient to me at this time, perhaps too convenient."

"The harm caused by giving it is less now than the good it might do."

"I see. There is one thing more. I have known and trusted you all my life, Devota, and cannot stop now, but the fact must be faced that by absolving me of blame in the poison deaths you also absolve yourself."

The other woman considered this in silence. She shook her head. "I never thought, when we took ship for New Orleans, that it would come to this."

"Nor did I." Elene's breasts rose and fell in a difficult breath. There were tears creeping from the corners of her eyes. She wiped at them with the heel of her hand. "I don't really think you told me this to remove suspicion."

"Yes, I know. You fear I may be lying to help you."

Elene gave her a watery smile. "You always did know me too well. Leave me now, please, so I can think."

The maid hesitated as if she would say more, but finally did as she was asked.

It made no difference. Try as she might, Elene could discover few reasons for belief in Devota's confession, and many to doubt it. Distrusting both doubt and belief, she sat once more in clouded confusion.

It occurred to her after a time, however, that if what Devota had said were true, if Ryan had been under no compulsion to stay with her, then there was one thing that was changed. It was possible that he had been the man with whom M'sieur Mazent had begun negotiations for the hand of his daughter, the one Flora had spoken of as her fiancé. That would explain why the girl had not wanted to put a name to him in front of Elene. She might have wanted to spare her, or else had feared that as his mistress Elene would attempt to stop the engagement. Certainly it would explain the girl's excitement over the prospect of her marriage.

There was nothing unusual in the impending announcement being postponed due to the death of Flora's father, but what had happened then? This phantom fiancé should have been in evidence, on hand to support and direct the girl. Flora had made it plain that his absence was his choice, not hers.

Why should her fiancé have failed to remain interested? Had he found himself unable to face life with such a colorless female for a wife? Or was it something else, something to do with money, perhaps, the dowry being of crucial importance to many would-be suitors? Had the future groom discovered that the Mazent property in Louisiana was not so rich as supposed?

On the other hand, what if M'sieur Mazent had discovered something about the suitor that was not to his liking? Suppose the thing he had discovered was so distasteful that he had forbidden the man to speak to his daughter? Might the rejected fiancé have been so incensed at seeing a fortune slipping from his grasp that he had arranged to dispose quietly of M'sieur Mazent, choosing poison because it would mimic the man's gastric problems that were known to all?

A shudder ran over Elene. Not Ryan. He could not. Could he?

Certainly not. Even if he could, that did not explain the deaths of Hermine and Serephine. There had to be a connection between them. It made no sense otherwise.

Hermine had known Ryan before the rescue from Saint-Domingue. He and Morven were friends, had met each other often about the islands as they all moved from place to place. It was possible that Hermine had known some tidbit concerning Ryan that he might not have wanted Mazent to discover. Perhaps she had teased him about it, or else suggested he pay her to hold her tongue. Perhaps he had killed the actress to prevent her mischief.

Serephine's death was more difficult to explain. Her whole purpose, it seemed, had been to live for Durant.

She had, of course, been a fixture of Durant's life for years, and was therefore knowledgeable about what happened on Saint-Domingue. She might have been killed for the same reason as Hermine, then, because of what she knew. It was a most unsatisfactory idea, however, mainly because it was so unlikely that Serephine would, of her own accord, threaten anyone. The only thing that gave it weight was the possibility that she might have been tempted to tell Durant what she knew. Durant, one could be fairly sure, would have used the information against Ryan without a qualm.

There was a problem with that line of reasoning. It was that Durant had just as much access, in general, to the gossip of the island as Serephine. It seemed unlikely that Serephine would know something to Ryan's discredit that had never come to Durant's ears.

Unless, of course, it was a matter of women.

Men gossiped among themselves, there could be no doubt of that, but they did not do so in such graphic detail as women. Also, there were problems and intrigues that never came to the ears of men at all because they were not of general concern, never involved the law or medicine, the public streets or the field of honor that were the provinces of men. It could be something of the bedchambers and boudoirs, of the slave quarters or even the nighttime meetings and rites of the Voudou.

No. It was not possible. The man she knew, the man who had held her in his arms and bathed her body while she was desperately ill, could not have caused the violent and degrading deaths by poison of three people. If she was going to concoct games of secrets and blackmail, then any one of the people who had left Saint-Domingue aboard the *Sea Spirit* might be guilty, from poor middle-aged Claude Tusard to girlish Flora Mazent. So might any of the people they had met since then in New Orleans, an acquaintance such as Rachel Pitot, a servant, a vengeful citizen who did not like islanders, any madman with access to poison.

She must stop such thoughts. They did not help, served no purpose except to distract her from what she should be doing.

She must decide where she was going and what she was going to do. That was it. Nothing else mattered right this minute. Nothing.

But suppose Ryan had killed no one, had only spoken of marriage to Mazent? When would these negotiations have taken place, before he asked her to marry him, or after she had refused, perhaps out of pique for that rejection? He had made his abrupt proposal on the same afternoon that he had told her about the vauxhall party planned by Mazent; she remembered it well. The party had been held three days later, and it was then that the first mention had been made of Flora's betrothal.

Still, there had been nothing on that evening to indicate that Flora was any more aware than usual of Ryan. Her attention had been centered on Durant, her escort by default since neither had a partner. How long ago that night seemed, with its scent of orange blossoms and its laughter. And afterward, in the courtyard—

She would not think of that.

She must leave, she really must. But how was she to make her way? She had been given a better education than most due to her lengthy sojourn in a French boarding school; it should be possible for her to hire herself out as a governess. However, she had discovered that schooling was not considered a great advantage here, certainly not a necessity for the enjoyment of life. The one public school maintained by the Spanish king, along with a handful of private establishments, was considered adequate for the education of boys. Girls were schooled by the Ursuline nuns to the age of twelve or so, after which additional learning was thought to be a detriment to the making of a good wife and mother.

What else was there? The menial jobs of house maid, nurse, laundress, or cook were held by slaves or free women of color. Free women of color also made up the majority of the vendors of trifles on the streets, the candies and cakes, nosegays and sunshades. There might be employment to be had with a milliner or seamstress, but it would most likely be on a piecework basis. Elene's talent with a needle was adequate; still, she lacked the speed and polish required to make enough to keep herself and Devota, even with Devota's help.

There was a single possibility, and that was the perfume. If there were no special powers in it, then all her efforts to retrieve the little that had been sold, her staunch attempt to destroy the rest, were for nothing. She still had the empty bottles and a few of the ingredients to make a scent of some kind. Why should she not return to the original, if the money could be found? Or would the effort be wasted since she had given out the stories of a rash caused by the perfume? Would it take so long to build sales that she and Devota would starve amidst their wondrous scent?

No matter, she would not give up.

She still had her earrings. She would sell them, take the small amount they might bring, and buy minute amounts of the flower essences, enough to make no more than two or three bottles of perfume. By selling these, she should then have the means to make five or six more. It would be a weak beginning, much more so than she had planned, but it would suffice. Eventually, perhaps even before Ryan returned, she would make the money to afford Devota and herself a small room somewhere, a place of their own.

It occurred to her, fleetingly, that she would have ample funds to proceed if she sold Devota. She could as easily have bartered away her own mother, of course, on top of which was the fact that Devota held the secret of the final ingredient of the perfume. The idea was dismissed almost before it was born. She and her maid would make their way together. The sooner they started, the better.

It took nearly a week to arrange the best price for the earrings, six days of tramping from jeweler to milliner and back again. They were bought, finally, by a grande dame with kindly eyes who heard Elene haggling with a goldsmith. That evening, Elene and Devota counted the money with care, and made an even more careful list of what they would need to recreate the perfume.

Morning brought a caller, Durant. Elene met the news with impatience, since she was on the point of going out with Devota. Taking off her bonnet again, smoothing her tightly braided coronet of hair, she went out onto the gallery to greet him.

Durant bowed over her hand. She murmured something polite. It was a beautiful day, cool and pleasant with the poignant blue of the autumn sky arching overhead, so she indicated with a nod to Benedict that refreshments were to be served overlooking the courtyard. Leading Durant to a pair of chairs on either side of a small table, she sat down.

In the bright light, she noticed that he had grown thinner since leaving Saint-Domingue, as if the heat of a New Orleans summer and the loss of his mistress had shrunk his body and his features. His air of dissipation was gone, and in its place was an impression of self-discipline. There was still arrogance in his bearing, however, and a covetous look in his eyes as they rested on her.

"I understand Bayard is away," he said.

"Yes, a matter of business."

"Business for Laussat? We must hope the trip to Washington City doesn't prove too dangerous."

"Is it common knowledge then, Ryan's mission? I thought it a secret."

"I have no idea how common it may be, though I heard it myself at the Café des Réfugiés. Perhaps Bayard was merely giving himself airs? After all, how secret need a mere courier's journey be?"

Elene gave him a level stare. "It's more than that, I believe."

Durant shrugged his disinterest and changed the subject to ask after her health. As she answered, Benedict arrived with the wine. While the manservant was present, they continued in that innocuous vein, commenting on the fever cases reported of late, the numbers of which were declining as the cooler fall weather continued. Durant told her which families had returned from their visits in the country in response to the return of salubrity, and of the amusements being planned for the fall and winter, many of them centered around celebrations of the expected change in government.

When Benedict had gone away, they spoke of the retreat of the French before the British on Saint-Domingue, and the growing power of the Negro general, Dessalines.

"It begins to look as if there is no hope of the French ever returning," Elene said. "Have you decided what you will do if nothing can be regained from what you own?"

"Do?" he inquired with a lift of his brows.

"What activities you will pursue, whether you will buy land and raise sugar cane like everyone else, or perhaps read law or delve into commerce?"

"I have no intention of soiling my hands with commerce, that much is a certainty. And the law is for pettifogging types who love disputation."

"You will be a planter again, then."

"We shall see," he said, taking a careful sip of his wine, "though I am flattered by your concern. But what of you? I have expected at any time to hear of your marriage."

"My marriage?"

"To Bayard. Serephine had it from your maid some time ago that he had proposed, though she only mentioned it to me just before she died."

There was no need to explain herself to Durant. "I don't care to marry, as I told you on the ship."

"That may prove to be a mistake."

"What do you mean?" There was a tone in his voice she did not like.

"I am assuming you enjoy your position here, as a wealthy man's kept woman. It appears to me that Ryan is looking to the future in his quest for a wife."

"The future?"

"The Americans who will be coming to power are not as forgiving of irregular living arrangements as the French, or even the Spanish. They will frown most sternly upon a man openly keeping a mistress. To keep one secretly is, naturally, a peccadillo to earn a wink and a slap on the back."

"I doubt Ryan is concerned with what the Americans think."

"That's where you are wrong. He has been doing business with them in a small way for years, and no doubt expects to increase the commerce greatly when they come to power. Unlike us, who make distinctions between business and social acquaintances, the Americans will expect to be entertained in his home. This he cannot do without a wife."

Elene gave him a straight look. "Are you trying to say that I will hinder his prospects with the Americans?"

"Oh, I doubt Bayard will allow that. I'm trying to hint that the betrothal you were so obliging as to lay at my door the other day may have been contracted by him."

"You mean with Flora Mazent?" Her voice was blank.

"Is it so shocking?"

"Not exactly. The possibility was mentioned by someone else."

"These things have a way of becoming known."

"I didn't say I believe it."

"Only consider, there was her father, a man of means ready to invest in Bayard's operation, and a young and impressionable girl who could be expected to do as she was told and not make a fuss if he chose to set up his inamorata in a separate establishment, or even keep her under the same roof. What could be better?"

"He wouldn't." She could not quite keep her voice steady.

"No? He is a privateer, remember, used to arranging matters to suit himself, bending the rules here and there."

Was it possible? The blood drummed in Elene's ears as she tried to decide. There was logic in what Durant said. Ryan's trading interests were important to him, consuming much of his time and a great deal of his thoughts. He was also vocal in his opinions of the benefits to be gained by coming under the American flag. He had, after all, undertaken this arduous ride to Washington City for that reason.

That did not mean he would allow the Americans to dictate his way of life; still, he might enjoy appearing to conform while adjusting his household for his own pleasure. If he had intended to marry Flora instead, the plans had gone awry. It was just as well, for Elene could never have consented to being a part of a *ménage à trois*. She could hardly blame him for the attempt, however. He had asked her to marry him first, after all.

The idea that she might be harming Ryan's interests by living in his house without benefit of marriage was also abhorrent to her. It would be a poor return for the way he had saved her life twice over. He had never mentioned the problem to her, but then he wouldn't; it was not his way. Madame Tusard had tried to warn her for her own sake, but she would not listen then. Now, coupled with the painful knowledge of the muddle she had made of their liaison and the fact that he was holding her without love, it served to strengthen the resolve she had already taken.

She drew a deep breath. "You need not darken Ryan's character to me. I already intend to leave him."

The words hung in the air, stark, resonant with finality. For a panicked instant, Elene wished them unsaid. That was impossible, and unwise.

Durant's brows went up. "You mean—what will you do?"

"Find a room somewhere," she said with deliberate vagueness.

"And do what?"

"Begin again with my perfume. I must have something of my own to make the money to earn my way. Otherwise I will always be a kept woman, dependent on some man for every bit of food and rag of clothing I wear. I can't bear that."

"Your perfume? Are you sure?"

She gave a hard nod. "I'm sure."

He tilted his head to give her a doubtful look, but went on. "Bayard would come after you the instant he returns."

"It will do him no good." She lifted her chin.

He got to his feet and moved to the railing. Over his shoulder, he said, "There was a time when I came very near to having the right to take care of you."

"I somehow doubt that in those days you would have given your consent to my becoming a perfumer."

"Very true," he said in dry tones. "Nor do I approve of it now. According to Serephine, it's not just perfume but a witch's potion you make with that woman of yours."

"You believe it, of course?"

He shifted, as if uncomfortable. "I've seen and heard of stranger things on the island. I threw out the bottle Serephine had the minute she told me."

"Just in case." She had not known he believed in the Voudou. Serephine must have told him of the perfume after her visit trying to get it back.

"As you say."

"I suppose you know your disapproval makes no difference to me."

He shrugged, his gaze on the gently moving leaves of the oak tree. "Anyway, I hope, for old times' sake, that you will permit me to be of assistance in this move."

Surprise held her silent for a moment. "If you are offering money, it's very generous of you, but I prefer to manage myself."

"My God, Elene," he cried, swinging on her, "must you be so proud? I don't expect anything of you in return!"

"I never thought you did."

"Didn't you? All right, I said some things on the ship coming from the island that I shouldn't have, that I didn't mean." He raked his fingers through his hair, his face dark. "But now I have this need to turn back the clock, to have everything as it used to be, for it to be as it once was between us."

"You must know that's impossible."

"Is it? Suppose I said to you, come live with me?"

"I never lived with you before." The objection was instinctive, without force as she searched for a way to refuse him without hurting his pride.

"A small matter. We were so much together we may as well have been under the same roof."

"It isn't my purpose to exchange one man for another. Besides, you must know that I . . . that my affections are elsewhere."

"I expect you think you are in love with Bayard. That's of little importance."

A flush not entirely of anger heated her cheekbones. "It may be to you, but it isn't to me. Anyway, I don't need a protector."

"I think you're wrong," he said, his jaw muscles tightening, "but I won't argue about it. If you won't come to me, where will you go? Have you found a place?"

"Not yet." She had not looked, though she would not tell him so.

"There is a room available where I live."

"I feel sure it would be more than I can pay."

"Not so. In fact, the rental is paid for more than a month, until the first of December."

"Let me guess," she said in tight suspicion, "the room belonged to Serephine?"

"What an opinion you have of me. As a matter of fact, it's a servant's room, one I took because I was looking for a maid for Serephine. It's small, but comfortably furnished, and has the advantage of being safer than some rat-infested hovel on the edge of town."

"Because you will be near?"

He made a sound of exasperation. "Because it's on a decent street, one lighted at night. Come, don't be foolish. Say yes, and I will speak to my landlady and have her save it for you."

As she stared at him without reply, he went on. "I'm not an ogre, Elene. Our fathers were friends and neighbors, you have known me forever. I only want what is best for you."

Put that way, it seemed childish to insist on finding her own accommodations. Still, she hesitated.

"Think," he said, his tone cajoling, "if you don't have to pay for your room and board, you will be able to advance with your perfume that much faster."

"I don't care to stay in a room paid for with your money."

"That's ridiculous!"

"It may be, but it's the way I feel."

"Then you can pay me for it, if it makes you feel better, but only after you have begun to sell."

Her lips tightened. "It's seems odd of you to be so intent on aiding me. I thought you scorned commerce."

"I feel sure you will grow tired of it," he answered with a smile. "Then I hope to persuade you to listen to my proposal after all."

"At least you're honest, even if you're wrong."

"Prove it." The challenge was quiet. He stood straight and tall against the morning light.

If she agreed, it would mean she could leave Ryan's house now, without having to wait to earn the money. It would be taking action at once, before she could weaken and sit supinely waiting for him to come back.

"Show me I'm wrong," Durant urged again, his eyes narrowing as he watched the expressions on her face.

A decision must be made. She gave an abrupt nod. "Very well. I will."

"If anyone can, *chère*, I don't doubt it's you."

The words were satin smooth, the expression in his eyes clear, but the clasp of his hand on hers when he took his leave was held a shade too long, and the kiss he placed on its back was fervid.

CHAPTER 18

"I'm not going."

Elene was almost packed. She had decided to remove to her new lodging immediately; delaying would only make it harder. Gathering her belongings together had not taken long since they were so few, hardly enough to fill a small trunk. She had hesitated over the gowns, but since the materials for them had been purchased with the money from her mother's necklace, her right to them seemed clear enough.

She had never considered that Devota would not wish to go. Her maid was a woman of strong opinions, Elene knew, but the will of her mistress had been her own for so long that it had not occurred to Elene it could be otherwise. She had not expected Devota to like what she was doing, and had even thought she might have to persuade her, but she had certainly not thought to hear a flat refusal to leave Bayard's house.

"Tell me why?" Elene straightened from placing her nightgown on top of the items in the trunk that sat on the bed and turned to face her maid.

"I have made a place for myself here. I would rather not leave it."

"Your place is with me!"

"Your place, *chère*, is here also."

"How can you say that? There is nothing to hold me, no obligations, no vows."

A stubborn expression moved over Devota's face. "Maybe not spoken ones, but they are there."

"You don't know," Elene said in pain, looking away from her.

"I know a great deal, and part of what I know is that M'sieur Ryan will be in a fury when he finds you gone. Then maybe that's what you want."

Elene ignored the suggestion, refusing to even consider it. She didn't think so. In any case, it was the last thing she expected. "I still don't understand why you won't go. You can always return if you're so sure Ryan will come after us."

There was a movement in the open doorway. Benedict stepped forward. "Forgive me for the intrusion, Mam'zelle. Forgive me also for taking the allegiance of your woman; it was not intentional, I promise you. She does not wish to leave here, I fear, because of me."

A glance at Devota's face, impassive and yet flooded with unaccustomed crimson, was enough to confirm what the manservant said. It came to Elene, looking from one to the other, that it had been some time since Devota had been heard railing against the man, longer still since they had looked daggers at one another. They had both begun to be quite circumspect, in fact, from the night they had stood guard together in the dark courtyard.

Elene looked back to Devota, the flecks of silver dim in her gray eyes. "This is a true attachment—not as it was once before?"

"You mean as it was with Favier? I have no secrets, you see, from Benedict. No, it is not at all as before. Benedict is a man who, if the perfume had power, would be worthy of its use."

Elene lifted a brow a fraction at such praise. "I see. Why could you not have said so, instead of making excuses for staying here that had to do with Ryan?"

"They were not excuses, *chère*, believe me."

Elene could order Devota to go, and presumably she would be obeyed. She did not like going without her; it would be like arriving at Durant's house without an essential protection. She had no desire to force her will on her maid who was also her aunt, however, nor to be cumbered by a rebellious companion.

She said, "Stay then, if that's what you want."

"What I want is for us both to stay."

Elene shook her head with an attempt at a smile. "I can't do that, but I can wish you happiness."

"Ah, *chère*," Devota said, and coming forward, wrapped her arms around Elene and stood rocking her slowly from side to side. When at last she released her, she said, "About the perfume. I will come and help you whenever you send word."

"I may well send," Elene said wanly, "though I have the notes I made, the recipe, and I think I would like to try it on my own."

"There should be no difficulty. You should take this, just in case, for comparison." Devota reached to pick up the last small bottle of perfume left of the batch they had made from where it sat on the table near the bed. Tucking it into Elene's hidebound trunk, she closed the lid.

"There is that last ingredient that I don't know, of course." Elene's inquiry was tentative.

Devota met her gaze a long moment, then gave a nod. Leaning, she whispered in her ear.

Benedict gave them a scathing look, muttering under his breath before stepping around them and latching Elene's trunk. He hoisted it up onto his shoulder. With great dignity, he said, "Since you will not stay, Mam'zelle, we will walk with you to your new place, Devota and I."

There was an instant when Elene felt a wayward impulse to ask the manservant what he thought his master would do when he found her gone, to demand why Benedict himself did not try to persuade her to stay. At the same time, she knew it would change nothing. Taking up her bonnet and gloves that lay ready, she put them on, then moved from the bedchamber with her head high.

The rooms Durant occupied were located on the top floor of a three-story house. There was a salon and dining room with attached butler's pantry, and a pair of bedchambers with a single dressing room between them. He insisted that Elene see them, showing her about with derogatory remarks for the inconvenience of the stairs that led up from the lower front gallery then through a stair hall in his mulatto landlady's apartments on the second floor. He also made excuses for their small size and lack of a view, in comparison to the houses he and Elene had known on the island.

Elene did her best to reassure him, praising their airiness and freedom from noise so far above the street, and the charm of the decorations. As she walked through them, however, it was not the drawbacks that he pointed out that struck her but how very much they reminded her of Serephine. The woman's presence was in the vivid colors of the wall hangings and the exotic richness of the coverings on the floors, in the faience shaped like palm trees that graced the salon's mantelpiece, and especially in the miniature of the young boy, her and Durant's son, that hung over the bed in the second bedchamber. It was a presence Elene had not reckoned with, though not a disturbing one.

Her own room was on the floor below, with its own entrance from the stair hall. It was small and simply furnished with no more than a four-poster bed, a plain dressing table, and a wing chair, but was as comfortable as Durant had promised. Best of all, it was adjoined by another even smaller room, a cubicle meant for the storage of trunks and boxes. This cubicle, with the addition of a worktable, would serve admirably as a place to mix her perfumes.

The mulatto landlady owned a dozen slaves as well as the house, the legacy of the gentleman whose mistress, or *placée*, she had been for twenty years. Her servants cleaned the rooms and she provided meals from her outdoor kitchen for her tenants. The arrangement was convenient, according to Durant, though it meant that tasks were done only when the landlady had no need of her servants herself, and that food sometimes arrived lukewarm. All that was lacking was someone to run small errands and attend to personal needs, which was why he had been considering a maid for Serephine.

For those times between meals when he required something light to stay the pangs of hunger, Durant relied on the sellers of meat pies, pastries, and candies who roamed up and down the streets outside. He respected Elene's wish to pay her own way, he said, but if ever she should need funds for such purchases, or even for her larger expenditures, there was always a bowl filled with coins and paper money of all denominations on the central table in his salon. It had been a custom in his father's house on the island, a tradition it was his whim to continue. She must take what she wished. Elene refused the largesse, of course, but appreciated the gesture.

Despite Elene's misgivings, there was little in her removal to Durant's rooming house of which she could complain. He was everything that was considerate, seldom intruding, issuing only an occasional invitation to join him for dinner. He inquired after the progress of her perfume making with what appeared to be real interest, but did not encroach upon her work area or the time she spent in it. Coming and going on his own affairs by day and by night, he disturbed Elene hardly at all.

There was once, however, in the middle of the night at the end of the first week, when she had awakened to the quiet rattling of her bedchamber doorknob.

"Elene?"

It was Durant, his voice slurred with drink. She lay still, listening.

"Elene, let me in!"

She could hear his heavy breathing. The doorknob rattled again and there came the thump of his shoulder hitting the door. It was securely locked; she had made sure of that. He cursed with ragged virulence. After a time, she heard his footsteps as he moved away, ascending the stairs with slow care to his own rooms.

When next they met, Elene waited to see if Durant would mention the incident, or perhaps make some demand. He did not. It seemed best not to speak of it herself for fear it would precipitate the very confrontation she wanted to avoid. If it was repeated, she would be forced to make it plain that he had no automatic right to her bed. It was not, and it passed over as if it had never happened.

September turned into October and the heat of summer finally faded into autumn. The days grew slowly cooler, but sunny and smoke-flavored, colored with the yellow and rust of leaves that clung stubbornly to the trees, the gold and lavender of the spikes of goldenrod and tangles of black-eyed susans and ageratum in the ditches. The open air market near the levee began to be flooded with fall greens and also with pumpkins and sweet potatoes, sweet figs, persimmons, and pecans, both the tame variety of the last as well as the small and rather bitter wild pecans preferred by many.

The news of the outside world penetrated slowly but surely to New Orleans. That from Saint-Domingue was not good. As Ryan had predicted, the British had blockaded the island. The French soldiers under Rochambeau were holding their own but were expected to surrender before many weeks were out. From the planters and their families left on the island there was, ominously, no word.

It took longer than Elene had expected to gather the ingredients of the perfume once more. When they were assembled, she proceeded with caution, mixing minuscule amounts of the various essences as she experimented with them. She was by no means sure that she had a perfumer's "nose," that ability to distinguish individual scents and to blend them into wonderful combinations. In truth, her sense of smell seemed strangely off of late, so that a mixture which seemed delicious in the morning could make her nearly ill as evening fell. She grew cautious, afraid to waste the precious fluids. More than once, she considered sending for Devota, but that would be to admit defeat, something she was not quite ready to do.

Nor was she ready to attempt to copy Devota's perfume. The cause was not just her growing mistrust of her sense of smell, but also a curious reluctance to put the special properties of the scent to further tests. The longer she put it off, the more afraid she became, though whether from fear that the perfume would not sell, or what it might do to those who bought, she could not tell. Neither did she use her carefully hoarded stores to make any useful quantity of the scents she had fashioned, however. She could not decide which would be best, to gamble that women would buy what she had made, or to put her energies into making and selling a perfume she knew that men enjoyed and women craved.

One day, in the effort to make up her mind, she took the last tiny blue, beribboned bottle that Devota had pressed upon her into her work cubicle and drew out the stopper. It was not just a scent that was released, but an assault of memories. One after the other, they crowded in upon her. The moment when the two black revolutionaries had appeared in the woods on Saint-Domingue. The feel of Ryan's arms in the darkness of the hole under Favier's house. Hermine's pleasure over the bottle of perfume given her. Ryan's last half-violent, half-tender possession, and the way he looked as he kissed her good-by. With the images came an inundation of terror and joy, ecstasy and regret.

A chill ran along the surface of her skin followed by the prickling of gooseflesh. With it came a perilous certainty that no scent which could evoke such powerful reactions at a single whiff could be powerless.

She was going mad. It was just a perfume. Only a perfume.

It made no difference what it was. To make it again would be to mix together and bottle up tiny doses of purest pain and most virulent desire. Whether that result was in the perfume or in her mind was of no consequence. She could not do it; it would make her ill. Even the breath of its smell that lingered brought a strange nausea. No, she could not. Sometime soon, perhaps, but not now.

Pressing the stopper back into the bottle, Elene pushed it from her to the back of the worktable. She left the workroom, closing the door firmly behind her.

All Hallow's Eve came and went, the time of reverence for the dead, of flowers and candles in the cemeteries. Elene visited the graves of Hermine and Serephine and even M'sieur Mazent. As expected, the authorities had not troubled themselves greatly over the affair of the deaths by poison.

Elene still mulled over them from time to time, but even for her, the passage of time and the unlikelihood of her perfume being a factor made finding the killer less urgent. Now and then, however, like pulling out a too-complicated needlework pattern that has been cast aside, she attempted to fit what she knew into some recognizable framework.

It was no use. If the perfume was eliminated as a common thread among the three people, then the only thing left to connect them was the fact that they were all from Saint-Domingue. Regardless, they had not known each other there, had not met until they left the island together aboard Ryan's ship. It was possible something had happened on the ship itself, but try as she might, Elene could not think of what it could have been. Hermine and Mazent had exchanged no more than common civilities, while Serephine had hardly spoken to anyone at all.

In a spirit of curiosity, Elene questioned the maid who cleaned the rooms about Serephine's last day, asking if she had received any visitors, any messages, if anything at all unusual had happened. She learned exactly nothing. No one had come and there had been no notes or anything else delivered. Serephine had gone out shopping in late afternoon, but returned after little more than an hour, having bought nothing more than a half pound of chocolate bonbons. She had been found dead by Durant when he returned for dinner.

It crossed Elene's mind to wonder if Durant might not have done away with his mistress after all. He was the one who knew her best, indeed almost the only one who could be said to really know her. On the other hand, why would he have brought her with him if he cared so little for her that he could kill her? Why kill her when it would have been so easy for him to simply discard her? More than that, Durant might have lashed out in rage, but it did not seem likely that he would resort to poison. There was also the immutable fact that even if a reason could be found for his destruction of Serephine, there was no apparent reason for him to effect the other deaths. Sometimes she wondered if the truth would ever be known.

In the first week of November, Colonial Prefect Laussat, certain that the official confirmation for which he waited would be delayed at least another two weeks, left New Orleans for a trip up river to see more of the countryside before his departure. It was said that Madame Laussat, midway in her pregnancy and no longer going into society, was beginning to make lists of the items to be packed when they left Louisiana.

Elene saw Madame Laussat at the market one morning a few days later. The prefect's wife was standing to one side while her majordomo bought redfish and her youngest daughter played with a monkey being offered for sale by a seaman just off a ship from South America. Her figure, though concealed by the style of her walking dress, had thickened since she was last seen; still, she was not yet ungainly with her condition.

Elene smiled and spoke as she passed the woman, but did not pause. There was no reason the wife of the prefect should recall her from their one chance encounter, and she did not want to seem encroaching.

"Mademoiselle Larpent, isn't it? Good day," Madame Laussat said.

Elene, like most people, was charmed to be remembered. She inquired after the other woman's health, and they stood chatting of inconsequential things.

Finally, Madame Laussat said, "I must not keep you. I only wanted to say how sorry I am that my husband took M'sieur Bayard away from you, and that I trust you will discover that the benefit to Louisiana outweighs the inconvenience."

Elene could feel the heat of a flush climbing into her face. The other woman apparently did not know that she had left Ryan's house. Rushing into speech to cover her embarrassment, she said, "I'm sure he was happy to be of service to your husband."

Madame Laussat laughed. "I don't know that he was happy! Indeed, he seemed a bit distraught at the necessity when he left us. He is a loyal citizen, however, and as such is performing his duty at the expense of his own desire."

Had the choice of words been deliberate? Elene, glancing back at the prefect's wife after she had moved on, could not be sure. She took another step, then looked back again. How very attractive Madame Laussat was in her pregnancy, her skin blooming with health, her face serene, her carriage showing an upright and dignified grace. In a few short months there would be a child, much desired, infinitely loved, no matter the mischief its inconvenient conception might be causing with the couple's traveling plans at the moment.

Whereas her own child—

Elene was pregnant. She had suspected it for some time; had wondered in fact that Devota had not guessed before she left Ryan's house. Perhaps she would have, if she had not been busy with her own love affair.

The baby was her responsibility. She would take care of it. Nor was it undesired, or unloved, though she would admit to a certain inconvenience. Now and then she permitted herself to wonder what Ryan would think when he knew. The possibility had never been mentioned between them. They had chosen to ignore it, as if it could not happen. That had been obtuse of them, she freely admitted. No matter. She could not expect a man who would leave her, just to show her he could, to care that she was carrying his child.

Soon Durant would notice. It was not a moment she looked forward to with pleasure, not that she was afraid of him or what he might do. In truth, she hardly knew what to expect. Once she would have expected him to jeer at her; now she was not so certain. He had changed, becoming more lax in his notions of behavior, both his and her own since leaving the island. She should have been glad of it, since it had made these last weeks more bearable. Instead, it affected her with increasing unease.

There was nothing in the jovial mood with which Durant announced his soirée four days later to reassure her. He seemed excited, and at the same time, on edge. He had invited everyone he knew, including the men with whom he drank and gambled, several planters who were in the city with their families, and naturally those who had come with them from the island. He insisted that Elene be his guest of honor, refusing to listen to any excuse. Propriety did not matter, he told her frankly. Everyone knew they had rooms in the same house. That their rooms were on separate floors made no difference to the gossips. The *on-dit* floating about the city was that they were lovers, anyway.

It crossed Elene's mind to wonder who could have spread the news of her removal to the same house, unless Durant had happened to let it fall. She had told no one herself, had scarcely seen anyone to tell. She did not accuse him, however; the possibility that the tale had been spread through the servant grapevine was just as good.

Elene had little inclination for gaiety. She was never ill in the mornings as were most in her condition, but late afternoons and early evenings had become times of trial of late, when any stray odor could bring a wave of sickness. To concoct perfume had become so wearing that she had almost ceased to try, hoping it would be better in a week or two.

It was just dusk when she began to dress for the party. She sat in her wrapper at her dressing table, braiding her hair before putting it up, while waiting for Devota, who would be on hand for the evening, to come and help her into her gown. When there came a soft scratching on the door behind her, she called out for the maid to enter. The door opened and closed. Intent on what she was doing, Elene did not look up until something in the quality of the silence drew her attention.

Reflected in the surface of the dressing table mirror was Durant. He was already dressed in a black swallow-tail coat with gray breeches and a blindingly white shirt. She swung to face him.

"I didn't mean to startle you," he said, his voice strained. "I only came to tell you that your maid has been delayed by an accident in the kitchen at Bayard's house, and to offer my services instead."

"I can manage, I think. Thank you."

His gaze was not on her face, but rested instead on the opening of her wrapper that she had not bothered to close since she was alone, and on the curves of her breasts that had grown fuller in the past week. As she gathered the wrapper edges together in a defensive gesture, he stepped forward. "Do you feel well?"

"Yes, of course." It was not quite true, but the lie might send him away.

"I've noticed lately that you are rather quiet in the evenings, and not too anxious for your dinner."

"Am I?"

"One would almost say you were ill."

"Oh, I don't think so."

"Nor do I. Serephine was like that when she was *enceinte.*"

She forced a laugh. "What an extraordinary thing to say."

"Oh, it's perfectly ordinary, for a young and healthy woman who has been sharing a man's bed. I have been wondering how long it would be before the symptoms appeared."

Elene was tired, suddenly, of the pretense. She said in hard tones, "Now you know."

He smiled. "Yes, I do. How soon can we be married?"

"Married!" She did not know what she had expected, but it wasn't this. She would have said Durant had too much pride to take another man's child as his own.

"Don't sound so surprised. It's only what would have happened months ago, if not for the revolt and Bayard's interference."

"Things have changed."

"We can put them back the way they were."

He had said as much before, as if taking her as his wife would bring back the position he had once held, the wealth and power. She shook her head. "They can never be the same."

"They can be close enough for me."

Was that true? She was not the only one who would be affected by her decision; there was her child to think of also. What kind of father would Durant be to it? Was he accepting its presence for her sake, or was his offer simply to be revenged on Ryan for taking what he considered to be his?

"Why are you doing this?" she asked softly, almost to herself. "You never pretended to be overflowing with devotion for me on the island."

"It will grow, just as it would have grown if we had wed as our fathers wished on Saint-Domingue. You are my chosen bride. Whatever else changes, that remains."

He had not said he loved her. In one way she was grateful, in another, sad. "It won't work, you know. I'm different now, and so are you."

Annoyance crossed his handsome face and was gone. "I think you might try to make it work, for your child's sake."

She gave him a wry smile. "That's one of the differences."

"If I don't mind, why should you?"

It was a point she should, perhaps, consider. She said at last, "I will have to think about it."

"There isn't much time, if we are to avoid scandal."

What he meant was, there was not much time if he was to claim the baby as his own. Could she permit him to do that, to deny Ryan all knowledge that he had fathered a child? The answer was no. She would wait, at least until Ryan returned. If Durant had any concern for her at all, he would allow her that much.

"There is time enough," she said.

The thing that brought Durant's New Orleans friends to his rooms, Elene thought two hours later, was the promise of cards, food, wine, and stronger drink. What brought the refugees from the island was primarily curiosity. They had heard of her change of abode, and suspected a change of protector, and could not wait to see how she and Durant would behave, what they would say. The only thing that would have made it better for them was if Ryan had been there so they could see his behavior also.

Devota presided in the dining room, seeing to it that everything was ready, from the polish of the crystal to the centerpiece of nougat shaped like a fleur-de-lis nestled in golden autumn leaves, and also that the service was smooth and timely. Germaine, arriving with Flora Mazent, set herself to help Devota, and their voices in low murmurs could be heard at intervals.

Flora had bloomed, there could be no other word for it. She still wore black, but her gown had style in its cut and drape, and in its rolled collar of ecru lace that rose in the back to frame her face and neck. Her hair was nicely dressed with curls about her forehead, and her cheeks and lips delicately reddened with carmine. More than that, she smiled

and laughed in a fashion that bordered on the coquettish. If the rein-
statement of her betrothal was the cause, however, she gave no indication of it.

Morven, Josie, and Madame Pitot presented themselves together, the
last to appear. Morven left the two women to find their own pleasures
the moment they all came through the door. As handsome as ever, and
as raffishly charming, he made his way around the room in a shower of
compliments given and received, until he came to a halt beside Elene's
chair.

He bowed over her hand, told her she looked incandescent, then
under the buzz of conversation said with a mocking smile, "Are you
sure this is an improvement over Ryan?"

The words were not meant to sting, she thought, but they did. She
could not be surprised the actor thought the worst, but since he did,
pride forbade that she attempt to set him straight. She lifted a brow.
"As much as the widow was an improvement over Hermine."

"Ah, I see. A financial arrangement."

"You might say so."

"I thought Ryan merely out of town, not bankrupt. What a pity that
his service to the colonial prefect should be so costly."

"I don't know what you mean."

"Don't you? It was always his practice in the past to avoid grand
gestures. I wonder what made him do it this time."

"Grand gestures?"

"Such as this tiresome journey. It can benefit him nothing except
saddle sores."

"And the thanks of his country?"

"Now there's an object. Do you mean Spain, France, or the United
States?"

"France, of course!" she answered, annoyed by the repeated flick of
his irony.

"For gratitude alone, no doubt. Who can have persuaded him it
would be worth the risk of his neck?"

Elene stared at Morven. She had persuaded Ryan of France's importance. In which case, if anything happened to him, it would be her fault.
Or would it? She had been certain Ryan had his own reasons for his
wilderness trek to Washington City, reasons that had nothing to do with
her. She could, of course, be wrong.

"Would you care," she said with extreme politeness, "for a glass of
wine?"

Morven laughed in quick understanding. "Very well, I'll change the subject. Slightly. I was hoping you weren't happy. I have an opening again in my troupe."

"An opening? For an actress?"

"Our ingenue has left us. She and Josie didn't get along."

"While you got along with her perfectly?"

He smiled down at her with febrile charisma. "I get along with most women."

"So I've noticed!"

"Have you?" he asked in lazy appreciation for the flash of tartness. "Then you won't be surprised to know that I was enchanted to hear you have left Ryan. I don't poach on my friends' preserves, but Gambier is no friend of mine."

His casual declaration, coupled with the assumption that she would be pleased, took her breath away. Her tone abrupt, she said, "I have no talent as an actress."

"I can teach you the craft, among other things."

"Thank you, no. I am also no ingenue."

"Then you shall have the lead part. You will make a magnificent tragedienne."

"Over Josie? She will hardly permit that!"

"She won't have a choice," he said with a shrug. "In truth, she isn't equipped for the roles, and she is becoming too plump."

"I couldn't displace her. Besides, there is Durant."

"Loyalty is a lovely trait, but are you sure that with Gambier it isn't misplaced?"

Elene gave him a straight look without appreciation for the slow smile he permitted to curve his mouth. "Tell me," she said, "do you ever feel any responsibility for Hermine's death?"

"Should I?" he asked, his insouciance intact, though there was a shadow in his dark eyes.

"It seems possible she died for love of you, whether by her own hand or some other."

His face hardened. "I withdraw my offer of an acting stint. I fear that in the death scenes between us you might use a real dagger."

He inclined his head and moved away. Elene watched him go, watched him join Josie who was laughing in a corner with Durant.

Josie was indeed more embonpoint, though not yet to excess. Her face, her shoulders and breasts and arms were rounded, the skin pink and white and firm, just as some men liked them. One day she would become blowsy and fat, with petulant features, but for now she was a comfortable female, with just enough vivaciousness to make her interesting to those who did not expect wit. Was it possible for such a woman to kill Hermine in order to take her place?

Madame Tusard and her Claude were sitting alone. Elene moved to join them, and they exchanged a few banalities about the weather and the various guests. Madame looked once at Josie and gave an audible sniff, but said nothing. She did not release her hand from her husband's arm, however. For his part, M'sieur Tusard studiously ignored the actress. It was enough to make Elene wonder if he had come to his senses, or if Josie had found another paramour. A moment later, she had to laugh at herself. If she wasn't careful, she would become as prone to conjecture as Françoise Tusard herself.

The woman's rampant curiosity was exposed as she began to drop broad hints concerning Elene's living arrangements. Since Madame Tusard was eyeing the door of Durant's extra bedchamber at the time, Elene thought it prudent to lead the way down to the second floor to show her own Spartan quarters. To her surprise, the two of them were joined by several of the other ladies. They professed an interest in seeing where her perfume experiments were being conducted, though it soon became apparent that most were merely inquisitive and the rest in search of a private place to adjust their clothing and attend to the needs of nature.

There were twenty seated for dinner. The cook of the mulatto landlady had excelled herself, presenting a deliciously light oyster stew followed by squabs in wine sauce, which in turn were superseded by grillades of beef served with herb rice and a cabbage soufflé. The meal was topped off by a dessert of crepes filled with pecans and cream and flamed in cognac. It was a menu Durant had chosen himself in consultation with the cook. That his guests were enjoying his choices was attested by the relative quiet.

Elene sat at Durant's right hand, valiantly sampling the dishes placed before her. She caught Durant's gaze upon her once or twice, and managed a wan smile for him, but she was glad that M'sieur Tusard, on her right, was concentrating on his food, for she was not at all inclined toward conversation.

It was as the dessert plates were being taken away and the cheese and nuts brought out that Durant got to his feet. He rapped on the table for quiet, then lifted his wine glass.

"My friends," he said, "it is with pleasure that I see you gathered around my table. Happiness should be shared, and I invite you to join with me this evening in my happiness at the coming nuptials uniting the lady at my side and myself as man and wife. Ladies and gentlemen, a toast to the woman who was once my bride-to-be and now holds that title again. To the lovely Elene!"

CHAPTER 19

THE thunder of hard knuckles on the door of her room brought Elene surging to her feet with her heart pounding in her ears. The hour was late. Durant, she thought, was out for the evening. On the other side of the door could be some ruffian who had stumbled upon the rooming house. There was also one other person it could be.

She swallowed hard, then moved forward. "Who is it?"

The voice that answered was rough with anger, but achingly familiar. "Open this door, or I'll kick it down!"

Ryan.

She stepped to turn the key, then had to move quickly back out of the way as he strode into the room. The harsh look on his face, the sight of his clenched hands at his sides, brought the rise of her own temper.

Pushing the door shut, she turned to face him. Her voice acid with irony, she said, "Do come in!"

Ryan swung to glare at her, and felt the sheer rage that had gripped him as he made his way here begin to fade. Her face was slightly fuller than when he had left, but the features more refined. Her eyes were fathomless gray pools, and her skin had the color and sheen of mother-of-pearl. She had been getting ready for bed, for her hair lay across her shoulders in a thick swath, shimmering with the light of a branch of candles beside the bed.

He looked away deliberately, his gaze sweeping about the room. Turning, he crossed to the door to the small cubicle and pushed it open. That it was empty could be seen at a glance. "Where is Gambier?"

"Not here, nor will he be. These are my rooms, mine and no one else's."

There was no relenting in his face as he wheeled back to face her. "What in the name of heaven are you doing here?"

"I had to have somewhere to go." She clasped her hands before her, keeping her words steady by hard concentration.

"Did you? What was wrong with where you were?"

"I couldn't stay there forever. I have my own way to make, and there was no point in putting it off any longer."

"Going with Gambier is making your own way?"

Elene heard the contempt in his voice and responded to it. "I didn't go with him, not as you mean. He had paid for this room—"

"Oh, you admit that?"

"I admit nothing! It's just a place to stay until—"

"Until you are married."

"We aren't going to be married!"

He flung away from her. "Oh, come on, the rumor is all over town. I was told of it twice before I could tie up my horse before Laussat's house this afternoon, and twice more after I stepped through the city gates."

"Durant made an announcement. That doesn't mean I agreed."

"One thing usually follows the other."

"He thought to force my hand."

Ryan felt relief move over him in a sudden wave of heat. He frowned to keep it from showing. "Then there will be no wedding?"

"I didn't say that," she corrected him.

"I don't understand you."

That was fair enough; she hardly understood herself. She had been incensed at Durant's high-handed attempt to use her condition against her. She had told him plainly she would not be coerced, though it had failed to dent his self-assurance. In truth, she felt trapped between un-palatable choices, between marrying a man she didn't love and raising her child alone. If she told the man before her he was going to be a father, he might renew his offer of his name, but did she want to marry him for that reason?

She lifted a shoulder. "I have told Durant I will not be married except under French law. Spaniards have too much power over their wives."

"You can set the date then. The transfer of the colony from Spain to France will be made on the thirtieth of this month."

Her excuse had been facetious, purely for Ryan's benefit. On an indrawn breath she said, "So soon?"

"Laussat has reason for haste. The plans have been made for weeks."

His wife's pregnancy was the reason. Was it her imagination, or was Ryan's gaze assessing as it moved over her? She turned away. "I'm not sure it matters. I may yet decide I prefer my independence. You will be interested to know that I have made up my mind once more to be a perfumer."

"With Gambier's backing," he said in flat tones.

Her eyes flashed as she swung to face him. "By no means! With my own."

Ryan stood listening to the tale of the earrings. When she had finished, he stared at her a long moment. He had meant to snatch her up and carry her back to his house by main strength. His muscles ached with the need to do just that. She faced him with such resolution, such dignity, that he could not bring himself to destroy it. Abruptly he said, "You would have more room to work with me."

It was as near to an appeal to return to him as she might ever hear, he wasn't the kind to beg. But neither was she the kind of woman to meekly pack her bags and follow a man.

She raised a brow. "That's hardly a respectable suggestion."

"Respectable? When have I ever cared for that?"

It was true, in its way. Carefully, she said. "You are a respected man of business among those you trade with, and there's nothing to say you won't wish to appear more so when the Americans come."

"What have they to do with anything?" There was puzzlement in his eyes as he watched her. She was trying to tell him something, he knew, though what it could be he could not see.

"You . . . you will be wanting a wife, and I don't—" Her throat closed on the words, gripping so tight she could not go on. She lowered her head to stare at her hands.

"I know. You don't want to be married, at least to me."

"Nor do I care to be your mistress while you wed someone else!"

"I don't know what you're talking about. Wedded or not, you're the only woman I've ever wanted to see at the head of my table or beside me when I wake in the morning. Since you have refused, that's the end of it. Make your own way, if that's what you want."

She could feel the inner force of him battering at her sense of control. It gave her voice a defiant edge. "It is what I want!"

Ryan swore softly, then moved toward the door. The need to turn back, to seize her and carry her off after all, warred within him with grudging appreciation for her stand. He could bend her to his will, but what good was that if he earned her hate?

A muscle clenched in his jaw. His voice grating, he said, "Then I'll leave you to it."

The door closed behind him.

Elene took a step after him, then stopped. There were a lot of things she could say, but pride and fear would not let her. Even if she could bring herself to say them, there was no guarantee he would listen. Let him go then.

By the end of the third day, Elene had accepted that Ryan was not coming back. She had also determined once and for all that she could not marry Durant. If there had ever been any doubt, seeing Ryan again had routed it. She would have given Durant her decision, if he had allowed it, but he was busy celebrating the coming transfer with his friends during the afternoons and evenings, and sleeping off the effects in the mornings.

Elene, balked of her object, began to think of the baby. If she was going to be its sole support, she must begin. It was time to make Devota's perfume, no matter what effort it took. The ribbon ties on the bottles had been ruined when they were emptied, however, and must be replaced. She decided to begin with that small task.

The purchase of the ribbon, no more than enough for four bottles, did not take long. Reluctant to return at once to her quiet room, she walked toward the river. Standing on the levee in the cool wind, she stared at the rippling stretch of eternally flowing water. She thought fleetingly of the many women who, in her situation, had plunged into rivers the world over. Such an easy end held no allure for her. Life was not good, but its promise was greater still than its pain. She thought that for her it would always be that way. She turned homeward.

As she neared the rooming house, Elene saw a praline seller coming toward her. The quadroon woman was singing a catchy tune of praise for the confections she carried in a tray on her hip. There was a swing to her skirts as she walked and a saucy smile on her face beneath her red silk tignon, while wide gold earrings swung against the pale cream of her cheeks. Her pralines were covered by a crisp white cloth to discourage the flies, and when she lifted it their rich, milk-and-sugar smell wafted on the air, mingling with the smells of wood smoke from evening cook fires, the taint of the effluvium from the gutters, and the scent the quadroon wore.

For a wonder, the smells did not make Elene queasy, perhaps because of the freshness of the evening air and her hunger after her walk. She bought a flat, round piece of the candy studded with lumps of pecans. The quadroon gave her a flashing smile from under her lashes along with a soft word of gratitude, then moved away down the street, singing.

Elene nibbled at the edge of the praline as she climbed the stairs to her bedchamber. That small taste did not make her feel ill, as so many things did at that time of the day. When she had removed her bonnet and gloves, she broke off a larger section with a small pecan half embedded in it and placed it in her mouth.

A bitter taste assailed her tongue. She screwed up her face. The pecan was from wild trees, it must be. Nausea washed over her and perspiration erupted across her brow. She crossed quickly to the bed to drag out the china chamber pot that sat underneath, then spat the mouthful of candy into it. In an uncontrollable rush, the tiny bit of praline she had swallowed earlier, as well as everything she had eaten at lunch, spewed forth. She dropped to her knees, racked by spasms that seemed to go on and on.

At last they passed, but the cramping in Elene's stomach did not. She was frightened at its violence. She was being foolish, she knew; it was just a little sickness. Women had suffered such indignities from the beginning of time. Still, she was afraid. Holding to the bed and the walls, she staggered out into the stair hall and called out for the landlady.

Devota came at once, with the servant girl who had been sent to fetch her trotting wide-eyed behind her. Her maid took one look at Elene as she rolled back and forth on the bed with her hair damp with sweat, and sent the servant to bring hot water and a cup. From a bag she had brought with her, she took dried herbs and white and yellow powders, which she mixed in small pinches in the hot water. Standing over Elene, she bade her drink, then drink again and yet again.

The spasms passed. Elene could straighten her legs, could breathe easier. She did not let go of Devota's hand, however, until night came and sleep claimed her.

When Elene awoke, it was morning and Devota had gone. A light rain was falling; she could hear its gentle patter on the roof overhead. She lay in bed, staring up into the gauze folds of the mosquito netting around her with her hand on her abdomen. The child inside her, tiny and drifting as yet, was quiet, safe. There had been moments during the afternoon before when she had been afraid for it; she had not known the illness that was a part of pregnancy could be so violent. But once more Devota had worked her magic and all was well.

Magic of another kind had taken place, for suddenly the child was real to her. Until this moment her condition had seemed like an illness or a problem to be solved. She had spoken of the baby to Devota, had thought of the baby, but it had had no more substance in her mind than a small ghost. If she had lost it, she would have been as much relieved as saddened. Now it was her flesh and blood and also a part of Ryan, and therefore an infinitesimal being to be fiercely protected.

It also deserved the chance to know its father.

Elene could feel the apathy that had gripped her sliding away, being replaced by purpose. She had allowed circumstances to overwhelm her for too long, had spent too much time mourning what once was, what might have been. No more. It was time she made up her mind exactly what she wanted and then went after it. If she could not order her own life, how could she ever hope to order that of her child?

Ryan must be told. It had been sheer cowardice not to let him know at once. What he might choose to do about that knowledge was beyond her control, but he should have it. Procrastinating over the perfume, such as buying bits of ribbon for it, must stop. She would have to get on with what must be done.

The deaths by poison were another problem altogether. They nagged at her, and she could not forget them. Still, they were the concern of the authorities and none of hers. She must not allow the shadow they cast to darken her own future. She had, she thought, concentrated upon them as a defense against the necessity of facing her own difficulties. That was something else she must put behind her.

The clatter of a tray outside the door heralded her morning coffee. The young maid opened the door and put her head around it, then seeing Elene awake, pushed inside.

"*Bon jour*, Mam'zelle. You had a nice sleep? Your woman who was here last evening said I must not wake you until far into the morning. Now M'sieur Durant instructs me to tell you that the people are gathering in the Place d'Armes already. He will be going himself in half an hour and wishes to know if you feel like joining him."

The transfer ceremony, that ceding Louisiana from Spain to France, would be held this noon. Of course she must go. She flung back the sheet. "Yes, I will join M'sieur Durant. Tell him to please wait for me, then lay out my tan poplin and my shawl."

"But your *café*, Mam'zelle?"

"Leave it there on the table. Quickly now!"

The rain still fell, a steady silver drizzle from a heavy gray sky. The crowd waiting at the Place d'Armes sheltered from it as best they could, standing in the interior portico of the Church of St. Louis and under the arcade of the municipal building known as the cabildo, where the official exchange of government would take place in an upper room, or else huddling under the few trees along the converging streets. Some few ladies held oiled silk parasols over their heads or covered their bonnets with their shawls, while the gentlemen stood with the rain dripping from the narrow brims of their hats. Many of them wore the tricolor of France, a jaunty symbol of loyalty.

The Spanish troops were drawn up in formation to one side of the Place d'Armes where their red uniforms and the white cockades on their bicornes made a brave show. Opposite them, with the flag pole still flying the lions and castles of His Most Catholic Majesty of Spain between them, was a militia made up of the citizens of the town, men of a dozen different nationalities. Many of them, so the talk ran among the crowd, had fought with the Spanish governor Galvez some years before, heroically defending Louisiana against the British in what the Americans called their revolution.

A cannonade boomed out in salute from a ship on the river. Laussat was coming, walking along the levee. Now the colonial prefect could just be seen passing the guardroom of the military barracks, striding amidst perhaps fifty or sixty Frenchmen. A drum roll began, portentous, stirring. An order rang out and the troops in the square, both the Spanish and the militia, snapped to attention. Laussat walked with his head held high and his face impassive, a strong and competent representative of France. The drumroll rumbled louder and louder; then, as Laussat and his escort disappeared inside the cabildo where the Spanish officials waited, it suddenly stopped.

There was little to be heard except the quiet murmuring of those assembled and the spattering of the rain. The soldiers in formation stood stiffly enduring. A light wind whipped the flag above them so that it gave a soft snap, and also clattered among the fronds of the palm trees that lifted their dark green crowns beside the church.

Slowly the crowd began to ease out into the Place d'Armes, surrounding the soldiers, gathering under the balcony of the cabildo. Elene and Durant moved with them. There came a hail, and Elene saw Josie waving, making her way in their direction with Morven in tow. They exchanged greetings as they came together, then Josie, turning this way and that, caught sight of the Tusards and Flora Mazent and beckoned to them.

At that moment, Laussat, with the elderly and white-haired Governor Salcedo and the urbane diplomat acting as commissioner, the Marquis de Casa Calvo, appeared on the balcony before them. As at a signal, the Spanish flag began to descend the pole and the French flag was raised. As the tricolor of France reached the top and unfurled in the breeze, a rousing cheer rang out. It frightened the pigeons on the rooftops so they took flight, wheeling in the gray rain, but soon died away. A Spanish officer took the flag of his country and bore it off from the square. The Spanish troop wheeled and marched away at double time behind the officer.

Beside her, Elene felt Durant stiffen. She glanced at him, then followed the direction of his narrow gaze. Not ten paces away, shouldering through the mass of people just behind Flora Mazent, was Ryan.

He came toward her, his broad shoulders cleaving a passage, his advance steady. The planes of his face were carved into hard lines, and his eyes were dark blue, direct and relentless. Alarm touched Elene, then faded to a waiting stillness. She lifted her chin.

Ryan saw that gallant gesture, so well remembered, and felt his heart compress as if in a vise. He had tried to renounce her, had damned her for a fickle, hard-hearted jade, and sworn he could live just as well without her, but his house felt empty and lifeless since he had found her gone, and his bed was a lonely place. He recalled the glory of her hair, hidden now under her bonnet, spread out over his pillows; could feel in his memory the silken smoothness of her skin and see the rich sheen of satiated desire in her eyes. She had been yielding grace, fresh challenge, and sweet content made whole in female form. More than that, she had been his, and would be again so long as the strength to make it so remained in his body.

He barely nodded to the others, touching his hat brim as he came to a halt in front of Elene. Without preamble, he said, "I hear you have not been well."

Devota had told him, of course, though surely not the cause. The words of concern, no matter how hardly spoken, were so unexpected that her reply was short and toneless to prevent her voice from shaking. "A minor ailment."

"No stomach upset can be minor, not among those of us who came from Saint-Domingue, not now."

Her gaze was clouded as she caught his meaning. The thought had occurred to her, but had been pushed aside by the implications of her pregnancy. Was it possible? Was it?

"Oh, Elene," Josie said, her eyes huge in her face as she came nearer. She reached to push back Elene's bonnet that shielded her face. "I should have seen it before. You have the look of Hermine when she was taking arsenic. You really do."

The look of Hermine. That pale translucence of the skin. Arsenic. If she died, then so would her baby. Elene swayed on her feet.

Concern leaped into Ryan's eyes. He moved with the swift agility of well-oiled muscles, brushing Durant aside as he would a pesky mosquito. With one hard arm at her back and the other under her knees, he caught her up.

"No, no," she protested. "It was only a moment of giddiness. I had no dinner, and no breakfast."

Durant reached to clamp a hand on Ryan's arm with anger smoldering in his face. "No, is right. The woman you hold is my fiancé. Put her down."

Ryan swung from him. "I believe we have gone through this once before on the *Sea Spirit*. And settled it."

"Maybe. This is different."

Durant snatched at Elene's arm, his fingers biting into her wrist as if he would tear her from the man who held her. Elene pulled against his hold, trying to prevent herself from becoming a part of a tug-of-war between the two men. With one part of her mind she registered the avid faces of the onlookers, the heads turning to watch. For the rest, she was only aware of the hard, secure clasp of Ryan's arms around her, and the mortification of her intense pleasure in it.

"Stop this," she cried. "Stop it, both of you! Put me down at once."

Instead, Durant grasped her shoulder, thrusting his arm between Elene and the man who held her in his determination to wrestle her from his arms. He glared at Ryan over Elene's form. Through set teeth he demanded, "Give her to me!"

Ryan gave a derisive laugh edged with recklessness. Stepping back, he lifted one long leg, placed his foot against Durant's abdomen, and shoved.

Durant's hold on Elene was wrenched free. He went staggering back with arms flung wide, careening into the crowd, landing flat on his back. He thrust himself up on one elbow. There was a white ring around his mouth and rage in his eyes as he stared at Ryan through narrowed eyes. "For this," he said thickly, "you will meet me again. I demand satisfaction."

"No," Elene whispered, and heard her shock echoed in the gasps that ran through the people gathered around them. Vaguely she was aware of Josie's moan and Flora's thin scream.

Ryan paid not the slightest heed. His gaze raked the man on the ground. "A meeting you will have, but whether you will be satisfied is another matter."

"I am easily suited. All I require is your life." There was venom in the words as Durant pushed himself erect and straightened his sleeves.

"Try and take it." Ryan looked toward Morven. "You will act as second for me?"

"That I will. Have you another choice?" As Ryan gave him a name, he inclined his head. "Never fear. We will arrange it."

Ryan gave a nod, then turned on his heel and began to push through those gathered around them, striding without effort. The crowd parted, leaving a long, open lane. Ryan marched along it with Elene clasped against him. In the street near the edge of the open square, Devota and Benedict appeared and fell in behind them.

At that moment in the Place d'Armes, a cheer arose as Laussat emerged from the cabildo. Cannons boomed and muskets were fired in salute. As the echoes died, the new governor of Louisiana began to speak. His voice faded with distance as Ryan left the square behind.

"What do you think you're doing?" Elene asked in breathless demand. "People are staring."

Ryan's voice vibrated deep in his chest as he answered. "I'm taking what I want. After all, I'm Bayard the privateer; what can you expect?"

There was an odd singing in her veins. Her chest felt tight and tears burned the back of her nose. His shoulder and chest against which she lay were rock hard. The male vitality of him surrounded her, sapping her strength. "I'm perfectly capable of walking. Put me down this minute!"

"Not until I have you where you should be."

A shiver ran along her nerves. Her voice tight, she said, "This is intolerable."

"Is it now? Too bad, because it's going to get worse."

Around them the rain still fell, misting their faces so that droplets clung to brows and lashes and glittered like diamonds on their mouths. It dripped from Ryan's hat brim, landing on Elene's shoulder, and spattered in the street to gather in noisome, muddy puddles. Through it loomed Ryan's house, silent and stalwart in the gloom.

The sound of raindrops and their wetness was cut off as Ryan ducked into the tunnel-like entrance of the portecochere. Gaining the courtyard, he climbed the stairs to the gallery. At the top, he turned to speak to the two servants who still followed.

"Go to the rooming house. Bring her things, everything."

"I'll take one of the maids and go," Devota said to Benedict, exchanging a long look with the manservant. Benedict gave a nod, as of some communication made.

Ryan appeared not to notice their exchange. Swinging about again, he moved to the open door of his bedchamber and shouldered through it, kicking it closed behind him. He crossed to the bed and placed Elene none too gently onto the yielding surface of its mattress.

Elene caught herself on her elbows. Before she could push to a sitting position, however, Ryan flung himself down beside her and leaned to brace an arm on either side of her shoulders. His voice hard yet etched with pain, he said, "Tell me again, why?"

"Why what?" she snapped in return, incensed at his use of his strength for mastery, angry too at the flicker of gratification inside her at his show of rampant determination to have her with him.

"Why did you go with Gambier?"

"Maybe I was tired of having you decide my life for me! As you're doing now. You can't just cart me here again and expect me to stay."

"I can," he said, the words grim with certainty. "And I will keep you here until the gate to hell drips icicles, unless you can give me some good reason for why you left this house."

The impulse to strike out at him was strong, but to struggle would be useless, if not dangerous, in her condition. As much as it went against the grain, she must think of such considerations now. More than that, there was a matter or two that required some clarification between them, for her sake as well as his. She lowered her lashes, staring at the pulse that throbbed in the strong brown column of his neck. Finally, she said, "It seemed best."

"Best? Best for whom?"

"For both of us."

"You might have consulted me before deciding my life for me." He mocked her earlier complaint with bitter sarcasm, and despised himself for having to fight the urge to kiss away the drop of rain that fell from the thick fan of her lashes to her cheekbone.

"Oh, very well! It was best for me. It seemed a good thing to remove myself before I was thrown out. There are few wives who care to share their homes with their husbands' mistresses!"

His face hardened. "You said something similar before. I think you had better explain."

"Flora Mazent."

She had succeeded in surprising him, if nothing else. As his expression remained uncomprehending, she was forced to continue. "Flora was supposed to be engaged, but her fiancé withdrew from the arrangements after the death of her father. You were seen in a close business discussion with M'sieur Mazent."

"That makes me the fiancé? Gambier was with Mazent more, both before and after we landed here."

"He denied that he was the chosen groom."

"And that's all that's required?"

"I have no reason to doubt him."

"Suppose I deny it, too."

Was he denying it or not? There was no way to be sure. "But it had to be one of you. The Mazents knew no one else."

His voice neutral, he said, "There was always Morven, or one of the men on my ship."

"Morven and Flora? Don't be absurd! As for the men on your ship, I think M'sieur Mazent would have chosen a gentleman."

"For that much," he said in irony, "I thank you."

"In any case, there was nothing said when you left to indicate that you wanted me here when you returned."

"The unpardonable sin, I took you for granted."

She flashed him a sharp look. "You rode off without a backward glance or thought."

"What was I supposed to have done? Given you my undying love and begged you to wait?"

She did not answer. She could not. Nor could she look at him.

"Ah," he said softly, "I begin to see."

Panic seized her, panic based on fear of what he might guess, and what he might say in response to it. If it was the wrong thing, it might be too painful to bear. "You needn't think I am breathlessly waiting for a declaration of your intentions."

"No, I would never think that. I have not forgotten that you are a woman of ambition."

She clenched her jaws together, a reaction of sheerest nervous agitation, one that kept her lips from trembling. Her words when she could speak were brief. "Is that so wrong?"

"Not at all. But I see no reason why you cannot also be my woman." The deep tone of his voice, the caressing look in his eyes made it difficult to breathe. He shifted, resting his weight on one hand while with the other he released the tie of her damp bonnet and drew it off, flinging it aside. He loosened her shawl, sliding it from her and disposing of it also since it had absorbed the rain, leaving her walking dress fairly dry.

Seeing his gaze move next to the buttons of her walking dress, Elene moistened her lips and spoke in a tumbling rush. "To be your woman would mean I would always have to be afraid of losing you."

"Never, except in death, and to live in fear of that loss is to turn your back on the joy of living." He touched her cheek, as if marveling at its smoothness, then trailed his fingers along the curve of her jaw line to the point of her chin.

With a catch in her voice, she said, "I can't help it."

"Can't you? Only someone with no fear of death would risk her health by taking arsenic, even to produce such fragile loveliness."

"I didn't!" she cried in indignation, snatching her chin from his grasp with a toss of her head. "I wouldn't! It would be too dangerous for—"

A knock came on the door.

Ryan cursed under his breath, then pushed himself away from Elene to sit erect on the end of the bed. He called out a command to enter.

Benedict stepped into the room. "M'sieur Morven Ghent and another gentleman are here, on the matter of the duel."

"Morven is prompt, for an actor," Ryan said in dry acknowledgment. "Tell him I will be with them in a moment."

As Benedict went away to do as he was bid, Elene sat up. She put her hand on Ryan's arm. "There is no need for you to fight Durant again. Please, won't you do something to stop it?"

"It was Durant who issued the challenge." There was the sound of steel in his voice.

"Because of your actions. You could apologize for knocking him down."

"I somehow doubt that will satisfy him. There is the small matter of taking his bride."

Her lips tightened. "For the last time, I'm not his bride! If you would only be reasonable!"

A smile curved his mouth, one that struck chill into her heart. "I am perfectly reasonable, so long as no one tries to take what is mine. If Durant wants you, he will have to kill me first."

He gave her no chance to reply, but pushed off the bed and strode quickly from the room.

A short time later, Ryan and his seconds left the house. They gave no indication of where they were going, but it was assumed their departure was on the business of the duel.

In their absence, Devota returned with Elene's belongings. The maid did not ask if the things should be unpacked and put away, but bustled about the bedchamber restoring them to their accustomed places. Elene lay watching her, and wondering at her own quiescence.

Perhaps it was the effect of the poison, if she had somehow ingested such a thing? Or of her pregnancy? Or even the paralysis of fear, her fear for Ryan and what she had caused?

Those explanations were real possibilities, but she knew differently. She stayed where she was because it was where she wanted to be. And because there was still something unfinished between her and Ryan Bayard. That it might never be finished was something she refused to consider.

Devota paused in her tasks, looking at Elene. "You are all right, *chère*?"

"Yes, fine."

"You don't look fine."

Elene forced a smile. "You are so good for my conceit."

"Humph. You're sure your stomach doesn't cramp?"

"Don't fuss, Devota, please." As her maid turned away, taking the last items from Elene's small trunk, she went on, "I suppose you're happy now."

Devota gave her an oblique look. "It depends."

"On what?"

"On what happens."

Elene looked away. "Yes."

"He's much man, M'sieur Ryan. He won't be beaten."

"But if Durant dies because of me, how will I live with it?"

"You will live," Devota said, pausing in what she was doing. "It's only a little for you, his challenge, *chère*, and much for his pride. To lose both you and his home, his island kingdom, has been too much."

"And also Serephine. Yes, I suppose so."

Devota returned to her task without comment. Emptying the trunk, she moved to a small wooden crate from which came the clank of glass.

After a moment, she straightened. "I thought you took the last bottle of the perfume with you?"

"I did. Did you want it for something?"

"Only to set it out for you before I take the rest of this to the workroom. But it isn't here."

"It must be. It was on the table in the smaller room, with everything else."

"It wasn't there. I packed those things myself."

"I don't suppose it matters," Elene said, her tone soothing as it seemed Devota was becoming upset.

"Someone has taken it."

Was it possible? Elene frowned in the effort to think. The last time she remembered seeing it was the afternoon before Durant's party. If it had been stolen, the list of those who might have done so was long, from the mulatto landlady and her servants, to any of the men and women who had been in Durant's rooms on that evening. There had been much coming and going as the evening advanced.

"It was only perfume," she said at last.

Devota met her gaze across the room, her own somber. "There are those who don't know that, or don't believe it."

She could only agree.

A part of her lethargy, Elene discovered, was due to hunger and weariness. Benedict had brought her a light meal after Ryan had gone. By the time she had eaten it and watched Devota set the bedchamber to rights once more, she could barely keep her eyes open. However, when she awoke two hours later, she was only slightly refreshed and too on edge to lie on the bed any longer.

The rain had not long been stopped. The evergreen leaves of the oak in the courtyard glistened, and water still dripped from the tiled roof to splatter on the paving below. The cool breeze that blew across the gallery was so laden with moisture that it brought the rise of chill bumps. The lingering grayness of the day made the afternoon seem further advanced than it was, and there was the glow of lamplight spilling from the kitchen below where dinner was in preparation.

People were beginning to move about the streets once more. Through the porte cochere could be heard the sound of a horseman going by, the barking of dogs chasing what sounded like a stray pig, and the song of a praline seller crying her wares. There also came the firm sound of footsteps, evenly paced, purposeful.

Elene smiled a little. She would know that stride anywhere. She got to her feet and moved to the head of the stairs, waiting for Ryan to emerge in the courtyard.

He did not appear immediately. There could be heard the soft murmur of an exchange. It lasted no more than a moment, then his footsteps began to echo in the porte cochere.

His head was bent as he entered the courtyard, so that the dying light gleamed in the walnut waves of his hair. He was looking at something he held in his hands. He broke off a piece and put it in his mouth, beginning to chew.

"What do you have there?" The words broke from Elene without her volition, spurred by a vagrant idea, a faint memory.

Ryan looked up with a smile curving his mouth as he began to mount the stairs toward her. He swallowed before he spoke. "Only a praline. The pecans are bitter, but I'm not complaining. What with one thing and another, I missed my luncheon. Would you care for some?"

He broke off another piece of the candy and the smell came to her, milky and sweet and sickening. She hurled herself down the stairs toward him. "Don't!' she cried, "Oh, don't!"

His eyes widened, startled, but he was already lifting the next piece of praline toward his mouth. And then she was upon him, knocking his hand aside so that the candy he held crumbled, wrenching the rest of it from his grasp to fling it into the courtyard.

Staring at him with her eyes wide with fear, searching for the first signs of illness, she whispered in horror, "Poison. It was poisoned!"

CHAPTER 20

"WILL he be all right?"

Elene asked the question as softly as possible. She did not want to disturb Ryan who slept, at last, with his hand resting between two of her own. It had been bad, the effort to rid his system of the poison, but Devota's herbs and powders had finally done their work.

"I told you, *chère*," the woman said, "he is strong. In the morning he will hardly know he was sick."

Elene gave a soft sigh, then shivered. "Suppose I had not been on the gallery? Suppose he had eaten all the praline before anyone saw him?"

"He would be dead. But he isn't, nor is he going to be. Don't think of it. You should go and have your dinner, then find a bed."

"Not here," Elene said, indicating Ryan's bed, the one they had shared for so many weeks. "I . . . I wouldn't want to disturb him."

Devota gave a nod. "Benedict can have another chamber made up for you while you eat."

"It will be my pleasure," the manservant said from where he stood on the other side of the bed.

Elene made no move to go. She stood staring down at Ryan, at the hollows caused by pain under his eyes and the pallor of his skin. Other than that, he was little changed. The force that he held inside him was apparent in his features, and yet there was tenderness in the curve of his mouth, and passion.

She said, "The duel will have to be canceled." As Devota and Benedict remained silent, she looked up at them. "Won't it?"

Benedict shook his head. "I would not presume. It's a matter of honor."

"Surely he can't appear on the field. He will be far too weak."

"It's for him to decide," Devota said. "You must not worry yourself about it, it isn't good for you."

"How can I not? Oh, Devota, isn't there anything that can be done to stop it? Anything at all?"

Devota met Elene's eyes across the long, straight form of the man on the bed, her own soft brown gaze infinitely receptive, cogent with thought. She pursed her lips. "It may be there is a way."

Elene drew a quick, silent breath of hope. She glanced at Benedict who was suddenly as oblivious of the two of them as if he were deaf, as he busied himself tidying the room. Softly, she said, "But without harm?"

Devota came toward her. She took Ryan's hand and placed it on the sheet, then grasped Elene's shoulders and turned her toward the door. "Go eat, *chère*, and don't fret. It's possible something may occur to halt this affair, but if not, you must accept what happens, for there are things we can't change all through life."

Elene sat alone in the dining room picking at the food prepared for her, but she was not hungry. It was all very well for Devota to tell her not to fret—her maid could have no real idea of how she felt. To see Ryan brought so low filled her with horror. Since it had occurred so soon after she had returned to his house she must be to blame, had to be to blame. Just as she was to blame for the duel.

Her thoughts ran in circles. It was a distraction from her fears for his health and of what would happen in the morning to think of the poisoner. It almost seemed that if she could discover why Ryan had fallen a victim, she would know who was doing this terrible thing to people.

What exactly had happened, then, to make him a target? First, he had returned to New Orleans. He had taken her from Durant and installed her in his house once more. Finally, he had accepted Durant's challenge.

Was it possible Durant had tried to kill him to be certain that the meeting would never take place, that Ryan's death which he so violently desired was achieved?

There was the praline vendor. What role did she play? She was the same one who had sold her the candy, for Ryan had been able to describe her. Was she no more than some pretty free woman of color paid to sell poisoned confections to the chosen victims? Or was she the killer herself?

Elene put down her fork and sat back in her chair. She closed her eyes. Slowly she brought to mind the evening she had bought her praline, the quiet street, the cool wind blowing from the river that had fluttered the skirt of bright cloth worn by the quadroon with the praline tray on her hip. She could almost see the red silk tignon the woman had worn, intricately tied, and the gold hoops of the earrings hanging from her ears with only the lobes visible where the tignon covered her hair. She had not been tall, not quite as tall as Elene herself, and her hands had been rather short fingered. Her features were vague, however. The quadroon had kept her head down, almost as if she were afraid of being noticed too much—though people seldom really looked at the street sellers, being more interested in their wares. But there had been the smell of seafood cooking and kitchen fires, and the milk-and-sugar smell of the pralines. Milk and sugar, and the girl's skin so translucent yet creamy with the gold earrings against it—

Elene's eyes flew open. Of course. That was how it had been. How could she have missed it? And there had been that other time. She knew. Dear God, she knew. It was unbelievable, but she knew the one person with a reason that led in a straight line from one victim and near victim to the next. The only person.

Elene sprang up from the table. If she was right, then something must be done, now, tonight. If it was not, then the killer would surely strike at Ryan again, and next time might succeed.

The night had turned colder after the rain, with a biting wind funneling down the streets. She was not prepared for such a weather change, and she hugged her shawl around her. She was grateful for that much. It was the purest luck that she had remembered that Devota had thrown the wraps they had worn earlier over a rack in the laundry to dry. She could not have retrieved one from Ryan's bedchamber. Devota was still there, and her maid would have made a great noise about her leaving the house if she had discovered that was what she meant to do. She had left a note on her pillow to ease Devota's mind if she found her gone, but prayed she would be back before it was found.

The streets were dark, lighted only by the lanterns on their ropes slung across the streets. The way was not long, however, and soon the inn loomed before her.

Germaine opened the door to her knock. Elene gave the quadroon woman as pleasant a smile as she could muster. "May I come in?"

"It's very late, mam'zelle—for visiting."

"I will only be a moment."

It was difficult to see the face of Flora Mazent's maid with the light coming from a candelabrum in the room behind her; still, Elene thought the bones had grown sharper since last she had seen her. As the woman inclined her head and stepped back, there was a stiff reluctance in her movements, but also a shading of resignation.

Flora Mazent rose from where she was sitting on a settee with a novel in marble covers in her hand. "Why, Elene," the girl said brightly, "how nice to see you."

"Please forgive the intrusion, but I have come on a matter of importance, and I believe you may be able to help me."

"Really?" The girl indicated a chair across from the settee and resumed her seat, waiting with interest and expectation on her plain features.

How to begin? Elene had made no plan. The only thing she could think of was to plunge into it. "You told me once that your father had arranged a marriage for you before his death. I wonder if you would give me the name of the bridegroom?"

Color flooded the girl's face. She opened her mouth as if she would answer, then looked around her and jumped to her feet. "I haven't offered you refreshment, have I? Where is Germaine? She will bring us coffee or perhaps tafia or wine. What would you prefer?"

"Nothing, really."

"Oh, please, you must have something warming. You look chilled."

"Coffee with milk then." Anything to get back to the subject that consumed her.

"Yes, it does sound good. Germaine!"

The maid had left the room, going into the bedchamber. Flora did not wait for the woman to answer her call, but went with quick steps from the room to find her. There came the faint sound of their voices through the half-open door, then a moment later, Flora came back into the parlor.

The girl had regained something of her composure in her brief absence. As she resumed her seat, she said, "Now where were we—oh, yes, my fiancé. Your question is very personal, isn't it? Perhaps if you will tell me why you want to know?"

"I believe it may have a bearing on the deaths among those of us from Saint-Domingue."

"Oh, dear." The girl waited, her hands folded in her lap like a child who has been well schooled in manners.

"This man, I am almost certain, is directly involved. It would be of enormous help if you would give me his name."

Flora stared until her eyes began to water, then looked slowly down at the floor. Quietly she spoke. "It is—was—Durant Gambier."

Relief washed over Elene in a wave. She had known it must be so; still, there had been a lingering doubt. Durant had lied, or at least, misrepresented the truth. It was possible that, because no betrothal ceremony had been performed before witnesses, no contract signed, he had not considered himself bound. It was clear, however, that Flora thought otherwise.

Taking a deep breath, Elene squared her shoulders. "This evening, someone tried to kill Ryan. A praline vendor sold him poisoned candy. The reason for this, I think, was because he was to meet Durant Gambier on the field of honor."

"But that's terrible. Do you mean M'sieur Gambier—"

"No. Durant has too much pride to stoop to such measures to defeat an opponent. I believe it happened because someone was concerned that Ryan might best Durant with a sword as he had before, might actually kill him."

The girl blinked. "It's so . . . so unlikely. People don't do such things."

"Some do, especially those who have learned that death is an easy solution. Only consider Serephine."

"You mean the woman who came here with M'sieur Gambier?"

"His mistress, yes."

"But . . . what has she to do with anything?"

"Durant was fond of her, perhaps more fond than he knew. They had been together for years, had raised a son to an age to send to school in France. If there was a problem with Durant's marriage plans, it might have been because Serephine represented another possible impediment to the nuptials. And so Serephine had to die."

"I can't believe—"

"And then there was your father."

"Please, don't," Flora said, her face crumpling with distress. "I would rather not speak of that."

"I'm afraid we must, though I am somewhat mystified about his death. I can only assume that once more it was caused by the snag in your marriage arrangements. Possibly it was something your father discovered, or something he said to Durant, that caused the breach. I can't think what it might have been; even to me it seems a flimsy cause for murder. However, there was a large sum of money involved. Durant's affluence was not in evidence on the ship, but appeared about the time these negotiations for your hand in marriage began. It appears that instead of borrowing on his estates, not an easy thing, he may have accepted a loan from your father on the strength of the proposed engagement. At any rate, it seems almost certain that your father's history of stomach disorders suggested an easy manner of either shutting his mouth before he could do more damage, or possibly of revenge."

Flora's pale eyes were wide, staring. At the sound of the door opening as Germaine returned with their refreshment, she jumped up in such obvious relief that Elene felt the stir of pity.

The next few minutes were filled with pouring out the steaming hot coffee, adding hot milk for Elene and milk and sugar for Flora. The smell of the brew was delicious in the cool air, and the feel of the cup so welcome in Elene's cold hands that she sat holding it between them. There was in her mind a reluctance to drink, but the coffee and milk for both Flora and herself had come from the same containers so that it was unlikely to be dangerous. The coffee, as she took a cautious sip, was smooth and mellow, without a trace of bitterness. She avoided the small cakes that had been brought on the tray, however.

Flora swallowed a mouthful of her coffee as if in need of its strength. She drank again. "Everything you have said seems to have come from your imagination. You can't expect people to pay attention unless you have proof."

"True, and I have none. I must go to the authorities, of course, but I have no idea whether they will act on what I say. My best hope is that if the person becomes aware someone suspects, the murders will stop."

"How very magnanimous."

The girl's tone was strained, but then her father had been killed. In answer to the implied criticism, Elene said, "What I want most is to protect others who might become victims, particularly those I love."

"You are very lucky. I think . . . I think perhaps Durant Gambier was not a suitable husband for me after all."

There seemed no answer to that. Elene took another sip of her coffee to cover the pause. After a moment, she said, "There is still Hermine's death."

Flora sighed, rousing herself. "Yes, what of it?"

"I think . . . I'm almost sure she died because of something she said on the night we all went to the vauxhall. If you will remember, she spoke of using arsenic to keep her skin pale. While she was talking, she looked at another woman there, and it was almost as if she knew they shared a secret. I think they did. I think Hermine knew, because of the look on her face, that the other woman used arsenic, too."

Flora looked from the dregs of coffee she swirled in the bottom of her cup to Elene's face, then down again. "You are speaking of—"

"Let me tell you something that happened," Elene interrupted her. "I had been shopping, taking the evening air along the river yesterday afternoon. As I returned toward the rooms where I was staying with Durant, I met a vendor of pralines, a pretty quadroon. She was dressed with a certain bright, cheap stylishness, with a red turban and gold earrings. Her face was painted with white lead and there was carmine on her lips and cheeks, but the skin underneath was creamy and fine, pale enough, almost, to be white. There was one thing more about her that I didn't notice at the time for the smell of the street and the poisoned pralines she carried—and perhaps because it was so familiar to me. It was her perfume. She was wearing my perfume, the scent made by Devota and myself."

Flora made no answer. She only sat listening, watching Elene from under her lashes, her gaze intent. Elene drank the last of her coffee and set the cup aside. She went on. "Later, this evening in fact, I remembered that scent. I also recalled a woman who had begged me to sell her some of it, a woman I had been forced to refuse. With these memories I put the fact that, on the night of Durant's soirée, the last bottle of this unusual perfume was stolen."

"How very clever of you."

"Not at all. It was just that I was able to recognize what others might not." Elene's tone was flat. She waited.

Flora pursed her lips. "I see. I suppose you came to some conclusion?"

"I did. I came to the conclusion, Flora, that the quadroon who sold the pralines was you."

A sound left the girl that was something between a laugh and the expelled air of a blow. "Oh, but I thought—that's ridiculous!"

"You thought I was accusing Germaine. It was what you hoped anyone would think, if the praline seller fell under suspicion."

"But I'm not a quadroon!"

"No, not precisely." Elene gazed at the other girl with clear and steady understanding. Elene was of the islands where mixed blood was a constant possibility, one which could be detected in myriad small ways, in the slight fullness of a mouth or broad base of a nose, the texture of skin and hair or sound of a voice. The sum of such small clues meant much to those familiar with them, those with reason to look for them.

Flora straightened, and the retiring air she wore fell away from her like a veil. A smile curved her soft lips that gave them a cruel twist, making her seem much older than she usually looked. She patted the knot of her blonde hair with its crinkling waves and laughed, a soft sound of virulent satisfaction that raised the hair on the back of Elene's neck. Her movements suddenly supple rather than awkward, languid in their grace, she put down her coffee cup and reached to take a cake, biting into it with sensual pleasure.

"I may as well tell you," the girl said, leaning back on the settee. "I am an octoroon, almost as white as you. Germaine is my mother, of course. As for what happened to that stupid cow, Hermine, she brought it on herself. She knew my father in Saint-Domingue, and I'm certain she knew about me. That night at the vauxhall she was laughing at me, almost telling me in front of everybody that she knew my secret. Killing her was ridiculously easy; I only had to visit her and give the arsenic to her in chocolate. Naturally, I had to give her more than a normal person since she was used to it, but no one would think anything of it if the way she died was discovered. And they didn't. She was buried as a suicide, wasn't she?"

"But you killed your own father! How could you?" That was the question that had haunted Elene, making what she had thought seem so impossible.

"Papa was an honorable man, too honorable. On Saint-Domingue, I was betrothed twice—men are attracted to me and I like them, so it was easy to arrange. Each time, papa took the man who wanted to marry me aside before the wedding and told him the truth. The men withdrew, and who could blame them? I couldn't allow that to happen again, could I? I had been taking steps to prevent it even before we had to leave the island. Papa's stomach, you know, the cause was arsenic, a slow and sure death that would seem natural. I used my own powder, the same I took every week. Then came Durant. He was so handsome, so much the gentleman. I couldn't take the chance that Papa would tell him. I just couldn't."

"Then poor Serephine was also in the way."

Flora's face hardened. "I took the chance of killing Papa in haste for nothing. When he was dead, Durant told me he didn't care to marry after all. He had taken money from Papa I thought, though he denied it. Anyway, he had what he wanted, so why should he wed me? He mentioned his attachment to his mistress, but I think it was only something to say. I think what he really wanted was to marry you. I knew it when you moved into his rooming house the minute Bayard left you. It was necessary to kill both Serephine and you."

"So you sold Serephine chocolate bonbons."

"And you pralines. It took a while to think how to give the poison to you since you don't care for chocolate. It didn't work nearly as well to cover the taste, did it? That was my mistake."

The conversational tone of the girl's voice, as if the topic was one of ordinary interest, made the hairs rise along Elene's arms. Skirting the question, she said, "But even if I had died, what made you think Durant would go back to you?"

"The perfume. You were right, I stole it at the party. Germaine said it had the power to drive men mad with desire. When I use it again with Durant, he will be mine. After he has had me, he will be captivated, anyway. I told you, men are attracted to me."

In the bright-colored guise of the praline seller, Flora had been seductive, even amazingly pretty. However, the way she dressed and wore her hair, the washed-out colors she affected as Mazent's daughter, gave her so plain an appearance that her conceit over her looks was ludicrous, her assurance of her attraction for men a bizarre fallacy. Elene had felt it without clearly recognizing it that night at the vauxhall when Flora had insisted the Americans were watching her. So had Josie, which was why the actress had laughed at her. It was a great wonder Josie was alive.

Elene got to her feet, gathering her shawl that she had allowed to slip from her arms back around her. "I don't think there is any more to be said, except this. You failed to kill Ryan, just as you failed to kill me. The duel is in the morning and will, it seems, be held as planned. There is no way you will be able to harm Ryan further since we will all be on our guard. I suggest you not interfere, but let happen what may."

"Good advice, I don't doubt," the girl said with derision. "What a pity you will never know the outcome."

Elene was on the point of turning away. She swung back sharply. "What do you mean?"

"Germaine, as you so carefully figured out, is my mother. It has not been so long since she discovered what her daughter has been doing, only since Serephine died, but she has my best interests at heart still. I told her to put arsenic in your coffee cup. She has the habit, you know, of obeying me implicitly, as a servant should obey her mistress."

It was natural for Elene to place her hand on her abdomen where her child rested. There was in that region a little queasiness not unknown at this time of day, but no cramping, no real nausea. Not yet.

"Why?" she asked in puzzlement. "You must know I am no longer with Durant. You saw Ryan take me away this morning."

"It's always possible Durant will kill Ryan and turn to you again. Besides, I don't think you have told anyone what you know, such as Ryan or your Devota, or they would be here with you. It will be just as well, then, that you don't have the chance to—"

Flora broke off at the opening of the door. Her face froze into a mask of shocked surprise as Germaine walked into the room followed by Ryan, and also Durant. She sprang to her feet, then stood wavering, uncertain.

"Sit down, my love," Germaine said, going to her, taking her hand, drawing her back down upon the settee as she seated herself beside her.

Ryan moved with swift strides toward Elene and took her in his arms. They closed warm and safe around her. She stood there a long moment, leaning against his strength, savoring his comfort, before she stepped back to look into his face. "The coffee, there was—"

"There was nothing in your coffee," he said, the words deep-voiced, sure.

"You don't understand. I have to get home, home to Devota—"

"There was nothing in the coffee," he repeated, "at least, not in yours."

Elene stared into the deep blue of his eyes. Slowly she turned her head toward Flora. Flora looked at her with wide eyes, then shifted her gaze to Ryan, and beyond him to where Durant stood in stiff dismay with his face flushed. By infinitesimal degrees the girl moved her head until she was staring at her mother.

She screamed.

There was ancient sorrow in Germaine's face as she took her daughter into her arms, rocking her gently. A sob caught in her voice. "I couldn't let you do it, my love, not again, not anymore. It was wrong, so wrong. We made a mistake, your papa and I, bringing you into a world like this, but it was a mistake of love. You shouldn't have killed him. I loved him so much. Just as I love you. Just as I love you."

Silence gathered in the room. Abruptly Flora stiffened, throwing her head back.

"Devota," Elene said urgently, "someone must go for Devota!"

Ryan shook his head. "Too late, I think. Just as it would have been too late for you."

How long had they talked, she and Flora? Long enough. There had been no natural nausea of pregnancy to make the girl's stomach instantly reject the vileness. She whispered, "We have to do something."

Germaine looked at them over her daughter's shoulder. Her voice thick, desolate, she said, "Leave her to me, I beg of you. Just—leave her to me."

"Come." Ryan turned Elene toward the door. Her muscles were rigid so that it was difficult to move. It seemed, still, that there must be something to be done. A part of her mind stood aghast at the swift turn of events. She had not meant to precipitate anything like this; she had not meant it at all.

Durant stepped forward, blocking their way. He paid no attention to Ryan, speaking only to Elene. "I have to talk to you."

"There is nothing to be said." Elene started forward, but he would not step aside. She stopped again.

Ryan's voice held a hard rasp. "This is not the time, Durant."

The other man looked at him. "When is? We may kill each other in the morning." He turned back to Elene. "I know I am at fault. I should never have let the business with Mazent go so far. But I needed the loan of his money, and didn't realize how tightly the strings were attached until it was too late; he was an old fox, though basically an honest one. Since I had been fooled, I felt no need to hold myself bound by a pact with a dead man."

"You owe me no explanation," Elene said, trying to stop the flow of words.

"I do. I have to tell you. I swear I didn't know what Flora had done, what she would do, to get what she wanted. My thoughts were always of you. You have been like a dream before me since we left Saint-Domingue, a vision of happiness just out of reach. I have lived for the life we had planned together, you and I. I have tried to be patient, to wait until you were ready to begin. Why can't it be now?"

How desperately people needed love. There was not much they would not do to achieve it from those they desired. Desire, however, was a poor exchange for the love they professed to crave. Some never seemed to understand that to be loved, one must first love. Even then, love could not be forced in return, did not come with guarantees. She had learned that much.

"I'm sorry," she said.

"That isn't enough. You have to—"

Ryan moved forward. "She doesn't have to do anything, not now, not ever. This has been a trying evening. If you have any concern for her, you will let her go home."

"I have to make her understand."

"Wait until tomorrow. If you are the victor in our meeting, you will have all the time in the world to convince her. If not, it won't matter."

Ryan pressed passed Durant, taking Elene with him. The other man gave way, though there was bitter enmity in the glare he gave Ryan. Then they were out of the rooms, out of the hotel, out in the clean, cool night air.

Devota was waiting for them, her face creased with anxiety, when they reached the house. Behind her Benedict stood as impassively as ever, but his hands were twisted together in front of him and he started forward before he could catch himself as he saw Ryan.

There was some mention of coffee to warm them, but the very idea made Elene shudder. They had small glasses of pale gold sherry instead, while they sat around the small fire burning in the bedchamber and Ryan told the other two what had taken place.

When he had finished, Devota shook her head. "Poor confused girl."

"She was a murderess several times over for nothing more than her own protection, her own gain," Ryan said harshly. "So sure was she of her own superiority that no one else mattered."

"You are wrong, M'sieur Ryan," Devota said. "So doubtful was she of her worth, she could see value in the life of no one else."

He lifted a brow as he considered it. "You may be right."

Elene entered the conversation, her gaze on the man at her side. "What I don't understand is how you, or Durant either for that matter, came to be at the inn. When I left the house you were asleep."

"The commotion when Devota discovered you were gone woke me— you and Devota were so quick to rid me of the arsenic, both before and after I swallowed it, that there isn't much wrong with me a fair-sized meal won't cure."

What he meant, but would not say, was that his strength was such he had recovered quickly. Elene permitted herself a smile, but did not comment as he continued.

"You said in your note you were going to see Flora Mazent, but Devota was afraid it was a ruse, that you were going to try to persuade Gambier to stop the duel. I knew where the Mazents had been staying, since I had met him there once to discuss a business venture that didn't materialize—the proposition you assumed was a proposal. I went on ahead while Benedict went to check with Gambier. At the inn, I was intercepted by Germaine. I think Gambier may have guessed more than he admits, for he joined us shortly, looking as if he expected to see a corpse. Germaine led us into the bedchamber where we could hear. Neither of us liked our position as eavesdroppers, but in seconds we were too involved in what was being said for it to matter."

Devota shook her head, frowning. "Germaine is a strong woman, stronger than I could have been. What will be her punishment for this? Have you any idea?"

"I think Flora's death will be an unfortunate accident, the last in a series of dangerous deaths involving arsenic. For my part, I feel that for Germaine to be forced to so terrible a deed is punishment enough. There is no need to involve the authorities during this time of changing power."

Benedict, gazing at Elene who was valiantly smothering a yawn with her fingertips, nudged Devota and tipped his head in her direction.

Devota took one look and got to her feet. "I think it's time, *chère*, that you were in bed. Let me help you off with your dress, then I will bring you, perhaps, a glass of warm milk?"

"There is no need for your services," Ryan said in lazy contradiction as he lifted a hand in restraint. "I'll do whatever she needs."

"She needs rest." Devota's brown gaze held concern.

"Really, Devota," Elene said in quiet reassurance, "I'll be all right."

"I'll see that she gets rest," Ryan said, rising and moving toward the door which he held open.

Devota would have said more, but Benedict rose, touching her arm, and glided from the bedchamber. His gesture for her to follow was polite, but imperious.

Ryan smiled at Devota as the maid looked at him once more. "She will never take harm from me."

Devota gave a hard nod, as if to say she would hold him to his word. Finally, the door closed behind her.

Ryan returned to the fire, turning to stand with his back to the flames. He looked down at Elene, at the flickering glow of the fire reflecting on her pale face and dancing in her hair, at the shadows of fatigue under her eyes. Bending with sudden decision, he scooped her up in his arms and moved with her toward the bed.

She should protest, should declare that she did not want to be in his arms. It would be a lie. Morning would come soon, and with it the duel. Against such a threat, what use were promises and pledges of future intentions? There might be only tonight for the making of memories.

He took down her hair, spreading it in molten gold splendor over her shoulders, and unfastened her gown before easing it from her with petticoats, stockings, and shoes. Stripping away his own clothing, he pinched out the candle flames and joined her on the mattress. She held out her arms and he drew her against him. Their bodies melded together, heart to heart, hollows and curves, legs entwined. Gently they rocked each other.

Home, he was home, Ryan thought, home to comfort and content in the arms of this woman who always smelled of flowers and who above all others could fill his soul. Whatever came, she had been his for a time, and was once more, at least for this night.

To Elene, the warmth and strength of his body was a haven, one she wanted to wrap around her and, at the same time, to encompass. Nothing mattered except this closeness. His lips tasted of wine and restrained desire. It was the restraint for which she had no need.

"Love me," she whispered. "It's been so long."

He caught his breath. "Are you certain?"

"Never so certain in my life."

She touched him in wonder, in encouragement, in free exploration. Pleasure was a bright blossoming, familiar, yet strangely new. Love was effervescent in her veins, and she whispered it against the strong column of his neck. She was wild, she was wanton, she was out of control and did not care. She eased upon his hardness, taking him, giving herself. That the exchange was secret was her joy and her pain, and in the end, her solace.

She knew when he slid from the bed as dawn crept through the shutters. She heard the sounds as he gathered his clothing from the armoire and left the bedchamber. She lay still, staring dry-eyed into the dimness with one hand covering the ache of pain in her chest. The urge to leap up and follow was near unbearable. It would be best, however, if she remained here, waiting. She could not interfere in the duel without making a fool of herself, or else having the seconds pull her away from the two men with silent curses for hysterical females who did not understand the code of honor. For her to stand pale and distraught on the sidelines would be a distraction that could not be allowed. She should dress herself and sit on the gallery, patiently waiting for Ryan to return, or until news was brought that he would not be coming. That was the way of dignity and quiet, courageous acceptance.

She could not do it.

She threw back the covers and left the bed. Moving with care to keep from alerting Devota or Benedict to her purpose, she began to dress.

The duel would most likely be held in St. Anthony's garden at the rear of the church of St. Louis. This was the traditional place for bouts with swords, she had heard, though those involving pistols were settled outside the town where the noise and pistol balls were less disturbing. The meeting place was no great distance from Ryan's house. The street on which he lived ran directly behind the church.

Elene slowed her steps as she drew near. The garden was a large rectangle centered by a small statue of St. Anthony and enclosed by shrubs that had grown well above head height, though the lower limbs were sparsely leafed. She stopped behind this cover.

The men were already gathered on a grassy area in front of the statue. The seconds were measuring the swords for length, while the doctor checked his bag of dressings. There was a handful of spectators in evening dress, as if they were just winding their way homeward from the party given the night before by Prefect Laussat in celebration of the transfer. They talked among themselves in low voices, commenting on the affair, the identity and prowess of the two men. There was also the exchange of what had the sound of discreet bets.

Ryan stood nearby, with his back to her. He had removed his coat and was adjusting his shirt sleeves. Durant was directly opposite Ryan across the grass. Glancing at his opponent, he began to remove his coat also.

One of the tails of Durant's coat swung heavily against his knee. He reached down to feel the bulge in the tail pocket, a look of puzzlement creasing his forehead. Putting in his hand, he drew out what looked to be a doll. He stared at it an instant, then uttered an oath and flung it from him.

The doll landed in the grass in front of St. Anthony's statue. It was the small wax figure of a man. On its head was a patch of fur the exact color of Durant's hair, and it was dressed in a miniature version of a black tailcoat. Protruding from its chest was a tiny brass sword that was thrust through the area of the heart. Durant stood staring at it, his face pale and his eyes fixed.

Elene stared at the figure also. Her throat was tight and her heartbeat throbbed in her ears as she thought of Devota's promise, and of how Benedict had gone to Durant's rooms the night before, supposedly in search of her. This was the answer then. How pathetic it appeared, lying there in the dew-wet grass, a gray lump with legs twisted and bent and its tailcoat all askew. But the small, sharp sword glinted in the first rays of the rising sun.

Ryan appeared to have his gaze fixed on the wax figure, as did one or two of the spectators. The seconds, Morven among them, were intent on their duties; none of them paid it the least attention. Moments later, their discussions and arguments completed, they turned and approached the duelists. The actor, taking the lead as usual, was their spokesman. With a masterly bow, he asked in formal language for the final time if there could be a peaceful settlement of the differences between the two men.

Durant raised his gaze from the gray form in the grass. For a moment he looked blank, as if he had forgotten where he was, what he was doing. Perspiration beaded his forehead in spite of the cool morning. Finally, he shook his head. Ryan perforce, as the challenged party, did the same.

The swords were shown to the two men. They approved them. Ryan made his choice. The other blade was presented to Durant. The seconds stepped back out of the way, each pair gathering behind their man. Ryan and Durant took their stances, facing each other.

Quiet descended, broken only by the soft murmur of a breeze in the hedge and the low warble of pigeons on the eaves of the church rising above them. The sun, stretching higher, glittered on the grass, on the blades the two men held, and on the hilt of the tiny sword impaling the wax figure in the grass between them.

"Salute."

The swords swept up then swiftly down again in unison.

"*En garde!*"

Ryan took the swordsman's position, right leg forward, slightly bent, left hand back, sword presented in his right. Durant did not move. He looked from the doll in the grass to Ryan, then back again.

Ryan eased upright again with the grace of firm muscles. He turned to the seconds. "There seems to be trash of some kind here on the ground. Perhaps it could be removed before we stumble over it."

Elene heard his words with a stifled moan of distress. Almost, she had begun to hope that Durant would withdraw because of the doll.

Ryan's action was scrupulously fair, and therefore admirable, but misguided.

Morven came forward. He picked up the wax figure, turning it over curiously. "Where did it come from? I assure you we checked the field for impediments."

"It . . . fell out of my pocket," Durant answered, his voice a croak.

Morven gave him a bright smile. "From my travels in the islands, I would say someone wishes you harm. Better you than me."

The actor stepped back into his place behind Ryan. Glancing once more at the doll, he fingered the small sword, moving it back and forth, then gave it a little push that sent it deeper into the soft wax.

Durant uttered a gasp and clamped his hand to his heart. His sword tip trailed in the grass.

Morven looked up with lifted brow, then with magnificent disdain, tossed the doll aside. Durant swayed on his feet.

"Gentlemen, are you ready to proceed?" the actor intoned.

Ryan gave his assent. Durant said nothing. He looked around the garden, as if searching for something, or someone. His gaze touched Elene, narrowing in recognition. A white ring appeared about his mouth.

A rumble of comment moved among the men gathered to watch. Durant looked back toward the seconds, to Ryan, to the clear morning sky overhead. He hefted the sword in his hand, then let it dangle again.

He moistened his lips. In compressed tones, he said at last, "I believe that we should postpone this meeting. I . . . I am not well."

Durant's seconds, men he played cards with on occasion, looked at each other with lifted brows for the irregularity of the request. One of them stepped toward Ryan, clearing his throat. "Is this acceptable to you, sir?"

Elene could not see Ryan's face. All she could see was the straight set of his broad shoulders and the proud tilt of his head. She wondered what he was thinking, if he knew what she had done. She wished, suddenly, that she had not encouraged Devota to interfere, that she had shown her faith in his ability to best Durant. She knew he could, for she had seen him do it before. But that was before he had been weakened by poison, before she realized she loved him. There were chances that should not be taken.

Ryan was long in answering. His words when they came were quiet and even. "It is not acceptable."

Not acceptable. He was refusing Durant's capitulation. The anguish of it was like fire in her mind.

"What is your pleasure, then, sir?"

"To begin again," Ryan said in incisive tones, "from the presentation of the swords, and the question of settlement."

Before the second could answer, Durant threw down his sword. His face twisted into a mask of fear and fury, he stared at Ryan. "Very well then. Let me stand as admitting myself at the fault in our quarrel and assert that honor is satisfied."

"Thank you." Ryan inclined his head in a bow. "Please accept my apologies for any injury to your self-esteem I may have caused."

It was a gallant gesture toward Durant's pride which Ryan had forced him to shed. Durant's departure from the code of honor had been galling for him, that much was plain, but his fear had overcome his reluctance to make it, just as fear of poverty had overcome his reluctance to take money from Flora's father.

Elene, hearing the echoes of Ryan's voice dying away, felt the bursting surge of love and glorious relief. She wanted to run to him at once, to touch him, to be sure he was safe. Instead, she waited decorously until only Ryan and Durant and Morven were left in the garden before she joined them.

Durant, still facing her, watched her approach. His lips flattened and his black eyes turned opaque before he said, "Did you come to gloat?"

"No." Her voice was quiet as she answered. "Only to see what you would do to each other."

"For your sake? Who has a better right to watch? I hope you were satisfied, as I must be now."

"Yes, I think so." Reaching Ryan's side, she stopped. He looked at her as he shrugged in his coat. There were equal parts of concern and irritation in his eyes, and something more that warmed her to the center of her being.

"So you have made your choice, or was it made for you?" Durant glanced down her still slender form. "Nature has a way of lending a hand in these affairs."

Morven, glancing at the grim cast of Ryan's features, began to make his excuses. When he saw no one was attending to them beyond Ryan's brief thanks for his services, he bowed and strolled nonchalantly away.

Elene was watching Durant, seeing plainly for the first time the petty malice and jealous possessiveness in his face. He had been so diminished since the days on the island that an odd compassion for him moved inside her. Her father had chosen this man for her, her dead father, and perhaps he had a right to a certain consideration. Even Ryan had given him that.

Her gaze clear on Durant's face, she said, "Tell me the truth. Do you love me?"

Beside her, Ryan took her arm. "Don't do this," he said, his voice rough, "not here, not now."

Her gray eyes were fathomless, unfaltering on his as she turned to him. "There will never be a better time or place than now. Because of it, I ask you, too. Do you love me?"

Durant, scenting a possible advantage, a possible change in his fortunes to be had by a swift answer, edged forward. The words taut, he said, "Yes, Elene, I do love you."

Ryan held her gaze, his own seething, darkly blue. "I have loved you since I first saw you standing gilded by moonlight in a dark wood, since I held you in my arms through three days of living entombment. The smell and taste and feel of you enchants my heart and is engraved on my bones, and will follow me into the purgatory I will surely find because I put you above all else. But if this is no more than a trick to wring a like admission from Durant, I swear I will—"

"If I asked you to let me go to him, would you?"

The garden was quiet, the sun brightly shining, drying the dew on the grass. Ryan stared at her with his blood congealing, gathering in cold and gelid weight in the hollow of his chest. The seeping pain gathered there also, spreading outward until it inhabited every mangled fiber of his being. He held his breath against it, then closed his eyes as he let it have its way. Raising his eyelids with determined effort, he said. "If you could swear to me that you loved him and only him, and could love none other your life long, then, I would."

She shifted her stance toward Durant. "And you, would you let me go to Ryan if I required it?"

"God, no!" he answered in scorn. "If you were mine, I would never let you go, not for any man!"

A wry smile flickered across her mouth, then was gone. "Then perhaps it is as well that I am not yours." To Ryan she turned a countenance naked of pretense, openly vulnerable. "Please," she said, "take me home?"

Devota and Benedict were horrified that Elene had gone to watch the duel. They scolded and insisted that she sit down on the gallery to rest while they arranged a special breakfast to celebrate the wonderful outcome of the dawn meeting. Devota refused to be diverted by compliments for her part in the event, or to attend to Ryan's demands to know why she had interfered. She was not concerned for him, she said, only for Elene should anything happen to him.

When Devota, with Benedict in tow, had bustled away to the kitchen, Ryan moved to stand against the railing in front of Elene's chair. He crossed his arms over his chest with deliberation, though his voice was light as he spoke. "It seems to me that everyone is solicitous of your health to the point of foolishness, even Benedict. I know you were nearly poisoned, but so was I, and they aren't hovering over me. Can it be there is something I should know?"

She lifted her gaze from her contemplation of the water sparkling in the courtyard fountain. She thought of falling in with his bantering manner, of making a jest of the matter, but her growing attachment to the life within her would not permit it. Quietly she said, "I'm going to have a baby, our baby."

"Ours," he said as if testing the word. "You thought it necessary to let me know it's mine?"

"I didn't want you to have to ask."

He leaned over her, bracing his arms on the back of her chair. "Dear God, Elene, I have told you I love you. Don't you think I know this child is mine without having to be informed of it?"

"After the way I wrung an admission of love from you—"

"Which you wouldn't have got if I hadn't meant every word! Let me tell you, I knew you were carrying my child the minute I took you in my arms in the square. How could I not, when every inch of you is as well known to me as my own hand? I will grant that there hasn't been much time for you to tell me I'm going to be a father, but I didn't expect to have to force the news from you, or to have it treated like a death sentence."

"A death sentence?" she echoed.

He knelt at her feet, taking her hand. "I know a child is brought into the world in pain and indignity for the mother, and I'm more sorry than I can say for it, but isn't there any joy in you for the prospect of holding it? Have you no love for it, even if you have none for me?"

"Of course I love it," she said in amazement. "But what makes you think—"

He would not let her finish. "Then why won't you marry me? If you will take my love, why not my name for the child's sake? How many times do I have to ask before you will say yes?"

She opened her mouth to explain, but the words wouldn't come. She had refused him before because she had thought she wanted to control her own life. She had discovered, however, that life, like death, defied control. What she did with her hours, where she went and when, had nothing to do with being in control, but simply with being true to herself and her goals. She could do that now, married or unmarried. In any case, she understood now that it was never control itself which was important, but the need to conquer the fear of loss, of being left alone. What she had need of, then, was the security of loving and being loved, and that she had, would always have in her heart, even if death should end it.

She moistened her lips, finally finding an answer for him. "Twice. You will have to ask me twice."

"Before and—"

"And now. Or if it will make it easier, I will take what you just said as a proposal."

He unfolded his arms and stepped to take her wrists, drawing her up to face him. His voice implacable in his determination to have a full answer, he said, "Why now?"

"What?" She stared at him, at a loss, while inside her there emerged a slow and spreading throb of desire to be held close inside his arms, pressed against him from breasts to ankles until they merged beyond separation.

"You would not marry me before, I think, for lack of love. Why now?"

She swallowed hard on the press of tears. "There was never any lack of love."

"From me, you mean."

"No," she said with a quick shake of her head, "from me. I love you, Ryan."

"You mean, all this time—?"

"All this time." The tears brimmed in her eyes, overflowing. "But I was afraid."

"There is nothing to fear. I will always be with you. Always."

A watery smile curved her lips. "Then there was the perfume. I would not have you only because of it."

He caught her to his chest, clasping her gently yet with the firm hands of one who keeps what he holds. "It was never the perfume, I swear it! I enjoyed it, yes, but I was more enthralled by you, by what you are, what you can be."

"I know that, now." Pushing her arms around his waist, she smoothed them up the ridged muscles of his back, pressing close and closer still.

He smoothed her hair with unsteady fingers, and bent his head to taste her mouth. Silence descended broken only by the tinkling of the fountain and the rattle of crockery from the kitchen below the gallery. At last Ryan raised his head. The words rich and warm with promise, he said, "On the other hand, if you were to wear your perfume tonight, I might be a willing slave."

"There's none left," Elene murmured.

He sighed. "Too bad."

"But I have the scents here for it, and it's a long time until dark."

"Too long," Ryan said, and turned with her into the house.

EPILOGUE

I⊤ was twenty days later, on a balmy morning with the feel of spring though it was in December, that Ryan and Elene stood in the Place d'Armes once more. In a ceremony very nearly identical to that which had taken place the month before, Colonial Prefect Pierre Clement de Laussat appeared on the balcony of the cabildo following the transfer of Louisiana from France to the United States. This time, however, the commissioners at his side were Americans, a fairly young and distinguished-looking gentleman named William C. C. Claiborne, who would be the new governor though he knew no French, and General James Wilkinson, who was portly and abrasive and spoke the language of the new territory execrably.

On the flagpole in the center of the square, the tricolor of France slowly descended while the red and white bars and circle of stars on a blue ground of the United States was raised. As the flags met at the halfway point, there was a small pause while the flag men jerked at the ropes, almost as if the banner of France were reluctant to give up its sway. The minor halt was highlighted with drama a moment later as salvos of cannon sounded from the forts and batteries of the city walls and from the ships in the harbor to salute the country giving way and also that gaining ascendancy.

Then the American standard surged upward, catching the breeze at the top of the staff so that its circle of stars and its stripes shone in the sun. There arose a ragged cheer. For the most part it came from the Americans, some in the toggery of gentlemen, some in the rough leather clothes and coonskin caps of the "Kaintucks" from the backwoods, or else it was raised by small boys. The French stood silent, somber at the loss of civilized rule, certain that they were being given over to barbarians.

Elene had few such reservations. She had come to see that Ryan was right. Let the Americans come with their energy and lust for commerce and their money. The wives of these men would need perfume as much as the French.

She was anxious to get back to her workroom where she had begun a new scent that she meant to call Louisiana Garden. And she must get Devota to help her make up a new mix of the Paradise perfume as she had sold the last of the most recent bottling, her own personal store, just before she set out for the square. She did not want to be without; the perfume was still Ryan's favorite, and tonight there would be a grand ball given by the Laussats to celebrate the events of the day and the prefect's new posting to Martinique. There would be many lovely ladies present, no few of them Americans. A woman who was growing more obviously *enceinte* every day needed all the help she could get to compete. Besides, perfumes were always more noticeable in the heat of dancing. It would be a good time to discreetly display her scent.

Behind Elene stood Devota, holding Benedict's arm. The mulatto woman watched the couple before her with indulgent eyes. The scent of perfume wafted on a breath of wind and she breathed deeply, a smile hovering about her mouth.

Elene turned in time to catch the soft, almost secretive expression in her maid's brown eyes and the quiet pleasure on her face. Her own lips curved in return. "What is it? Did I miss something?"

"No, no, *chère*. I only caught a breath of our perfume, and was thinking how perfect it is."

"Perfect?"

"The name, Paradise."

A shadow of suspicion flitted over Elene. She raised her hand to clasp her mother's cameo at her throat, one of Ryan's many groom's gifts to her before their wedding, as if clutching a talisman. That Devota might have lied to her about the perfume and its effects for her own good was perfectly possible. Hadn't she done it once before? Or had she?

Elene didn't want to know. The perfume was special, that much she understood. There were many who had quickly grown to love it and depend on it. If there was harm in it, it was not apparent. No, she didn't want to know.

"Yes, quite perfect," she said, and turned back to the spectacle before her.

Devota smiled again, then schooled her features to blandness as Benedict tilted his head to stare down at her. But he only said to her in soft tones, "Perfect for you."

Laussat had come down into the square to address the French militia. Now he and the American commissioners were reviewing the troops of the United States drawn up in impressive formation. In a moment the transfer of Louisiana to the United States would be done and they could all go home. Already, men and women were milling and shifting, making their way back toward the streets and the cafés and drinking establishments where they would discuss this momentous occasion and toast the past.

Ryan breathed deeply of Elene's scent, and his lips twitched in wry acknowledgment of the desire it always kindled inside him. He pressed her arm against his side. "Ready to go, *chérie*?"

"Always, with you," she answered, and smiled into his eyes with her own shining silver gray in the winter sunlight.

AUTHOR'S NOTE

THE raising of the American flag at the Place d'Armes in New Orleans on December 20, 1803 was the culmination of the most fabulous real estate deal in history. For approximately four cents per acre, the United States received nearly a million square miles of territory containing the largest and most valuable river system in the world, an area bounded on the west by the Continental Divide of the Rocky Mountains, on the north by the head of the Mississippi in Minnesota, and on the south by the Red River and the Gulf of Mexico. The purchase more than doubled the size of the young United States, giving it the base upon which to build a strong and enduring nation.

One of the most amazing things about the transfer of this immense domain is that it was accomplished without wars, without treaties, without compromises or strife of any kind. It was the result of quiet and diligent diplomatic effort—and a great deal of luck. The desire of the United States for unimpeded access to the gulf coincided nicely with Napoleon's distraction over European affairs and his urgent need of funds. The American emissaries were close at hand when the decision was made to exchange land for money, and the deed was done. It was, perhaps, one of Napoleon's most inglorious mistakes. The question will always remain of just what he had in mind originally when he wrested Louisiana from Spain in the Treaty of San Ildefonso, and what would have occurred, what Louisiana would be today, if he had directed his ambition toward the New World instead of Europe.

The Louisiana Purchase and the inauguration of American government in New Orleans, then, were not dramatic events filled with fury and bloodshed and the sound of cannons. They were, in fact, as tedious and time consuming as indicated in *Perfume of Paradise*. The summer and fall leading up to the transfer occurred as given, including the forty days of rain, the yellow fever epidemic which very nearly claimed the life of Colonial Prefect Laussat, the pregnancy of his wife which complicated his plans for departure, and the inexplicable and embarrassing delay of the confirmation of the cession by Napoleon. This, too, is the way history marches, slowly and surely.

The events in Saint-Domingue also followed the pattern shown. General Jean Baptiste Rochambeau, who had taken command after the death of Leclerc, surrendered to the British in November of 1803. On January 1, 1804, the Negro general, Dessalines, declared the independence of Saint-Domingue under the name of Haiti. Most of the whites left on the island at that time were massacred. The property of the former French landowners was forfeited to the new government without compensation.

The young black republic founded with so much bloodshed has since had a shaky history, including a long period of dictatorship in modern times under the Duvalier family. It is currently far from stable, but valiantly struggling to retain its autonomy as a black nation.

Publications consulted for research material were many, but none was so helpful as *Memoirs of My Life*, by Pierre Clement de Laussat, translated by Agnes-Josephine Pastwa, O. S. F. I am indebted to the long line of people who aided in the rescue of the moldering manuscript of these memoirs from the tower of a French chateau at Bernadets and saw to its publication. I am also grateful to the staff of the Louisiana Collection, Louisiana State University Library for their cooperation; to Lawrence Lynch, archivist of the Louisiana Archives, for his time and trouble; and to the staff of the Jackson Parish Library, Jonesboro, for their unstinting effort.

The people mentioned in the book who actually lived and played their parts are many. On Saint-Domingue there was the Negro governor-general, Toussaint, and his successor, Dessalines, also Napoleon's brother-in-law, General Leclerc, and his successor, Rochambeau. In Louisiana, there was Colonial Prefect Laussat with his wife and their three daughters; the Spanish Governor Salcedo, Intendant Morales, and Commissioner the Marquis de Casa Calvo. Etienne de Bore made a fortune in sugar and became the first major of New Orleans. Bernard Marigny, later in life, established a faubourg, or suburb, in New Orleans with streets named Desire, Bon Chance, and Good Children. William C. C. Claiborne was an able governor who married a Louisiana Creole lady and collaborated with Jean Lafitte and Andrew Jackson during the Battle of New Orleans. General Wilkinson gained honor in serving the United States in the territory, but died amid whispers of treason over the Aaron Burr affair. All other characters are purely fictional.

And so, regrettably, is the perfume called Paradise.

Jennifer Blake
Sweet Brier
Quitman, Louisiana

ABOUT THE AUTHOR

JENNIFER BLAKE was born near Goldonna, Louisiana, in her grandparents' 120-year-old hand-built cottage. It was her grandmother, a local midwife, who delivered her. She grew up on an eighty-acre farm in the rolling hills of north Louisiana and got married at the age of fifteen. Five years and three children later, she had become a voracious reader, consuming seven or eight books a week. Disillusioned with the books she was reading, she set out to write one of her own. It was a Gothic—*Secret of Mirror House*—and Fawcett was the publisher. Since that time she has written thirty-two books, with more than nine million copies in print, and has become one of the bestselling romance authors of our time. Her recent Fawcett books are *Surrender in Moonlight, Midnight Waltz, Fierce Eden, Royal Passion, Prisoner of Desire, Southern Rapture,* and *Louisiana Dawn*. Jennifer and her husband live in their house near Quitman, Louisiana—styled after old Southern planters' cottages.